ПЯТНО
THE STAIN

ПЯТНО
THE STAIN

A NOVEL FOR WOMEN

CATHERINE IVERS NORTON

DEDICATION

For Sean, the inspiration for Sergei's electric blue eyes.

CONTENTS

ACKNOWLEDGMENTS

This novel took nearly twenty years, from the first word in 2002 to publication in 2021. I could not have done it without a lot of help and support, especially from my sister, Susan Norton, who read through each version and provided feedback, including proofreading the final copy. I appreciate you so much, Susan. Thank you for believing in me and my beloved characters. You are far more than just a sister; you are my best friend. This story would never have become the novel it is without you.

I attended Sunday services several times at St. Mary's Russian Orthodox Church in Jamesville, NY, in 2002. The priest and his wife were very friendly and happy to answer my questions. I was impressed by the rich beauty of the small church, the deep traditions, and the peace that lasted throughout the day afterward. The members were friendly and inclusive, generously giving me blessed apples and bread to enjoy at home. I felt the presence of God profoundly in those services, and I was moved to tears by the beauty of the church. The description of Kazan Cathedral is based on my experience at St. Mary's, as was Slava's observation that when it comes to spirituality, Cassandra 'thinks too much and feels too little.' This insight is true of me also, and it was under the onion dome at St. Mary's that I had this realization. When I finally make it to St. Petersburg, I will light a candle in Kazan Cathedral in remembrance of your contribution to this story. I will always be grateful for the peace you gave my heart during the troubled period of my life when this story was born. May God bless you all.

Also, in 2002, as a result of an online inquiry about Russian family names and heraldry, I began an email friendship with a man named Valery in Moscow, who became interested in this story. He explained families do not have heraldry in Russia, but they do have symbols. Valery suggested Karpov for Sergei's surname and a carp fish symbol, so the leaping fish was born. He also predicted Sergei's love of black tea and made sure I knew about *zakuska*, the snacks eaten while drinking vodka. He imagined Sergei would call Cassandra by different names depending on his mood and suggested

'Sandra,' 'Sandrochka,' and 'Sanka.' Valery's photo showed a strikingly handsome, distinguished blond man with deep blue eyes. I wrote him into the story as the man Sergei is speaking with at the St. Petersburg party the fateful night Cassandra wanders into the laundry room with Slava. Reading that passage always makes me smile and think of my friend in Moscow. Thank you so much, Valery. I am sorry we lost touch, but I am glad I knew Yuri Gagarin was the first man in space when you quizzed me. I have learned so much more about your beautiful country since we last communicated. I sincerely hope you are doing well. Большое спасибо, мой московский друг.

Many friends read and gave me input on the early edits of the manuscript. Silvie Semenec Ward was there from the very beginning. Silvie helped me nail down Sergei's unusual psychiatric diagnosis. Susan Jaromin Kane, Kelli Edwards, and Johanna Theetge Morgan gave it a read-through once I finished the initial manuscript in 2015. Carol McCaskill and Connie English read both the first and second books. So many edits followed, and everyone's input was valuable. I am very grateful to all of you, thank you.

My French sister-in-law, Aude Rabault, assisted with French phrases early on to ensure the grammar and expressions were authentic. *Merci beaucoup, Aude. J'aimerais pouvoir te voir plus souvent.*

Kirk Barker helped with some of the phrasing when I rewrote the original story in 2015. Whenever I read the sweetly innocent line, "the beginning of a quiver that might make my knees buckle," I think of you. Thank you for this adorable contribution. I also appreciate the support you gave me when I relaunched this project.

Una Moneypenny is a dear friend in the Ithaca, NY area who volunteered to edit the book. Una has a bachelor's degree in English from Wells College in Aurora, NY, and is my go-to person for proper grammar, etc. She describes herself as a student of the world and 'seat of the pants' editor. Una is far more than that. She is the kind of friend who drops what she is doing and comes with a chainsaw when a tree falls on your house. Friends like this are rare, and I am deeply grateful you are in my life. Thank you, Una.

Damaris Vazquez is another sweet friend in Ithaca, NY, who shot the photography for the book cover. Damaris is a fine nude photographer, blacklight body painter, ultraviolet photo and digital artist, videographer, spoken word poet, who works as a visionary, oracle, and all-around Squix. She can often be seen dancing in Ithaca, a charming muse who inspires others to follow their dreams with the same passion she follows hers. You are a treasure, Damaris. Thank you for everything you do to make Ithaca the mystical portal it is.

Cassandra feels blessed to have friends with skills, and so do I. Two of my old friends and published authors, Lisa Marsh and Janet Margot, arrived at precisely the right time with publishing advice. Oh ladies, thank you so very much. Publishing a first novel is a feat of endurance. I am so very grateful to have your expert support.

I also want to thank Ivan, my longtime friend in Russia and fellow St. Petersburg SKA hockey fan. He has been wonderful, sharing cultural information about the city, cluing me into entertainment trends, and providing me with the kind of insider hockey news I crave. It means so much to me to have a friend in Russia. Спасибо, Иван. Вы первый, кого я хочу видеть, когда приезжаю в ваш прекрасный город! Пойдем вместе на матч СКА!

Finally, I would like to acknowledge you, the reader, for daring to take this journey. If you wonder what Cassandra looks like, know that she is beautiful because she looks like you. I hope you like the story.

BENEATH A CRESCENT MOON

New York City, United States, October 1996

Fortune flung me from the sheltered waters of academia onto the island of cultured savages. A fish out of the water, about to be eaten alive.

This fashion show of an Upper East Side cocktail party was hosted by my new boss, Dr. Jerome O'Neill, the owner of a busy psychotherapy practice in midtown Manhattan.

Jerry was tall and stocky with a big smile and a bright sense of humor that immediately put people at ease. He introduced me lightheartedly to the socialites as "Dr. Cassandra Abbington, my latest acquisition." I immediately forgot their names, of course.

What a nightmare.

I told a middle-aged woman wearing a blue dress I'd just moved to the city after completing my Ph.D. at the University of Rochester.

"Where is that?" She asked.

Rochester is the third-largest city in New York. How can an adult not know the major cities in her state? Some New Yorkers are so self-involved, it's as if life does not exist anywhere else. I might have been astounded, but I was already used to this phenomenon after a month in the city.

"Upstate," I simply replied.

That was Siberia as far as she was concerned.

She smiled with disinterest and began talking about herself and her series of husbands. I encouraged her to continue and relaxed into the safe harbor she provided. I dreaded the moment between conversations when I suddenly found myself standing alone while everyone else gathered in groups.

A late arrival caught my attention. The blond man had a medium build, stood less than six feet tall, and appeared in his mid-thirties. He surveyed the crowd as if he was searching for someone. Our eyes met, and I felt a chill, like icy fingers stroking the innermost reaches of my abdomen. The last time I had that feeling was when I lost control of my vehicle and skidded off a winter road.

I shivered at the memory.

I quickly looked away and realized Blue Dress had stopped speaking. She was eyeing me quizzically.

"Do you know him?" She asked in a hushed tone.

"No," I replied.

"Well, I've never seen him before," she harrumphed, "I would have remembered that outfit!"

He was wearing a smart-looking black suit with a dark gray dress shirt unbuttoned at the neck. Glancing to the other men with their necks bound with conservative ties, it seemed an unusual choice for this affair.

My glass was empty, so I excused myself and went to the bar.

The Cabernet Sauvignon rose in a red tsunami as I lifted the glass. The wine threatened disaster but did not breach the rim.

Don't worry; it's just nerves, I told myself.

Hand tremors were a bad sign. I was not adjusting well to the city. The constant noise rattled me, the crowds made me uncomfortable, and I felt pressure to perform well at the party.

To make things worse, I felt like a bumpkin among the sleek and fashionable New Yorkers. My dress was lovely, but it came from a clearance rack in a discount store. I didn't know the designer because the garment tag was missing. To me, it didn't matter, but I worried everyone knew I went the cheap route and judged me. I reminded myself that people constantly evaluate other people; this was true. The fault in my thinking was the assumption that their assessment of me would be negative.

Knowing that did not make me feel any better.

I retreated through a French door that opened onto a delightfully deserted balcony. A chilly breeze from the west felt crisp, clean, and smelled faintly of apples. The view was impressive from the 11th floor. The dark expanse of Central Park was only a block away, while city lights dazzled in every other direction. The sky was slightly overcast, with a hint of the crescent moon visible through the clouds. I leaned on the railing, closed my eyes, and took deep breaths, exhaling slowly to release tension.

A peaceful feeling gradually settled over me.

Freshly composed, I decided to return to the party. At the door, I paused to take one last look at the moon, which was more visible now. On a whim, I lifted my wine glass in grateful salutation for the gift of peace I had just received.

The door suddenly opened behind me, jolting me with a start. A crimson wave crested the rim of the glass, spilled onto my left breast, and then flowed down the front of my cream-colored dress.

"Oh no!" I cried and immediately began to dab my dress with the tiny paper napkin from the bar. What a catastrophe!

"I am very sorry," a man's voice said, with a European accent I could not quite place. I looked up to find the face of the late arrival.

As our eyes met for the second time, everything stopped. I took in every contour of the stranger's countenance. I was sure I'd never seen anyone like him before, and yet he seemed oddly familiar. He had Slavic features, of that I was sure. If he was taller and stockier, I might have imagined him to be a hockey player. His eyes were brilliant sapphire blue, the shade of a clear January sky high in the mountains. They blazed with rare intensity beneath finely cut eyebrows that ruled over a long straight nose with a slight bump in the middle. He had prominent cheekbones and a high, proud forehead graced by a short mane of fine sandy-blond hair. His closely shaved skin revealed a flawless porcelain complexion. My attention lingered on his smooth, pale rose lips, which seemed pressed into a tight expression of concern.

Concern?

I suddenly realized he was offering me his handkerchief.

Feeling the hot flush of embarrassment rise to my cheeks, I glanced down and accepted the cloth. A golden fish leaping above three stylized lines of blue water was embroidered on fine white linen. I handed it back to him.

"There is no need to ruin your lovely handkerchief. I will take my dress to the cleaners tomorrow," I said.

"No, no," he insisted. "I cannot allow a beautiful woman to be seen in society with a stain of my doing."

It seemed strange he was so concerned.

3

"Actually," I admitted, "I am a stain magnet. Please do not blame yourself. I should not be allowed to drink red wine with my clothes on," I added and chuckled softly at my inane attempt at a joke.

He did not laugh. There was a studious expression on his face. Perhaps my jab at humor missed the mark.

"Look, I think I have a solution," I said as I reached up and pulled out the large rhinestone studded comb to release my French twist. My hair cascaded down past my shoulders in loose waves.

"See? If I move my hair around to the front and am careful not to move around too much, I can cover most of it," I explained, pleased with my handiwork.

He did not reply.

I lifted my head and looked directly at him for the third time. His lips parted slightly, and his face wore a strange expression of wonder. He seemed to be looking through me as if he remembered something from long ago. I searched his face until his gaze returned. Our eyes locked, and I shuddered, feeling the icy fingers return to stroke my belly once again.

I felt like running, but I was transfixed.

"What is your name?" He asked, finally releasing the tension.

I blinked and glanced away, stunned.

"Cassandra," I replied softly.

He motioned to a small table with two chairs and pulled one out.

"Please. Sit down, Cassandra," he said.

I took the seat, grateful for the opportunity to give my knees a rest. His intensity was a bit much, and I was beginning to feel shaky again.

He set his half-full glass on the table.

There was a tiny red puddle left in mine.

"You must be freezing," he observed with concern. "It's barely 4 degrees."

I knew he meant Celsius. It was about 40 degrees Fahrenheit.

"I am comfortable," I said, and it was the truth. "I am from the North Country – Lake Placid, in the Adirondack Mountains, near the Canadian border. I love the outdoors, even in winter. Nothing can keep me inside."

He removed his jacket and wrapped it around my shoulders.

"Mountain girl or not, I will not allow you to freeze on my watch," he replied.

His jacket smelled manly with a hint of cologne, and I enjoyed the feel of the satin lining caressing the bare skin on my shoulders. I would usually decline such an offer. But I had to admit it felt good. I did not want to take it off.

So I simply said, "Thank you."

Somewhere in the back of my mind, I heard my mother cheering. Graciously accepting compliments and always saying 'please' and 'thank you' were essential lady lessons.

He watched me for a moment before he spoke.

"Your glass is empty," he stated bluntly.

"Try some of mine," he said. "It will warm you."

I lifted the glass to my lips and sniffed the clear liquid. One whiff told me it was vodka. Straight, no ice. Ugh, how horrible!

I glanced up and noticed an 'I dare you' playful expression on his face.

Not one to back down from a challenge, I tried it. To my surprise, it was so smooth it slipped down my throat, albeit with a slight burn on the back end. This vodka was rather polished for such hard liquor.

"Good," he said encouragingly. "Have some more."

"Vodka does not stain," he added with a slight wink.

A sweet smile crossed his face that melted my defenses. He said, "I am Sergei."

Sergei retrieved a bottle of Ketel One and two shot glasses from the bar. A server trailed behind him carrying a tray of hors d'oeuvres. The man glanced at me with a slight smile as he set it on the table and quickly retreated.

Sergei didn't sip vodka; he threw it back with an impressive flair. He ate a little something after each shot. He called it 'zakuska,' a bite of food to make the vodka behave. It was exciting to see someone drink like that. Of course, I couldn't keep up with him, but I drank a few shots to be a good sport.

A calm curiosity settled over me.

I learned his full name was Sergei Ivanovich Karpov. The golden fish on his handkerchief was his family symbol, a carp. He told me he was a private investor in town on business and frequently traveled to oversee his holdings. He said he served on the board of directors for a consumer health products manufacturer with Jerry O'Neill. Jerry's grandfather started the company years ago, and Sergei had a substantial investment in it now. He said he'd just come from a meeting at another New York company, which was why he was late to this gathering. Business seemed to be good.

Sergei earned a Master's in Business Administration at Nyenrode University in the Netherlands. He was fluent in several languages. Sergei lived in Russia near St. Petersburg on a farm with horses. His parents were deceased, he had no siblings, he'd never married, and he had no children.

There wasn't anything fascinating to tell about me, but he wanted to hear it all anyway. I didn't mind answering Sergei's questions. I was flattered he seemed so interested.

I'd been in school for most of my life and just started my first professional job four weeks ago. I had a Bachelor's degree in Psychology from Alfred University and recently completed the Clinical Psychology program at the University of Rochester. At 28, I was young for a Ph.D. I made many sacrifices to do it. I'd never married.

"I never met a man who could compete with my passion for my work," I explained.

Recalling the fumbling attempts at romance I experienced over the years made me nauseous. I spent the last few years avoiding dating entirely, finding it far easier to be alone.

Of course, I didn't mention this to the attractive man sitting across from me.

I studied his hands as he refilled the shot glasses. They were square with medium-length fingers. His nails appeared to be professionally manicured. He wore no visible jewelry except for a gold watch that peeked out from under his sleeve as he slid one of the glasses toward me.

He held up a finger to indicate a pause and declared, *"Za fstryé-tchoo!"* before we tossed back our shots in unison.

"A toast to our meeting," he explained afterward. "Please continue, Cassandra. Tell me about your job."

Warmth spread through me as I described being a therapist helping people sort through their problems, noting how the city seems to create higher rates of depression and anxiety than anywhere else. But then again, I conceded, maybe city people are more open to talking about their problems than country folks.

I told him about my dissertation, which examined the family structures of people with severe psychological disorders like schizophrenia and catatonic depression. I was searching for dynamics that lead to positive outcomes to develop social interventions at the family level. I interviewed hundreds of people to illuminate the findings from the aggregated data I analyzed, using their stories to describe data trends in a human, relatable way. I'd already published several academic papers on the topic and had two additional manuscripts under review. As if the dissertation hadn't kept me busy enough, I co-authored an abnormal psychology textbook with my mentor in Rochester. We were in final edits with the publisher. If it sold well, I might make a little money. My goal was to become a university professor, so every publication helped build my credentials. Psychotherapy provided helpful field experience in the meantime, but it was not my true passion.

With the liquor easing my inhibition, I leaned in and playfully confessed I was a New Jersey Devils hockey fan. My love of hockey was a secret none of my colleagues knew, and no one would ever guess. We were deep in New York Rangers territory, and the Devils were the enemy team across the river. I joked I might be run out of Manhattan by an angry mob if they found out. I made a show of looking over my shoulder conspiratorially to make sure no one heard, then lightly touched his forearm and laughed flirtatiously.

Sergei's electric blue eyes sparked with amusement as he assured me my big secret would be safe with him. It was silly, but I was pleased with the thought of trusting a Russian with a secret. Why not? Doesn't doing something 'forbidden' always make it more exciting?

We drank another shot together. This time he toasted in English,

"To your beauty!"

I smiled and laughed as I tossed back the drink.

He needs glasses! I thought, but something about this man made me feel more feminine and attractive.

Before I knew it, I was telling him everything about my life. I even told him about the rusty Jeep Wrangler I sold when I moved to the city. Sergei seemed amused by the idea of me four-wheeling a Jeep through snowdrifts on backcountry roads, but he didn't laugh. He raised his eyebrows and exhaled loudly through his nose instead, shaking his head from side to side with a controlled grin. That seemed unusual. I wondered if all Russians laughed like that.

I also noticed he didn't show his teeth when he smiled. I saw normal-looking teeth when he spoke and wondered why he would want to hide them. His facial expressions were more reserved than most Americans, so I paid closer attention to things like the creases at the corners of his eyes to gauge how he was feeling. I had to look closely, but I didn't mind.

Sergei intrigued me.

We seemed to connect easily despite coming from opposite sides of the planet. And there we were, the only crazy ones sitting on an 11th-floor balcony on a cold autumn evening. The temperature was dropping. Even when our exhalations turned to vapor, neither of us wanted to go inside.

Most of the guests were gone by the time he escorted me indoors with his arm around my waist to help hide the stain. He made a point to say good night to Jerry, who shot me a big smile and flashed two thumbs up as soon as the Russian's attention turned. I'd planned to take the subway home, but how could I refuse Sergei's offer to give me a lift in a limousine?

He walked me up to my third-floor East Village apartment door, where we chatted in the hall for another hour. Sergei insisted we meet again before he left town in two days. He also insisted on paying for my dry cleaning. When I tried to refuse, he pressed a stack of twenties into my hand. We agreed to have dinner the following evening.

Before he left, he took my hands in his and leaned in to kiss me. As our lips touched, warm fluttering sensations lit up my belly, and I felt the beginning of a quiver that might make my knees buckle. Being so close to his face was thrilling. And those lips! After furtively watching them for hours, the feeling of their smooth warmth touching mine was exquisite.

Later, I stripped off the ruined dress, left it on the floor where it fell and slipped into bed nude. I relived the kiss over and over again until I began to wonder whether Sergei was real or just a phantom in my twisted imagination.

2

CHARDONNAY S'IL VOUS PLAÎT

The clock in my office ticked slowly above the depressed sales manager's head as he spent his hour lamenting his inability to attract women. I encouraged him to keep talking and occasionally summarized what he said. Sometimes all clients need is to speak and feel heard to let the truth of whatever is bothering them hit the air and dissipate. His mood improved significantly by the end of the session, and he seemed more attractive too. Funny how that works, I thought with a chuckle.

I considered canceling my other afternoon appointments, but I wasn't sure how that would go over with my new boss. I fought to stay focused, but my unruly mind kept trailing back to Sergei's lips and the words he said to me. As soon as my last client left, I hurried out of the office, vowing to type my therapy notes later.

I stopped at Filene's Basement on Broadway and found a bargain on a sexy red satin dress. An Asian pattern wove through it in golden thread. Peacocks and pheasants. That might catch the eye of a Russian, I thought, feeling pleased. The dress fit me perfectly, showing off my curves in the right places while retaining a fair amount of modesty. I went to another store and found a matching pair of four-inch heels. They cost more than I wanted to spend, but I was out of time. With less than two hours left, I dashed home to get ready. I secured my hair into a loose bun with two silver chopsticks leaving a few flirtatious tendrils along the sides of my face and at the nape of my neck. I put on the last touch of makeup, red lipstick, and was frantically waving my wet fingernails to dry when the buzzer rang precisely at 8:00 pm, right on time.

He is here!

Sergei's warm smile showed how pleased he was with my appearance. I twirled slowly in the lobby to let him admire me from all angles. On an impulse, I curtseyed before him, extended my arm, and said,

"Your Majesty."

He took my hand and kissed it. The red nail polish was a little bit smudged from my haste. If he noticed I wasn't perfect, he didn't seem to mind.

Our dinner reservation at Pó wasn't until 9:00 pm, so we went for a walk to pass the time. We strolled down West 4th Street for a few blocks and sat on a bench by Washington Square Park. It was a warm evening for that time of the year, perhaps 65 degrees. Although it was a clear night and the moon had not risen, I could not see any stars. There is too much light pollution in the city for starlight to shine through. The thought made me sad. I mentioned this observation to Sergei.

"Someday, you will come to my home in Russia. The stars are so close you can touch them. We will dance on a carpet of snow beneath the lights of the Aurora Borealis. I will show you magic," he said.

I didn't know what to say, so I said nothing.

I just gazed at him and smiled. His eyes were so intense that I began to feel embarrassed after a few seconds and had to look away. I pretended to be interested in the people passing by on the sidewalk.

My mind was racing. Sergei intrigued me. He wasn't a big man, but something was commanding about him. Power exuded from his every pore. It was more than his perfect posture and the purposeful way he moved. He chose his words carefully, precisely communicating as intended. The intelligence required to do that impressed me, even more so for a foreign speaker.

I became aware of his body heat emanating in waves beside me. I detected the slightest hint of his scent beneath his cologne and fresh clothing. The thought of his body excited me. He touched my hand lightly, breaking me from my reverie. He gently took my cheeks in his palms and turned my face to his.

"I want to look at you," he said, "because I never want to forget the way you look tonight."

His eyes were softer now. I had a strong urge to kiss him, but I held back. God, I hope you can't read my mind. He winked, and for a moment, I thought that he could.

At last, it was time to claim our reservation.

Sergei ordered a bottle of French Chardonnay for me and a double vodka for himself. I was surprised and a little annoyed he didn't ask me what I wanted. I don't care for white wine. Chardonnay? I shot him a question mark in the form of a raised eyebrow. He explained,

"It goes best with the grilled salmon. Pó is famous for this dish. It is the best you will ever have."

I wasn't satisfied. I wasn't fond of fish either.

"I insist you try it," he said, showing me his sweet smile.

Ah, those sweet lips warmed my heart, and I let the issue go.

To my surprise, the wine was delicious. So much better than the oaky Californian chardonnay I tasted in the past. I complimented the selection.

"See?" He said, smiling. "I know what I am doing. You need to trust me."

When the waiter returned, I ordered the salmon as Sergei recommended. He ordered lamb paillard for himself and a glass of merlot to go with it.

The salmon was excellent, and the wine paired beautifully.

We strolled the city for an hour after dinner, finally arriving at my building around midnight. We lingered in the hall by my apartment door for some time, unwilling to let the evening end. I was too embarrassed to invite him into my tiny studio apartment and wasn't sure if it would be appropriate on a first date anyway.

Our conversation paused when we heard someone singing the Star-Spangled Banner, but only the first two lines, on repeat. The volume increased sharply as an intoxicated neighbor rounded the corner and staggered toward us, sliding along the wall for support. "Ohhhhh say can you seeeeee? By the dawn's early liiiiight!" followed by an impressive belch that filled the corridor with the stench of beer and pepperoni pizza. I rolled my eyes and chose the lesser evil. I hastily unlocked the deadbolt and waved Sergei inside before the wretched beast came any closer.

11

Sergei surveyed the interior of my apartment with great interest. There wasn't much to see – it was one room and a bath with antique plumbing fixtures. The lone window didn't need a curtain because it faced a brick wall. If the kitchenette was any smaller, it might fit in a shoebox. A dining table with two chairs, a desk, shelves overflowing with books, a garage-sale dresser, and a bed filled the space. More books stacked beside the bed served as a makeshift night table. At least my bed was elegant. The queen-size walnut sleigh bed once belonged to my grandmother. Thankfully, I remembered to make it this morning, so it looked tidy topped with a puffy white comforter.

The heat kicked on with the sound of groaning pipes, and the old steam radiators began to hiss as they warmed. The old building seemed alive, possibly possessed.

Sergei took it all in and appeared to be very amused.

He studied the three photos displayed on my dresser. One picture was of my father and me on skis at the head of a black diamond trail on Whiteface Mountain. The sun was shining, and we were both smiling. I was about 10.

Another was a snapshot taken on my doctoral graduation day. My mother and father's faces beamed with pride, and I seemed full of hope and looked impressive in my cap and gown, wearing the full university regalia.

He said he liked the one of me swimming in Mirror Lake with my black lab the best. Her name was Jenny, and she had a big stick in her mouth. She was my first dog. I must have been about six years old.

A plastic model of a red Jeep with a tan soft top rested on the desk by my laptop. Sergei picked it up and peered through the tiny windshield.

"Why do you have this toy?" He asked.

I imagined he thought it was foolish for a grown woman to have such a thing.

"Life cannot always be so serious," I explained. "Sometimes, I get over-involved in my work. When I need a break, I take that little Jeep and pretend I am driving. See?"

I placed two fingers on the roof and drove it around the desk, making rumbling sounds. I went over the bumpy keyboard and attempted to drive up the slant of the laptop screen sideways. The Jeep rolled, but I recovered and continued to drive. The toy truck trundled over his hand and then up his arm. The folds on his suit were hard to negotiate, and the terrain was steep, but my little Jeep managed. He was the Rubicon Trail, the ultimate adventure for four-wheel drive enthusiasts.

He smiled warmly.

Oh my God. This man is gorgeous.

My cheeks bloomed with the warmth of attraction.

Look away!

There was no time to plan, or I would have splurged on a bottle of expensive vodka. Luckily, I had half a bottle of Smirnoff Orange Twist in the freezer. I poured some into a juice glass for Sergei. Straight up, the way he likes it. I cut mine with cranberry juice.

"Who puts vodka in the freezer?" He teased.

"It gets thick," I explained earnestly, "but it doesn't freeze. It's great when you run out of ice cubes."

He said, "Ha! In Russia, we do not use ice cubes. We drink vodka to stay warm!"

Sergei was enjoying himself. I loved to see his smile, especially the way it softened his eyes and made them sparkle.

I did not have much food on hand, two frozen Lean Cuisine entrees, a few unappetizing cans of diet shakes, and a leftover pint of General Tso's chicken. I warmed the chicken in the microwave for Sergei for a little something to nibble on with his vodka. Probably not a very impressive zakuska for a Russian, but it was the best I could do.

The hour was late, so we made plans to see each other again. Then we exchanged telephone numbers and email addresses. He promised to keep in touch while he was traveling.

Sergei held me for a moment by the door. I pressed my cheek against his collar and inhaled his manly scent, which I found highly arousing. I'd waited my entire life to meet a man I wanted to be romantic with, and I didn't want to wait any longer. This was it. I wanted him. Right here. Right now. All he had to do was say the word, and I would be his.

He gave me a simple kiss on the lips instead.

My awakened libido raged for more. I slipped my arms beneath Sergei's jacket and wrapped them around his back. My eyes pleaded for another kiss, and he obliged. This time I was ready, and I kissed him passionately. I became conscious of my hands gripping his buttocks, pulling him closer. His male arousal pressed against me. Encouraged, I slipped my tongue into his mouth, and it found what I wanted – connection.

"No!" He shouted, pushing me away and taking three steps back. He looked stunned. He gripped the back of a chair to steady himself.

Confused and hurt, I simply stared as a wave of emotion crossed over him. His beautiful face contorted into a scowling mask, but only for a moment, and then his features relaxed. His eyes found mine. They burned with a fire that I cannot describe.

"Don't ever do that again!" He scolded angrily.

"I'm sorry, I don't understand," I whispered.

Don't all guys want sex?

As I lowered my eyes, I knew he thought I was a slut. The rancid taste of shame rose in my throat. Tonight was only our first date, and here I was, not only willing to have sex but throwing myself at him.

"Look at me," he ordered.

I felt tears beginning to form as I lifted my eyes.

"I am sorry, Sergei. I did not mean to offend you," I choked in apology.

The tears were flowing now, and they would not stop.

"I thought you wanted me," I squeaked. My mouth suddenly felt parched.

He folded his left arm over his abdomen and stroked his chin with his right hand. He studied me like an artist does a painting. I waited. Finally, he took my hands in his.

"I desire you more than you know, little bird," he said softly. "But it is too soon. Please do not kiss me like that again. I may not be able to stop myself the next time."

He hugged me and kissed my forehead.

"I will see you in two weeks," he said. "Good night."

And with that, he left. He was flying to Istanbul in the morning.

In the weeks that followed, we spoke on the phone almost every day. He described the places he visited and told me about his business deals. His strategy was to buy weak companies with problems he knew how to correct. He would reorganize from the top-down to make them profitable. Then he would sell and make a bundle. He diversified his holdings by selecting investments in various industries around the globe. If one market or industry went down, another would go up so he would never lose.

Sergei painted himself as a tough negotiator who never left any money on the table. He was highly competitive, celebrating his victories like a conqueror but accepting defeat poorly, taking disappointments hard as personal failures. I listened to him vent his temper with verbal tirades many times. I was happy to hold space for him and glad he didn't feel a need to hide his emotional struggles from me. He didn't present a façade to impress women as most men do. I valued his honesty. He needed my support, and of course, I wanted to help.

In the end, business was just a game to him. He loved the agency it provided because he was the one making things happen and could think steps ahead of everyone else. His brilliant mind thrived on the analytical challenges, and his heart loved the drama of high-stakes finance. When tough men crumbled under the pressure he applied, Sergei felt even more alive.

We developed a relationship with depth and mutual respect. I had no desire to repeat the embarrassment I experienced on our first date, so I did not push the intimacy issue. I saw Sergei enough to say I had a boyfriend, which kept people from setting me up on blind dates with their lovelorn relatives. I had all the solitary time I needed to rebound from the intensity of the psychotherapy practice. I spent my free time writing and exploring New York's numerous museums and art galleries on my own.

A long-distance relationship was the perfect arrangement.

Whenever he had a chance to come through New York, he did. Sergei brought gifts from far-off places – a handcrafted jewelry box from Turkey, a winter hat from Germany, a silk bathrobe from San Francisco. By far, the best present was a world atlas he bought at the bookstore down the street from my apartment. The oversized, heavy book had colorful fold-out maps jammed with information on every place in the world. I'd never taken an interest in geography, so this became a valued resource to feel closer to him as he traveled around the globe.

Sometimes he would surprise me by coming to my office to take me to lunch or buzzing my apartment when I didn't expect him. He always seemed to know where to find me. Often he had just a few hours layover on his way to someplace else. I was never sure when I would see him next, but I was always glad when I did.

He caught me unprepared one rainy December afternoon. I'd left the apartment wearing black yoga pants and a fitted tank top beneath a red plaid vintage men's flannel work jacket I found at a thrift shop. Leather knee-high

15

lace-up work boots completed this reckless ensemble. A chewed-up yellow #2 pencil held my hair in a wild absent-minded bun on top of my head, and I had my glasses on. They had small lenses, a style that conveyed 'intellectual with an attitude' to the world. At least that was the look I was going for when I bought them. I may have looked more like a crazy librarian, but I wasn't worried. East Village is funky, so I fit right in.

The sidewalk was full of people looking down, dressed in overcoats and carrying umbrellas. I was on a single-minded mission: Coffee. I was focused on my new project, still editing the words in my mind. I'd forgotten to grab my umbrella and decided to trudge on in the rain rather than go back up the two flights of stairs to get it.

I did not see Sergei in the crowd.

He almost didn't recognize me either.

"Sandra?" He asked tentatively, touching my arm as I passed.

I turned at the sound of his voice, and my heart leaped in my chest when I saw his face. He was striking and perfect as always in a dark business suit and fine wool overcoat.

"Sergei!" I cried in surprise.

I was so delighted to see him I completely forgot my appearance. He wrapped his arms around me and kissed me right there on the sidewalk with pedestrians flowing around us like a river. Cold rain drizzled from a lead-gray sky. My hair fell in a shameless waterfall as the pencil dropped, forgotten to the wet concrete below. I looked at him through my glasses and watched him take in the sight of me. As raindrops obscured the lenses, I realized I did not look my best and began to feel embarrassed. I was always dressed and wore contact lenses in the past. I wasn't wearing any makeup. This moment was the first he'd seen me in my 'natural' state.

What does he think of me? I wondered apprehensively.

"Sandrochka," he stated, his warm breath teasing my face. "You are full of surprises. What else do you have in store for me?"

Ah, I thought, relaxing. Sergei said it in a way to let me know he still found me attractive. I noticed he called me 'Sandrochka' only when he was feeling affection for me. And it was always said in a deeper tone than usual. The rest of the time, I was 'Sandra' to him. No one ever called me Sandra. 'Cassie' is the American version of my name, but I didn't correct him. Sergei's names gave me clues to how he was feeling.

"If only you knew, but I will not divulge my secrets. There is only one way for you to find out!" I teased as I bit my lower lip, raised an eyebrow, and then displayed a frisky smile.

"You play with me, Sandra," he warned.

I didn't care. I could play with this man for the rest of my life and never get bored. I took off my glasses to view his face without obstruction. He was close enough to see, but the world beyond him became a blur.

"Yes," I admitted, "but not nearly as often as I would like to!"

We locked gazes, and all the noise, sights, and commotion that is New York City vanished beyond the perimeter of his eyes. We went to a place where only we existed.

It was a quiet place.

His eyes held mine just as his hands were now holding my shoulders, guiding me backward. My feet and legs moved as if hypnotized. My back came up against a wall, and my nerve endings drew the outlines of cold, damp bricks through my clothing for my brain to read.

Sergei brought his face so close to mine our noses almost touched. Sergei's eyes were so close, so intense, so incredibly blue. His pupils were large, and through the void, I imagined I saw the universe expanding within him. I couldn't look away even if I wanted to. After not seeing him in weeks, the power of his proximity overwhelmed my senses. I forgot to breathe. This moment of feeling lost within his eyes stretched on into eternity.

He closed his eyes and kissed me. The heat between us was incredible, like standing beside a bonfire on a cold winter night. The front of me was burning hot, but my backside was freezing. He was the sun, and I was the earth, caught in his gravitational pull. We were two heavenly bodies floating on an ancient path through the universe, bound to each other by forces I could not comprehend.

Sergei pulled back and examined my face. I was awash with emotion and wonder. My cheeks were burning, and I was breathless. He smiled with satisfaction.

"Where are you going?" He asked bluntly.

"W-what?" I stammered.

"You were leaving the building," he prompted.

"Oh," I stalled.

The sounds of the city flooded back to my awareness, and I suddenly remembered where I was. I felt like I just woke from a dream. I looked around and saw we were standing beneath the service entrance to my building. The rain was coming down harder, just inches beyond his shoulders. How could I have not noticed before? He brought me in from the storm! I looked at him and wondered why it seemed like he was expecting something.

"You were going somewhere?" He prodded. The deep crinkles in the corners of his eyes revealed the pleasure he took in his ability to produce such a powerful effect on me.

"Oh yes," I replied.

I felt like an idiot. Why wasn't my brain working?

"To Starbucks for coffee," I finally answered. "I am editing the article for Psychology Today. The final draft is due on Monday."

He already knew the magazine acceptance was a significant win for me to break out of academic writing and widen my audience.

"Let me get some caffeine into you then," he said. "I only have three hours. I won't take much of your time."

"No," I said. "Only three hours?"

I felt crushed. I would rather miss the deadline to have more time together. Sergei smiled and took me by the hand.

"Let's go," he said.

I put my glasses on, and we stepped out into the rain. New York never seemed more exciting or beautiful than on that dreary December day. I could have walked to Albany with him, but our destination was only a few blocks away.

We looked like an unlikely pair at the coffee shop, he in his perfectly-tailored business suit and me dressed as a rogue student philosopher, but I didn't care. It was enough to be together.

Sometimes, he called to ask my advice on dealing with difficult people or motivating someone to sign a deal. I used active listening to help him talk through problems. He usually figured the problem out on his own, but it delighted me to lend psychological insights. I could see situations from different perspectives, and that often helped him sharpen his strategy.

We spent so much time talking on the phone I grew to love the sound of his voice. I began to hear him in my dreams. He spoke 15 languages fluently, and I was thrilled to listen to them all. He began to talk to me in French, my only other language. French with his accent was the sexiest I'd ever heard. I was inspired to practice and become better.

My French was rusty, so I spent my free time reviewing old class notes and listening to audiotapes. I watched every French film with English subtitles available at the public library. He noticed I was improving and promised to take me to Paris once I became fluent. That was motivation enough for me, and I worked hard to polish my skills. An excellent teacher, Sergei gently corrected my errors and always remembered to tell me he was proud of my progress.

When the British Psychological Society invited me to speak at a three-day conference in London in February, Sergei rearranged his schedule to meet me there. Once my talk was over, I blew off the rest of the events to spend more time with him. We did a little sightseeing, but the damp cold from the unrelenting rain quickly became tiresome. By the time we saw the Crown Jewels at the Tower of London and walked across the London Bridge, we had had enough. We stayed indoors and enjoyed long conversations that traveled from topic to topic. When we ran out of words, we snuggled on the couch in front of the television in my hotel room and watched cricket matches. I loved to lay my head on his warm lap and feel his fingers stroke my hair.

"You are soft like a kitten," he spoke tenderly, gazing down at me with half-closed eyes.

My heart purred as I met his gaze.

"Thank you for coming to London, Sergei. I'm so glad you are here," I softly replied.

"Why don't you call me 'Seryozha'? 'Sergei' seems so cold coming from you," he explained.

I sat up and looked at him, surprised. It never occurred to me he had a pet name.

"Seryozha?" I asked.

He nodded and smiled. I pronounced it correctly.

"Seryozha," I repeated, feeling the way the name rolled off my tongue. "I love the way that sounds."

It was so much better than 'honey.' I rested my cheek against his chest to listen to his heartbeat and feel his warmth. I loved to be close to him.

"Seryozha, Seryozha, won't you kiss me handsome, Seryozha?" I sang with a giggle and turned to look at him again.

Sergei kissed my lips and lightly exhaled over my face. I breathed in his breath, drinking in his very essence. He was everything I ever wanted.

Being with him felt so right.

"I am completely in love with you, Seryozha," I admitted quietly.

His face beamed with delight as he wrapped his arms around me, pulling me even closer.

"Oh, Sandrochka, You make me so happy! Of course, I love you too!" He cried.

He kissed me again, and at that moment, I knew he was the one for me. He was my first love, and he felt the same way! I did not comprehend love intellectually, but the undeniable truth of it filled my entire being. All I wanted to do was melt into him, to become one with this incredible man and love him forever.

I was astounded when he did not lift the ban on intimacy. Being in love was more than enough justification for physical relations, and I was Catholic! Russians must be total prudes, I thought, but I did not push the issue. There was nothing wrong with being old-fashioned. Moral values, integrity, and self-control were good traits in a partner. As much as my frustration was growing, I loved him enough to wait until he was ready.

And yet, it seemed bizarre he would put off sex for so long – not just intercourse, but French kissing, sensual touching, and everything else. I had never seen him without all of his clothes. Tattoos could cover his body.

Lurking in the back of my mind was an irrational fear he was hiding a hideous deformity. That is ridiculous, I told myself, he would have told me. Besides, we were in love! That would have to be enough for now.

I hoped he wouldn't make me wait forever.

It was making me anxious.

3

VEUX-TU?

By April, I'd become much more comfortable in the New York social scene. That's when I met Jack Hawthorne at an uptown dinner party hosted by one of my new connections. He was a handsome angular man in his early 50s, with dark brown hair marked by broad swaths of gray at the temples. Most people would describe him as 'distinguished,' but Jack reminded me of Clark Kent's newspaper boss in the Superman comics. The observation amused me so much I initiated a conversation to find out more about him. I learned he was a publisher with wit and intellect to match his good looks. We fell into a lighthearted exchange, and before I knew it, we were bouncing project ideas off each other. I told him how much fun I had weaving real human stories into my otherwise dull dissertation data.

"You know what would be a lot of fun?" I asked excitedly. "Doing the same thing for personality disorders, with a twist of using historical figures and celebrities to showcase each one… the disorders will provide a construct for analyzing famous people the general public is already fascinated by!"

I was supercharged. I couldn't believe I had never thought of this idea before. Several celebs sprung to mind immediately. Jack was just as excited about the project, calling it "refreshing" and "completely new and different," which sounded a lot like the positive tagline reviews we might receive on the final product.

He called later that week to offer me a job. People with personality disorders are interesting characters who interact with the world in unusual ways. They can be very successful, but how they go about their business varies dramatically depending on the disorder.

The ten personality disorders cluster into three groups. There would be one book for each group – the Eccentric, Dramatic, and Anxious types.

The project would take two years, and I would be paid a quarterly advance for meeting my deadlines. I would be free to travel anywhere in the world that had internet access. I knew this was a golden opportunity. The idea of traveling around the globe with Sergei was appealing, but I wanted to talk it over with him before deciding.

He was home in Russia when I called. The tone of his voice and faster speech told me he was excited. He congratulated me and said,

"Of course, you should take the assignment. Aren't you getting tired of listening to those New Yorkers complain about their problems anyway? Now you have a chance to do something worthy of your intellect."

They were beautiful words to hear.

"I am so happy for us," he continued, "I must see you right away so we can celebrate. I will be on the next plane out of St. Petersburg. Look for me tomorrow afternoon."

I didn't have to ask. I knew it would be a 16-hour flight with a connection in Western Europe, probably Frankfurt, to JFK. He'd made the trip many times before.

Sergei arrived at my office as I was clearing my desk for the day. It was Friday, and he could spend three entire days with me. He was not flying out again until Monday night.

I told him I turned in my resignation letter. The bad news was Jerry was upset because I hadn't given him a year on the job. It would be a hassle to rearrange the caseloads in his growing practice. All of the other therapists were overloaded already. I felt guilty, but what could I do? The good news was I would finish transferring my clients within a month. Then I would be free.

Sergei smiled and said,

"Don't worry. I will find a way to compensate him for taking you away."

It seemed like a strange thing to say, but I didn't dwell on it.

We stopped by my apartment to freshen up before going out to dinner. I took a shower and dressed quickly, leaving my hair to dry in loose natural waves. When I came out of the bath, I was surprised to see a crystal vase filled with red roses on my tiny dining table.

"For you, my princess," he said with a smile, standing beside the table.

THE STAIN

"Thank you, Seryozha. They are beautiful," I replied as I sniffed the blooms. They were lovely. On closer inspection, I noticed there were 15 roses. That's odd. They usually sell them by the dozen.

"Read the card," he said.

There was a small white card tied among the stems. Inside was a note handwritten in French:

"*Veux-tu m'éspouser?*"

I wasn't expecting a marriage proposal. Stunned, I looked at Sergei and saw he was waiting for my reply.

"*Oui, absolutement! Je t'adore, Seryozha!*" I cried.

Sergei took my hands in his as he kissed me without restraint. There was nothing between us but our clothing. His chest rose and fell against me as he explored my mouth with his tongue for the first time. The kiss was more intense than I imagined in all of my longings over the past five months. My body responded with pulsing waves of heat and electricity.

As he withdrew from the kiss, my entire being cried out for the lost opportunity. I counseled myself to calm down. I waited five months for that kiss. Surely I could wait a little longer. I prayed he wouldn't want a long engagement.

"The flowers are from the shop on the corner," he said as he dismissed them with a wave.

"The vase is Waterford crystal from Ireland. I had the pattern custom-cut. An original, like you."

"But this, my dear Sandrochka," he paused, "this is 100 percent Russian, like me. This is a gift from my heart. It once belonged to my mother, Sofia."

He took a little black box from his pocket and placed it in my hands. I looked up at him, unsure, and he nodded to encourage me to open it.

The top popped open, revealing a colossal oval diamond surrounded by 16 rubies in an antique ring setting. It looked priceless, and I imagined it probably was. I was speechless. Sergei took it out of the box and placed it on my finger. My hands were trembling – a perfect fit.

The diamond looked huge and stunning on my hand.

"Oh, Seryozha, I love it!" I declared as I displayed my hand for him to see. The diamond blazed with internal fire. He smiled. I threw my arms around his neck and covered his face with kisses.

A cloud of sadness passed over him as he explained the ring was the only thing that remained of his mother. The original opal had fallen out, its spark gone and lost to time. His voice deepened and quivered as he spoke. Knowing my beloved man was on the verge of tears touched my heart deeply. I understood this was a profoundly sentimental gift, priceless and irreplaceable.

"The new diamond symbolizes our love. My love is for you and you alone," he said as he gazed into my eyes, connecting with the deep place in my heart where there are no words.

I was so overwhelmed it took a minute to speak,

"Thank you, my love. I will cherish Sofia's ring always."

Satisfied, he took out a notepad and a pen from his briefcase and sat down.

"Sit," he said. "We have planning to do."

I glanced at the vase and noticed the crystal was cut with peacocks and pheasants, which seemed familiar. The same pattern as the dress I wore on our first date! I was amazed he remembered that level of detail. I couldn't imagine how much trouble he had gone through to have it made for me. When did he have the time? I was touched. I gazed at him with wonder, but he was wearing his business face.

I knew that look. It was time to negotiate.

I placed my feet firmly on the floor and sat taller in my seat.

The first item on the agenda was the wedding.

We discussed the service. I was Roman Catholic, but I only went to church when visiting my parents. The church would require a year-long engagement, the groom's conversion, and pre-marriage counseling.

I couldn't wait a year!

Luckily, Sergei wanted a simple wedding. He insisted on a judge because he didn't believe in God. My parents will freak out when they find out I'm marrying an atheist, I thought, but they would probably be happy someone finally took an interest in their bookworm of a daughter.

We reached an agreement quickly. The ceremony would be in one month, in New York. I was assigned to find a venue and make the arrangements. He didn't care how much it cost and encouraged me to plan the event however I wanted. He said he would invite his guests, two or three friends in the States, by phone.

The second item was the honeymoon. He asked,
"Parles-tu bien le français, ma petite?"
"Est-ce que je parle couramment le français?" I replied flawlessly.
Paris it was.

The third item to be discussed was my finances.

He started with debts. I reluctantly told him how much I owed on student loans and credit cards. The total was just under 100 thousand dollars, a shameful sum to confess to anyone. I found it hard to speak the words and braced for his reaction.

"Are you sure that's everything?" He asked with one raised eyebrow, seeming to know I was holding something back.

I took a deep breath, exhaled, and confessed to one more loan that took me over the 100 grand mark.

"Good," he calmly replied to my utter amazement. "Get the last statement for each account and bring them to me."

I looked at him like he was crazy.

"Now!" he commanded.

I jumped up and quickly retrieved what he wanted.

"I will pay the balances, and we will close all of these accounts next week," he said.

"Give me your credit cards," he ordered. I pulled them from my wallet and watched in disbelief as he took scissors and cut them up. He did it so dramatically that it seemed more of a symbolic gesture than a precaution. Then he pulled a black credit card from his billfold. 'Cassandra Karpova' was stamped on the front. I was shocked to see my married name in print. We had not discussed changing my name. Most professional women keep their maiden names or use a dashed name like 'Abbington-Karpov.' I looked to him for an explanation.

Instead, he said,

25

"I want you to start using this immediately. Be sure to sign with your new name. It will be official soon enough."

He made sure I was listening and dipped his head slightly to get me to nod my agreement. Within the span of a second, I decided I didn't care about my last name. I couldn't argue with the man who just removed the heavy yoke of my student debt. I nodded.

"You are to be my wife," he continued with a smile of satisfaction, "and I expect you to have fine things. Go shopping. I don't care how much you spend. This card has no limit. I will provide for you completely starting today."

He paused for a moment, choosing his following words carefully.

"I want you to keep your income and any savings you have in your name. Each day we are together, you will choose to be with me. I want you to have a measure of security in case it does not work out," he stated, looking at me with a wry smile. "But it will work out, won't it, Sandra?"

I nodded and smiled. I could not believe this was happening. This day was better than all the Christmases of my life put together. I got the gorgeous man, my debts were 'poof,' there was a rock the size of Texas on my finger, I was living in the most exciting city on earth, and I was about to go on a shopping spree.

Life could not get any better than this.

"Finally," he said, "we need to discuss where we are going to live."

I hadn't thought about that. This discussion was moving so quickly.

"We cannot live here," he said, dismissing my tiny apartment with his hand as he had done to the roses.

"Any suggestions?" He asked.

I shook my head, no.

"Well then," he said, looking at me intently. "I want you to live with me in Russia."

I must have looked unsure about the prospect of moving to his country without knowing how to speak the language. I spent the last four months watching silly French films and practicing to become fluent in French. Had I known this was coming, I would have spent that time learning Russian.

I knew very little about life in Russia, except for what I read by Tolstoy. Of course, that was super outdated. I learned about Catherine the Great, how Napoleon's army was defeated when winter came early, and the Romanov family's demise during the Revolution. I knew the Soviet Union was devastated by the Nazis in World War II but was pivotal in ending the war. Then there was Communism, the Cold War, and the threat of nuclear annihilation with the United States. The Soviet Union broke up a few years ago. Russia was known for its space program, and Yuri Gagarin was the first man in space. They have world-class chess players and scientists. Russia invests heavily in education, which I admire. Oh, and I knew Russian bad guys in movies say *"do svidaniya"* before they kill someone. That's about it. I was embarrassed by my ignorance, but I wasn't a history buff. In my defense or complete lack of it, I didn't know that much about American history either.

My impression was that chaos reigned in Russia today as the country struggled to move from government-run everything to a market economy. The administrative and economic shift was a considerable change. Surely it would take time to work things out.

Sergei seemed to sense my uncertainty and said,

"I will teach you Russian myself. We will give it one year. If you don't want to stay, we will move anywhere in the world you want. I only have one requirement – to be near an international airport."

Sometimes, I swear the man could read my mind. Russia couldn't be that bad if he lived there and wanted me to join him. He had horses. I love horses! What was a year anyway? Nothing.

It was a deal.

I agreed to his plan and contemplated my life as 'Mrs. Sergei Karpov' or 'Dr. Cassandra Karpov.' Would it be 'Dr. & Mr.' or 'Mr. & Dr.'? Why did it say 'Karpova' on the credit card? I suddenly realized how little I knew about his culture. I didn't care. I would love the way our names sounded together in any possible way.

My entire life just changed in one hour.

I noticed Sergei patiently waiting. I smiled to show he had my attention.

"Sandra," he said. "It is time for me to meet your parents."

Oh, Lord. Here we go.

We flew south to Tampa the following day, and Sergei drove a rental car northeast to my parents' condo in the outer suburbs. Their housing complex was typical of Florida, hastily built homes lining a golf course landscaped with ponds into which golf balls and small dogs disappeared. I still could not believe my father had traded his lifelong passion for skiing for this. He did it for my mother, who wanted to retire someplace sunny. There was no shortage of sunshine in Florida that day. It was hot, 85 degrees in the shade. The air was oppressively humid, and the sun seared our skin. Sergei was uncomfortable. Perspiration peppered his brow. I suspected it wasn't just the heat that was bothering him.

The oversized American flag and Chevy pickup with a Dole-Kemp bumper sticker in the driveway left no doubt this home belonged to 100 percent red-blooded Americans. They were conservative Republicans whose worst nightmare was coming true.

Bill Clinton was in the White House for four more years, and their liberal daughter was marrying a Russki.

My father's red face and swollen midsection betrayed his love of scotch. Thankfully, he was sober enough and in a good mood. If we could just avoid the subjects of politics and religion, we just might prevent an international incident. Unfortunately, those were my father's two favorite subjects.

I prayed for divine intervention.

As my Dad took a step back to make a show of appraising my boyfriend, I cringed, praying he wouldn't humiliate me severely. After what seemed an eternity, he shook Sergei's hand.

"Mr. Abbington," Sergei said politely. "I am honored to meet you. Sandra has told me much about you."

"Call me David. And this is Mary," he said, nodding to my mom.

Her eyes nearly popped when she saw the size of the diamond on my finger, but she was careful not to say anything. She knew why we were there. We sat in the living room sipping sweet tea as my father drilled Sergei with questions about his background. He answered them all as politely as possible, but I noticed that, as a lawyer would, he did not offer any additional details beyond the specific question asked. My parents were embarrassing. Before retiring, my father worked as a ski instructor in the winter and cut lawns for wealthy people in the summer. The only job my mother ever had was working in a gift shop. Neither of them went to college. I watched in horror as my father grilled my future husband like he was some sort of criminal, but I was proud of the way Sergei handled himself.

He was a true gentleman.

When the interrogation was over, Sergei asked to speak to my father privately. They went into the den and closed the door. As soon as the door clicked shut, my mother rushed to inspect the ring up close. She said,

"He's handsome and obviously wealthy, Cassie. But I am worried about you marrying a foreigner. Weren't Russians our worst enemies just a few years ago? You don't know anything about his customs."

"I love him, Mom," I replied, "and I would love him just as much if he was poor. I don't care about cultural differences. He is a man, and I am a woman. He loves me. That's all that matters."

I filled her in on the wedding details, my new assignment, and then reluctantly, our plans to live in Russia. I knew she would not like any of this and would object to our choice of residence the most. Her grave expression revealed the depth of her concern. She said,

"To get married so soon is lunacy. You've only known this man for five months. What can you possibly know about the strength of his character in such a short time? Why aren't you getting married in the church? And I can't believe you're ready to run off to Russia with him! People come to the United States to get away from Russia. It's horrible there. Stray dogs run loose on the streets, and people have to stand in line to buy stale bread. Why do you want to go there? What if they go Commie again? What happens to you? You are insane!"

"Mom, I'm a psychologist," I said, playing my sanity trump card. "Remember all those years at the university? Believe me. I know a good person when I see one. He loves me. I know it with all of my heart."

"You're pregnant!" She exclaimed.

I laughed out loud, thinking of the impossibility of that particular situation. It certainly was not my idea to play the part of a virgin bride.

"Nope. That would be virtually impossible, Mom," I said.

She nodded her understanding, probably thinking old-world Eastern Europeans must be very traditional. No sex before marriage. That was the one selling point for her.

A wisp of scotch painted a scented trail through the air as the door of the den flung open. Sergei emerged first. He wore a satisfied smile and flashed me a reassuring wink. My father looked a little less cheerful as he announced,

"I have given Mr. Karpov permission to marry our daughter."

Mom looked stunned. He said,

"You know Cassie. She has a strong will. She has already said yes. Have we ever been able to stop her from doing anything she wants to do?"

She shook her head, 'no.'

That was true, I thought with satisfaction. How frustrated my parents had been over the years trying to raise a stubborn daughter! I questioned everything, did research, presented facts, anticipated counterpoints, and won every argument. My husband was going to have his hands full.

"Besides, she's 28. It's time she married. Sergei has the means to provide for her and has promised to treat her well. Let's not make this any more difficult than it has to be," he added.

As Sergei took a seat beside me on the sofa, my father faced us and announced,

"Sergei and Cassandra, you have our blessing."

We stayed for a classic American dinner of Mom's homemade meatloaf with mashed potatoes and gravy and flew back to New York late that evening. On Monday, we applied for a marriage license and visited a clinic to run the whole battery of STD tests. The tests were not a requirement for marriage, but Sergei insisted. I knew nothing about his sexual history, but I was sure a 36-year-old male certainly would have one. He'd never brought up the subject, and I never asked. I didn't want to know about his old girlfriends, and it seemed rude to ask anyway. I was relieved when we both came back with clean reports. Whatever happened in the past did not matter.

There was nothing to hold us back.

4

LOVE AT LAST

The month leading up to the wedding sped by as I wrapped up my therapy work, made plans for the wedding, and packed my belongings into boxes. Before bed, after one long day, I opened the world atlas Sergei had given me to contemplate my life in Russia. The first thing that struck me is the Russian Federation is the largest country in the world. Nearly twice as large as Canada, which is number two.

Russia stretches from Finland in the west to Alaska in the east. Kazakhstan, Mongolia, and China follow its southern border. To the north lies only the Arctic Ocean. The country spans two continents. The westernmost fifth is part of Europe. This area is bordered in the east by the Ural Mountains, which run north and south to form a physical barrier that marks the boundary between Europe and Asia. Russia has a long coastline along the Pacific Ocean. I noted there are a great many seaport cities and towns. I imagined life in Eastern Russia is very different from the place I was going.

St. Petersburg is Russia's westernmost city and also the furthest north. Comparing the latitude line (60 degrees) to North America, I was surprised to see the city is in the same position as the northern tip of Labrador. St. Petersburg is further north than all of the major cities in Canada. It even beats Juneau, Alaska.

The topography is not mountainous, but it did not appear to be perfectly flat either. St. Petersburg is a port city on the Gulf of Finland, the eastern end of the Baltic Sea, which flows south of Norway and Sweden to connect with the Atlantic Ocean. There is a big lake just north of the city called Ladozhskoye Ozero. I inferred the word *Ozero* means lake in Russian because

31

the other lakes are named the same way. The Neva River runs from the lake through the city and out to the Gulf of Finland. Sergei said he lived about 80 miles southeast of St. Petersburg, near the town of Chudovo. A surge of excitement coursed through me as I traced the highway route on the map with my finger.

My publisher, Jack Hawthorne, met with me several times over the month to iron out the details of my assignment. Like my parents, he had reservations about my rush to get married and move overseas. I reminded him Russia had changed a lot since the cold war ended. They are not communists anymore. Besides, I was marrying the most capitalist man I'd ever met. That seemed ironic. Jack laughed and agreed because he met Sergei through Jerry O'Neill and was already familiar with his financial rhetoric.

Of course, I would be fine.

I assured him writing would not be a problem and promised to send weekly updates. Jack agreed to the arrangement and told me I could count on him if I got into any trouble. Jack felt more like a friend than a boss, so I invited him and his wife Jean to the wedding.

I chose an old-fashioned white wedding gown with a high collar and long fitted lace sleeves. A lace-covered cut away at the bosom offered a tasteful peek of cleavage. The skirt had several layers of taffeta beneath to make it fuller at the hip, and the bodice fit closely to show off the curve of my waist. A long row of buttons led down to a generous bow at the small of my back. I felt like a fancy gift, eager to be unwrapped. I indulged in daydreams about Sergei untying that bow as I waited for our big day to come.

My best friend from college was stuck home in Ohio with newborn twins, and I didn't have many friends in the city, so I skipped the bachelorette party. My mother, Aunt Lucy, Cousin Lisa, and friend Kelly from work joined me for a luxury weekend spa getaway at Mirbeau Spa in Skaneateles. Sergei insisted we take a limousine to the Finger Lakes from Manhattan, making the trip even more special. He made all of the arrangements and had his driver, Uvar, take us. Champagne, roses, fine chocolates, and several wrapped gifts from Sergei greeted me when I arrived in my room. The card read,

*Relax and enjoy, my love. No one deserves the royal treatment more
than you.
~S.*

The morning of the wedding, I had my hair professionally done in an elaborate formal style of loops and curls accented with hundreds of miniature pearls, a project that took two hours. My bridal party joined me to have their hair and makeup done too. We enjoyed a catered lunch of healthy fare – salads, avocado slices, organic grilled chicken, fresh, plump strawberries dipped in chocolate, and refreshing chilled herbal teas. Finally, a professional makeup artist transformed me into a beauty queen. I'd never thought of myself as particularly beautiful, but looking in the mirror, I was stunned to see a picture-perfect bride looking back at me.

Although my mother objected to the 'bad luck' of the groom seeing the bride before the wedding, my father and Sergei joined us, and we spent the afternoon taking photographs in front of iconic New York City landmarks. We took the VIP elevators at the Empire State building to be photographed at the top, holding champagne flutes with a panoramic view of the city behind us. Then we were on to Rockefeller Plaza, Times Square, and the Brooklyn Bridge to further document our day. Sergei's driver, Uvar, pulled the limo up to the hotel to drop us off and later joined our party as a guest.

The Waldorf Astoria Hotel provided an elegant setting for our Tuesday evening wedding and dinner reception. My father escorted me down a white rose petal-strewn aisle and gave me to Sergei beneath a rose-covered arbor. The ceremony was everything Sergei wanted – simple, legal, and no mention of God. We said "I do" and exchanged wide gold bands, placed on our right hands in the Russian tradition since that was where we were going. 'Sergei & Cassandra Forever' was inscribed inside of both rings, along with the date. The officiating judge proclaimed, "By the power vested in me by the City of New York, I now pronounce you husband and wife." The ceremony took less than ten minutes.

A solo pianist at a black baby grand played two traditional songs, Wagner's Bridal Chorus on my way up the aisle and Mendelssohn's Wedding March on our way back down. Those in attendance rang silver bells engraved with our names and wedding date once the official proclamation was made.

Fourteen guests seemed like a small party for such a significant event in our lives, but we had fun drinking champagne toasts and celebrating with those in attendance all the same. The hotel catering did not disappoint. The eight-course meal offered menued choices and wine pairings at each step. Attendants fussed over us, making sure everyone had everything they desired. Dinner stretched to three hours.

Before the dessert course, my mother pulled me aside and said,

"Cassie, you are a beautiful bride and an easy person to love. I am sure you will make him very happy. Open this."

She handed me a small gift wrapped in white paper with a golden ribbon. I hesitated because Sergei and I should open our presents together.

"This is just for you," she insisted. "Open it."

I carefully untied the bow and peeled back the paper to see a cookbook of traditional Russian recipes. I flipped through the pages and was surprised I had never heard of most of the dishes. The only thing I recognized was Beef Stroganoff, and there was something that looked like pierogis but had a different name. I smiled as if a child had just handed me a bouquet of wilted dandelions. The gift was a nice gesture, really, but I did not see why I needed this on my wedding day. A cookbook?

"Learn what he likes," she advised, "and cook for him. Do this, and you will have a long and happy marriage."

Sergei did not care about my cooking. But she was so insistent I took her message to heart. My mother would know. She had been married to my father for 30 years, and they were still together.

"Aren't you going to give me some sex advice?" I teased.

She laughed and said,

"No. I have been watching you, and I think you know what to do. I don't believe I have ever seen a bride with so much desire for her groom. Trust your heart, and you will not go wrong."

I smiled and thought of the sexy things we would be doing later on. I could not wait to be alone with Sergei, and I'm sure it showed. It was nearly six months from the day we met, but it seemed like I'd waited my entire life for him. I tingled all over, thinking about what was coming.

"Well," I said with much bravado. "I did take those human sexuality courses in graduate school. At least I know how the parts work!"

She laughed and said,

"I am more than a little jealous, Cassie. Your husband is handsome, but I had this moment with your father, and I will never regret it. Good luck!"

At last, it was time for Sergei to take me to our bridal suite.

Sergei asked me to sit on the bed and not move or say anything. He stood above me for several long minutes, gazing down with his mysterious blue eyes. They were soft. So soft it seemed he was about to cry.

"I want to burn this image of you into my mind forever," he explained, "so I will never forget the happiness I feel today."

When he was satisfied he'd done that, he sat down beside me and took my hand. In a serious tone, he said,

"I love you with all I am. I never want to hurt you or do anything to make you doubt me. Your trust is essential to me. I will protect and care for you. I want what we feel today to last until we are both old and gray and our grandchildren have children."

I lost myself as I looked into his eyes. I whispered,

"Oh, Seryozha, I love you, and I am yours now. Will you please release me? I have waited so long."

My husband kissed me softly at first and then more aggressively. I felt rapture, for the moment I long anticipated was finally coming. We embraced fervently, his hot tongue searching for mine and finding yielding bliss. A warm expectant glow spread between my thighs as a chorus of 'Oh my God, it's finally going to happen' sung through my mind. No one could want anyone more than I desired Sergei that night. He reached around and tried to undo the buttons on the back of the dress. They were not yielding to his touch. Frustrated, he flipped me over onto my stomach and bit off the buttons one by one, spitting them across the room.

Once my back was bare, Sergei paused to savor the moment. Then he rubbed my back gently and slipped his hands beneath to cup my breasts. He gave my desperate nipples a hard pinch.

I was on fire!

He slapped my rear playfully and told me to stand. He removed the dress and lingerie and threw everything on the floor in a crumpled heap. I stood before him completely nude and let him appreciate my bare flesh for the first time. I knew from my studies that men love to look at naked women, even

35

those who are not entirely perfect. I decided I was close enough and did not feel any shame because I knew he loved me. He made a spinning motion with his finger, asking me to twirl as I had done that evening in my apartment lobby. I obeyed and followed with the same curtsey. But this time, I said,

"Your loving servant awaits you, my King."

Sergei had a strange smile on his face, and he took his time looking over my body while I performed my little act. When his eyes reached mine again, they looked like the flames of hell lighted them. I felt the sensation of icy fingers in my belly, but I did not want to run away this time.

He snapped his fingers once and pointed to the bed. I walked over to it slowly and reclined on the pillows, watching to see what he would do next. He removed his clothing piece by piece, folded them neatly, and carefully placed them on the back of a chair. What a tease! I nearly burst with anticipation.

Sergei was lean with defined muscles. A light layer of fine blond hair covered his body, with somewhat thicker hair on his chest. There were no tattoos or signs of deformity. I felt silly for having worried.

He was perfect, not a scar, birthmark, or mole.

My eyes traveled down his body at a slow pace until I saw his arousal. I gasped, seeing his erect penis at last. He smiled as I took in the sight of his manhood for the first time. Then he turned to the side so I could enjoy it in profile. He pressed his hips forward to impress me even more. He was not circumcised, but his thin foreskin was fully retracted and resting at the base of the head like a snug sweater. It was about average size, but it looked so much better than 'average.'

I was finally seeing the penis of the man I loved.

And it was all for me!

I began shaking with anticipation.

When Sergei came to claim me, he moved fast. He kissed me and ran his fingertips gently over my nude form, sending my nerve endings into high pleasure alert. By the time his kisses reached my belly, my legs had parted naturally, allowing him to explore my feminine folds up close. I leaned back into the pillows and tried to relax, but I felt exceedingly self-conscious with the lights on. I hoped he didn't notice.

"Oh, Sandrochka," he said with a pleased smile, coming up to kiss my lips. When he pulled back, he looked deeply into my eyes, the tug of a smile still on his lips. "Is this really your first time? I am so glad we waited!"

I nodded shyly. This situation was beyond embarrassing, but at least the shame of being a 28-year-old virgin would be over soon, and I would no longer have to guard this ridiculous secret.

"Don't worry, I'll be careful," he promised as he dimmed the lights before kissing me again, his warm lips and frisky tongue reigniting my passion and easing the anxiety within me. He retraced his path of kisses, more leisurely this time, teasing as much anticipation as he could until his face was once again between my thighs.

His warm tongue licked the entrance of my vagina, which he teased open with his fingertips, careful not to probe too deeply. When he started sucking on my clitoris, warmth flooded my interior, and I felt the slick lubricating fluid ooze outward.

"Are you ready?" He asked, placing elbows beside my shoulders as he rose into the missionary position. The firm head of his penis pressed a sexy offer to the excited circle of nerves at the mouth of my vagina.

I nodded.

He kissed me lightly on the lips once again before his beautiful blue eyes locked onto mine, and he pushed his penis into me, so gently the first time. My mind focused intently on the single point of sensation – a pinch of pain as the wrapper tore on the gift of this new part of our lives beginning, followed by the exquisite feel of the interior of my vagina stretching and expanding to receive him fully. Sergei watched my face for signs of distress, taking the time to create an indelible mark in my memory so that I would never forget the importance of this moment with him. At last, he was fully inside, fitting us together snuggly. He ground his hips into mine playfully, and we spontaneously laughed with joy. We were complete, at last! Feeling my husband merged within me was the culmination of a journey over oceans, continents, cultures, and time.

I was the one he'd searched for, and he was the one I waited for, without knowing I was waiting for anyone at all.

Sergei was my King. I was his Queen.

We held hands while he slowly stroked his penis in and out, our eyes connected, soft gaze never breaking. The words "I love you" spontaneously spilled from our lips, repetitively, a divine mantra weaving spells of love around our souls and knitting our hearts together for eternity.

We were both overcome with emotion. Sergei's tears flowed unrestrained. They dripped onto my face, where they joined with mine, the Neva River flowing straight into the Hudson, our ancestries dancing and forming new alliances with every subtle movement and shift in energy.

Making love for the first time on our wedding night was the most profound experience of my life. All those months of longing charged this moment of ultimate intimacy with far more power. Sergei Ivanovich Karpov was my husband, and I was his wife. We were joined together, at last. When Sergei came inside of me, the magic was complete. There would be no undoing this love spell. We were one, forever.

After feeling alone for most of my life, I'd finally found my home with him.

Sergei was already up and in the shower when I woke the following day. To my horror, there was a crimson bloodstain on the pristine white bedsheet. Praying he didn't notice, I quickly made the bed and wrapped myself in a fancy terrycloth hotel robe.

"Husband," I called nervously from outside the open bathroom door. "May I join you?"

He opened the glass shower door and welcomed me into the steamy interior with a bright smile.

I dropped my robe by the door and ran to his open arms.

I felt a pang of regret as the plane took off and banked a wide circle around New York to cross the Atlantic, giving me one last view from my seat on the Concorde. As soon as I'd become accustomed to life in the city and was starting to enjoy myself, it was time to move on. The ultrafast plane felt like a metaphor for the speed with which my life had taken a new direction. As luxurious as it was, I felt unsettled.

Sergei's smile assured me our future together would be far better than anything we left behind. We clinked our champagne glasses, held hands, and spoke in French about what we would do in Paris. I wanted to spend a few days at the Louvre, and he wanted to show me Versailles, the country palace of Louis XIV. We had two entire weeks, so we could easily do both and have plenty of time alone together.

The plane approached Charles De Gaulle International just as the sun was setting. The lights were on in Paris, and I was thrilled to catch a glimpse of the Eiffel Tower from the plane. Sergei had the driver tour the city to orient ourselves before settling into our hotel for the night. After studying French throughout my school years, I was finally in France. I never imagined I would see Paris by limousine, and yet, there I was gushing and pointing excitedly at the places I'd read about in books to my new husband, who had seen it all already.

La Tour Eiffel!

L'arc de Triomphe!

Notre-Dame!

There was something wrong with the hotel room. Sergei objected,

"Non, Non, Non! Qu'est-ce que c'est? Tout est faux!"

The suite looked acceptable to me.

"What's wrong?" I asked.

"It was a surprise for you. Now it is ruined."

He took me back down to the lobby and instructed me to wait in the bar while he straightened out the problem. Twenty minutes later, he came for me, and we checked into *hôtel numéro deux*. This time Sergei was satisfied. I looked around, trying to figure out what he didn't like about the first room. This suite was slightly larger but had pretty much the same view. The only difference was that this one had antique furniture with a four-poster bed. Perhaps he felt the old-fashioned decor was more romantic for our honeymoon.

Sergei could be a bit high maintenance at times, getting upset over insignificant details. I recalled him nearly losing his mind when he couldn't find a specific kind of black tea in New York City. I didn't question him. I just chalked it up to European quirks. He had plenty of them.

I was just glad he was happy.

The hour was late, so we decided to order room service for dinner. Sergei selected chateaubriand for two and ordered three bottles of Bordeaux. It seemed like a lot of wine, but I did not say anything.

We took a long, hot shower together while we waited for the meal to arrive. I enjoyed the pleasure of washing my husband's body with soap and shampooing his hair, lavishing him with loving, tender caresses from top to bottom. I worked my way down to a kneeling position. As I washed his feet, I playfully teased the head of his penis with my tongue and took him into my mouth, serving him in a dirtier way. The warm water streamed over my face as tendrils of my wet hair threw off little sprays of water as they swayed possessed in an erotic love dance. I glanced up over his abdomen and chest in time to see his eyes roll back and his lips purse as his semen exploded into my mouth. I savored the taste of his salty Russian cream and swallowed it, taking time to lick the last few drops before gazing back up to the face of the man I loved.

"Oh, Sandrochka," he breathed, pulling me up and kissing me deeply. He spun me around and slipped his still hard cock into my hungry pussy from the rear. I was sore from making love the night before and again in the morning. He seemed impossibly huge. And yet, I welcomed the discomfort, trying to enjoy the sensation even more for having to wait for so long. I bent over at the waist and put my hands on the wall, shifting my legs further apart to give him deeper access. He took advantage and pounded me thoroughly for what must have been 15 minutes. His cock stretched me wide, and his hardness scrubbed the inner walls with each stroke, forcing me to expand and lengthen as his testicles slapped my pleasure nub in rhythm with my desire.

My mind went blank, and my soul soared through the cosmos, all reason lost as I tipped over the edge into an orgasm. There was nothing but Sergei and me, intertwined and convulsing as one. This time his love burst deep inside of me. He slowed his pace until he came to stillness, but then he carefully remained inside. He reached around and stroked my clitoris in circles until I came once again. He breathed into my ear,

"You deserved one more, *mon petit oiseau*."

We heard a loud knock on the door, the agitated sound of someone whose previous attempts went ignored. He smacked my rear playfully, jumped out of the shower, and threw me a hotel robe, winking.

"Hurry," he urged.

I peeked around the corner to see a male server dressed in a white shirt, black vest, and matching bowtie roll in a cart and arrange dishes on the dining table. Sergei thanked the man and said he would open the wine himself. The server wished him, *"Bon appétit,"* before rolling the cart back out of the room. Hearing the familiar phrase uttered in France for the first time gave me a schoolgirl thrill.

Sergei opened a bottle of wine and poured two glasses. He lifted the domes, set them aside, and beckoned me to dinner. I sat down, suddenly starving and savoring the aroma of the roasted beef tenderloin.

As I lifted my glass, Sergei said,

"*Non!*"

Startled, I looked at him.

"It's red wine," he explained flatly.

My face had an expression of 'So what?' written on it.

"You have a bad record," he explained with feigned seriousness. "You are a stain magnet. You said so yourself."

Oh my God, you are going to say it.

And he did,

"If you want to drink red wine, you have to remove your clothes first."

His expression playfully teased me as if this was a game of truth or dare. Not one to back down from a challenge, I stood up and gave him a striptease he would not soon forget, throwing my robe across the room as a grand finale. Feeling nude, but not necessarily naked, I sat back down. I drank the entire glass of wine in one motion and slammed the empty glass down on the table like a gunslinger in a western saloon. The wine tasted even better for having earned it the sexy way.

"Aaahhh!" I proclaimed.

Then I stuck my tongue out at him.

Sergei's odd smile told me he wasn't hungry for dinner anymore. He put the domes back over the plates and stood quickly. I was faster. I ran around the suite shrieking and giggling as he chased me. I ran like a naked gingerbread girl, taunting him with near catches and confounding him with sudden changes in direction. There was nowhere to run in the end, and we made love right on the floor in the spot where he brought me down.

His eyes locked onto mine. I lifted my hips to receive him, and he plunged inside, taking me to the hilt on the first stroke, plundering my bounty like a pirate. His ruthless fingers pinched and stretched my tender nipples while his rock-hard dick hammered me into yet another supernova

41

orgasm. Then he screwed me slow with deep hard thrusts. My breasts jumped with each ramming. The carpet burned my back, but I didn't care.

All the while, his eyes never left mine. Perhaps Sergei was watching my reactions, or maybe he was as lost in love as I was. I never felt so close to another human being in my entire life.

His eyes closed when he came, and then he hoarsely spoke,

"Promise me you won't ever forget you are my wife, Sandra."

The blue of his eyes searched my face, expectantly.

I was stunned by his request. How could I ever forget him?

"Promise," he insisted, eyes pleading.

"I promise, Seryozha. I will never forget you are my husband."

My husband collapsed onto me and wept into my hair.

We spent the following day shopping on the Champs Elysees. Sergei encouraged me to buy clothing. The eager shop assistants at the pricy designer stores brought everything they had in my size to my dressing chamber. I modeled outfits as he sipped champagne and bought everything he liked. I noticed he seemed to have a preference for the color red on me. He also favored very feminine clothes that showed off my figure. Shoes, bags, jewelry, lingerie, nothing but the best money could buy. We bought so much we had to have the purchases delivered to the hotel.

Sergei bought a pair of sunglasses that made him look like Arnold Schwarzenegger in the 'Terminator' movie. I told him they looked hot on him, and they did. But I felt uneasy because I felt cut off from him. With his eyes covered, I couldn't see what he was feeling.

We stopped for a late lunch at an outdoor café and ordered champagne. The café wasn't busy, and the service was glacially slow. I must have drunk the wine too fast because I got a bit tipsy. I started to giggle and could not stop.

I kept saying, "*Hasta la vista,* baby!" and cracking up. It seemed funny at the time because he was wearing those ridiculous sunglasses.

I married a cyborg.

Most husbands would be embarrassed by drunken behavior like this. But Sergei didn't mind. He watched me with an amused smirk on his face and ordered another bottle of champagne.

I think he liked to see me lose control.

On the way back to the hotel, Sergei stopped to look at a display of long silk scarves. He insisted I pick one out. I wasn't the silk scarf type. What was the point? Silk wouldn't keep me warm in the winter.

I teased him about being into the *'babushka'* look and said I would never wear it. But he was serious and asked me again to select something. So I picked out a red one, thinking of his favorite color on me. He added five more and bought a total of six. I had no idea why he wanted the scarves, but I did not say anything. We'd already burned through an ungodly amount of cash. Why should I care if he spent a little more?

We returned to our room around six and uncorked a bottle of Beaujolais. Sergei poured two glasses. I glanced to him for approval before I picked mine up this time. He gently shook his head, 'no.'

He wanted me to take my clothes off again!

Something in me rebelled. I crossed my arms and looked away. Sergei came closer and put his face directly in front of me, forcing me to look at him.

I closed my eyes.

His nose was just a millimeter away from mine, and I smelled the fragrance of his skin. I loved being this close, and he knew it, but I would not yield. He waited for a long minute. Then he said,

"You can't hide from me. Open your eyes."

His breath played over my face.

It was warm and smelled sweet, like wine.

I felt ridiculous in this untenable position, but I would not budge.

So I squeezed my eyelids tightly shut.

Sergei put his lips on mine and kissed me softly, slowly. I resisted as long as I could, but then excitement gripped me, and I responded automatically. I opened my eyes and saw him looking at me. A smile turned up the corners of his eyes. That turned me on even more. Before I knew it, my clothes were gone, and I was wantonly making love to him as he lay on the floor beneath me.

When we returned to the table, he handed me the glass of wine.

The cold war was over. The Russian won.

We talked at length about the issues of trust and loyalty. Sergei insisted they were the foundation of a happy marriage. We had no problem agreeing to maintain a solid partnership and present a united force of 'us' against the world. We also decided never to allow anyone to come between us, not even my parents. Is loyalty the cornerstone of trust? Check. Should we always be truthful and not hide secrets from each other? Check. No argument.

"No one is perfect," he reflected sadly. "We are going to make mistakes. We should promise to give each other another chance as long as there is a sincere effort to make things right."

I wasn't sure what scenarios came to his mind, but this request seemed pretty standard. Like if I went on a shopping spree and blew our budget, I could cut back on spending the next month and make it right. I didn't want to think about him having an affair, but we were married, so of course, we would work through it and try to rebuild trust if he did. I would always give marriage counseling a try before turning my back on him, no matter what happened. Or if he developed a drinking problem but went to rehab to quit, of course, I would stand by him. I wasn't worried about that happening. If he were going to develop alcoholism, it probably would have happened by now. He didn't seem interested in other drugs.

"Okay, I agree. Do you want to put this down on paper?" I teased.

He laughed.

"No, my little bird, this is an oral contract, but it is just as binding."

It was my turn to laugh. We were simpatico – a perfect match.

My newly minted spouse then brought up other, more unusual, thoughts about marriage.

"When wives withhold sex, couples grow apart," he claimed. "If a woman holds this power in the relationship, she will inevitably deny herself and her man the physical satisfaction and emotional connection needed to work through problems and stay together. The love dies. I have seen it happen many times in the lives of my friends. Wives should not have the right to refuse their husbands."

Whoa! I thought, but I understood the basis for the argument. I'd seen it happen too. Sergei had a point, but that didn't make his solution fair. He watched as I processed the logic.

I did not like the idea.

I could be an equal partner in a mature sexual relationship.

I desired him just as much as he did me.

Facts.

Why should I give up my right to refuse?

He read my face and said,

"Eventually, you will become angry about something and pull away from me. You will cut me off, and our love will die. We need sex to stay connected, even more so when we argue. We do not have a religion or the fear of God to bind us if our love fails. Our marriage will end. You don't want that to happen, do you?"

"This is something you should have brought up before we married," I stated bluntly, thinking the Catholic pre-marriage counseling and extended engagement didn't seem so silly now. My husband expected me to be a mindless sex slave? Oh, hell no. That was not going to happen.

"So? We are discussing it now," he calmly replied, eyeing me with a steady, level gaze.

Sergei was a professional negotiator with iron-clad nerves. I shifted uncomfortably in the hot seat, feeling his strong will bore holes through me as the seconds ticked.

He had a valid concern, one I could not deny, and he saw this as a real threat to our lasting relationship. He was determined. I knew I would never win this battle with a flat refusal. If I was going to agree to this, I wanted something in return. So I came up with a compromise.

"If I don't have the right to refuse, then neither should you," I argued. "This doesn't have to be a 'Man has all of the power and Woman has none' arrangement. Surely there will be times when you become angry with me and want to pull away. If you adjust the terms so that neither of us can refuse each other, ever, that we will always make love, even more so when we fight, then I will gladly make this deal with you."

Sergei considered my amended terms.

"It's a deal," he declared.

I put out my hand to shake on it, but he clasped my wrist and pulled me in close to seal the pact with a kiss instead.

After spending a day touring Versailles and a fancy dinner out, he had a playful look in his eyes I now recognized meant something special was coming. I was already nude from drinking a glass of red wine in our suite, so I knew it was only a matter of time before things became steamy. When he asked me to sit on the bed, I complied, wondering what new pleasure he would exact on me next.

"Let's play a game," he said mysteriously.

He withdrew the red silk scarves from a drawer and approached me. I brimmed with nervous anticipation, not knowing what he was going to do. I watched as he secured my left foot to a bedpost. He looked to see if I objected. I said nothing. He repeated the procedure with the right foot and then each of my wrists. Each time he checked to see if I trusted him to continue. I was frightened, I admit, but I tried not to show it. I was now spread-eagled on the bed, open for his pleasure.

I felt vulnerable but strangely excited at the same time. Being tied up was a first for me. The cool air pulled the heat from my most intimate anatomy and lifted my nipples to high peaks. I felt deliciously naughty, allowing a man to splay my legs open and fully expose the parts a lady is supposed to keep covered. It was a crime against God, or at least my upbringing in the Holy Roman Catholic Church where a woman's modesty is of utmost importance.

If Sergei was going to hell, he was intent on taking me with him.

I tested the silk restraints. The knots were secure. The tight pull of the twisted material pressed against my wrists and ankles. The bonds were waking up nerve endings I had never noticed before, creating new areas of sensitivity.

I breathed deeply to calm my anxiety. I could trust my husband not to hurt me. He loved me, right?

Sergei stood silently by the end of the bed, taking in the scene and perhaps enjoying the signs of turmoil playing out on my face. After a few minutes, he sat beside me, stroked my hair, and told me he was happy I trusted him. I could tell he was pleased by the smoky tone of his voice. Sergei untied the scarves before he made love to me. It was the best sex we'd had so far, and I'd thought it could not get any better. Seeing me tied up was a real turn-on for him. Afterward, he held me in his arms and told me how much he loved me.

The scarves appeared several more times before the end of the trip. Each time he tied me in a new position. Sometimes he would use one to blindfold me while he touched my body. The bondage would not last long, it never hurt, and he always made love to me afterward. Kinky, but why not?

I admitted to myself that I kind of liked it.

WELCOME TO RUSSIA

We said *au revoir* to Paris and caught a Russia-bound connection in Frankfurt. The final leg of the trip took seven hours. The sun was still up at 11:00 pm as we approached St. Petersburg. I recognized the Neva River snaking through the city, just as I had seen on the map in my atlas.

The passenger cabin erupted into applause as the plane landed safely on the ground. I was stunned by this unexpected burst of enthusiasm and turned to see my husband chuckling.

"It's what we do," he explained with a slight shrug of his shoulders.

The airport was disorienting, with signs spelled out in indecipherable Cyrillic letters. I could read none of it. Fortunately, Sergei was there to guide me, and we moved through customs quickly with minimal questioning.

Sergei's bodyguards met us at the airport. I recognized Uvar from his trips to New York City. The burly man had light blue eyes, blond hair and seemed to be in his late 40s. His thick build reminded me of a retired football player – long legs, barrel chest, and muscular arms. He smiled warmly, showing off a complete set of crooked, discolored teeth.

"Welcome to Russia, Cassandra Davidovna Karpova," he spoke in English.

I knew he didn't speak English well and probably practiced that statement just to make me feel at home. I appreciated the gesture and said,

"Thank you."

I looked to Sergei, who said, *"Spasibo."*

"Spasibo," I repeated to Uvar.

I was totally unprepared for this!

People did not always have the surnames we use today. In Russia, they used patronymics – your father's first name, with '-ovna' generally added to the end for a female and '-ovich' for a male. The name is similar to English names like 'Johnson' that started as 'John's son.' The patronymic moved to the middle position in Russia. Addressing someone with all three names together, as Uvar just did with me, is a sign of respect. Using the patronymic without the surname maintains confidentiality in case anyone is listening to a private conversation. Privacy is more of a concern than in the States, where people tend to be more open about everything. Sergei explained this tradition to me in an earlier conversation.

I remembered a sign on one of my psychology professor's doors that said, "Just because you are paranoid doesn't mean they aren't out to get you." I took it to mean there is a grain of truth in everything.

Karpov is a male surname in Russia. Karpova is the female version. The language is simply more gendered than English.

My new name meant Cassandra, daughter of David, a female of the Carp people. I laughed to myself. The original Cassandra was a Trojan princess with a gift of prophecy. The Greek name means 'She who shines over men.' Put that all together, and it sounds like the name of a fantasy role-playing character.

Sergei's other bodyguard, Ilya, was younger, in his mid-twenties. He had rich brown eyes and loose brown curly hair to match. Strong jaw muscles added a certain intensity to his lean face, giving him a determined appearance. The way he held himself felt threatening, as if poised for a fight. He looked like he spent whole days in the gym with his thick arms, powerful legs, and muscular torso. Perhaps these are good traits for a bodyguard, but he made me nervous. I assumed he was single because he did not wear a wedding band. While Uvar was very friendly, Ilya avoided eye contact and did not speak to me at all. He nodded in my general direction and looked away as we were introduced.

"Ilya is a little shy," Sergei whispered into my ear as we settled into the backseat of a black Mercedes SUV with dark tinted windows while the men loaded our luggage into the back. He told me it was an armored car with bulletproof glass. My husband was just a businessman, not a politician or a celebrity.

"What are you worried about?" I asked.

"Just a precaution," he replied cryptically.

Against what? I wondered nervously.

Just outside of St. Petersburg, the police pulled us over. An officer shined a flashlight in each of our faces and asked to see identification. I was petrified because he looked so commanding in his military-style uniform. When you don't understand the language, anything a policeman says sounds threatening. I had a bit of a phobia of law enforcement in my own country, but this was far more frightening. Sergei gave my hand a reassuring squeeze and told me it was not a big deal. We were pulled over for speeding. That fact seemed debatable, but Uvar paid the 'fine' on the spot, and we were on our way. This sort of thing happened frequently.

There was still a two-hour drive ahead of us, and it wasn't long before Sergei fell asleep. I was much too nervous for napping, so I studied the passing landscape. The area around St. Petersburg is coastal and flat. I'd read the city was built on reclaimed marshland by Peter the Great only 300 years ago, young by European standards. The city's name changed to Leningrad during the Soviet era, and the original name returned after the Soviet Union disbanded.

The landscape gradually began to change as we drove to higher ground. The land was still relatively flat, but there was some variation in the relief. I was surprised to see there were many rivers, streams, and wetlands. Occasionally, I glimpsed a low hill. Birch and pine forests alternated with farm fields. I smiled when I saw fields planted with potatoes, a common crop in New York State.

I remembered a time I made a midnight raid on a farmer's field with my college roommate. We had been drinking beer and came up with the crazy idea to steal potatoes. Before I knew it, we were out in a farm field, digging up the golden tubers with our bare fingers. The earth was wet from the rain. We carried the illicit harvest using the fronts of our shirts as slings. We were filthy, but we did not get caught, and it was a thrill to get away with the crime. Once we got back to our apartment, we fried potato slices in oil and ate them with ketchup. They were the best-tasting potatoes I'd ever had in my life – all the better for having stolen them.

I wondered what Sergei would think if he knew about that incident. It seemed strange I had no idea how my husband would react to a story like that. Would he think it was funny college hijinks, as I did, or would he believe it was wrong to steal and make me send $10 to the farmer to make amends? I didn't want him to think less of me, so I decided not to tell him.

My thoughts returned to my unknown destination, and I started to worry. The peculiar light of the after-midnight twilight started to seem creepy, casting threatening shadows on the passing landscape outside the window. I started chewing on a rough patch of cuticle on my thumb, wondering if my mother was right. Did I rush into this too quickly? Uvar could see I was nervous and gave me a reassuring smile through the rearview mirror. I smiled back and put my hands in my lap. I glanced at Sergei's face, gently twitching in his sleep, and focused on the steady sound of his breathing to calm my nerves. The road went on endlessly, taking me farther away from everything I'd ever known.

Uvar finally pulled off the highway onto a secondary road and then into a driveway that led to an enormous brick home with a high peaked roof set on a slight rise in a forest clearing. A matching 10-foot high thick brick wall completely encased the house. Uvar pressed a button on a device that resembled a garage door opener. The massive iron gate rolled sideways and disappeared behind the wall, then automatically closed behind us after he drove in.

We passed a turn that led to a formal entrance in front of the house. That driveway looped around an illuminated fountain featuring a sculpture of the golden Karpov fish leaping above an arched crown-shaped curtain of flowing water. There was a three-story columnar architectural feature at the center of the home, a Beverly Hills mansion but, oddly, no landscaping. There was nothing but lawn right up to the foundation.

I squeezed Sergei's knee to wake him.

"This is your farm?" I asked excitedly.

He nodded and smiled sleepily. Uvar pulled around back into an enormous attached garage that could easily fit ten cars. Inside there was only one other car, a red BMW M6. Sergei explained he recently built the house and had not given much thought to his car collection. Then he said he would order a vehicle for me as soon as I decided what I wanted.

We sat on a bench in a mudroom where we changed into house shoes. There was a pair of cozy pink sheepskin slippers waiting for me with a bow on top. He thought of everything!

"Thank you, Seryozha," I said with sincere appreciation.

Sergei hugged me warmly and said,

"Welcome home, Sandrochka."

The staff greeted us in the kitchen. None spoke English, but I listened with interest as Sergei introduced me to them in Russian. Beluka was the house manager, overseeing housekeeping, household supplies, and cooking. Vasily took care of the house and grounds, and Demeshko tended the horses and farming. They radiated such genuine warmth I instantly felt welcome. I wanted to talk to them, but all I could do was smile. I needed a crash course in Russian!

Beluka set out a steaming pot of black tea and plates of sandwiches and cookies. She poured the tea into crystal glasses that fit into heavy golden holders decorated with the Karpov family fish symbol. I said *"Spasibo"* to Beluka and sipped from the glass of tea as Sergei gave me a tour of the house. The first floor contained a large modern kitchen with a generous four-seat built-in breakfast bar overlooking the prep area, a spacious dining room with a long oak table surrounded by 20 high-back oak chairs with padded leather seats, a large formal parlor with a bar, and a comfortable western-style family room with big cozy sofas and a wide-screen television. Next on the tour was a library with etched glass doors that Sergei used as an office. A concave wall of interior windows overlooked the rounded three-story central hall. There were two other large unfinished spaces on the first floor. Sergei opened the doors to let me peer in, but there was nothing to see but drywall and plywood flooring inside.

There were fireplaces in all of the main rooms downstairs, even the kitchen. I felt better knowing we'd be able to stay warm in the event of a power outage. Storms happen everywhere, and I could only imagine how cold it was going to be in winter. I grew up in the bitterly cold Adirondack Mountains, but this was so much farther north.

Sergei must have read my mind because he said, "We have generators with enough fuel to last six months if needed."

That assurance put me at ease.

A one-story wing off the back of the house near the garage provided quarters for the staff. There were four bedrooms with a kitchen, dining area, and lounge. Sergei noted most of the team lived with their families and rarely spent the night. Demeshko and his wife lived in a separate cottage on the farm. Only Ilya stayed at the house full time. He told me Ilya monitored the home security and drove Sergei on local trips within Russia to give Uvar a break. Sergei whispered conspiratorially,

"Uvar likes to travel abroad to get away from his wife, Lana."

I made a 'that's crazy!' face. Sergei chuckled.

We looped back around to the cavernous center hall, where an elegantly curved staircase rose from the white marble-tiled floor to a gallery on the second floor. The round hall rose to a height of perhaps 40 feet and featured long vertical windows. An enormous crystal chandelier with hundreds of individual lights hung like a pendulum from the center of the ceiling. Our footsteps echoed on the marble floor. I followed my husband up the stairs, then paused by the railing to view the magnificent round hall from above.

Sergei began opening the doors along the hall to the right of the staircase, and I hurried to catch up with him. There were eight guest bedrooms, each with a private bath. The rooms were appointed with fine furniture and decorated with rich textiles. In one room, the bed was missing, and a mattress was leaning up against the wall. I was puzzled.

"For your sleigh bed, Sandra," he explained.

"Oh yes," I said.

I'd forgotten it was coming.

Having seen the guest rooms, we returned to the landing, where Sergei opened a door to another staircase leading to the unfinished third floor. He flicked on a light switch, but we didn't bother going up.

"There's nothing to see," he explained.

Then we crossed over the landing and passed through a set of oversized oak doors. Both doors swung inward to the master suite.

The bedroom was spacious, surpassing the square footage of five of my New York apartments combined. The most prominent feature was the bed, which stood beneath a 20-foot vaulted barrel ceiling. It was a king-size piece of furniture with massive oak posts that went up to support equally solid horizontal rails that held up a flat canopy. The canopy's fine ivory cloth folded to form a sunburst pattern that gathered in the middle behind a star-shaped golden button. There were sheer matching drapes along the sides held back to the headboard by small golden ropes capped with tassels. The exquisite coverlet was deep red woven with a traditional Slavic folk pattern in gold. Pillows in various colors, shapes, and sizes offered comfort at the head of the bed. I'd never seen a piece of furniture like it and imagined it had been crafted right in this very room.

The room itself was very masculine and dark, with oak-paneled walls and polished oak floors. The chamber felt like a protective embrace from an enormous man.

Two oversized comfy chairs faced a large fireplace with a fine round Persian rug defining the space in-between. The exquisitely detailed design of the carpet culminated in a circle with playful white birds at the center.

Carved into the front of the fireplace mantle was the familiar leaping Karpov fish. Two silver candelabra with white tapered candles rested on top of the mantel in front of a large mirror. A fireplace in the bedroom seemed very romantic to me. A decorative cloth screen dressed the firebox for the summer.

I was surprised to see a bar with a bottle of high-end vodka on top beside two crystal cocktail glasses on a silver tray. Who has a bar in their bedroom? I peeked behind to see an impressive selection of vodka and fine wine. Sergei's stash of the good stuff, I thought with a chuckle.

Sergei patiently waited to show me two full baths set off the main chamber, accessed by a short hallway. Each had a dressing room within a walk-in closet.

His bath was very masculine, dressed in dark polished stone, and featured a steam shower with massaging water jets.

A mosaic of pretty floral vines set within a field of fine white tile decorated my bath. I was surprised to see a built-in vanity with ample storage for beauty supplies and a free-standing glass shower enclosure with an overhead rain feature. But it was the porcelain pedestal tub set into an alcove with large windows on three sides overlooking the forest that took my breath away.

A soaking tub with a view! No neighbors! Just for me?

"I love it!" I gushed.

Sergei smiled, clearly pleased with my response.

Finally, he showed me my office, a medium-sized room off the farthest end of the master suite. There was an oak desk with a comfortable swivel chair and an empty bookcase built into the wall. A phone rested at the ready on the desk. My books and other possessions were on a ship crossing the Atlantic Ocean and would arrive soon.

I was overwhelmed and overjoyed by the beauty of the home and all he had done to make me comfortable. Sergei held me and said,

"A house is not a home without love. Now that you are here, Sandrochka, my life is complete."

"Your home is so beautiful, Seryozha, far beyond my greatest expectation. I honestly do not know what to say. I have never seen anything like this before. I can't believe I get to live here!" I replied excitedly.

I recalled my tiny childhood home. I always thought my family was lucky to have a house on the lake, but the two-bedroom cottage would look like a dollhouse in the yard next to this palace.

"Sandrochka," he said finally. "This suite is our special place. I do not want anyone to intrude here. Beluka and her girls will clean the house and do the laundry, but I would like you to maintain these rooms. The staff will not disturb us while we are here. Will you do that for us?"

"Yes," I replied.

I understood his desire to create a sanctuary and was relieved he did not expect me to clean the entire house. As much as I appreciated the beauty of the large chandelier in the center hall, I cringed as I passed beneath it, knowing what a pain it would be to dust.

Before retiring to bed, Sergei went to the hall and clapped his hands twice to summon his canines. Two large black dogs appeared. They were stockier than German Shepherds but smaller than Rottweilers, with long black wavy fur and floppy ears. They ran to their master and circled him, trying to steal his attention from each other. They adored him. After lavishing attention on their master, they gave me the old sniff-down assessment, concluded I was acceptable, and then presented themselves to me for petting. Sergei said they were a brother and sister from the same litter. Velikan was the male, and Kukla was the slightly smaller female.

They were Hovawarts, a German breed popular on farms in the Middle Ages. They had the qualities he was looking for – intelligent, loyal, good instincts, and do not stray. He cautioned me to keep an upper hand with them. Hovawarts require consistent subordination training, the only drawback to the breed. I grew up with dogs, so I was not concerned. We would get along just fine.

As I snuggled in bed with my husband for the first time in my new home, a sense of relief embraced me. The dogs lay on the floor beside Sergei, protecting the king as he slept in his castle.

After waking me with a leisurely round of sensual lovemaking, Sergei dressed in his equestrian gear, padded tan breeches with inside knee patches, a coordinating polo shirt, and dark brown knee-high polo boots. My riding pants were still on the ship from New York, but it didn't matter. I wore my knee-high black patent leather English riding boots, blue jeans, and a white blouse. A fine outfit for trail riding.

Beluka was out shopping by the time we made our way downstairs in the early afternoon, so I oriented myself to the kitchen and prepared a brunch of ham and cheese omelets while Sergei sat at the breakfast bar sipping his favorite black tea and reading a newspaper. The kitchen was immaculately clean. After we ate, I hand washed and put the dishes away, then carefully wiped down all surfaces I'd used. I was keen to stay on Beluka's good side.

Sergei gave me a tour of the grounds afterward. We exited through the kitchen and stepped onto a large stone patio accessible from both the kitchen and family room via triple-insulated glass French doors. I was surprised to see a fine collection of outdoor cedar furniture, just as you might see in the States. The summers are lovely in this part of Russia. Why not spend as much time outdoors as possible? I do not know why this surprised me so much. Perhaps I assumed it would always be winter here.

The ten-foot wall surrounded the house, with room for a generous lawn on every side. Sergei explained he had not had time to plan the landscaping. The broad swaths of green grass showed off the architecture in a stark way. I had a brief mental image of children playing on the lawn. We would not have to worry about them wandering off. That was a definite plus. There were only three openings in the wall, and the gates remained closed for security.

We drove through the main entrance last night, which opens with a keypad or remote control. A callbox for visitors operates just like the buzzer in my old apartment. A chime sounds inside the house like a doorbell. Visitors then speak with someone inside who can press a button on the intercom to open the gate. I'd noticed the intercom in the kitchen earlier. There were a few others on the first floor.

Another iron driveway gate led through the rear wall to the barns. All traffic coming in and out of the property had to pass through these gates. I looked up and noticed security cameras at each entrance and imagined Ilya watching us on a monitor. That thought made me nervous, but the feeling passed when I caught up to my husband, who slipped his hand into mine.

The third opening in the wall was a person-sized arched doorway located in the middle of the backyard. The door itself was cast-iron with a hand-painted design of a river scene, featuring the golden Karpov fish leaping high above shadowy water-bound fishes in the river.

"This is a stunning work of art!" I declared.

Sergei accepted the compliment with a modest shrug of his shoulders and tapped 3-9-9-3 into the keypad. The gate unlocked with an audible click. Then he pushed the door open.

"The same code is used for all three gates. We change it once in a while," he explained.

Velikan and Kukla followed us through the door, which closed behind us and locked automatically with a metallic clink. I saw an identical keypad mounted on the wall on the other side of the door.

We walked down a stone path, passing first through an orchard of hardy young apple, pear, and cherry trees, and then onto a large vegetable garden. Sergei explained the wall protected the trees from the winter wind. There were several outbuildings, stables for the horses, and a big barn to store hay. We went to see the horses first. There were six in a variety of colors. The stables smelled wonderful in that earthy natural way they always do. I had not been horseback riding in years, but I felt right at home. The stables were clean, and the horses seemed healthy.

I was surprised to see that each one had the Karpov fish branded onto its left hindquarter.

"Is it the convention in Russia to brand horses?" I asked.

He shrugged and replied,

"How else would I identify my horses if someone steals them?"

It was my turn to shrug. I'd never seen a branded horse in New York State and had no idea how they stopped horse thieves back home. The farmers used plastic ear tags to identify their cattle. Which is crueler – a passing moment of pain or big plastic tags in your ears for the rest of your life? I concluded the ear tags were probably more annoying.

After we visited with the horses, Demeshko saddled a white stallion named Pobeda for Sergei and a chestnut mare, Milaya, for me. Swinging up into the saddle felt as natural as if years had not passed since I last went riding. The sun was shining, and it was a warm 72 degrees. Just about perfect. We continued the tour by horseback.

The farm was about 1200 acres, twenty of which were surrounded by a fence tall enough to keep deer and other large animals out. The garden, orchard, barns, an indoor-outdoor arena for horse training, and pasture filled the fenced enclosure. There was plenty of room to expand the protected growing space and build more barns as the farm grew.

The land beyond the fence had active hay and fallow farm fields but was primarily forest and meadows through which he was cutting a network of riding trails. Sergei dismounted to open a cattle gate in the fence, and I rode through.

Sergei explained he had to sacrifice being near the city to get this much land and was lucky to have it at all. The government leased the land for 100 years as part of an agricultural deal because it was once a farming collective. As long as someone wanted to maintain the farm, they could renew the lease indefinitely.

He told me how much he enjoyed spending time at a *dacha* when he was a child, reminding me how fond city-dwelling Russians are of their summer cottages. The cities were too crowded for him, so he decided to live in the country full-time. Not having to worry about a daily work commute made that possible.

Velikan and Kukla ran beside the horses and entertained themselves by chasing each other and stalking small prey. We followed a trail through the woods until we came to a place where there was a soft grassy patch beside a creek. We dismounted and relaxed on a blanket for a while, enjoying the sunlight filtering down through aspens and birches. The canopy of leaves reminded me of an outdoor cathedral with green lights of every shade filling the space below. As a slight breeze stirred, the leaves fluttered cheerfully, making a sound that reminded me of a gentle waterfall. I felt buoyant.

We heard a commotion in the tree above us and looked up to see what was happening. Two small birds were fighting, chirping loudly and hopping from branch to branch. One seemed to be chasing the other. Suddenly, the pursuer mounted the little runaway for several seconds, and then they flew off together. It was springtime, and they were mating. What a romantic event for us to witness! Sergei smiled, put his arm around me, and pulled me in close for a kiss.

Love was everywhere!

6

PRIVATE TUTORING

When he was home, Sergei managed his business affairs from the library. We spent the evenings relaxing with each other and making love, deepening our connection with each passing day. Once he fell asleep, I'd slip out of bed, wrap myself in the shirt he'd worn that day, and go into my office and write. The warmth and manly scent from his shirt inspired me. Then I would slip back into bed before Sergei woke around 5:00 am, and we would often make love again. He did his best work in the mornings and early afternoons. I was still on New York time and slept until noon. We reconnected around 3:00 pm each day to share an early dinner prepared by Beluka.

My writing was always best after an evening of playing Sergei's sexy games. Not only was it prolific, but it was inspired. I saw connections between things I had never imagined before. My intellect was blooming, and my writing flowed easily.

Jack Hawthorne was amazed by the material I was putting out. We spoke at least three times a week. I'd call around 11:00 pm after my husband fell asleep and catch Jack in the office before leaving for the day. There is a seven-hour time difference in the summer, so it was only 4:00 pm in New York. I loved to hear his tough-guy New York accent. The connection with Jack made me feel closer to home.

Perhaps the distance fostered a sense of privacy between us, or I am just the type of person people love to tell their secrets. Jack confided he had fallen in love with a Japanese girl half his age. She was now his mistress, and his wife didn't know anything about it. I was too excited about my news not to reciprocate, so I told him about the kinky romance I was having with Sergei. I'd graduated from silk scarves to soft ropes and was finding bondage to be a major turn-on. No one else in my life knew or would ever guess I was into that sort of thing. Jack and I never criticized each other for deviating from the traditional path, and we were both glad to have someone open-minded to share our private joys.

As blissful as our home life had become, Sergei still traveled most of the time. His trips lasted about two weeks, and then he usually worked at home for a week before taking off again. I missed him terribly while he was gone. I was glad to have my work, and I took daily walks around the farm with Velikan and Kukla. The dogs were good company. Riding wasn't much fun alone, so I spent time talking to the horses and brushing their coats instead. Sergei did not want me to leave the fenced enclosure without Ilya, but I wasn't about to ask him to go with me.

Although I loved the house and country life, I became very lonely on Sergei's farm without him there. I had no in-person contact with anyone who spoke English. I made some progress with Russian by practicing with a program on my computer. But I was not good enough to engage anyone in conversation. I had so much trouble pronouncing the words. American mouths just can't seem to produce certain sounds. The Cyrillic alphabet was proving to be a significant obstacle to my progress too.

After a particularly lonely week, I heard the driveway gate open and rushed to the garage to greet Sergei as he emerged from the car. I was stunned when he treated me coldly.

"Go upstairs," he commanded angrily.

A nervous hour went by. I paced the floor in the master suite and tortured myself, trying to figure out what I had done to provoke him. I could not come up with anything. My hands trembled as he came through the door. I was sitting on the edge of the bed, watching to see what he would do. He ignored me and went to use his bath. When he came out, he poured vodka into a glass and sat in his chair by the fireplace. He looked lost in thought. He seemed to be in a foul mood. After a few minutes, he suddenly turned to look at me and simply said,

"Come."

I went to him. He pointed to the floor, so I knelt beside his chair. He placed my head in his lap and stroked my hair.

"Sandra," he said. "Never run out to meet me like that again."

Sergei continued to pet my hair. My eyes welled with tears.

"When I am ready, I will come to you. Wait here for me," he directed.

My tears were flowing now, and they were dripping onto his pants. The water pooled on the surface at first and then swiftly disappeared into the fabric. I had longed so much for him to come home. Now we were together, but he seemed a million miles away. I took a ragged breath.

"It is not that I don't want to see you. I do," Sergei explained. "Let me come to you."

I did not understand his logic, but at least I knew why he was angry. I started to feel a little better because I could avoid this mistake in the future.

"Look at me," he ordered.

I lifted my head to meet his eyes.

"I love you," he said, but he did not smile. His lips looked cruel, and his blue eyes were cold.

I'm sure my face showed fear because I felt it. The dissonance between Sergei's words and expression was unnerving.

His eyes grew a half-degree warmer.

"I have missed you, little bird," he said before rising to his feet.

Sergei tore off my clothes and then his own. He threw me on the bed and entered me savagely, rutting like an animal. I wrestled with him, but he managed to pin me down on my back. His hands held my wrists high above my head. He was rough, and I was not ready. It was the first time he hurt me. I felt nothing but pain. When he finished, I rolled away from him, crying, and buried my face in the pillows. He touched my shoulder, but I refused to look at him.

"I'm sorry," he said, "I don't know what came over me."

I ignored him.

"I lost a lot of money in a business deal today. You know how much I hate to lose. I did not mean to take it out on you," he explained.

I said nothing. I pretended not to hear.

"You know I never want to hurt you," he tried.

There was still no response from me.

The moments passed.

I started sobbing.

60

"Sandrochka?" His voice sounded weak, like a little boy.

My heart broke to hear it. Sergei touched my shoulder gently, as a child might wake his mother. I turned to see his face drained of color and painted with a frightened expression. He softly confessed,

"There is something wrong with me."

There was an eerily innocent and fragile look on his face, resembling a lost child. I took him into my arms and soothed him, and he laid his face on my chest and wept. I stroked his hair until he calmed.

"What is going through your mind right now, Seryozha?" I asked.

"I am going to lose you," he replied softly.

"Why will you lose me?" I asked.

"I lost control," he said as he looked up at me. There was a well of sorrow in his eyes, "Our trust is broken. I do not deserve you anymore."

"I love you, Seryozha, and I always will," I consoled, "we will find a way to work through this."

"You don't understand. This has happened before," Sergei stated, "I thought I had it under control."

"What happened before?" I asked.

"I hurt a girl," he replied.

He sat up suddenly, so I did too. He searched my face for the slightest hint of judgment or shock. He did not find any.

I wanted to put him at ease, so I asked an easy question,

"What was her name?"

"Yasmina," he replied. "She was a prostitute in Amsterdam."

"Tell me about Yasmina," I prompted.

"Yasmina," he repeated and paused, recollecting. "I went to see her many times over oh, five years. I liked her because she would let me tie her up. But I never loved her," he hastily added, looking at me to see if that mattered. It did not.

"I paid her well. She was happy to get the money," Sergei explained.

He paused longer, perhaps 20 seconds or more. I said nothing and waited for him to continue. He checked my face to see if I could handle what he was about to say. Satisfied, he took a deep breath and spoke,

"One night, while we were fucking, something came over me, and I started to beat her. I bit her so hard she bled. I tasted her blood in my mouth. I hated her, but I was having sex with her anyway, banging her up against a wall. I could see myself doing this, but I couldn't stop. By the time I finished, she was unconscious."

He quickly added,

"I did not kill her."

Sergei looked at me for a response. Fortunately, my placid therapist mask hid my shock. I heard a few doozies in New York, but nothing quite like this. I calmly nodded for him to continue.

"They took her to the hospital. She had a concussion and needed stitches," he confessed. "I was arrested."

"When I was released, I went to see her," he continued. "Her face was black and blue, and she was missing a tooth. There was a row of stitches near her eye. She will have a scar on her face for the rest of her life."

His eyes became glossy. He sadly whispered,

"She was such a pretty girl. I took her beauty."

Fat teardrops rolled from his eyes. I touched his shoulder and asked,

"Do you want to stop?"

"No," he said, "I want to tell you everything."

"The worst part was how terrified she was to see me," he continued. "I just wanted to apologize. She screamed at me to leave. She said she never wanted to see me again. I felt evil."

His face went vacant as if recalling the scene.

"How old were you?" I asked, pulling him back.

"28," he replied.

I noted this happened eight years ago, long before we met. Thank God.

"What did you do next?" I asked.

"My attorney paid her to drop the charges," he said with a sigh.

He looked me straight in the eye with a grave expression on his face.

"I don't understand why this happened," he said. "I could never hurt a woman. Impossible. It goes against everything I believe. One woman is more precious than ten men. I would fight to my death to protect you."

Sergei's eyebrows pinched together tightly as he strained to understand what had happened. To me, it was incomprehensible. This revelation was enough for one night. I didn't want him to feel over-exposed. That could undermine the feeling of safety I wanted to provide so he would remain open to tell me more.

"Let's stop here, for now, Seryozha," I said softly. "We have plenty of time to figure this out together. I'm not going anywhere," I added with a reassuring smile.

"How can you love a monster?" He asked.

"I don't love a monster," I replied. "I love you."

I remained with Sergei until he fell asleep. Looking at his face made peaceful by rest, I had a hard time believing he was capable of the violence he told me he committed. And yet this news had come from his mouth, so I had to accept it. I was in bed with a violent offender. That thought gave me the willies, so I changed it to a 'former violent offender, never convicted.' Not much help. He paid the victim to drop the charges. If anything, using wealth to evade legal consequences was even more despicable.

And yet, I believed he was a good person. He was pretty tough in business and could be very demanding, but he was not antisocial. I would have seen that. Besides, he seemed to care about people, and he felt deep remorse for what he'd done to Yasmina. Antisocial personalities don't feel any guilt or shame.

What would drive a person to behave in such a violent way? What triggered it after having a relationship with this woman for five years? Was he still dangerous? Could he be helped? Even as a psychologist, this was entirely new to me.

He mentioned he lost a deal today – did this bruise to his self-esteem have anything to do with his behavior?

I went back over the other details he told me and tried to piece an explanation together. I knew his mother, Sofia, died of heart trouble when he was five years old, and his father raised him until he passed when Sergei was 13. I didn't know exactly how either of his parents died. I gathered his father was a heavy drinker and a smoker who did not treat his only child well. Sergei mentioned he had risen through the ranks of the Communist Party.

Then there was Sergei's expression when he talked about his father. I concluded hatred and fear would not be too strong of words to describe his feelings for his father. Sergei had spent two-thirds of his life outside the borders of his country alone with no family. That must have been very difficult for him, but it wasn't enough to explain the violence.

I suspected something terrible happened to him as a child.

I gently kissed Sergei's cheek and slipped out of bed. As I bent down to pick up his shirt from the floor, I saw he'd torn some buttons off. He was usually fastidious with his clothing. Interesting, I thought as I wrapped myself up in it anyway. I summoned Velikan and Kukla and then went to my office to work. I called Jack to get the latest update on his scandalous sex life, but I did not mention what happened to me tonight or Sergei's startling revelation. Then I logged into the university library system back home and dug into the scientific literature on sexual sadism and sadomasochism but found nothing that fit the situation. Sergei was a little kinky, a harmless sexual preference, not a sadist.

We did not speak much during supper the next day, and he retreated to the library afterward. I went upstairs and took a long soak in a hot bubble bath. I enjoyed the sensation of the water relaxing my muscles and absently watched as little waves lapped at the side of the basin. I remained in the tub until the water grew cold and my skin became quite wrinkly. Then I dried off with a towel, coated my body in rose-scented lotion, combed my hair, and dressed in the pale pink silk kimono robe he bought in San Francisco as a gift for me.

I retrieved the red scarves myself for the first time, placed them on the bed, and waited for him to come. I wanted to show I still trusted him. I lounged on the bed, exploring a book about Russian religious art to pass the time. Unreadable Cyrillic hieroglyphics comprised the text, so I gazed at the photos of icons. I was struck by how much information the images conveyed without needing words, telling whole stories in the depth of the feelings they inspired in the viewer.

I must have dozed off because I woke to the sensation of fingers stroking my hair. I slowly became aware of Sergei sitting beside me on the bed. I looked at him sleepily and said,

"I am still yours, my love."

He graced me with his sweet smile, and his eyes were tender and warm. He lifted me into his arms and kissed me softly.

"Tonight is just for you," he pledged.

His fingertips ignited tiny sparks of electricity wherever he touched me as my robe fell open, exposing soft, pampered skin. I drank in his essence, his scent, his warmth. I listened to the sounds of his kisses and the rustling of the bedsheets as he slowly worked his way down my body, taking time to love every square inch. He finally settled between my thighs, sucking on my clitoris until it was swollen and pulsing. Once roused to high sensitivity, he began flicking it with his tongue while he massaged my labia and gently teased the opening of my vagina with his fingertips.

I closed my eyes and concentrated on the sensations he created for my pleasure. There was nothing for me to do but relax and enjoy it.

The tension in my body slowly rose to such heights that I saw bursts of fragmented colors like looking through a kaleidoscope at the sun when it finally released. I opened my eyes and gazed up at the golden star at the center of the canopy while my body quaked with the lingering traces of his gift.

Sergei kissed my forehead. He put the scarves away and then went to sit in his chair, where he opened a book and read.

I continued to work on my polite Russian phrases with the computer program, then practiced with Sergei over dinner and in general conversation. He gently corrected my errors, and I made progress. I could now converse a little with Beluka and her daughters, who seemed eager to help. When I pointed to household objects, they said the word, and I repeated it, earning a 'Da' as a reward. My Russian vocabulary slowly began to grow.

Sergei taught me phrases that were not in my language program. He asked me to stand at the center of the round rug in the master suite to begin my lesson as he sat in his chair.

"Повернись ко мне!" He said.

"Face me," he translated. "Repeat it to me."

"Povernis' ko mne," I said as I looked at him.

"Good," he said with a wry smile.

He was enjoying this.

"Разденься!" He exclaimed.

"Undress!" He translated again. "Repeat"

"*Razden'sya,*" I said and slowly began to undress, tossing my clothing piece by piece outside the stage set by the perimeter of the carpet.

"Excellent," he complimented.

I stood nude before him and waited for his next instruction. He smiled as he took in the scene. His eyes lit with a fire I already knew so well.

"Стань спиной и нагнись," he said.

"Stand with your back to me and bend over," he advised. "Repeat."

"*Stan' spinov i nagnis.*" I said as I turned and bent from my waist.

"Nice pronunciation," he praised.

I was becoming very aroused. This kind of foreign language instruction was much more fun than you get in school. A few moments passed. I could not see Sergei, so I looked at the circle of playful birds on the carpet by my feet. They seemed as happy as I was.

"Раздвинь ноги, пожалуйста," he instructed.

"Spread your legs, please," he interpreted. "Repeat."

"*Razdvin' nogy, pozhalyuista,*" I said as I walked my feet wide apart.

"Super," he said.

"Еще нагнись, ниже!" He ordered.

"Bend over lower!" He translated. "Repeat."

"*Escho nagnis', nizhe,*" I repeated.

I placed my elbows on the floor in front of me, giving it everything I had. I was a living Playboy centerfold for an audience of one.

"Well done, Sandra," he commented in the rich amber tone of arousal.

Sergei's face was visible now. The image was upside down, but his smile was unmistakable, and his electric blue eyes sparked with desire. I knew the lesson was over. He stood and shed his clothing as he came to collect my overdue tuition.

His practiced hands slowly played over my back, teasing their way down to my most vulnerable female flesh. My body burned beneath his touch. I cried out in pleasure when he entered me, slowly, teasingly, forcing my attention on the sensation of a prolonged penetration, millimeter by millimeter. My vagina stretched and lengthened to accommodate him perfectly. I was hot, wet, and hungering for more. Once he was all the way in, he delivered, thrusting fast and deep.

I remained in that awkward position as he brought me to one quivering climax after another. When he could take no more stimulation, he pushed the entire length of his swollen cock into me as far as it would go. His hands gripped my hips, holding me tightly against his. He paused, again, centering my awareness on his testicles convulsing against my clitoris as they shot a payload of his love deep inside me. He said nothing as he continued to hold me tightly afterward, penis still embedded deep within me, his semen pleasantly stinging internal sensitive skin sore from overuse.

He playfully slapped my rear when he finally withdrew and chuckled at the sight of his semen running down my legs as I struggled to stand, pushing up from the floor with sore forearms and aching, overstrained thighs.

With my back still turned to him, he held me warmly, absently teasing my left nipple with his deft fingertips. He kissed the back of my neck lovingly and whispered in my ear,

"Ты мой любимый ученик."

Ty moy lyubimyy uchenik. I already knew this phrase meant,

"You are my favorite student."

My private tutoring lessons continued like this night after night. I soon developed a repertoire of naughty things to say and respond to in Russian.

7

LET'S DO LAUNDRY

After spending the summer months secluded in the country, I finally had a chance to make my Russian social debut in September when Sergei announced he was taking me to a party in St. Petersburg. I wanted to make a good impression but wasn't sure what to wear, so I asked for his help. Sergei selected a low-cut black satin cocktail dress. I added matching four-inch heels with tiny spaghetti straps, thigh-high sheer black stockings with a line up the back, and a black lace garter belt to hold them in place. The entire outfit came from our shopping spree in Paris.

Oversized hot rollers transformed my hair into a wild pile of riotous bouncy curls. I encouraged one coil to dangle flirtatiously over my left eye. Black mascara, smoky gray eye shadow, and red lipstick completed the look. I felt like a French woman, sophisticated and powerfully alluring.

Sergei stroked his chin as he admired my transformation from newlywed homebody author to party-going vixen. The upturned corners of his mouth and his sparkling eyes told me he was delighted. Before we left, he slipped a small wrapped box into my hand. I was surprised, and he nodded for me to open it. Inside was a pair of diamond earrings. They had eleven diamonds each and dangled a full three inches in a line that swung freely on a flexible gold assembly. He took off the earrings I was wearing and put the new pair on.

I posed with a big American smile and placed my open hands by my ears, showcasing the dazzling jewels like a model showing a prize on a TV game show.

"Now you are perfect!" He declared with a chuckle.

Ilya dropped us off in front of a building adjacent to a yacht club on one of the islands in the central part of the city. I was nervous walking into the surprisingly large and lavish apartment. There were no other Americans in attendance, but I felt safe with Sergei. He placed his palm on my lower back as we made our way through the crowd to say hello to our hosts, a couple who appeared to be in their mid-50s. They seemed surprised Sergei had a wife, but I couldn't follow their conversation, so I didn't know what my husband told them about me.

The party was already in full swing, and the guests were stunning. The men dressed in black suits, and the women wore black dresses. The Russian women looked like supermodels to me. I wondered why Sergei chose an American bride. Did I seem exotic to him? It was hard to believe, but I admitted that might be true. I certainly felt different than the other women here.

Sergei introduced me to many of the guests who seemed eager to meet me. I smiled brightly and tried my best to be charming. I could pick out certain words and phrases in Russian, but I could not put the whole thing together and felt like I was drowning in my ignorance. Fortunately, some guests spoke to me in English, and others could speak French, so I managed to engage in some conversations and not feel entirely lost.

My social anxiety threatened to pierce the calm surface of my self-presentation, but I managed to keep my thoughts under control. I have an unfortunate tendency to become spastic when nervous, so I made a plan to make it through this evening without becoming a mess. Having learned the hard way, I drank only white wine and did not eat to prevent any unfortunate mishaps.

We eventually became separated, but Sergei always seemed to keep me in his line of sight. We made eye contact frequently, and he flashed a muted smile to let me know I was doing well. So far, my social debut seemed to be a success.

The sophisticated atmosphere began to break down around midnight. Some of the guests had already gone home. The ones that remained were getting drunk. The men took off their ties and loosened their shirt collars. I was surprised when they began to use foul language. I was familiar with some of these words from Sergei's private tutoring sessions, and I could figure out some of the other ones because they had common root words.

They seemed to be challenging each other, each one trying to outdo the last one's insults.

Sergei did not participate in this rude behavior. I noticed he seemed more polite and better educated than his friends. He was in another room engaged in a deep conversation with a dignified blond man in his early 50s. The women, while curious to meet me at first, shied away from me now. They huddled together, and I strongly suspected they were talking about me. It wasn't just paranoia. They were looking at me and talking to each other with their hands covering their mouths.

As if I could lip-read Russian.

I was becoming very uncomfortable. I was an outsider and realized I always would be. It wasn't easy for me, but I was used to not fitting in. At least the feeling was nothing new.

The German riesling I'd been drinking turned my stomach, so I asked the bartender for a shot of Jägermeister over ice to sip. I hoped the medicine-like liqueur would ease my discomfort and clear my mind. I sat alone on a sofa and entertained myself by watching the men playing cards. They passed a bottle of vodka around, and I noted everyone took a good, long drink as if it would have been a great embarrassment not to. They were getting louder and more out of control.

One of the men kept staring at me. I met him earlier in the evening when he'd spoken with Sergei. He seemed to be looking for investors for a casino in *Gretsiya*, which I inferred meant Greece. The discussion was serious, yet he seemed more interested in me than Sergei's wallet. His furtive glances made me feel uneasy. Sergei did not seem to notice, so I didn't think much of it. American visitors were a novelty here. Perhaps he was simply curious.

Someone put techno music on, and the pulsing, repetitive beat made my head throb. The room hung with a dense layer of cigarette smoke that stung my eyes. The walls began to close in on me. I was hot, my palms sweaty, and my heart began to race. I recognized the razor-wire edge of panic beginning to build and tried to distract myself by examining details – the curtains, art, and carpet – anything to focus attention outside of myself. I glanced around for more distractions, and there he was, waiting.

Our eyes met again.

A warm, welcoming smile lit his face.

I smiled back nervously. It would have been rude not to.

I didn't mean to stare, but I'd never seen a man like him before. He was enormous, over six feet tall, and broad. He was muscular but not inflated like he spent time pumping up his muscles in the gym. He was just a powerfully built man with a lot of meat on his bones. He'd tossed his suit jacket aside when the formality of this party broke down an hour ago. His white dress shirt was unbuttoned at the neck, revealing a gold chain that disappeared out of view.

Wavy dark brown hair framed his broad face and set off his large greenish-golden hazel eyes. His thick black eyelashes were extremely long, but they did not make him look feminine. Instead, they gave him a sultry appearance so convincing I imagined he was a master of the carnal arts. His strong nose was long and straight. It led down to full cherry lips that glistened with light as if he just licked them. My gaze lingered there a little too long, so I looked down at his hands.

The long fingers of his right hand tapped the beat of the dance music playing in another room. There was a hefty gold signet ring on the middle finger of his left hand with a prominent Cyrillic letter В, which corresponds to a V in the English alphabet.

Vladislav Pavlovich Valkov.

His name was a mouthful, but I had no trouble remembering it. Everyone called him by the familiar name, 'Slava.' He seemed to be well-liked by the people here. Some of the men clapped him on the back as if he'd recently won an award, a gesture of affection and respect perhaps.

He was not wearing a wedding band.

I quickly glanced back up to his waiting eyes.

His smile was even broader now.

I found him perilously attractive.

My unease sharpened suddenly, and I had an urgent desire, to leave. I looked to the right to see my husband still steeped in a conversation with the dignified blond man in the next room. He was facing the other way, but his hands gestured as if he was making an emphatic point. Politics. I knew better than to bother him when he was in the middle of a rant. That conversation would probably take a while.

71

I did not want my first night out in Russia to end early, especially after spending the first three months isolated in the country, but I could not sit here any longer. I glanced at the handsome stranger one last time. He nodded his head slightly to his right and shot me a wink. I laughed.

The attention was flattering.
Too bad I wasn't single.

I was surprised to feel the floor undulating beneath my feet as I rose to stand. I bent down to remove my strappy black heels and carried them casually on a finger, trying to look nonchalant. The other guests were drinking vodka late into the evening. Surely no one would notice if the American was a little tipsy from a few glasses of wine.

I made my way to the kitchen and found it mobbed with people smoking and talking. My eyes burned in the haze. I decided to find a quieter place to collect myself. I remembered seeing a modern laundry room nearby, so I picked up a bottle of mineral water and set off in search of it, praying it would be dark, deserted, and cool.

Thankfully, it was. I marveled at the fine honey maple cabinetry and white marble countertops. There was no sign of Soviet austerity with two washers, two dryers, and a sink with a waterfront view. This laundry room was the poshest I'd ever seen.

I stood at the sink and gazed at the city lights twinkling outside the window as I swallowed two tablets of aspirin from my purse and drank the entire bottle of water. Hopefully, it would be enough to stave off a hangover.

I closed my eyes and inhaled deeply, pausing to hold the air for a moment before releasing slowly. I repeated the breathing exercise for several minutes. Feeling clearer, I turned to leave.

My heart jolted to discover a wall of a man blocking the exit.

Vladislav Valkov!

The big man eyed me with mischievous intent but said nothing. His powerful presence held me like a deer frozen in the headlights of his eyes. We gazed at each other for a long moment until I blinked and looked away. I could not speak Russian, so I shot a little embarrassed smile and tried to step around him. I was tired and wanted to go home with my husband. I certainly didn't want to deal with a behemoth drunken admirer.

Vladislav put his hands on my shoulders to stop me from leaving. My shoes fell from my finger and clattered to the floor as I took a step backward. I was stunned, but I felt no fear.

I did not cry out for help.
I did not say no. *'Nyet'* was one of the Russian words I knew.
I was so stunned. I did not say anything at all.

He wrapped his large hands behind my head and grabbed two fistfuls of my hair. As he pushed his body against mine, his enormous erection pressed a lewd promise into my ribs.

I tried to turn my face from him, but he held my head forward.
I tried to pull away, but my back wedged against the counter.
I had no choice but to let him kiss me.

Electricity coursed through me as Vladislav's broad face came closer to mine. I was awestruck, as if I was watching the moon suddenly crash into the earth. His green eyes sparkled with golden fire and the corners crinkled with satisfaction to see my eyes go wide, and my mouth open in astonishment.

His hot cherry lips brushed against mine, igniting an instant wildfire.

Vladislav quickly found my traitorous tongue to be a willing playmate for his. I knew it was wrong. I was married, but I could not stop myself. I couldn't even think with all of the blood rushing from my head to my lady parts. I felt drugged within an erotic dream. All I could do was respond with primal, animalistic desire.

I returned his kiss with equal passion. Once I relaxed, he lifted me onto the counter. He maneuvered between my legs and pulled me close, kissing me wildly while stroking his fingers through my hair and down my back. Then he began to grind his erection into me. My dress slid wantonly past the tops of my stockings, leaving only a thin layer of black satin to protect my honor. If not for the presence of clothing, he would have easily penetrated me. He was right on the mark. It felt so much like the real thing I rode upward on a spiral of sensation, nearly to the point of climaxing.

CATHERINE IVERS NORTON

Just as I was about to go over the edge, an image of my husband's scowling face flashed through my mind. I stiffened, shocked by my behavior. What was I doing? I began to resist with all the strength I had.

I was sick, confused, and lost in the moment. I must have forgotten who I was and, perhaps, more importantly, to whom my heart belonged.

I started to panic.

Oh God, what can I do?

Vladislav's lips completely covered mine. I could not cry out for help with his tongue in my mouth.

Why didn't I do that earlier when I had the chance?

I leaned back as far as I could and banged my head on the upper cabinet several times, trying to summon attention. But he did not stop. My action only made him more aggressive. One of his large hands cradled the back of my head, and the other gripped my lower back, pulling me even closer. I beat his chest with my fists and squirmed to break away. He crushed his body into me, pinning my arms between us. All the while, he continued to push into me. He was stimulating me in a way I could not ignore, even though I knew it was wrong. I teetered on the edge of orgasm but valiantly held myself back.

I was married and did not know this man.

I certainly did not love him.

I absolutely could not allow myself to come.

I see-sawed between the pleasure pulsing through me and the shame of being a married woman in a stranger's arms.

How could something that feels so good possibly be so wrong?

The more I struggled, the wider he managed to spread my legs and the more intimate his thrusting became. There was absolutely nothing I could do. His sizable erection pushed deeper, inches into me, constrained only by the taut material of his pants. My delicate French panties were useless, soaked through, and forced deep inside.

74

My God, he is screwing me with his pants on!

I struggled to stay at the top of the cliff, clinging to my dignity. But one more thrust proved too much. My entire body tensed, and I shuddered as I went over the sinful waterfall, my eyelids squeezed tight under a cloud of darting stars. The moment my body relaxed, he drove even deeper, and my panic returned. His pants were on. It made no sense.

Was he just screwing with me, or did he intend to screw me for real?

The house is full of people, I suddenly thought. Where is everyone? How can this be happening? My mind fought to find a way out and could think of nothing. I prayed someone would come into the room and stop this depraved situation before I betrayed my husband a second time.

A few seconds later, I received an answer to my prayer, but my heart sank at the sound of his voice.

"Sandra!" Sergei shouted.
"What the fuck is going on?" He demanded in Russian, followed by a torrent of exceptionally foul swear words I couldn't spell even if I could recall them all.

Vladislav backed away from me with a guilty grin on his face. His smug expression challenged Sergei. He was a much larger man and confident he would win a fistfight. I quickly slid off the counter, wrested the panties from my snatch, and smoothed down my dress. I struggled to regain my composure. I wiped saliva from my bruised lips and raked my hair with my fingers. I looked at Sergei to see what he would do. His eyes blazed with anger. He stared at the big man, then at me, and then back again. He was struggling to understand what he had just witnessed.
"I like your new pet, Ivanovich," Vladislav said provocatively in a deep husky voice.
Sergei glared at the big man and motioned his flat hand at his throat, left to right in the head being cut off, 'you're dead!' threat gesture. Then he took my hand brusquely, turning his full attention to me.
"We are leaving," he stated.

75

"Put your shoes on," he ordered.

I stole a glance at Vladislav as I bent down to put my heels on. He caught my eye and gave me a covert, self-satisfied smile that told me he was not done with me yet. His boldness was unbelievable. I looked down and saw he had a massive glistening wet spot on the front of his pants. I didn't know if it was all from me, but it looked condemning regardless of the origin. Could he have climaxed? Lost as I was in my arousal, I did not even know. I desperately hoped my husband had not noticed the stain.

As Sergei dragged me away, I turned once more to see the face of my assailant. Vladislav met my eyes as he touched the telltale stain on his trousers and brought his fingers to his nose. He smiled broadly as if this was funny and winked just before I turned the corner and could no longer see him. Then I heard his laughter, deep and rich, a warm, joyful sound that may have induced a happy response in me in any other than this unbelievable situation.

In an incredible act of self-control, Sergei calmly walked me through the party, cordially said goodnight to our host and hostess, and led me out through the front door. Once in the backseat of the Mercedes, I said,

"I am so sorry, Sergei. I don't know why he did that. I was just trying to clear my head then all of a sudden, he was there. Right behind me."

He didn't say anything. He just looked at me with a disgusted expression on his face.

"It's not my fault!" I pleaded. "Please talk to me."

Tears sprang from my eyes.

He said nothing. He looked straight ahead with his lips pressed tightly together and nostrils flaring with each inhalation. His breathing was fast and shallow. Sergei was fuming with anger.

"Please?" I begged.

He looked out the window and ignored me. I tried to touch his hand, but he jerked it away. The silent treatment lasted the entire ride home. It was the tensest two hours I'd spent in my life.

I looked forward and noticed Ilya nervously watching me in the rearview mirror. The concern on his face was evident, but as soon as we made eye contact, he quickly glanced away.

My mind replayed the scene again. Why did I allow it to happen? I asked myself repeatedly. I could not come up with a good answer. I was doing so well until midnight when I began to feel sick. I realized now that I could have bit Vladislav's lip or tongue to make him stop. The thought never occurred to me. Nothing like this had ever happened to me before.

Sergei finally broke his silence in the master suite with the heavy oak doors closed and bolted into the floor and ceiling behind us.

"Take a shower," he ordered.

I looked at him in disbelief. I wanted to talk about what happened.

"When you are clean, you are to brush your teeth and rinse your mouth thoroughly with mouthwash," he directed.

"This is important. Do you understand?" He asked.

I understood he thought the big man polluted me, so I nodded and did as he instructed. I scrubbed myself until my skin was pink and tender. I scoured my teeth, gums, tongue, and even the roof of my mouth with my toothbrush for 10 minutes. Then I carefully flossed my teeth. I gargled the nasty Listerine-type mouthwash until I began to choke.

I was as clean as a sinner could get, wrapped in a large white towel when I returned to my husband. Sergei was sitting in his chair with a glass of vodka in his hand.

He did not look happy to see me.

It was nearly 4:00 am. He was never up this late.

"Floor," he stated, pointing to the carpet.

I knelt at the center of the carpet, inside the circle of playful birds. They did not seem so cheerful tonight. I cast my eyes down and waited.

"You are attracted to him," he stated.

"No," I denied.

"Look at me, Sandra," he ordered.

I lifted my eyes to him as I had done so many times. His face had no expression, but the squint in his eyes betrayed his anger.

"I know you better than you know yourself," he said. "I saw the way you looked at him when I introduced you. Your smile and the blush on your cheek gave you away. Valkov saw it too."

"No, Seryozha, I love only you. I do not want him." I said.

He was not buying it.

"You lie to me, Sandra. You wanted him, and he made you wet. I could smell your pussy in the car all the way home," he said with disgust.

He spat on the carpet.

"He forced himself on me!" I cried emphatically.
He said nothing.
"What is a kiss, Sergei? Nothing happened!" I tried, even though I knew something sexual had transpired between us. I just did not know how to define it. Could it have been 'sex' if we had clothes on?
Sergei looked at me for a long minute, reading my face.
"You may be educated, but you are a stupid girl," he stated sharply.
The insult stung. I glared back at him but said nothing.

"If I had not come when I did, you would have let him fuck you. You cannot deny it," he accused.

His words were as harsh as a slap to my face. Worse.
I chose my argument carefully for maximum impact. I said,
"No. I had no choice. It would have been rape. And it would have been your fault. You are supposed to protect me. Those were your friends, not mine. Where were you?"
He looked wounded, and I immediately regretted blaming him. It was not wise to fuel his anger. I should have kept my mouth shut. A moment passed. I could see he was thinking of just the right thing to say. Finally, he said,

"You like to fuck, Sanka, and you would like to fuck Valkov. That fact is obvious. It would not have been rape because you wanted it. You left the evidence of your desire all over the front of his pants. You are a whore."

The blunt statement knocked the wind out of me like a blow to the solar plexus. Sergei's point came across loud and clear. He downed his drink, set the glass on the table, and poured more. Calling me 'Sanka' was a punch to my ears. He only used this opposite of a pet name when furious with me. 'Sanka' was a personalized version of 'bitch,' just for me. There is no equivalent in English.

78

"Please, Sergei. Stop," I pleaded. "I love you, and I cannot bear this."

Silent stone-faced minutes passed before he dealt the final blow.

"Tell me, Cassandra," he said, "Did you ever say 'No' or tell him to stop?"
I could not respond in the affirmative. I said nothing.

And then the question I most feared to hear,
"Did you come?"

Looking down with shame, I could not deny it. I was guilty.

The hot tears streaming from my eyes did not affect him. He just watched me without expression and drank more vodka.

I cast down my eyes, trying to conceal the depth of my misery. I did not want to give Sergei the satisfaction of knowing how much his words injured me. I hid my face beneath my hair. The lump in my throat grew to such proportions that I had trouble getting air to my lungs. I could not breathe.

My head flared with pain. It felt like there was a knife lodged in my brain, causing white-hot unendurable agony. My entire body racked with sobs. The towel fell to the floor, but I did not care. I could hide nothing from him anyway. My soul lay bare for him to study and criticize.

I could not deny it.

I knew I was a vile and worthless human being. I did not deserve to be loved by this man or anyone else. It was over. I thought about going back to America, but there was nothing for me there. I loved him too much to leave.

He was so much better than me.

The tears fell from my chin onto my breasts and rolled down my thighs to the floor. There was a deep well in me, and I cried until they stopped coming. For the first time in my life, I ran out of tears and could not make more. My head was ready to explode from the pain, and my body continued to convulse with ragged sobs. My empty stomach twisted tightly, pushing bile up into my esophagus to burn my heart. My chest ached in agony.

I wished the hand of God would come down and strike me dead.

I stopped thinking and simply experienced the deep anguish and utter humiliation of this devastation without reflection. It was the lowest I ever felt in my life. I had no pride left, only shame.

Suspended in a pause of time, I slowly became aware of the pain in my knees and realized I'd been kneeling for a long time. I felt discomfort but no emotion. I was empty. My tears had long since dried, and the crust from their salty tracks tightened the skin on my cheeks. The rest of my skin had goosebumps from the chill night air.

I brushed my hair back with my hand and looked for Sergei. I'd forgotten he was even there. He was still sitting in his chair, still watching me with vacant eyes.

The vodka bottle was empty. He looked equally drained.

"Come," he softly spoke as he patted his lap.

Arrows of pain shot from my knees as I crawled to him. I did not care. My penance was over. I placed my head on his lap and reveled in his touch as he stroked my hair. Seeds of hope sprang in my heart that he still accepted me.

We remained like that for some time. Finally, Sergei helped me to my feet and guided me to bed. I burrowed under the covers and watched as he summoned the dogs, undressed in his usual careful way, and came to join me.

He took me in his arms and brought his face close to mine. He looked into my eyes, and I gazed back, wondering what he was thinking. My heart was bursting with love, and I desperately wanted him to love me still. I didn't know if what happened tonight changed his feelings forever.

Sergei kissed me tenderly, and my soul rejoiced. My body opened to him naturally, and he accepted the invitation. We made love slowly and never broke our gaze. I felt more emotionally connected to him at that moment than I had before. He'd seen my weakness and still loved me. He didn't have to say the words because I saw them written in his eyes.

I was forgiven.

I held off my orgasm until I sensed he was ready, and we came simultaneously. We continued to hold each other long after it was over. His eyes showed so much tenderness. I couldn't believe he'd ever been so angry with me.

I vowed never to hurt him like this again.

8

CAUGHT IN THE FUR TRAP

I woke to see Sergei enter the room and set a tray on the table by the two chairs. The midday light streaming through the windows burned my eyes.

"Good afternoon, Sandra," he said as he took his seat.

I sat up in bed and gave him a sleepy smile.

"Come while it is still hot," he requested.

A teapot and two bowls of hot oatmeal with fresh berries waited on the tray. I wrapped myself in a robe and sat down in my chair.

"Thank you for bringing me breakfast. I'd like to do this for you, but you are always up before me," I finally spoke.

He nodded slightly to let me know he heard, but he didn't comment.

I didn't feel like eating, but the oatmeal was good. The wholesome food untied some of the knots in my tender stomach. I should have eaten something instead of drinking the Jägermeister last night. Thinking back over my drinking career, I couldn't recall Jäger ever having been a good idea. Jäger isn't medicine. What was I thinking? Never again, I promised myself.

"About last night," I started.

"No," he said firmly. "I do not want to discuss it."

We silently sipped the black tea. When the cloud finally lifted from my mind, I noticed Sergei staring straight ahead at nothing in particular. He appeared lost in thought. His face wore a sad expression, and his eyes seemed softer than usual.

"What are you thinking about, Seryozha?" I asked gently.

He broke from his reverie with a shake of his head and looked at me. He was on the verge of tears.

"My mother came to me in a dream," he said. "I was so young when she died. I'd forgotten what she looked like, only that she was kind. My father destroyed all of the photographs after he buried her. I had nothing to help me remember."

"Oh?" I asked. My heart broke for him. I couldn't imagine what it was like to lose a mother at such a young age.

"She had long hair like yours and gentle blue eyes," he noted. "My mother was the kindest woman I have ever known. She was very spiritual, like an angel. It was a gift to see her. I do not want to forget again."

His eyes glossed over, and tears began to roll softly down his cheeks. My heart ached to see him weep, but his fragile beauty in expressing such tender emotion moved me. He wiped his face absently with the back of his hand and continued,

"She came to comfort me, and her sweet expression told me everything would be okay. In her hand, she held an Orthodox cross. She opened her palm as if she wanted to give it to me. She said one word before she disappeared."

He stopped speaking, and his expression went blank as he seemed to be reviewing the vision. Perhaps he was trying to burn it into his memory. I waited. Finally, he looked at me with a sad smile.

"What did she say?" I gently inquired.

"Surrender," he replied.

He looked away, and I was left to ponder the meaning of this word on my own. Surrender what to whom? Did she want him to join the church, hence the presentation of the cross? I doubted he would ever do that since he was as hard-boiled as an atheist can get.

Sergei had an existential philosophy about life. He believed we are thrown randomly into this world to make our way alone through a chaotic existence. No doubt, his childhood experiences supported this belief. I accepted he felt this way, but I never understood the position. To me, it seemed devastatingly lonely. Even if it was the truth, I could not see how anyone could take comfort in such a harsh view. He believed when you are dead, that's it. There is no heaven, hell, reincarnation, or going back to a spiritual 'source,' no seeing deceased loved ones, nothing.

"Only weak-minded people delude themselves with those beliefs," he said to me in the past.

I was one of them, and he knew it. I believed in God with all of my heart. How could anyone deny the existence of God when we see so much beauty in the natural world around us? The fact we are here at all is a miracle.

How could he explain his mother's appearance in his dream? Was it just a trick of his mind or a random event that meant nothing? Judging by the look on his face, I suspected he felt it was much more than that. He was lost in thought again. I knew he would need time alone for contemplation, so I quietly dressed and took the dirty dishes downstairs.

I stuffed my pockets with dog treats and rounded up Velikan and Kukla for a walk. Colorful leaves were already beginning to drop, and the air was crisp with a chill that felt like a New York November. A hint of winter to come, I thought with a shiver. A light rain began to fall from the overcast sky. I pulled my jean jacket tightly around me, stuck my hands in my pockets, and trudged on.

Autumn is my favorite time of year, so I took my time enjoying the moist scent of the earth. I listened to twigs snapping beneath my feet and the sound of the falling leaves blowing in the cool breeze. I threw a big stick for Velikan to retrieve, but Kukla caught it in mid-air. "Interception!" I declared with a laugh and noted it felt like American football weather. If I had a cup of coffee and a hot dog in my hand, I would have been all set to watch the Saxons play a game on Merrill Field in Alfred.

I missed New York.

The stick-throwing game ended when Kukla would not give up the prize. She paraded around with it as a big trophy. Velikan stalked her ferociously and took strategic chomps on the ends of the stick, but she refused to yield. Eventually, he wore the prize down to only the part still in her mouth. She held on proudly and would not admit defeat. What a smart girl. I admired her resolve.

The rain started to come down harder, so I reluctantly returned. I wrung the water from my hair and dried the dogs in the mudroom before entering the house. As I passed the library, I noticed Sergei focused at his desk, writing with a pen on paper. I went upstairs to take a shower. Then I went into my office and called my mother. She complained about the heat and said the air conditioning wasn't working. She insisted she was "burning up" inside the house and upset because my father was supposed to fix it, but he was out drinking with his golf buddies again. There wasn't much I could do to console her, so we chatted idly for a few more minutes before ending the call.

When I walked back out into the master bedroom, I immediately noticed a substantial gold-tone box with a red bow on the bed.

I jumped as a bright flash with a simultaneous boom of a thunderbolt struck close to the house. Heavy rain and hail began to beat against the windows. I watched the storm for a few minutes and then turned my attention back to the box.

There was a card tied to the bow. Handwritten in English,

> "Sandra,
>
> This gift is something every Russian's wife should have. You will need it this winter. Put it on wearing nothing but your riding boots and meet me in the stables at 8:00 pm.
>
> S."

Curiosity gripped me. What could it be? I carefully removed the red ribbon and opened the box. Inside was a dark brown full-length fur coat that was super-smooth to the touch. I'd never felt anything so luxurious in my entire life. Fur was socially unacceptable in New York, where animal rights activists condemned the cruelty of trapping creatures and tearing off their skin.

On the other hand, it would be wrong not to appreciate the sacrifice these animals already made.

How could I refuse such a precious gift from my husband after what happened last night anyway?

I carefully withdrew the coat from the box and wrapped it around me. The fur was soft, warm, and smelled wonderful. I spun on the circular carpet, pretending to be a movie star. I put the collar up and felt the fur tickle my nose. Then I held out my hand to the air and said,

"Delighted to meet you, dahling."

I laughed at my silliness and went to look in my dressing room mirror. If it were not for my own eyes looking back at me, I never would have imagined it was Cassandra Abbington from Lake Placid under that magnificent fur.

I'd seen old mink coats in New York City thrift stores, and this was different. There were long wide strips of deep brown fur I thought might be sable. This coat was full length and must have cost a fortune.

The coat was a little too warm, so I reluctantly took it off.

I glanced at the clock and saw it was already after 7:00 pm. The storm front passed quickly, and the sun was shining. I found my riding boots and noticed they were scuffed, so I carefully polished and rubbed them to a brilliant shine.

Not knowing what Sergei was planning, I curled my hair, applied makeup, wore my best jewelry, and hoped I looked the part. Walking through the house nude under a buttoned-up coat felt ridiculous, but fortunately, I did not see anyone.

Sergei was already in the stable, brushing his white horse, Pobeda. He turned as I entered, and his eyes sparkled with delight. Saying nothing, I unbuttoned and held open the coat to show I followed his instructions. I was gloriously bare under all of that fur and ready for whatever he'd planned for me. There was a blaze of heat between us 20 feet away. His eyes slowly wandered over my body, and a lusty smile lit his face as if he had never seen a naked woman before. I knew he wanted me, so I was surprised when he said,

"Come, let me help you onto the horse."

I was expecting a romp in the hay, not a horse ride!

There was no saddle, so I could not use stirrups to mount the animal. Sergei gave me a boost, and I swung a leg over the top. I'd never ridden bare skin or bareback before, so this was completely new. The horse's hair felt rough on my tender skin, but there was no time to object. He tossed a large saddle bag across the horse's neck and jumped on in front of me. I secured the top two buttons of the coat and let the rest fall open. I inched up to him and wrapped my arms tightly around his waist. I snugged my legs to the creature's sides to avoid falling off. The coat flapped gently in the wind as we rode.

We were off!

Sergei left the property through the front gate and headed west down a *prosyolok*, a back-country dirt road off the paved secondary road. This one was in rough condition, and the horse carefully maneuvered around deep puddles and quagmires. The sun hung low in the sky directly in front of us, filling the landscape with golden light and illuminating Sergei's hair, spinning it into gold. After a while, the road began to even out, and he brought the horse to a trot. I tightened my grip on Sergei and used my knees and boots to latch tighter, but I still bounced up and down and felt the horse's powerful muscles moving between my legs.

There is no sensation for a woman quite like riding bareback in the nude. Certainly not one I ever imagined. It was rough, yes, but I didn't mind. I was sure Sergei planned for me to experience this deviant pleasure when he wrote his note earlier that afternoon. The wind whipped through my hair, and my coat fluttered up at my waist. I held Sergei tightly and breathed in his essence. He smelled manly, and his body was warm. I put my cheek flat against his back and succumbed to the many pleasures of the moment.

And what pleasures they were!

The sky dressed in brilliant streaks of oranges and violets as the sun began to set. Azure blue at the horizon faded to a deep royal blue overhead. Behind us, there was nothing but black. Some of the evening planets began to appear.

We turned left down a trail through the woods heading south and followed a narrow foot trail for perhaps a half-mile. Then we turned right onto another trail until we came upon an old cabin elevated on wooden piers. It had a small covered porch with steps leading down to a gravel walkway. A footpath to the right led to a crudely built outhouse. Sergei dismounted and tied Pobeda to a post. He used a hand pump to draw water from a well and used a bucket to fill a trough for the horse. It was already half-full of rainwater, so the procedure did not take very long.

Sergei came for me next and helped me down. My rear was very sore from the ride, so I stretched my legs side to side and then bent at my waist and held a toe-touch to release the tightness in the back of my thighs.

"Enjoy the ride?" He asked as I rose, looking me in the eye knowingly.

I smiled guiltily because he already knew the answer.

He nodded with satisfaction.

Sergei pulled the bag down and slung it over his shoulder. He opened a zipper and withdrew a bottle of cognac. He handed it to me and said,

"Wait here until I come for you. The brandy will keep you warm. Do not knock on the door and do not look in the window. Understand?"

"Yes," I replied.

This excursion was another of his many surprises, and I did not want to spoil it.

I watched him carry several armloads of firewood into the cabin. Then he closed the door. A dim light came on, and I guessed from the orange glow it was an oil lamp. I set the cognac down on the steps and waited. Twilight was fading quickly, but I could see the cabin sat within a grove of tamaracks, a common tree in my childhood home in the Adirondack Mountains. Each autumn, the needles turn golden and fall off. People unfamiliar with deciduous pine trees assume they are dead, but they come back to life in the spring. It is the cycle of nature – death, rebirth, life.

These tamaracks were beginning to turn.

The woods had a clean scent, and I breathed in deeply. I watched the horse drink his water and move around, grazing on the grass he could reach within the limit of his lead rope. He made soft sounds, and his breath turned white in the cold air. He was tethered to the post and did not question his position. A powerful horse could easily break the rope, but this one did not attempt to escape. Maybe he had nowhere else to go.

I supposed it was not so bad to be owned by Sergei. He treated his horses well, and they seemed to love him in return.

The temperature dropped below freezing as darkness fell. Even with the fur, I began to feel a chill. I was glad I had worn my warm riding boots.

I was bored, so I opened the cognac and drank a little. I have never been fond of brandy because it is too sweet and boozy for me, but it went down without a fuss, and I felt a little warmer. Sergei was always right about these things. I sat on the steps, took another sip, and gazed at the stars winking on in the sky. The brightest appeared first and then the myriad of lesser ones. Soon the sky was so full of stars I imagined I was gazing into a diamond mine. I recognized the constellations because they are the same ones that spin around North America.

The first I noticed was the big dipper. I remembered the right side of the cup points to Polaris, the North Star, the last star in the little dipper's handle. That told me which direction was north. The Milky Way appeared as a bright white road further south in the sky. Then there was my old friend Orion and my favorite star cluster, Pleiades. The starlight was bright enough for me to see and walk around without tripping over anything.

There aren't too many dark sky places like this left in the modern world, I reflected, remembering how much I missed seeing the stars when I lived in

New York City. I suspected humans need darkness to balance out the barrage of light from televisions, computer screens, and artificial lighting. There was less and less darkness. Our species evolved to live in harmony with the cycles of nature. Artificial light is a relatively recent development in our history. I pondered the effects the bombardment of artificial light has on our hormones, sleep cycles, and mental health. Then I realized how rarely we even think about darkness until we find ourselves in it. Without darkness, we would not even recognize light because it would be everywhere. How interesting.

I waited and waited for what seemed to be an hour. Still, Sergei did not come for me. I heard him moving around inside the cabin, and I smelled wood smoke. So, he started a fire. That made sense. Why was he making me wait so long outside?

He's testing me, I told myself and kept my resolve to patiently wait even though I felt like breaking down the door. I tried to imagine what his face might look like if I did something like that. Shock? No, he would just be angry and push me away as he'd done on our first date. I never wanted to give him a reason to be so upset again.

I remembered how angry he was last night and how remarkable it was he made love to me anyway. I felt more closely connected to him than I ever had before. He never said anything, but I perceived his forgiveness in a way that seemed more real than words. Choosing physical intimacy over silence was an act of love. I knew I was the beneficiary of the 'deal,' and he was right – the last thing couples should do is avoid sex when issues arise between them.

There was absolutely nothing for me to do outside. I entertained myself by observing the stream of thoughts that constantly march through my mind. I sipped some more cognac, but I was careful not to drink too much. I did not want to be drunk when Sergei opened the door.

I reflected on how much I hated being separated from him, whether it was his business travel or these silly games we played. He teased every ounce of longing from me so I would always be desperate to please him. It worked every time, of course, but this was the first time I felt manipulated. I did not appreciate waiting in the cold.

A seed of resentment took root inside my heart.

If I were any other woman from New York City, I might be terrified to be left alone in the Great Russian wilderness with such a long walk back to a paved road. But I was not afraid of these woods. I liked listening to the sounds of the night. A crow flew over my head as I gazed at the stars. Perhaps I should say I sensed the crow. I heard feathered wings beating in flight and saw a black object blot out a path of stars above my head. Once in a while, I heard one call out to its friend in the forest, "Caw," and the other responded, "Caw-Caw." Crows sound the same wherever you go. These crows seemed to be settling into their roosts for the night.

I observed Pobeda was calm. If there were any predatory animals around, the horse would sense it. All appeared to be peaceful in the forest.

So where is he? I wondered. I had not heard him move in a while and prayed he had not fallen asleep. It must be two hours now. I considered knocking on the door but remembered I promised not to. Fur coat or not, it was freezing. I wanted in!

What kind of man would leave his wife out in the cold this long? My anxiety started to grow, and I tried to drive it back with cognac. Stupid, dysfunctional thoughts began to race through my mind. For all of my psychological tricks, I could not stop them. All I could do was tell myself they were irrational and try to ignore them.

'Will he make me wait all night?'
'What if a spider bit him and he is lying on the floor unconscious?'
'Is he having sex with another woman in the cabin right now?'

The last one upset me the most. I silently shouted 'STOP!' to myself to disconnect my runaway thoughts. I was surprised it worked. I looked up at the stars and realized they had moved since the last time I checked. I wondered how much time had passed. I noticed I was hungry too. I had not eaten anything since the oatmeal. I had no idea what time it was.

I took another sip of the cognac and realized the bottle was half-empty. That was more than I planned to drink. I stood up and walked around. Good, I am not intoxicated. Sometimes it's hard to tell in the dark.

I walked around the cabin, down the path for a bit, and then up to the horse. I petted Pobeda's face and kissed him on the nose.

Finally, the door opened, and Sergei came out.

"How are you holding up?" He asked.

89

"Great," I answered calmly. "It is a beautiful night, Sergei. You don't know what you have been missing. The stars are amazing."

I imagine he smiled. The light from the cabin door behind him cast his face in shadow, so I wasn't able to see his expression.

"A long time ago, you told me you loved the outdoors so much nothing could make you stay inside," he said. "Remember?"

"Yes," I replied.

"Would you come inside with me now?" He asked sweetly.

I remained silent for a moment. Of course, I wanted to go inside!

I made a show of looking around to consider all I would be giving up by accepting his offer.

"For you, I will make this one exception," I said finally.

He held out his hand. I walked up the stairs and took it.

The first thing I noticed was the aroma of food. It smelled like meat and nutmeg. A strange combination, but I was impressed Sergei cooked something for dinner. I was ravenous!

The interior of the cabin was as bleak as the outside. I saw one open room, a table with two chairs, a cast-iron wood stove with a glass door, and a bench wide enough for one person to sleep on pushed up against a wall.

Hot air blasted my face, and I flushed. I started to unbutton the coat, but Sergei said,

"Not yet."

He led me over to the bench.

"Kneel on the bench facing the wall," he instructed.

I wondered what he was up to, but I did as he requested.

"Good," he said.

He took my wrists and tied them with rough hemp rope to a metal ring fastened to the wall. Then he lifted the back of the coat over my head and tucked it down in front of my face. I was bare from my upper back down and could not see anything but fur in front of me. I expected him to make love to me like that and was shocked he wanted to talk instead. His boots paced the floor as he spoke.

"The men here are nothing like American men," he lectured. "Most of them perceive a woman's flirtation as an open invitation. You are too open with your feelings. Maybe you feel safe because American men ask permission before they take a woman. But you are in Russia, and things do not work that way here. You must learn to guard your emotions. If you are attracted to a man, do not show it unless you intend to go all the way."

"What happened with Valkov was unacceptable," he continued. "I can't allow my wife to have sex with other men. I refuse to share you with anyone."

I thought we were past this.
I did not know what to say.

"You took my ring and my name, Sandra," he continued. "You belong to me like the horses, the house, and everything in it. If a man steals my horse, I will beat him. If a man touches you, I will kill him."
I was stunned.

"Marriage is not enough of a deterrent," he continued. "Valkov did not care that you are my wife. He is a competitor taking a jab at me. There will be others who will try to possess you," he paused. "And yet, they are not important. I am concerned about you. You must never forget you are my wife again."

He rubbed lotion on my lower back, and the area grew cold. Although I sensed he was still rubbing the skin, I could no longer feel his touch. I had no idea what he was talking about, but I strongly suspected he'd gone insane. I pulled against the scratchy hemp restraints and tried to break free. The knots only became tighter and cut off the circulation to my hands. I started to panic. The rope cut in deeper and broke my skin as I struggled. My wrists became wet with blood.

"Sergei, stop. Please," I begged. "You are scaring me. We need to talk about this face to face. The rope hurts. Please untie me."

He stood so close behind me his clothing brushed against my most sensitive exposed skin sending ripples of electrical currents throughout my body. Even my toes tingled with the sensation. My head began to swim from the heat and the cognac. I wanted him so badly, but not like this. He reached around and stroked my stomach with his fingertips. Then he slid his hands over my skin and touched my breasts. My nipples were hard, and he pinched and twisted them until they hurt, but in a pleasurable way that is hard to describe. A soft moan involuntarily escaped my lips. I was drunk, confused, afraid, and incredibly turned on.

"Sandra, you decide," he said softly. "Will you accept my mark as you have accepted everything else about me?"

My mind flashed to the horse patiently waiting outside. Sergei would never harm anything he loved, and he would never hurt me. Was this just another test of my trust? Still, I did not respond. What was this 'mark' he wanted to give me?

"I will ask you only one more time, Sandra," he said firmly, his fingertips traveling lower to rub the nub of my clitoris gently. "Will you accept my mark? Yes or no? Decide now."

I knew I screwed up by yielding to Vladislav Valkov. I broke Sergei's trust. If I refused him now, would it be over between us? I could never accept that. There was no way I could go back to America and spend the rest of my life dreaming about this crazy man. No. I could trust him. He never hurt me before, at least not very much, and I was sure he was sorry for that. This question was just another test. He was making a point.
Sergei's fingertips tapped my clit, prompting me to answer.
He was ringing my buzzer.
Time is up. Decide.
A dam broke in my mind. I leaned into trust and said,

"Yes."

Suddenly he was gone. I heard a metallic sound, but I had no idea what he was doing. A few minutes passed.
"Straighten up as much as you can and do not move no matter what," he firmly instructed. "This is very important. Do you understand?"
"Yes," I said and braced myself for whatever was coming.
"Good," he said. "Hold steady."
I heard his footsteps approach. My body stiffened.

I felt pressure on my lower back for a second, maybe two, then it stopped. I smelled my flesh burning. With more surprise than pain, I screamed his name with all the breath I had,

"SERGEI!"

I struggled against my ropes and kicked backward blindly, trying to give him a shot in a place that would hurt badly. I gasped for air. Tears streamed from my eyes. Rage filled my heart, and at that moment, I wanted to kill him. I continued to kick violently and desperately hoped my boot would connect. It did not. Sergei was an equestrian. He knew better than to stand directly behind a pissed-off animal.

"What the hell did you do to me? You sadistic fucking bastard!" I shouted.

"You will not forget who you belong to again, Cassandra Davidovna!" He declared.

His voice came from across the cabin, well out of my reach.

I knew I was defeated, so I stopped struggling.

I could no longer feel my hands. My wrists bled, cut deeper by the rope and the fierceness of my struggle. I tried but could not move my fingers. My focus turned inward. I was in hell, and I sobbed for my lost soul. I used to be a good girl – I went to Sunday school and was a straight-A student. What happened to me? My mind reeled to make sense of what just happened. It was beyond my ability to understand. I felt like dying, if only to end the misery of this cruel moment. At last, my thoughts stopped coming, and I became mentally numb.

I became aware of Sergei untying my wrists by the excruciating pain in my hands as the blood returned, stabbing its way through empty veins. The sensation was far more agonizing than the dull sensation on my back. My fingers ached when I tried to move them. I rubbed my hands together. They were cold and felt like marble.

I no longer felt human.

Sergei helped me out of the coat, wrapped me in a soft blanket, and guided me to a chair beside the old wooden table. I absently watched as he removed the lid from a pot on the stove, ladled something into a bowl, and placed it in front of me. Then he gave me a spoon and set a loaf of bread on the table. I did not comprehend any of this and looked to him for an explanation. I was in shock. He did not say a word as he uncorked a bottle of Cabernet Sauvignon and set it on the table. He poured two glasses and pushed one toward me.

"Drink," he said.

Out of habit, I looked to him for approval, and he nodded his encouragement.

I clumsily lifted the glass with my stone hands and drank. Cabernet is the queen mother of wine, and her familiar flavor filled my mouth with fond gustatory memories. I savored the rich, dry taste and forgot all about the pain.

"Are you okay, Sandrochka?" He asked softly.

His eyes were tender as if he felt remorse for what he had just done.

"Yes, I think so," I replied. "What just happened, Seryozha?"

"I have given you a gift, but you do not realize it yet," he said. "Wedding rings may come off, but now you are bound to me forever. You will never forget me."

"I could never forget you. Why did you burn me?" I asked.

"Burn?" He asked with a surprised lilt. "That was not a burn. It was a brand. I made it this morning while you slept. It is like a tattoo, only much nicer."

He proudly smiled as if he expected me to feel honored. I had never heard of such a thing being done to a person before.

"What does it look like?" I asked.

I turned my head and arched my back in a vain attempt to see it. A wreath of pain shouted to my brain as the skin stretched like a patch of sunburn. Sergei watched and waited for me to turn my attention back to him. Finally, he spoke.

"There is a circle containing the leaping fish," he said, "the Karpov symbol. Like the one on my horses, only yours is much nicer. It is red now, but it will become white. I used fine gauge wire for the design. The scar tissue swells four times thicker than the original brand. I wanted the fish to stand out but still look pretty. That is the point. I want it to be beautiful, like you. The delicate design turned out perfect."

94

I finished my glass of wine, and he poured another. I did not like this at all.

"Sergei," I said, "what is to stop you from taking your wedding ring off? Do I have the right to brand the Abbington 'A' on you? If your logic fits, then you know this is only fair."

He arched his eyebrow and displayed his most disarming smile. I was almost charmed, but his magic did not work on me this time.

"No, little one," he said with a light laugh. "There is no need. I am not the one we need to worry about leaving. I am not a flight risk. Where would I go? I am already home. You are my wife. You belong with me, and I intend to keep you. You will bear our children, and we will raise them together."

I knew so many bed-hopping couples in America. The husbands cheat just as often as the wives. Jack was probably with his Japanese mistress right now. Was Sergei saying he would never cheat on me? Or just that he would not throw me out to make room for someone else? I needed to know.

"Are you saying you will never take a lover?" I asked.

This time his smile was even brighter than before. My line of questioning was amusing to him. I saw how one-sided our relationship was, and it angered me.

He thought I was his property.

"Sandra," he said. "You are a tiger, and I am eight years older. Where would I find the strength? Other women bore me. I searched the world to find you, and there is only one. I have never loved anyone else, and I never will."

I noticed Sergei did not answer my question, but I was through talking. I needed to process what happened. I stared blankly ahead of me, trying to make some sense of it. Last year, I started my career with my newly earned doctoral degree, thinking only of my work. Now I was naked in a Russian shack in the middle of nowhere branded by a Godless primitive I was crazy enough to marry. And why did I deserve the brand? Because another caveman forced himself on me.

'Possessive' was not a strong enough word to describe Sergei. He had a 10-foot wall around his house. Nobody would do that in America. It cost too much, and the maintenance would be a nightmare. We trust our neighbors. He didn't even have any neighbors. I was surprised he did not keep me locked up in chains. Maybe that was next. Yet here he was professing his love and saying he wanted me to have his babies. He did not make any sense.

My thoughts started to run.

How did I let this happen? Where was my pride? My husband just branded me! What will my parents think? I am an Abbington, for Christ's sake. I am an American. A psychologist!

I needed some distance to think, but I was stuck here. If I had a car, I would get in it and drive. But there was no car, and I couldn't even get on the horse without Sergei's help. I had no clothing. He was my only way out, and I wanted to run from him most of all.

I was trapped!

I panicked.

Survival instinct propelled me quickly upward from my seat to bolt for the door. The sudden motion caused my head to swoon violently. My vision went black as I fainted.

I remember the sensation of falling but not hitting the floor.

Only the release as I dove headfirst into darkness.

When my eyelids fluttered open, I did not know where I was. I was lying on my left side on a blanket in front of a fire. It smelled like camping. There was a pulsing sensation on the right side of my head. I lifted my hand to touch it and felt something sticky. I was naked except for riding boots. A door opened, and a blond man entered carrying a bucket. He seemed familiar, but I did not recognize him. I protectively folded my arms over my breasts and closed my legs. A cold draft from the open door passed over my skin, and I shivered.

"Be still," he said quietly.

He knelt beside me and looked at my face. He asked,

"What is your name?"

"Cassandra Abbington," I replied.

"What day is it?" He inquired.

"I don't know," I said.

"Where are you?" He asked.

"I don't know!" I cried again, becoming upset.

I knew I should know the answers. At some level of awareness, I knew I'd posed these same questions to others. I was disoriented and terrified.

He touched my cheek softly.

"Look at me," he said.

Firelight lit his face. I looked into his blue eyes, winter sky in the Adirondack Mountains, a deep, deep blue.

"Think carefully," he said. "Who am I?"

His skin was perfectly smooth and pale, porcelain white. I didn't know his name, but I wanted to kiss his lips anyway.

"Kiss me," I requested.

The blond man leaned forward and placed his lips on mine. He ran his tongue over my bottom lip and sucked it gently, releasing it with an audible pop. His kiss felt familiar.

"Who am I?" He repeated as he pulled away.

I opened my eyes and recognized him.

"Seryozha!" I cried, feeling a flood of relief.

"What happened?" I asked, looking around.

"You fainted and hit your head on the table," he explained.

Oh yes. Now I remembered everything, the horse, the cabin, the brand.

"You branded me, you bastard!" I shouted furiously.

I tried to stand, but he firmly held my shoulders down.

"*Nyet*, do not move," he said. "Let me clean your wound first."

He dipped a towel into the pail of water and washed the blood from my hair. Then he lifted it section by section until he found the gash. He carefully cleansed the area. Then he washed the blood from my wrists and hands.

"It is not as bad as it seemed. You are lucky," Sergei stated.

I did not feel lucky.

"How do you feel?" He asked.

"Hungry," I replied.

"Good," he replied. "Stay right here."

Sergei brought a bowl to me and said,

"Eat. This soup is *Parcha Bozbash*, lamb with chestnuts. My favorite."

I tasted a spoonful. The spices were unusual, but I liked it. The chestnuts reminded me of potatoes. I had never had this dish before. Sergei smiled and encouraged me to keep eating. He broke off a hunk of bread and handed it to me.

"I'm sorry I did not feed you sooner, Sandra. It was my fault you fainted. Too much alcohol on an empty stomach is hard on anyone. Do you feel drunk?"

My mouth was full, so I shook my head 'no.' I took a bite of bread and looked at him. He seemed genuinely concerned for me. I felt like a little girl being cared for by her father. But this man was not my father. My father would never brand anyone. I finished eating and set the bowl down.

"Would you like some more?" He asked softly.

"No," I said and politely added, "thank you."

My mother taught me manners.

His parents did not teach him anything.

"Sergei, I cannot believe you branded me. You may think you own me, but you do not. I married you because I love you. That does not make me your possession. Objects can be put away and forgotten. I am your partner in this relationship. I have a voice, and I demand you hear it," I said.

He looked stunned but did not comment. I was not able to read his expression, and it made me uneasy. I never spoke harshly to him before tonight. But then I had a good reason to be angry. Did he honestly believe I would be happy to be branded like his livestock?

Although he'd never hit me, I realized he could beat me to death, and no one would ever know. No one heard my scream. They would never find my body out here. It would be weeks before anyone even knew I was missing. My publisher, Jack Hawthorne, would go to the police, but what would the Russian police do? Why would they even care about a missing American? They had much bigger problems to deal with here. My parents would never know what happened to me. I saw an image of my parents crying, and it made me feel sad and helpless. A hot stream of anger burst open inside me. I will not let him kill me. I will kill him first! My hands clenched into fists, and my whole body tensed, ready to strike.

I caught myself before this train of thought spiraled out of control and took a deep jagged breath, forcing it below my clenched diaphragm in an urgent attempt to relax. I counseled myself that these ideas were irrational. Sergei would not try to kill me. The evidence to the contrary was that he loved me. I knew it was true. I did not need to fear him, but it was not wise to trust him blindly either. I knew he was capable of great cruelty, but I had no evidence he was a murderer. Well, he did say he would kill anyone who touched me. But that was only to make his point more dramatic. At least I hoped so. I gave him the benefit of the doubt and tried to calm myself down. I took another deep breath that went down easier and held it for a few seconds before releasing it slowly. I made a conscious effort to relax my hands, and then I smoothed my hair with them as if there was nothing wrong.

Sometimes I hated all of my thinking about thinking. Metacognition. It is what separates us from the rest of the animals. Self-awareness and the ability to reflect on our thoughts is a curse. I was driving myself crazy with my constant self-analysis, but it prevented me from pouncing on him and venting my anger with violence. That certainly would produce a negative outcome and might even provoke him to beat me as I had feared. The fear would become a self-fulfilling prophecy.

I understood how the thought, 'he will beat me to death,' led to the emotion of anger, stimulating a behavioral impulse to strike first, which would probably lead to the outcome of him beating me, if only in self-defense. I short-circuited this chain of events with my ability to monitor and change my thoughts.

Still, I hated these mental loops. Cognitive introspection helped me cope with so many things in life, but I couldn't shut it off and find peace. No wonder I get headaches. 'SHUT UP!' I silently yelled with my inner voice. I looked outward for distraction and saw Sergei.

He was studying my face as I did my psychological exercises. His features were expressionless, but his eyes were intense and seemed darker than usual.

"Is there any more wine?" I asked to break the tension.

He nodded and said,

"Stay. I will get it for you. Do not move."

He eyed me carefully as he backed away to retrieve it. He thought I would run again, or maybe he sensed my impulse to attack him.

I hated being under his scrutiny. It made me feel weak, like a child.

There was only a half glass remaining.

"Thank you," I said, taking the glass, "but let's share it."

I took a few sips and passed it back to him. He drank the rest and set the empty glass down beside the woodstove.

99

He lounged on his side with his upper body propped up on his elbow. The light from the fire made his blond hair radiant. I moved close to him and put my cheek on his chest. His body smelled stronger than usual, but I did not mind. His scent smelled like home. I closed my eyes and inhaled his essence, and found the familiarity calming.

"Let's forget about everything tonight," I said softly. "I do not want to think anymore. I just want to be with you."

Sergei rolled onto his back and pulled me on top along with him. I looked at his face. The firelight danced merrily on his perfectly smooth complexion, illuminating his beautiful features.

He looked like an angel, but he was not.

I brushed my nose against his and gazed deeply into his eyes. He kissed me softly as I carefully unbuttoned his shirt. I stroked the soft fur on his chest and traced circles on his stomach with my fingertips. Then I slid my hand beneath the band of his riding pants and touched his penis. I checked for consent, and when he nodded, I unzipped and slid his pants off.

I started to remove my boots, but he put his hand on my arm to stop me.

"Leave them on," he said with a husky voice.

Sergei's eyes were shining, and he kissed me aggressively. He slipped his hands under my arms and guided me back on top of him. I eased onto his penis gently, and we screwed facing each other for a few minutes until I impulsively turned around and rode him backward with my feet on the floor. The brand must have been something to see with the light from the fire illuminating my back like a spotlight.

"Oh, Sandra," he sighed. "You are a beautiful sight. Thank you."

I didn't do it for him. I just didn't want to look at his face. In my current emotional state, Sergei was no more than a tool to feel better. Nothing drives back bad feelings quite like sex, and I had a lot of negativity to dispel. I ground on him deeply with a hard and fast pace, gripping his penis with my vagina for a nice pull on the upswing and releasing on my way down to take him as deep within me as possible, pulling and grinding my way to a powerful release.

My mental networks went offline almost immediately from the destructive power of our tectonic plates colliding. Each intense seismic wave of ecstasy burned off more pain, frustration, and tension. I was as rough on him as he'd been on me, and I did not care as long as he stayed hard. He owed me.

I stopped counting after my 15th orgasm and exceeded my knowledge of Russian numbers that I shouted out of habit as each quake struck. Sergei was moaning and calling my name, but I ignored him until I felt his right leg jerk violently, signaling his release. I didn't want to stop, so I kept going and popped off one more orgasm on his rapidly deflating dick.

Exhausted and covered with sweat, I dismounted and turned to see a wide-eyed bewildered expression on his face. I rested beside him on the floor with my head on his chest.

After my heart rate slowed and my breathing returned to normal, I said, "Tell me about your mother."

Sergei drew a deep breath and held it, releasing slowly.

"There is not much I remember," he finally replied.

He paused to think.

"She was very spiritual and took comfort in her faith. Of course, my father was an atheist. He forbade her to practice Christianity," he said.

"She had a bible and an icon hidden in the back of her closet. When my father was away, she would take them out and worship alone. Sometimes she read me passages from the bible. She taught me. I promised to keep her secret."

He stared at the ceiling.

"I do not remember any more than that," he said sadly.

"Which icon did she have?" I prodded.

He thought for a moment, trying to conjure the image in his mind.

"It was one of Mary holding the Christ-child," he said.

There were lots of versions of that image. I'd seen several in the book on icons I'd been reading, and we had seen many more at the Louvre in May.

"Where is it now?" I asked, thinking this would be a family heirloom.

A pained look crossed his face.

"It burned. I saw it burning," Sergei recalled.

He sat up quickly, and I went with him. His chest pitched violently, breathing fast.

"That *mudak* burned her icon!" He shouted.

He looked at me in disbelief.

"It was all she had to give her hope, and he destroyed it!" He exclaimed.

He was burning with anger at the memory. His eyes moved from side to side as if he were watching his memories on film.

I knew this was a golden opportunity. In psychotherapy, we call emotionally-charged thoughts like these 'hot cognitions.' They allow a person to access memories and connect things they have not been able to before.

"What else do you remember?" I prodded.

Sergei's eyes opened wide as he recalled the scene.

"I was sitting at the table with my father, and my mother was serving us dinner. It was my birthday! We had *Parcha Bozbash* – because it was my favorite! My father was going on and on about something and was very upset. He may have been drunk.

He asked me a question, and when I did not know the answer, he banged his fist on the table. My bowl flew into the air and broke on the floor.

'You are no son of mine,' he shouted. 'Eat off the floor!'

I picked up the broken bowl and ran to my mother. I buried my face in her skirt.

'Go to your room and wait for me,' she said. 'Quietly, so you don't upset your father.'

I hid behind a chair in the next room and watched them through the open doorway. My mother cleaned the floor where my bowl had fallen.

They were talking, but I could not hear what they were saying. Then my father started shouting at her. He rose from his seat and punched her face. Her nose bled. My mother! I was frozen, terrified. I could do nothing."

Sergei paused for a moment and looked at me.

"Can you believe it?" He asked. "He was a fucking asshole. He had no respect for women."

"I am sorry you had to see that, Seryozha. What happened next?" I asked.

He thought for a minute and continued.

"I think he hit her a few more times, and she ran into the kitchen crying. I went to comfort her and saw her face was swelling with red bruises.

'Mama,' I said. 'Are you okay?'

She smiled through her pain and hugged me.

'Jesus said to turn the other cheek, remember Mama?' I asked."

Sergei stopped talking, and his face twisted into a pained mask. I touched his arm gently and said,

102

"Tell me what you remember."

"Fear," he replied. "My father must have heard what I said. He came into the kitchen in a rage."

Sergei's eyes pressed into slits, and his eyebrows pinched tightly. Deep furrows appeared on his brow. His skin paled as he took fast, shallow breaths.

"I cannot remember what he said, but he pushed me down and pulled my mother to their bedroom by her hair.

'Where is it?' my father demanded. 'Where is it?!'

My mother cried out from the pain.

I heard loud noises coming from their room, things being thrown around and smashing. I was scared and hid again. I wanted to help, but I was too small. I just turned five years old! My father would have killed me if I got between them. There was nothing I could do.

He came out with my mother's bible, tearing out sections and throwing them into the fireplace. The flames shot high, and the room filled with a reddish light. I was terrified. It seemed like hell to me, and my father was the devil himself.

Then the *mudak* burned her icon.

She came into view crying, her dress torn open and her face bloody and beaten. The look on her face when she saw the icon burning was total devastation.

'No!' she cried as she threw herself at the fire and pulled it out with her bare hands. The icon was on fire. I remember the smell of her burning flesh."

He paused to think.

"Mama was on her knees trying to put out the flames with the hem of her skirt. That icon was all she had to give her peace."

The image I was forming in my mind was horrendous. As Sergei told the story, I saw him as a terrified little boy hiding behind a chair, powerless to help his mother. No child should ever witness such violence. He paused to look at me. There were streams of tears racing down his cheeks. I was weeping too.

"Sandra?" He asked. "It gets worse."

"I am here, Seryozha. Tell me," I assured him.

103

Sergei took a deep breath and continued,

"He kicked her hard, and she fell over on her side in front of the fireplace. She was clutching the icon in both hands. He kept kicking her back. She begged him to stop, but he was in a rage. He must have kicked her at least twenty times.

I hid behind the chair and prayed my father would not find me. I thought he would throw me in the fire next. There was nothing I could do!

When he finally stopped kicking her, he pried the icon from her hands and threw it back in the fire. This time, she did not try to retrieve it. She was lying on the floor with her eyes open. She watched it burn.

My father put on his coat and hat and left. I guess he went out drinking or maybe to see a mistress. I don't know. As soon as he left, I went to my mother, crying. I cried not only for her and her beautiful icon but for myself.

I betrayed her. It was my fault!"

Sergei stopped again, sobbing. I took him in my arms and said,

"It was not your fault, Seryozha. Believe me. Your father did this to your mother, not you. Do not blame yourself. She loved you and would never want you to feel responsible. You know that, right?"

He looked at me and nodded. I hated seeing him in so much pain, but I knew how good it was for him to recall this traumatic event.

"Do you want to stop?" I asked.

"No," he said. "I may forget again."

He fell silent and fixed his eyes on a point in the air directly in front of him. He spoke slowly and flatly, his emotions cut off from the memory,

"Mama stood up, but she could barely walk. Her eyes were dead, and she could no longer smile, not even for me.

'We should call a doctor, Mama,' I said.

'No, my son, I do not need a doctor,' she replied.

She put me in bed and kissed my forehead, but she never said another word. Then she turned off the light and left the room, closing the door behind her. I cried for a long time, but I could not sleep. Then I heard a noise. I wanted to be good and stay in bed, but I was afraid she'd fallen.

I found her in her bedroom.

She was on the floor.
Her blood was everywhere."

Sergei stopped speaking, his face frozen in a mask of horror. I gently touched his hand, not wanting to startle him.

"Seryozha?" I asked softly.

He turned his eyes to me. After a moment, I saw a flash of recognition that returned him to the present. His emotions flooded back, and he began to sob violently. I offered my open arms and wrapped them around him. He rested his cheek on my shoulder.

"Let it out, Seryozha. I am right here with you," I encouraged.

His tears soaked me as I hugged him tightly. His body shook with emotion. His skin was hot to the touch. As hard as it was to see Sergei so upset, I knew it was good for him to reclaim this memory his mind had repressed for so long. This painful work was necessary for him to heal.

When he met my parents, he told them vaguely his mother died of 'heart problems,' and I think he believed that at the time. This story sounded a lot like suicide to me, but maybe his timeline was off, and his father came home and murdered her. Did it even matter? You can kill a person's spirit or their physical body, and the result is the same. His father was a vile man capable of great cruelty.

Sergei was spent and could not go on. I stayed with him until he wound down. He was exhausted and fell asleep without saying another word. I put a few more logs into the woodstove and watched the firelight dance on the walls of the cabin for a long time before sleep came for me. I wondered if the odor of burning flesh combined with the unique nutmeg meat scent of *Parcha Bozbash* formed a key to unlock the repressed memory of his mother's death.

A French novelist born in the 1800s, Marcel Proust, observed that specific sensory combinations assist with childhood memory recall. Modern research has validated and expanded on this phenomenon. It is now widely accepted that sensory information, including the sense of smell, is closely tied to emotion and memory encoding in what is known as the Proust Effect.

Despite everything that happened, this was a significant breakthrough.
I was beginning to understand Sergei better.
There was hope.

9

MOM WAS RIGHT

The fire burned out during the night, and the cabin was cold when we woke. I was stiff from sleeping on the floor, sore from the horseback ride, and my wrists were severely bruised and raw from the rope burn. I could barely feel the slight discomfort from the brand on my lower back and began to forget about it. We silently packed up and set off for home before the sun came up. The temperature was below freezing, perhaps 25 degrees, with a clear sky. A thin layer of ice skimmed the puddles and shattered like lonely mirrors beneath the horse's hooves. Sergei slowly retraced the route we'd taken the night before. I held on closely and watched the landscape go by as I gathered the fur coat tightly around my naked body.

The sky gradually grew brighter as we made our way along the dirt road. A reddish glow bloomed in the eastern sky. Suddenly, a single beam of light appeared, shooting straight up from the horizon, like a searchlight. The area at the base grew brighter until the first gilded edge of the sun rose above the land. The beam vanished as quickly as it came.

I gasped at the beautiful sight.

"What a glorious morning!" Sergei declared.

I squeezed him tighter in agreement.

Every sunrise offers hope to those who get up early enough to see it, no matter how bad things seemed to be in the dark the night before.

Sergei tapped in the security code to open the front gate and then again as we rode through the back to the stables. He gave his horse a generous helping of oats and brushed his coat lightly before we walked to the house together.

I went upstairs and looked at my back in the mirror for a long time. The brand was about four inches in diameter and looked just like the Karpov fish on the mantelpiece. The mark was red and tender to the touch, but as Sergei described, the lines were thin and the design delicate.

Tattoos are so common. This wasn't much different, I rationalized. The brand was more natural-looking and probably hurt less than a tattoo would have. I was relieved to see it was low enough on my back to remain private. No one would ever need to know it was there. My parents would never see it unless I wore a bikini, which was easy enough to avoid.

Still, I never would have allowed Sergei to do it if we had discussed it in advance. That bothered me. Even though I said 'yes,' I felt he did it against my will. I was tied up, half-drunk and sex-crazed when he asked for my consent.

Would he have done it even if I said 'no?'

Remembering my encounter with Vladislav Valkov made me uneasy. I knew it wasn't my fault, but in truth, I enjoyed it a little too much. I closed my eyes and remembered – I felt the giant's hands on me and my lips parting, eager to taste his tongue in my mouth. I was thrilled when he lifted me onto that white marble counter. My brain scrambled to comprehend what power he held over me and kept coming up blank. Could my husband be right that I had a character defect deserving of a 'tramp stamp' reminder?

Sergei was leaving for Hong Kong at 11:00 am on yet another business trip. This time he would be gone for more than three weeks. While he prepared to leave, I made an American breakfast of eggs over-easy, fried ham chunks, hash-brown potatoes with onions and rye toast. I served the hot breakfast to him in the library and sat on the leather sofa, and watched him eat. He was behind on his preparation for the trip and didn't have time for me. My husband was right there in front of me, but he was already gone.

I felt empty inside. Hollow. A few tears slipped from my eyes. I wiped them away with my hand and stood to leave the room quietly. The past few days were rough, and I didn't want Sergei to see how emotional I was. My body was sore, and I was utterly exhausted. I almost made it to the door when he asked,

"Where are you going, Sandra?"

I turned to face him. When I met his eyes, the waterworks turned on in full force. My tears flowed like someone blew up the dam. I was ashamed of my feminine weakness and put up a hand to shield my face. I turned again to go.

"Wait," he said. "What is wrong?"

I was unable to speak. I could not even look at him.

I ran out of the library, across the pristine white marble floor of the center hall, into the powder room, and locked the door behind me. There I broke down completely, sobbing loudly between painful ragged breaths. My face was beet red and soaked with tears. I hated feeling this way, so out of control. Until recently, it had been a rare occurrence for me to cry at all. I sat on the floor, hugged my knees to my chest, and let it all come out. Sometimes that is the only way to release such strong emotions.

Sergei knocked on the door, but I ignored him. The lump in my throat was too big to speak.

"Sandra? What is wrong? Let me in," he pleaded.

I heard the concern in his voice, but I would not open the door. I didn't want him to see me like this. I buried my face in a towel to muffle the noise and kept sobbing.

"Open the door," he ordered, his tone firmer.

He was losing patience.

"Leave...me...a-lone," I managed to squeak out.

"Unlock the door now, Sandra, or I will knock it down!" He commanded. The urgency in his voice propelled me to action.

I crawled to the door and unlocked it but turned my face away when he entered. I was sure I looked even more hideous than I felt and the thought of him seeing me like this upset me even more. I didn't want to send him on his trip with this image in his mind. He would never want to come home!

He rubbed my back with his hand, trying to soothe me. After a few desperate minutes, my sobs began to come at less frequent intervals. My tears slowed and finally stopped. I wiped my face with the towel.

"There," he said. "That is better."

I turned and found his dry blue eyes. Mine were probably bloodshot and red-rimmed. My contact lenses were sticky and clouded over with protein, but what could I do? I had to look at him. He expected me to.

"What is wrong?" He asked again.

A few more tears leaked out as I choked,

"I don't want you...to go."

A slight smile crossed his lips.

"Is that all? You had me worried, Sandrochka," he said sweetly.

"I'm sorry, Seryozha. I miss you so much when you go away," I explained. "I am afraid you will never come back."

"I will always come home to you, I promise," he pledged, pausing long enough to get a nod of acknowledgment from me.

"Are you going to be okay?" He asked.

I nodded again and tried to look strong even though I did not feel that way.

"Good. Stand up," he said.

I rose to my feet. Sergei put his hands on my shoulders and looked at me directly.

"You look terrible. Go upstairs and get some rest. I'll call you when I get to the hotel tomorrow," he said.

Then he kissed me on the forehead and spanked my behind to send me on my way.

"Go," was all he said.

I waited until the Mercedes pulled out of the driveway and disappeared down the road before I got into bed. I was exhausted physically, mentally, and emotionally, but sleep would not come. The bed was too big, and I felt lonelier than I ever had before. I called Velikan and said, "Come on," as I patted the top of the bed. He was unsure at first, knowing it was forbidden, but eventually, he responded to the international 'call the dog to bed' code. Not even a well-trained Russian dog can resist. Once on top, he stood over me and licked my face with his big pink tongue, making me laugh and feel a little better. I rubbed my nose in his muzzle, gently pulled on the black ridges of his lips, and scratched behind his ears. He had such pretty brown eyes. Much warmer than cold blue ones. I got him to lie down next to me, and I rewarded him with lavish praises, petting him all the while.

"Such a good boy! So handsome. Just look at you. Who could ask for a better dog? You're so big and strong. I love your big white teeth. Oh, those fangs are impressive! I am almost frightened!" I poured it on, and he loved every minute of it.

Kukla joined us, and I became the meat in the middle of a dog cuddle sandwich.

Sergei had a thing about allowing dogs on furniture: he was 100 percent against it. The idea of sleeping with dogs was disgusting to him, and therefore allowing one on the bed, his bed was the worst offense of all. I was violating a fundamental rule with two dogs, and I knew it. He had all sorts of prohibitions – no pets on the bed, no shoes in the house, no feet on the furniture, no eating pizza with your fingers. I was always doing something wrong with my 'dirty American habits.' He drove me crazy. He didn't have to clean the house, feet aren't that gross, and pizza is meant to be eaten by hand!

He nearly lost his mind when I tried to explain the 'five-second rule' – that it is okay to eat food that has fallen on the floor as long as you pick it up within five seconds. The extreme look of disgust on his face was so funny I laughed at him. I couldn't help myself. Sergei didn't kiss me for a few days afterward until I promised never to eat anything off the floor again. It's not like I did it a lot, but if you drop an M&M and it lands in a clean place, what harm could there be?

His stupid rules were overbearing and ridiculous.

I grew up sharing my bed with a dog, and it seemed like the most natural thing in the world to me. As long as the dog is clean, what is the harm? I did not mind changing the bedding more often. I buried my nose in Velikan's fur while Kukla used my belly for a pillow. Then I fell into a deep, dreamless sleep.

I woke to the sound of the dogs whining. Disoriented, I didn't know what day it was. The bedside clock said it was 12:08 am. I realized I'd slept for more than 12 hours. I quickly dressed in a t-shirt and yoga pants and went downstairs to let Velikan and Kukla out.

Ilya was in the kitchen making tea. He was always around, but for some reason, I was startled to see him. He never spoke or made eye contact with me. This time he acknowledged my presence with a slight wave. I was sure he tried to avoid me as much as possible. I didn't mind because he made me nervous anyway. Ilya was rugged and hard-looking, maybe a killer. I had no way of knowing. But here he was, protecting me and the house while the boss was away. The bodyguard could not be that dangerous if Sergei trusted him to be alone with me for three weeks.

I decided to reach out to him.

"*Zdravstvujtye* Ilya," I said, using the formal hello to get his attention.

"*Zdravstvujtye Gaspazha*," he replied.

I couldn't believe he just called me 'Madam.'

"*Pozhaluysta*," I replied. "*Menya zovut* Cassandra. *Moy druz'ya zovut menya* Cassie.*"

He looked confused.

Gah! My Russian stinks. I probably said it wrong.

"*Ya* Cassie," I said, pointing to my chest like I was talking to a monkey.

"Cassie," he repeated with a shy smile.

"*Molodets!*" I exclaimed, using Sergei's praise word for me.

Then I did my best to say I was making a late supper and asked if he was hungry. He nodded and took a seat at the breakfast bar to watch while I cooked. How boring it must be for him to guard a farm where nothing ever happens. At least I could entertain him for a while with a bit of a cooking show. I put on one of my old-school party mixes, and soon I was bopping around the kitchen singing along to funky songs like Frankie Smith's 'Double Dutch Bus' and Morris Day and the Time's 'Jungle Love.' I was surprised when Ilya joined the chorus singing, "Oh We Oh We Oh."

Maybe he was more fun than he first appeared.

I browned chicken breast cutlets in a little olive oil with fresh garlic in a heavy cast-iron skillet. Then I smothered them in Portabella mushrooms, sweet red peppers, and onions and poured in a half bottle of leftover red wine. I was ready with the lid, for the steam plume rose rapidly. I reduced the heat and let it simmer while the pasta boiled and green beans steamed.

Cooking for two is always more fun. I would never have gone through this much trouble just for myself. Tonight, anything was better than eating alone. I was so lonely when Sergei traveled.

I thickened the sauce with corn starch and seasoned it with salt, pepper, and basil before spooning it over the pasta. Then I opened a bottle of wine and asked if he wanted a glass. He shook his head '*nyet*.' Drinking on the job was not allowed. I insisted and promised not to tell anyone, making the 'locking my mouth and throwing away the key' gesture. Who would ever know? We were the only ones here. He seemed surprised by the offer, smiled, and accepted the glass I held out to him.

I made two plates and sat beside him at the breakfast bar. He lifted his glass.

"*Za Amerika!*" He toasted.

"To America!" I repeated in English.

He held my gaze briefly as we clinked our glasses together. A grin lit up his face that changed his entire appearance for the better.

We ate in silence, but I sensed he enjoyed the dish. I got him another serving and poured two more glasses of wine. When we finished, I rinsed the plates and put them in the dishwasher. He smiled and said,

"*Spasibo*," which means 'thank you' in Russian.

I smiled and tapped a peace sign over my lips to ask for a cigarette in smoker sign language. I did not smoke, but why not? He pulled out two filterless Belomorkanal cigarettes and lit mine first. They have an empty cardboard tip that squishes flat for smoking. The tobacco was strong and tasted vile. Naturally, I loved it. And so I sat there smoking and polishing off the bottle of wine with my new friend. We didn't talk, but we didn't need to. I was glad to finally connect with this stranger who lived under the same roof as me. I enjoyed his company. Anything was better than thinking about the three weeks of crushing loneliness that lay ahead.

I caught Ilya looking at the ugly bruises and abrasions on my wrists. He touched my hand gently and said "*izvinite*" with genuine concern in his eyes. Embarrassed, I dropped my hands to my lap, lowered my eyes, and said,

"*Spasibo*, Ilya, I am sorry too."

I wished him a good night and went back upstairs to bed. My Russian was far too limited to explain those marks. No doubt he knew who made them.

Sergei called as promised the following day. I picked up the phone in the family room on the first ring, eager to speak with him. He sounded tired. I was relieved he made it to Hong Kong safely and told him I felt better. We spoke briefly, and then the line went dead, disconnected.

A few seconds later, the phone rang again.

"Seryozha?" I asked expectantly.

There was a pause.

"How are you, Cassandra?" His English pronunciation was poor and his accent thick, but I understood the speaker. A sharp knifepoint of fear twisted in my belly. I turned to make sure no one was listening. I was alone.

"Vladislav Valkov?" I whispered in disbelief.

"Yes. Please. Slava. How are you?" He asked.

'Vladislav' sure was a mouthful, I thought wryly, suddenly aware my nipples were pressing against my shirt. 'Slava' was a good nickname. More like 'Hot Slava,' I laughed to myself before pushing my inappropriate volcanic thoughts aside.

"Good. And you?" I asked cautiously.

"Good, I hear your voice," he replied.

His voice was rich and husky, reflective of a man his size. I drew a mental picture of his devilish smile and handsome broad face. I remembered the way it felt when he held me on the countertop.

An icy chill shimmied down my spine, followed by an unwelcome surge of heat even lower. A tight pinch of shame followed.

"Why are you calling?" I demanded.

"Your husband is… away, yes?" He asked.

"Yes, but…," I answered.

"I must see you, Doctor," he said. "I have problem."

I could imagine what his problem was and how he hoped I would help!

"I am married," I stated.

"You are, Psychologista, yes? You help people?" He asked.

I was not falling for this, but I was curious.

"What is the problem?" I asked.

"I not stop thinking. Make me crazy. My work, eh, suffers," Slava explained.

I could relate to that, but I knew this was just a ploy to get me alone again.

"You are a rich man. Why don't you go see a therapist?" I replied.

"You are psychology doctor," he insisted.

"I am not licensed to practice here. I cannot help you." I responded.

"I pay you well," he insisted.

"No. Sergei would kill me if I saw you again," I refused.

"Sergei is in China. He will never know," he replied.

How did he know that?

"Sergei knows everything. I cannot do it," I stated firmly.

"You are afraid? I promise not touch you. I am sorry. I was drunk. You beautiful. Not happen again," he promised.

I wanted to believe him, but did he think I had the word 'stupid' stamped on my forehead? No, just 'tramp' stamped on my back.

Unwelcome thoughts.

There was silence on the line. I listened to the faint sound of static.

"Did he beat you, Cassandra?" He asked slowly, sounding genuinely concerned.

I was shocked by the question and hesitated before I answered.

"No...of course not," I replied, trying to sound cool.

"What did he do? He must have done something," he said.

Visions of the late-night crying jag and scenes from the cabin paraded before my mind's eye. I took a deep breath. My hands were trembling beneath my ugly, bruised wrists. At least the rope rash finally scabbed over.

"What did he do?" Slava repeated.

"N-nothing," I stammered.

My anxiety shot through the roof. I had to get off the phone. Now.

"I want to help. Tell me. You feel better," Slava offered seductively.

"No," I said firmly. "The details of my marriage are not your business. I have to go. Goodbye."

I slammed the handset down in the receiver and took a step backward. I stared at the phone as if it might turn into a snake, coil back, and strike me.

A moment later, it rang.

I jumped!

I let it ring three more times before I cautiously picked up.

"*Allo*?" I asked.

The Russian phone greeting is surprisingly similar to the one in the United States.

"Who were you talking to?" Sergei asked.

"Um, nobody, Seryozha. Wrong number," I said.

I am a terrible liar! You have to practice a lot to be smooth, but I was an honest person and generally never had any reason to lie.

"You are upset. I can hear it in your voice," Sergei noted.

"I'm fine," I insisted, trying to force a smile into my tone. "How is Hong Kong?"

"You were not upset when I spoke to you 10 minutes ago. Who were you talking to?" He repeated.

"Really, Sergei, it was nothing. I am fine," I said, feeling annoyed.

"How was your flight?" I asked, desperately trying to change the subject.

"It was not a wrong number, Sandra. I called several times. The line was busy. Who were you talking to?" He demanded.

I heard the anger in his voice. He knew I was lying! I fell into a trap. My stomach dropped, and a cold chill stalked my heart. What could I say? I could deny it and dig the hole deeper or just admit it was his mortal enemy. But then he would think I was up to something because I lied about it in the first place.

I knew he would get to the truth. He was onto me and would not stop until he was satisfied. If nothing else, Sergei was persistent. There was no easy way out of this. I ran through the list of people I may have spoken to, but I could not come up with anyone to fit the situation. I simply could not think fast enough. My ability to deceive was severely underdeveloped from lack of use.

"Who was it? Tell me!" He commanded.

"If I tell you, will you promise not to be mad at me?" I asked. It was a weak statement, something a child would say, but it was the best I could do. I was stalling.

"You will tell me who you were talking to. Now!" He ordered.

I took a deep breath and said,

"Vladislav Valkov."

Sergei was silent. I imagined what his face looked like and shuddered at the image I saw. Good thing he was in China and not in the next room.

"It's not what you think," I assured.

"What is it?" He demanded, his voice brimming with irritation.

"He asked me to help him with a psychological problem. I refused, of course. I have no interest in seeing him again," I explained.

Sergei was quiet. Not being able to see him drove me crazy. I had no idea what he was thinking. I hated this. Why did Slava have to call at that particular moment? If he waited an hour, I would not be in this jam right now.

"You lied to me," he said. "I cannot tolerate lying."

"I'm sorry, really I am. But I knew you would be angry. It's not like I asked him to call. He just did. I refused to see him. What more can I do? Please forgive me," I pleaded.

"Listen to me carefully, Sandra. I will say this only once," he instructed. "Stay away from Slava Valkov. He is a criminal, and he wants to take you from me. He is a very dangerous man. I cannot protect you if you do not listen. If he calls again, hang up the phone. If you see him, run in the opposite direction. Do not go anywhere without Ilya. I mean it. Most importantly, do not hide anything from me. Do you understand?"

"Yes. There is something else you should know," I said.

"What?" He demanded angrily.

"I don't know how, but he knows you are in China. He knows I am here alone," I said.

Sergei inhaled sharply.

"Put Ilya on the phone. Now!" He ordered.

Shocked, I dropped the phone and ran to Ilya's room in the staff wing and knocked on the door. He was pulling on a t-shirt as he opened the door, a set of weights and a lifting bench in view behind him.

"Phone. Sergei. Now," I said. I held an invisible phone to my ear, forgetting the Russian word for it.

Ilya picked up the extension in the kitchen. I went back to the family room to hang up the phone. I listened for a moment and heard Sergei say,

"....monitor phone calls coming in and out of the house..."

At least, I think that's what he said. They were talking in Russian, and Sergei was speaking quickly. My Russian was still poor at best.

My heart froze.

I carefully cradled the phone.

My husband is going to spy on me!

116

I could not believe it. Would Sergei know everything I say to my parents, everything I say to my publisher, Jack? I say a lot of things to Jack I would not want him to hear. I worked at home. He had no right to tap my office phone! I suddenly felt cut off from the outside world. I looked out of the window and saw the wall. A quaint throwback to the old days when marauding tribes would come to rape and pillage the villagers. Something to keep bad people out?

Now I saw it as a prison wall. To keep me in. I started to panic. I realized Sergei could change the security code on the gates, and I would not be able to leave! I had a strong urge to escape before they could lock me in. But where would I go? I had no friends here. I would never make it to St. Petersburg without the police pulling me over. The idea of dealing with the Russian police on my own terrified me. My thoughts raced out of control. I ran to the kitchen and crudely indicated I needed to talk to Sergei again when Ilya finished speaking with him.

I opened a bottle of vodka and threw back a double shot. I didn't bother with *zakuska*. Once you get past the initial gag reaction, it's smooth sailing. I drank another shot for insurance.

Within a few minutes, the alcohol hit my brain. The panic began to subside. Drinking is probably the worst way to cope with anxiety, but it was the best I could do on short notice. I had no time for mental gymnastics. I did not believe in taking psychotropic medications, so I had none on hand. Too bad because a Xanax would have helped. It never occurred to me to bring meds from the States. I was expecting happily ever after, not this nightmare.

Ilya's Belomorkanal cigarettes were lying on the counter. I pointed to the pack and raised my eyebrows. He nodded. I pulled one out, squashed the cardboard tip, lit the smoke, and inhaled deeply. I nervously flicked the ashes into the kitchen sink.

What else are they talking about? Were there secret cameras around the house? Hidden microphones? I knew there were surveillance cameras on all the gates and the roof. The house had an alarm system, but I did not know much about the security beyond that. I'd never thought about it before, thinking the security measures were balm for a case of paranoia. Who would rob a house all the way out in the country anyway? There was always someone here, and we had two big guard dogs on duty.

I watched Ilya's face as he spoke to Sergei. He was taking notes on a piece of paper. He seemed serious as if he was finally getting mission orders after years of training. I did not see what the big deal was. So Slava called. So he knew Sergei was out of town. So he tried to lure me out of the fortress to meet with him. I am not stupid. I would not go.

For this, we needed a full-scale security alert with a complete stripping of privacy? We were not under attack. Trust and loyalty? Bullshit. This place was a prison!

Finally, I got my chance to talk to Sergei.

"Hi," I said lightly.

I was feeling a warm buzz from the vodka.

"Sandra, I want you to stay in the house until I return. Do you understand?" He said firmly.

"No. I am seriously freaking out, Sergei. You can't keep me locked up here like a prisoner," I said.

I knew how much he hated when I said 'no' to him, so I said it even louder.

"What are you talking about?" He demanded.

"No. I am not your prisoner!" I repeated with even more emphasis as if that would clarify my point.

Ilya looked at me like I was crazy, so I turned my back to him.

"Listen," he said calmly. "I am trying to protect you. Valkov is trouble, big trouble. I am sorry you feel I am locking you up, but I need to keep you safe. You do not know what he is capable of."

"I don't know what you are capable of either!" I snapped, stressing the 'you.'

"I am your husband, remember? Listen to me. You understand it is my responsibility to make sure you are safe, don't you?" He asked.

"Yes, but I heard you say you were going to tap the phone calls. You don't trust me, and I need you to trust me. I was not going to meet with him. I would not do that to you after what happened. I promise I won't go anywhere without Ilya. Please do not lock me in!" I pleaded and started crying again.

I was disgusted with myself, enough with the tears already! I'd cried more in the past three days than I had in the last ten years.

"What are you talking about, Sandra? No one is going to listen to your phone calls. I just want to make sure Valkov doesn't continue to harass you," he explained.

Oh. I suddenly felt quite foolish.

"I trust you. Believe me," Sergei continued. "I need to protect you because I love you."

Those were the words I needed to hear.

"Oh, Seryozha, you picked an awful time to go to China, but I will be strong for you. You are right, and I do trust you. I'm sorry I snapped, and I'm sorry I lied to you. I will not do it again. Can you forgive me?" I said.

"Yes, of course, Sandra. Are you going to be okay?" He asked.

"Yes. I love you. Do not worry about me." I said.

"Good," he said. "Put Ilya on."

I could tell by the tone of his voice he was worried.

"Goodbye," I said and handed the phone to Ilya.

I stared at the blank screen on my laptop for several minutes before pressing the power button. Work will take my mind off of all of this, I assured myself. I clicked the file, and the manuscript flashed onto the screen. I decided to pick up where I'd left off three days ago and scrolled down to the end of the document.

Then the most incredible thing happened. My fingers hovered over the keyboard, but they refused to type. No words came. This never happened before. Stacks of scientific articles, journals, books, and handwritten notes surrounded me. I had all the inspiration a writer could ever desire, but I felt nothing. No words came.

My fingers seemed oddly alien. There were no signals from my brain to drive my hands to work. My life, my academic career, and my writing had been so easy up to this point. I worked hard but never struggled to achieve. Work was natural for me.

Now I felt most unnatural.

What is wrong with me?

I rounded up Velikan and Kukla and headed for the small gate in the wall behind the house. I crossed my left fingers and anxiously entered the numbers 3-9-9-3 with my right. The gate clicked open.

Sergei trusted me! It was not a prison after all!

I tried to write again later that day, but still, no words came. I shut the computer down and closed the laptop like a clam. I could not bear to look at the empty screen. Then I noticed I had a voice message.

"Hi, Cassie. It's Jack. I haven't heard from you in days. How is the book coming? Give me a call when you get in. You know the number."

I did not return his call. What could I say to him? I'd written nothing since the last update. Now I could not write at all. I looked around my office, and my eyes fell upon the cookbook my mother gave me on my wedding day. I opened it for the first time. Perhaps this is something I can do to distract myself.

I imagined how happy Sergei would be if I surprised him with a traditional Russian dinner. Before I could do that, I needed to learn the recipes. Since I would have no idea if the dishes were correct, I could use the staff as tasters. They would not mind. Beluka could help me fix my mistakes. Yes, a project was what I needed to take my mind off writing for a while.

The kitchen was well-stocked, but I needed fresh ingredients. Beluka, Ilya, and I made several trips to the market in Chudovo as I took off on a culinary adventure. For the next three weeks, I experimented with the recipes in my book until I got them right. Mastering these dishes was not easy because Russian cuisine is full of dumplings, puff pastries, and sauces I had never prepared before. Many of the recipes featured cabbage, beets, and fish – ingredients far from the top of my list of favorite foods. I persevered and was surprised to find I liked most of the dishes despite their questionable contents.

There was a grand conspiracy in Sergei's house. I spoke with him every day but did not give him any indication of what I was up to and swore everyone to secrecy. I pretended I was hard at work on my book, even though I had not written a single word. I kept Jack at bay by telling him I was taking a vacation. There was no more trouble with Slava Valkov.

Finally, the day of my grand surprise had come. The flight was due to arrive in St. Petersburg at 11:00 am, perfect timing for dinner. Ilya promised to phone me when he picked up Sergei and Uvar to let me know they were on their way.

I asked Ilya to give a note to Sergei after they left the airport. It said,

"*My love,*

How long I have waited for your return! My heart aches for you, and I cannot wait until you hold me in your arms again. But first, I have prepared a surprise to demonstrate the depth of my feeling for you.

Please, will you meet me in the dining room upon your arrival? It will give me great pleasure if you honor my humble request.

Your adoring wife,

Cassandra"

I chose the red satin dress I wore on our first date and spun my locks into a deceptively simple swirl on the back of my head, leaving two sections of hair to dangle freely in the front. These I formed into long corkscrew curls that draped down each side of my face. I wore the long diamond earrings Sergei gave me, sexy red heels, and make-up complete with red lipstick. I bleached my teeth the night before, so my smile was brilliant. Looking in the mirror, I decided I looked even more attractive than when this dress made its debut. My red painted nails were perfect this time.

I was sure to get his attention!

Vasily lit the dining room fireplace so it would be cozy and inviting when Sergei arrived. I set a service for one at the farthest end of the table with the best dishes, stemware, and silverware we had. I placed fresh flowers in vases on the table and filled the room with candles to add more romance and warmth. I imagined him sitting at the end of the long table, watching me come and go with my assortment of tantalizing culinary offerings. Knowing how much my husband loved classical piano, I selected St. Petersburg composer Sergei Rachmaninov. I turned the volume on low in the dining room, testing the sound ahead of time. Rachmaninov was timeless and beautiful. So very Russian. Yes, this will be the perfect accompaniment to the meal I prepared. I hoped he would not mind eating alone. The table had seating for 20, but we never had any guests.

I intended to change that after today.

Ilya called a little after 11:30 am to let me know they were on the way. Uvar would honk the horn as they pulled into the driveway when they arrived. I immediately set to work on my final preparations.

When I heard the horn, I dashed into the dining room to pour a glass of chilled vodka, light the candles and turn the music on. Then I hid outside one door and listened as Sergei walked in the other. A thrill of excitement coursed through me, knowing he was there. I gave him a minute to settle, and then I entered the room carrying a tray full of small dishes – a splendid assortment of *zakuska*. I served *bitky* meatballs with sour cream sauce, hard-boiled eggs stuffed with caviar and drizzled with a creamy yolk-mayonnaise mixture, stuffed mushrooms with sour cream, *olady* fritters with black raspberry jam, and smoked herring fillets in a cream sauce. I'd come a long way from serving him leftover Chinese food, I thought with satisfaction.

Deliberately avoiding eye contact, I carefully arranged the dishes in front of him. It took every ounce of control I had to not look at him.

"Sandra," he said softly.

My eyes flashed to him briefly.

Oh my God, he is so handsome! Look away!

I lowered my eyelashes, put a finger to my lips, and whispered, "Shhh."

I turned and left the room.

A few minutes later, I returned to refill his vodka glass. This time, I left the bottle. I would not allow myself to look at him even though I was dying to know what he thought of the appetizers. Again, I turned and walked the length of the room away from him.

I set the timer for ten minutes and thought about Sergei as the powerless five-year-old boy who blamed himself for the brutality his father inflicted on his mother. How hard it must have been for him to grow up without her. The fact that he survived at all spoke to his inner strength. If I had the ability, I would travel through time, whisk that child away and raise him myself. Sadly, I had no time machine, so home cooking, compassion, and love were all I could offer him now.

When the timer dinged, I brought in a bowl of *borscht*, a cabbage-beet soup. I served it piping hot with a dollop of sour cream on top. His glass was empty, so I filled it again with vodka. Then I placed the first course dishes on a tray and carried them out of the room. I noticed he had tried everything, even the herring, which I could never bring myself to taste in a million years. He had different tastes than mine, and that was perfectly fine. We did not need to be twins to love each other.

I gave him five minutes for the soup and once again entered carrying the tray. I could not decide which one to serve, so I gave him two salads to sample. The first was a simple marinated shredded red cabbage salad. The other was fresh mushrooms pickled in wine and garlic I had prepared five days in advance to give the flavors time to meld in the fridge. As I lifted the soup bowl from the table, I glanced at him briefly. He was watching me closely and caught my eye. He smiled, and I could not help but smile shyly in return. I quickly looked away and walked to the kitchen. This time I put a little more swing in my stride.

Five minutes later, I arrived with the main entrée. *Solianka* is a mixed meat Russian gumbo cooked with salt fermented cucumbers, mushrooms, capers, and tomatoes. My recipe used veal, ham, and kielbasa. His eyes lit up when I set the bowl down in front of him. Good, he recognizes it! The idea of cooking with pickles seemed very strange to me, but it tasted great. This dish was salty and a little sour.

Once again, I made the long walk away from him. Halfway down the length of the table, I pretended to drop something and bent from my waist to reach the floor, hoping he was watching. My skirt was cut just above the knee, and I knew there would be plenty of leg showing. I arched my back as I straightened slowly, casually smoothed my dress, and then continued to the kitchen.

I prepared a pot of strong black tea and placed a generous piece of rum baba on a dessert plate with a pretty floret of whipped cream. Baba is a sweet yeast cake with raisins soaked in a rum-sugar syrup. I still had a few minutes and tapped my red fingernails nervously on the counter to pass the time. At last, the timer went off.

I carried in the grand finale and set the cake before him. I poured the strong tea halfway up the glass and held the pot of boiling water up. He made a left-to-right hand motion to indicate he did not want me to weaken it. So I filled the glass to the top with tea. I placed the other dishes on my tray and turned to go once again.

"*Nyet*," Sergei said as he took hold of my waist and brought me down to sit on his lap.

I was thrilled! When I gazed into his electric blue eyes, I fell in love with him all over again. I felt as if I was seeing him for the very first time. He was so sexy, and his soulful eyes spoke volumes. I saw his love shining as clearly as if the words were plastered on a billboard for me to read. When a man like Sergei looks at you this way, you perceive it with everything you are – heart, mind, soul, and all of your senses. The feeling is overwhelmingly positive. No wonder I went into withdrawal whenever he was away and always craving more. I was an addict.

"I cannot eat another bite," he said.

I smiled, soaking in his attention like warm rays of sunshine on my skin. What could I say? I certainly did not mind if he skipped dessert.

"Where did you learn to cook like that?" He asked.

"Oh, Seryozha," I confessed. "I have been so busy these past few weeks learning. Everyone helped me. And I can do so much more – *pirogs*, dumplings, *varenyky*, and *bliny*. Name a dish, anything, and I will make it for you."

He smiled with delight, and I saw how much this meant to him. My mother was right! I wondered why he never said anything to me about cooking Russian food for him before. I would have tried this sooner.

"I am also ready to entertain guests. Just let me know how many people to expect so I can plan. Isn't it about time we started to use this beautiful room?" I said as I waved a hand like a game show host.

"Yes," he said. "I would like that very much."

He looked at me for a moment, and a strange expression crossed his face.

"You have changed, Sandrochka," he observed. "You are not the same woman I left here three weeks ago."

Other than my bad case of writer's block, I didn't feel any different.

"What do you mean?" I asked.

He thought for a minute and shook his head.

"I'm not sure. But I like it," Sergei replied.

We gazed at each other for a long time without speaking, meeting again in a fresh moment borne of three weeks separation and contemplation. Our love was evolving. He wasn't perfect, but he'd trusted me to help him face the trauma of his past. That was an act of true intimacy. I loved Sergei even more deeply because he shared the darkest day of his life with me. Understanding what happened to him moved me closer to acceptance.

He kissed me gently three times – first on my nose, then between my eyebrows, and again on my forehead. I accepted his kisses with gratitude.

"Won't you try a taste of the cake, my love?" I asked. "It's rum baba."

He nodded, so I broke off a small section, dipped it in the whipped cream, and placed it in his mouth. I was stunned when he grasped my wrist and brought my fingers to his lips to clean off the sticky syrup. He took his time dragging his teeth sensually over my skin, swirling his tongue in circles, and gently sucking my fingertips. I closed my eyes and felt the sensation pulse through my electrical pathways and light up my body from the inside. My nerve endings tingled in anticipation, and my face flushed with warmth. When he stopped, I opened my eyes. I had to re-focus to see clearly, but the fire of desire was burning brightly in his eyes when I did.

"Let's go upstairs, Sandrochka," he said in a deep sexy voice.

I gathered the remaining dishes as he blew out the candles. I dropped the tray on the kitchen counter, ran through the house and up the stairs with him right behind me. Once inside the master suite, Sergei closed the heavy wooden doors and held me against them, kissing me passionately. I melted like butter in his scorching embrace. I kissed him hungrily as if I was starving, and he would be my last meal. We staggered toward the bed without ever breaking our kiss.

He lifted my dress over my head in one continuous motion. His breath caught in surprise when he saw I was not wearing anything beneath it. I unbuttoned his shirt while he shimmied out of his slacks. I fell back on the bed and pulled him down on me by his shirt collar. His chest rubbed against mine, and my fingers combed through his golden hair. My burning lips reached for his flaming kisses again and again.

Sergei teased me, touching me only on the periphery and deliberately holding back the one thing I most desperately wanted. He turned my entire body into one large erogenous zone. Less sensitive areas like the arms, legs, and back became surrogate sensual centers under the power of his caresses. Wherever he touched me, fireworks of sensation exploded. I realized he avoided direct sexual stimulation on purpose, but I did not know why. By then, I was incapable of rational thought. All I could do was feel his touch and respond.

My lover was finally home!

I found myself face down on the bed, feeling him trace the healed circle of the brand with a fingertip as he scratched my back lightly with his nails. He slapped my rear with his open hand several times, causing a loud sound.

Whack!

Whack!

Whack!

The spanking did not hurt, but it gave me goosebumps all over. Then he ran his fingertips lightly over the erect flesh creating a whole new tactile sensation.

He was a madman! Who else would think to do these things?

"I cannot take any more of this teasing, Seryozha," I said as I rose to my hands and knees and started to crawl away.

Sergei seized my hips and pulled me back. My knees slid easily over the smooth sheets until I was once again under his control. He held my hips firmly as he moved into position. As I felt the initial press of his penis against the tender opening of my vagina, my body tensed, and I shook with a violent climax. He said something especially nasty in Russian before he drove his cock in against the surging tide of muscle contractions, igniting another explosive orgasm that would only be the second in a series of prolonged ecstasy.

What a man!

I could not imagine ever wanting to make love to anyone else. I was the luckiest woman in the world to have Sergei for a lover. We could not get enough of each other.

Thinking back, it seemed strange he waited until we were married to initiate any kind of sexual contact. He had a strong libido and was no prude. He had absolutely no religious convictions. Why did he wait? He could have had me anytime he wanted before we married. I was hot for him, and he knew it.

His decision did not make sense.

Sergei's hair was wet with perspiration. He was lying on his side with his arm draped over me. His eyes were half-closed.

"Seryozha," I said softly. "I wanted to sleep with you on our very first date. Why did you make me wait so long?"

He looked up, surprised, blue eyes shining with amusement.

"You have a Ph.D. in Psychology, Sandra. Why don't you tell me?" He deflected.

I gazed up at the canopy and thought. He loved to play games like this with me. I looked to the golden star for inspiration and spoke freely.

"Well, Seryozha," I started. "You are a very horny man, and I know for a fact you wanted me on our first date. A woman knows. But for some unknown reason, you did not take advantage of the opportunity. At the time, I assumed you thought I was a slut and wanted to get to know me better, so I would not give you a sexually transmitted disease. Given your history, why would you be concerned about catching something from me? I should have been worried about you. We would have used a condom for birth control anyway. Hmmm. Were you offended I came on so strong? I know how much you like to be the boss. But that does not explain waiting for marriage either. There were countless other opportunities for you to have me on your terms, but you never did. You are not religious or old-fashioned. It makes no sense. Why did you wait?"

I looked to him for a bit of assistance and saw his smiling eyes sparkle with delight. His lips pressed tightly together. He would not give up his secrets so easily.

I was not even close.

"Okay tough guy, be a clam. I will get to the bottom of this with or without your help," I said.

I thought for a few minutes and had an 'aha!' experience.

"Seryozha, you devil, I have it!" I declared, looking at him. He waited expectantly to hear my theory with an amused grin on his face.

"You turned me on and deliberately withheld sex to trick me into marrying you. I would have done anything to get you in bed, and you knew it! I even consented to immediate marriage with no conditions. If we were already sleeping together, I would have insisted on a longer engagement, a church wedding including conversion to Catholicism for you, or if you refused, maybe that we live together in New York first to see how it went. I would have had the upper hand in all of this! Instead, you led me around by a little leash that was directly attached to my desire for you. What a monster you are! Only an evil mind would come up with such a wicked plot!" I stated with dramatic emphasis.

I poked him in the ribs and asked,
"What do you have to say for yourself? I am right. Admit it!"
Sergei smiled brightly. He said,
"You are onto me, Sandra. I got everything I wanted, and you fell for it completely. Oh, how you wanted me! Do you have any idea how hard it was for me to hold back when you were so obviously willing? I was dying! Fortunately, I have a lot more self-control than you do. I won. You are my wife, and we live in my house. Soon you will be pregnant, and I will have the family I have always wanted. Now you are even making me real food. But this is only half of the story."

Doing my best impression of a televangelist, I said,
"Speak, you demon. I demand to know how else you have deceived me!"
He smiled again, recognizing I meant to be funny.
I giggled and smiled back at him. He tricked me, but I was deeply in love with him. It did not matter how we got here.

He put his arms around me and gazed into my eyes.
"What you do not know, my dear Sandrochka, is how long I have been in love with you."
I looked at him soberly, suddenly feeling very serious.
"It took you four months to develop feelings for me, but I fell in love with you that first night on the balcony. In all that time, I tried to figure out how to convince you to marry me and move here. It seemed hopeless. What were my chances of getting a beautiful American with a Ph.D. to come to Russia? I knew you would never give up your New York career to become a country housewife. When you got the writing assignment, I seized the opportunity," he confessed.

He did scheme to get me to marry him! I did not know what to think about that. Why me? I was a nervous wreck with a big stain on her dress at that cocktail party. I never realized he felt so strongly, but thinking back, I acknowledged the evidence was there. Maybe I missed it because I did not know him. I assumed his intensity was a cultural characteristic.

"Did you think I was a slut?" I asked timidly.

"No," he laughed softly. "You wanted me, but you were so naïve about men. If you were a slut, you would have been there with someone else. Sluts have no trouble finding dates for cocktail parties."

"What do you mean by 'naïve'?" I asked.

I did not like that word because it implied 'stupid' to me.

"You trusted me completely. You were an ingénue, an innocent. You came to Russia without ever asking to see a photo of my house or how much money I have. You still don't know because you still have not asked. Think about it," he explained.

I could not believe he was telling me this, but it certainly explained a lot. Was I so naïve? Sergei inspired trust as much as he did love and desire in me. I never wanted to question his integrity. And I did not care how much money he had. Once you are comfortable, what good does any more do for you? I knew he was wealthy, but I would have come to Russia to live in an apartment if it meant we could be together. I believed in my ability to read people and felt my confidence was well placed.

"Well, Seryozha, you know I love you. Maybe I am naïve, but money is not important to me. You are. But you do owe me for your trickery. How will you ever make it up to me?" I asked innocently.

I showed him my best sexy smile and stroked the soft blond hair on his chest with my hand. He watched me with an odd expression but did not comment.

"Is there any way you can give me just one more thrill before we both collapse from exhaustion tonight?" I asked sweetly. "Then we'll be even."

He looked at me with mock disbelief and pulled back the covers to show me his rock-hard wonder. I smiled with appreciation. He was magnificent.

Oh yes, I was married to a sex machine!

My alarm went off at 5:00 am. Sergei was still sleeping as I quietly dressed and went downstairs. I cleaned up the mess I left the night before and set upon the task of making breakfast.

I carefully prepared *blinchiki*, which are similar to French crepes. I filled them with sweet cheese and raisins, folded them into triangles, and fried the packets in butter for a few minutes until they were golden brown. Then I put them in the oven to keep warm as I went upstairs to see if he was awake yet. No, he was still sleeping. I went back downstairs and prepared a tray for him. I sprinkled the *blinchiki* with powdered sugar and put a little sour cream on the side. Then I added small bowls of cubed cantaloupe and rinsed grapes, a pot of tea, and two glasses.

I set the tray down on the table next to the bed and sat down next to him. Sergei opened his eyes and looked at me dreamily.

"Good morning. I brought you breakfast, my love. Would you like to try my *blinchiki*?" I asked.

"*Blinchiki*?" He repeated, surprised.

He smiled, sat up, and looked at the tray.

"Why are you up so early, Sandra? You stayed in bed all night?" He asked.

"Yes. I have changed my ways. There will be no more late nights. I hope you don't mind." I answered.

"Why would I mind?" He asked as he rose and donned his robe and slippers.

I carried the tray to the table by the two cozy chairs. Eating in bed was probably another thing on Sergei's list of prohibitions. I did not ask.

I poured the tea and watched him take his first bite. I experimented with this recipe on Ilya, so I was confident Sergei would like it.

"*Molodets!* You have done very well," he complimented.

I happily sipped my tea and let him eat his breakfast in peace. I thought about the sour cream, cheese, and butter in these recipes and wondered what effect the rich foods would have on his cholesterol levels. I decided not to worry about it.

Vodka probably clears out arteries like drain cleaner.

10

DON'T DRINK VODKA WITH RUSSIANS

My social world began to open up as guests arrived for weekend visits. Sergei was proud of my newly developed hostess skills, and I loved the house coming alive with people. I had plenty of help catering to the needs of our guests. Beluka and her three daughters did most of the work.

Among our first guests were Piotr and Lena Orlov. Piotr was a short, dumpy-looking middle-aged man with a receding hairline and muddy brown eyes. He was swiftly building a fortune as an import-exporter. What he lacked in looks, he made up in personality. His ability to read people and diffuse tension with humor put me at ease right away.

Piotr's plainness contrasted sharply with his younger wife Lena, a tall raven-haired beauty with velvety midnight blue eyes and masterfully chiseled features. Everything about her dripped money, from the designer clothing and flashy gold and diamond jewelry she wore to her perfect makeup and poise. She always seemed to look like she just stepped off of a fashion magazine cover.

Once we discovered we both spoke French, I quickly warmed to her free spirit and saucy sense of humor, which she revealed only to her closest friends. She was intelligent, educated, and curious about life in the United States. She asked many questions about how I met Sergei, our relationship, and the circumstances that brought me here. Lena took me on as a project – coaching me in Russian etiquette and teaching me how to enjoy a life of wealth and leisure.

She took quickly to horseback riding, mounting and dismounting easily with her long legs. Lena rode like she was born on the back of a horse, and her newfound love of riding kept her coming back to visit.

131

We always spoke in French even though I could have used practice with Russian, and she knew some English as well. Conversing in French was one of the things that made our relationship special.

Having a friend took some pressure off Sergei, who began to relax and trust me a little more. We started taking more day trips to the city to shop, dine and visit friends.

St. Petersburg is a city known for a vast sea of apartment complexes. The older apartment buildings appeared utilitarian and dismal, reminding me of the housing projects for poor people back home in the States. Newer, more attractive buildings offered larger dwellings and more amenities. There were few, if any, single-family homes within the city. People with money seemed to combine multiple apartments or repurpose former office spaces into larger, modern homes for themselves. There were no exclusively wealthy or crime-ridden poor neighborhoods. I found this admirable, but I also wondered how long that would last as the economic gaps continued to grow. Russia was becoming more like the United States, and with that would come some of the same problems.

Lena and Piotr lived in a secure neighborhood for the ultra-rich well outside the city. Not many people knew about this exclusive community. The enclave was hard to find and completely concealed behind a wall of trees and privacy fencing. The entrance was gated and manned by armed guards 24 hours a day. Ilya stopped the Mercedes at the guardhouse, where a man checked our IDs against the Orlov's guestlist for the evening. Once cleared, the gate opened, and we drove in to see the elite neighborhood of mansions and meticulously kept grounds.

The Orlov house was obscenely huge and extremely gaudy, with shiny gold surfaces everywhere. Lena had to have the best of everything, even if the 'best' was hideous. But who was I to judge? How people spent their money was not my concern. I brought her a bouquet and told her how much I loved her home. A white lie, perhaps, but I adored her, so the feeling was authentic. Lena was proud, and she loved to entertain. I couldn't be happier to be there!

Thirty guests attended this dinner party. We drank vodka right through all the courses of the meal, stopping only for tea and dessert. Then the vodka came back out again, with everyone offering countless toasts to the hostess, to the ladies present, to Russia, and God-knows-what-else.

Once I accepted the first, I had to keep drinking the toasts, or it would have been insulting to stop. I tried to pace myself, but they kept coming, and the vodka was getting the better of me. Although I was an experienced drinker, wine was my preferred choice. I was not used to hard liquor.

I was getting smashed.

After dinner, everyone gathered in the parlor. Some of the guests played instruments and sang while others danced. It was riotous fun. I understood Russian dialogue better and was finally beginning to feel like I fit in. I laughed along with the jokes and revelry. I certainly was not the only one feeling the effects of alcohol.

I bummed a cigarette from someone without thinking. As I was taking my first drag, Sergei shot me a disapproving look from across the room. I waved to him with a guilty smile and kept smoking. He probably did not want the mother of his future children tarnished by the evils of tobacco. Hilarious! I was trashed on vodka and already as polluted as a person could get.

I knew I wasn't pregnant because I failed another pregnancy test just that morning. It was becoming a depressing monthly ritual – the hope, the test, the disappointment. Sometimes I suspected Sergei planned his trips so he would be gone on my fertile days. If he had a regular job, we would be expecting our first child by now. I was young and healthy. My doctor in New York said I could have children anytime.

It was his fault!

The cigarette was almost gone, so I took one last drag and put it out. I turned my attention back to the party. Someone handed me another shot of vodka, there was yet another toast, and I threw it back sloppily. I missed, and half of it splashed on my face and went down my chin. Oops! I wiped it away before anyone could notice. I looked around. Nobody cared. They were all drunk, laughing, and carrying on like frat boys and sorority girls at a college keg party. Even Sergei looked uncharacteristically smashed. That man had an iron liver. He could drink like a hippopotamus and get a good buzz going, but I'd never seen him completely intoxicated. Was I projecting my condition onto him? Even drunk, I was still thinking about psychology.

What a credit I am to my profession!

I caught the tail end of a joke and laughed so hard I could not stop, giggling like a schoolgirl. The weight of a heavy hand suddenly pressed down on my right shoulder. I turned and looked up, surprised.

"It's time to go home," Sergei said sternly.

He was not nearly as drunk as I imagined him to be. My attitude sobered quickly, although the rest of me could not. He was giving me the 'look.'

"Sure. Just give me a minute," I slurred.

He knew where I was going and nodded. It was a long drive home with no rest stops along the way. He took my seat and watched as I left the room. I was dismayed to find the restroom occupied and someone else already waiting in line. I remembered Lena had another one near the garage, so I negotiated my way down the long hallway past the kitchen. It was quiet and cool at this end of the house. Thankfully the door was open.

I heard the door handle jostle as I was washing my hands.

"Just a minute!" I sang out in English.

Then came a knock on the door.

"Ocupado!" I sang out in Spanish, bursting into laughter because no Russian would get the joke. Of course, it's just something stupid Americans would say, not even a joke, but somehow that made it all the more amusing.

I was a happy drunk.

When I stepped out, no one was there. I made my way back down the long hall to the kitchen.

As I passed an open door, someone reached out and grabbed my arm, drawing me gently into a pantry.

Surprised, I looked up into the face of Slava Valkov. He put a finger to his lips and said,

"Tssss. Quiet, Cassandra. I just wanted to see you."

He quickly closed the door behind me.

My jaw dropped in disbelief.

He gently put his right hand on my upper arm.

"How is Sergei treating you? Are you okay?" He asked, genuinely concerned.

I was so shocked I was unable to speak. I simply nodded and stared.

"Good. You have a friend in me," he said. "Take my card. Call me if you are ever in trouble. I will help you."

He seemed sincere. I did not know what to think of it.

"What are you doing here?" I finally asked.

"You do not know? Piotr and Lena are good friends. I live, uh, near," he explained, waving his hand in the general direction.

I took his card and carefully stashed it in my flirty red Chloé handbag.

I looked back up at him and saw his eyes, now golden, framed by those long seductive black eyelashes. I didn't feel the same level of animal attraction to him, although I would admit I still found him quite handsome.

Slava was gazing at me as if he were in love. I was drunk and did not trust this observation. This man assaulted me in a laundry room a few months ago. How could he possibly have any feelings for me?

"I have to go," I said and turned for the door.

"Wait," he requested.

I paused and looked at him again.

He cupped my chin gently with his hand and kissed me once lightly on the lips.

It seemed so innocent.

"I am sorry. I love Sergei. That is why I married him. I can't have an affair with you," I explained.

I turned again to go. Just as I reached the door, I heard a familiar voice in the hall.

"Sandra?" Sergei's voice searched. He sounded worried.

My stomach flipped, and I was extremely nauseous.

I turned to Slava with my hands up in an expression of 'what do we do?' Suddenly the tiny space seemed very crowded with two people in it. There was no place to hide and no other way out. I could think of no reason for me to be in there in the first place. I accidentally knocked a glass jar off a shelf in my panic. It crashed to the floor, smashing on impact. Plump green dill pickles went tumbling in every direction. The stink of vinegar filled the air.

The doorknob turned, and Sergei entered.

"Sandra?" He started to ask until his eyes fell upon Valkov. A storm of emotion passed over his face.

I immediately went to Sergei and tried to put my arms around him, but he shrugged me off.

He closed the door and leaned his back against it, blocking the only exit.

"No one is leaving until I find out what is going on," he stated firmly.

Sergei looked at the big man and then down to his crotch. No wet spot this time, I thought shamefully.

"Cassandra just told me how much she loves you," Slava said calmly.

Sergei was not impressed.

"Why are you in here with my wife?" He demanded. It was an obvious question that did not have an obviously good answer.

"I needed to speak to her," Slava replied truthfully, "to see if she is happy with you. Some men do not treat their wives with the care they deserve."

Sergei looked at me threateningly, and I took a step back, right into my would-be lover. I was trapped between the two of them with only a few feet to move in. I was overwhelmed by the closeness of the space and swayed, nearly losing my balance. Slava discreetly put his hands on my back to steady me.

"Are you unhappy, Sandra?" Sergei asked pointedly.

His eyes were knife-sharp, and his words cut me with their edges. A chill raced down my spine.

"I love you!" I cried drunkenly, slurring the words.

There was solid tension in the room. The acrid stench of the vinegar was blooming and burning my eyes. I flushed hot, and my head began to spin. I started seeing a double image of my husband. Two Sergei scowls were worse than one. I shook my head a few times to make my vision behave.

"Can we go home now?" I begged. "I am going to be sick."

My mouth became watery — a sign of impending eruption for me.

Sergei stood firmly. He said nothing.

"Please, I need air. Let me out!" I cried.

"No," Sergei refused angrily. "Calm down."

Looking to Slava, he asked,

"Did you touch her?"

A bolt of fear shot through my heart. I spun around and said,

"Say no!"

What an idiotic thing to say in front of my husband. Vodka does not increase one's IQ. My intelligence had taken a significant nosedive.

"Yes," Slava said calmly, eyeing Sergei directly, challenging him.

I watched his mouth form the tiny Russian word 'da' and felt helpless. I turned slowly to Sergei and found his eyes. They were ice cold. Twin frozen lakes embedded in his skull. A chill coursed right through the depths of my soul.

I fell to my knees and pressed my face against my husband's thigh.

"Please, Sergei, listen. He did not touch me. It was just a little kiss on the lips. No tongue. It meant nothing to me. Please don't hurt him," I begged.

Sergei pulled me up by the arm, saying,

"Stand. You are making an embarrassment of yourself."

136

I scrambled to a standing position. Sergei held me against him tightly and lifted the back of my party dress. Then he pulled down my panties roughly, exposing the brand, saying,

"Take a look, Valkov. See? She bears my mark. She belongs to me. If you ever touch her again, I will kill you."

If I were not so drunk, I would have been thoroughly humiliated. It was bad enough my husband was showing my bare bottom to a stranger, but I hated that brand and what it meant to him even more. The bile started to boil into my esophagus. An explosion was imminent.

I tore myself away from Sergei and shouted,

"Let me out! I am going to be sick!"

I tried to shove him aside, but he did not move.

So I turned and pushed past Slava and made it to a mop bucket just in time.

Tears streamed from my eyes as the contents of my angry stomach purged in heave after heave. My whole body convulsed with the involuntary effort. What a prize I was for two men to fight over!

At least I still had the power to clear a room.

Sergei and Slava argued outside the bathroom door as I rinsed the ends of my hair and bathed my face in cold water. I looked in the mirror and barely recognized myself. I looked frightful. My makeup was gone, my face puffy, and my eyes bloodshot. Drunk was not my best look.

I opened the door and said,

"Please take me home."

We did not bother saying good night to Piotr and Lena. As Sergei led me away by the hand, I glanced back at Slava and was stunned by the expression on his face. He wore a sad smile, and his eyes were wet with tears. Did I see that? What did it mean? I would have to consider it later when I could think clearly. My brain felt like it was floating in a glass jar full of liquid.

As soon as we got in the car, I passed out face down on Sergei's lap.

When I regained consciousness, I found myself lying on my back naked on the bed in the master suite. I immediately noticed the rope binding my wrists and ankles together. My skin was damp and smelled like soap, and the taste of toothpaste filled my mouth. How could I not remember bathing? Did Sergei brush my teeth? Could I have done it myself? How odd. I did not remember coming home either. I did a quick scan of my body. Thankfully nothing else seemed off except for a screaming headache and a raw ache in my gut.

I struggled to an upright position and saw Sergei sitting in his chair. It was just after 4:30 am.

"Ah, my drunken seductress has decided to join us!" He shouted. "How do you feel, whore?"

"Please do not call me that," I replied. "I don't feel well. Would you please untie me? I am not in the mood for games tonight."

"Oh, I think you are always in the mood for games. With me, with Valkov, or maybe you want both of us at the same time. Would you like two men to fuck you at once, whore?" He asked lewdly.

"Please stop. I don't want to fight with you. I don't have the strength. Please, I demand you untie me!" I replied.

"The whore is making demands!" He said sarcastically to an imaginary audience. The tone of his voice made my hair stand on end. That was not my husband sitting in the chair, but a demon in Sergei's form.

I struggled against the ropes but to no avail. Then I tried to slide off the bed to my feet, thinking I could hop to my bath and find something to cut my hands free. Instead, I fell to the floor and could not get back up to my feet. I looked up and saw a rope dangling from the horizontal rail at the end of the bed.

He was going to hang me!

I started screaming.

Sergei put his hand over my mouth to make me stop. I bit his hand deeply, drawing blood. He slapped my face as hard as he could, spinning my head.

I was stunned.

He hit me!

I could not believe it!

"Are you going to be quiet, or do I need to gag you?" He threatened.

The thought of being gagged was intolerable. I would not be able to talk him out of whatever he planned to do. I needed my voice.

"Who are you?" I whispered.

"Don't you recognize me, Sandra? I am the monster you married," he said coldly.

138

"No, you are not a monster, and I am not a whore. I love you. Please stop before you do something you will regret," I said softly, trying to appeal to his heart.

He wavered for a second but then said,

"No, you are worse than a whore. You are a drunken, disgusting animal. You need discipline."

He hauled me to my feet and secured my wrists to the rope hanging from the canopy rail. Then he pulled the rope up so tight I had to strain on my tiptoes to support my weight. I could not think. I just kept saying, 'Oh my God,' over and over in my head.

Terror consumed me.

He turned me to face the bed, and the first harsh bite of his leather belt sliced into my back.

Crack!

In that first agonizing moment, I knew I was not a masochist. The pain did absolutely nothing to stimulate me. I loathed the pain and hated the man who was delivering it to me.

Crack!

This time on my rear. It hurt less there, but I was dying. I started sobbing. I struggled to stay on my toes because my arms felt like they would pull out of my shoulders if I fell.

Crack!

My butt again. I changed my inner mantra to, 'Lord have mercy,' the shortest prayer I know. If I died tonight, I would at least go out asking for forgiveness.

Sergei stopped and ran his fingers over the welts, inspecting the quality of his work. I whimpered involuntarily but was careful not to say anything to inflame his anger or incur a gag. I could not afford to give up my voice.

It was all I had left to defend myself.

He slowly dragged the belt over my bare flesh and asked,

"Who are you married to?"

"You, Sergei," I replied meekly.

"That's right," he said.

"Why did you kiss Valkov tonight?" He asked, this time tapping the belt against my swollen skin, reminding me it was there.

"I didn't. He kissed me," I replied honestly.

139

"Wrong answer, Sanka!" He shouted.

That name hurt my ears almost as much as the belt on my skin.

Crack!

My upper thighs. The pain shot through me like bullets through paper. What did he want to hear? I told him the truth. My mind reeled through the stack of case studies on sadists I'd read. None of the profiles seemed to match him. They were predators, men no woman would ever marry. Sergei fit better with sadomasochism, a relatively harmless sexual preference rather than a psychological disorder. This scene was something else. He was out of control.

Maybe this was a drama he needed to act out, and I had to play the correct part. Righteous was not working. My mind sped to come up with a new plan. Perhaps the role of a penitent? I was not a martyr prepared to die for the cause of my innocence. I had nothing to lose.

"Why did you kiss Valkov tonight?" He repeated, tapping the belt against my rear.

This time I was ready.

"Forgive me! You are right. I am a whore, and I cannot deny it. I kissed that bastard because I wanted him to fuck me. I want every man to fuck me. I got drunk to act on my desires. I am not worthy of you. Save me!" I shouted as passionately as possible, hoping it sounded convincing.

A silent moment passed. The belt buckle rattled as the belt landed on the oak floor. Sergei spun me around to face him with tears flowing from his eyes. My 'good' husband was back.

"What have I done to you, Sandra?" He choked as he quickly untied the ropes. He helped me down to the bed and had me rest on my stomach.

"Don't move. I will be right back."

He returned a few minutes later with ice packs from the freezer and gently placed them on the welts.

"I am so sorry Sandrochka, can you forgive me?" He asked, tenderly stroking my cheek.

My husband was mentally unstable, and I could no longer deny I was at risk for serious injury at his hands. And yet, I loved him so much I could not imagine my life without him. I married this man and couldn't give up on him. I had a Ph.D. in Clinical Psychology. Of course, I had to try to help him.

"Yes, I forgive you," I said calmly.

I turned to look at him directly. The ice packs slid off, but I didn't care. The welts did not sting anymore.

"Please, come closer," I requested.

He lay down next to me and looked me in the eyes.

"I love you so much, Seryozha. I see so much good in you. I love your commitment to me, and I am glad you want to start a family. I am sure you want to be a good husband and father. But I am very concerned about your sadistic streak. I don't like pain, and I thought you were going to kill me tonight. I am afraid of you," I said as gently as I could.

A troubled look crossed his face. He started to speak.

"Shhh," I said, putting my finger on his lips. "I know you don't want to hurt me, but you lost control. I will be careful with my drinking, so I don't make myself so vulnerable. There is no excuse for drinking to the point of vomiting and passing out. I am not Russian, and I have no business drinking vodka."

"I'm sorry, but I can't allow you to tie me up anymore," I added.

He nodded his resignation. Our trust had broken, and the disappointment and pain evident on his face broke my heart.

"I think I understand what is going on. Remembering your childhood has reopened old wounds. It's common for people to feel worse before they get better. But you will get better, I am sure of it. You are intelligent and self-aware, which makes you an excellent candidate for therapy. I think it will help you."

He smiled sadly and said,

"I will try anything. I don't want to lose you."

"That is good to hear, but you should know I can't do this myself. I am too close to you, and I don't have experience with these issues. It would be better if we went to the States for a while. I know some great psychologists in Western New York. My graduate advisor, Dr. Marten, is brilliant and very open-minded. I am sure he has seen it all."

I paused to let him think about it for a minute. Then I continued,

141

"We could rent a house on the pretense of my doing research at the university for a semester. The weather is so much like Russia. You will feel right at home." I said, chuckling at the thought of anyone actually enjoying Rochester's horrendous lake effect snowstorms, frigid nonstop wind, and perpetually gray winter skies.

"We could ski, tour wineries, see Niagara Falls, visit Toronto, and go to faculty parties. We can even drive north to Lake Placid so you can see where I grew up and hit the big slopes. That would be a lot of fun. What do you think?"

"No," Sergei said, "I can't talk to anyone but you about this."

I was disappointed, but I tried not to show it.

"Don't worry, Sandrochka. I will get it under control. I promise," he added sincerely.

I studied him for a moment. People have to want to engage in therapy for it to work. Perhaps he wasn't ready now but would warm to the idea.

It is far easier to shove traumatic memories and negative feelings into a shoebox and hide it away deep in the mind's closet. Real strength is needed to take that box down and sort through the contents with another person. And yet, sometimes that is the only way to acknowledge what happened, understand how past experiences affect current behavior, process the feelings, let the past go, and finally be free.

Psychotherapy is effective, but it takes focus, determination, and effort.

He recently regained traumatic childhood memories. That was something solid to build on, and it gave me hope that he could have a complete recovery.

I didn't think he could control his rage at this point, but I wanted to believe he could grow beyond it. I wanted us to work together to become better partners for each other. We could take precautions to be safe in the meantime.

"Will you promise to give therapy more consideration?" I asked.

"Yes," he replied, gazing deeply into my eyes, giving me the solid soul connection I needed to believe in him.

Oh God, I love you so much. I know you love me.

Am I doing the right thing?

He kissed me, and any remaining doubt melted away.

142

THE STAIN

I woke well past noon on Sunday. The first thing I did was inspect my backside in the mirror. Four horizontal reddish-purple bruises marked the bite from the leather belt. They looked terrible, but the belt did not break the skin, and I was relieved there would be no scars. We showered together, usually a joyful activity, but the bruises were a reminder. Sergei kept telling me how sorry he was. He remembered hitting me with the belt but said it felt like someone else was in control of him at the time.

Dissociation.

Not a good sign, but I chose not to tell him. I wanted him to remain optimistic. If he was going to get better, he had a lot of work to do, and the more hopeful he was, the better the outcome.

I asked him to close his eyes while I washed him, taking my time and moving slowly to heighten the sensual experience, starting at the top and working my way down his body. I knelt and took his penis into my mouth to pleasure him as only a sexual goddess can, sucking, licking, and swirling my tongue around the tip. He put his hands on my shoulders to steady himself.

"Oh, Sandrochka," he choked as his hot semen shot into my mouth. I milked the rest out of him, licking up every precious drop. Then I washed his genitals with soap and continued my way down his legs to finish with his feet as if nothing happened.

Sergei's mood improved dramatically afterward, and we had a peaceful breakfast together. Sitting was painful, but I toughed it out and hid my distress so he wouldn't feel any worse than he already did. Then we went for a long walk with Velikan and Kukla in the new snow. Only a few inches had fallen overnight, but it was nice to see the landscape coated in a mantle of white. The snow reminded me of home. The air was crisp, clean, and energizing. Soon I would be able to cross-country ski, and the thought made me very happy. I loved winter just as much as the other seasons, maybe even a little more.

The world is quiet and peaceful when covered in snow.

I called Lena late in the afternoon to apologize for deserting her party without saying goodnight. She did not seem to mind. Slava must have told her I'd gotten sick because she asked how I was feeling. We spoke for a few minutes, and then she said,

143

"I have a message from your friend. He says he is concerned and will be in touch with you soon."

"Please, Lena," I said, "Tell my friend he does not need to worry and should forget about me. I am happy where I am."

"Are you sure, Sandra?" She asked.

"Absolutely," I replied.

"You can stay with me any time you want," she offered.

Why was everyone so worried about me?

11

WEAVING WEBS

Sergei canceled a trip to South America and withdrew his bid on a project. He was becoming depressed. The short days were not helping his mood, and I worried it would develop into a full-blown depressive episode. He said he'd never been depressed before, which I took as a good sign. On the other hand, depression in winter might seem normal to people who live so far north. I couldn't be sure. When I suggested he try an anti-depressant medication, he laughed, saying he would double up on vitamins and get a little more exercise.

He spent his days in the library, neither working nor reading, simply sitting in the dark listening to classical music. I checked on him from time to time but generally left him alone with his thoughts. He seemed to be in a cocoon. Perhaps he was processing his traumatic memories in his unique way.

In the evenings, we continued to talk about his past. He told me about his life after his mother died. There were a string of live-in nannies for a few years, each one driven off in succession by his father's sexual advances. No one stayed more than a few months, and Ivan Karpov never remarried.

His father continued to drink heavily and beat Sergei for even the slightest transgression. One 'accident' after another needed medical attention – a broken arm, a concussion. Each time, Sergei lied to the doctors about how he was injured, blaming himself for clumsiness.

Sergei coped with his miserable home life by throwing himself into his schoolwork, winning his teachers' praise, and moving to an advanced class. He described himself as a shy child with few friends. We were alike in this way, socially awkward brainiacs.

145

Finally, his father's excessive drinking caught up with him, and Ivan Karpov died of liver failure at age 39. Sergei described his father's skin as a frightening shade of yellow the last time he saw him. Only 13 at the time, Sergei did not cry. He said he felt nothing. There were no extended family members or friends to take him in.

Sergei was alone, an orphan.

A friend of his father took him out of the country to a boarding school in Austria known for its equestrian program. He received a sizeable inheritance stashed in a Swiss bank, but he had no idea how his father amassed such a fortune. There was also a safe deposit box full of diamonds. There was more than enough to pay for college and get a head start on his business ventures. The large diamond in my engagement ring came from that mysterious cache. No one had that kind of money in the Soviet Union, so whatever Ivan Karpov was doing before he died was most certainly illegal.

I called my old faculty advisor, Dr. Marten, for a case consultation. Using no names, of course, I explained Sergei's history of childhood trauma and abuse, his episodes of dissociative rage, and the deep remorse he felt afterward. He said it sounded like Intermittent Explosive Disorder, a condition treatable with medication, psychotherapy, anger management, and relaxation training. I asked him for referrals to specialists in Europe. He said he would look into it and get back to me. Meanwhile, I read everything I could find about the disorder, and the diagnosis seemed to fit perfectly.

Dr. Marten called the next day with three names – a psychologist in London, a psychiatrist in Marseille, and a psychologist in Geneva. All three were men. I thanked him and hung up the phone, allowing myself to feel a ray of hope. I wrote 'Rage Disorder Specialists' at the top of a piece of paper, followed by the three names and contact information, and put it in an envelope. Then I went to see Sergei, who was sitting in the dimly lit library listening to Mozart's piano concertos. I pulled a chair closer to face him. We looked at each other for a few minutes without saying anything, simply listening to the lovely calming music. I waited until the piece ended before handing him the envelope.

Tears welled in his eyes as he read what I'd written. He set the paper aside and opened his arms to me. I held him as he softly wept into my hair. We didn't speak. When the next movement finished, I kissed him on the forehead and quietly left the room, leaving him to his thoughts. It was up to

146

him to take this first step toward salvation. I was hopeful, but it seemed unlikely he would follow through.

My professional writing took a back seat to my other concerns, and I wrote sporadically. When I did, it was not my best material, requiring extensive editing. Every time I tried to work, my mind kept drifting back to Sergei and all of the horrors he'd experienced. I wanted to help him, but I didn't know how.

When I spoke with Jack Hawthorne, I downplayed my writing problems by claiming to have hit a lull. I assured him I would be back in a flow state soon. I lied and said we were settling into an easy married routine and had nothing interesting to report. He also seemed to be in a comfortable routine; of cheating. Jack was still seeing the young Japanese woman and keeping the affair from his wife. I wondered why he felt the need to cheat in the first place and why he didn't leave his wife for his new love, but I didn't ask. I simply wished him well and hung up the phone. I felt uneasy afterward, struck by the human tendency to become accustomed to harmful situations.

While I was kneading dough for bread one afternoon, I heard the chime from the front gate. I pressed the intercom button in the kitchen.

"*Allo?*" I asked.

"Cassandra? I need to see you," urged the deep voice of Slava Valkov.

I looked around to make sure I was alone. Sergei was in the library listening to Franz Liszt. I heard the melancholic melody of Consolation No. 3 drifting down the hallway to the kitchen. He listened to that particular piece so often I considered it his depression song. He probably did not hear the call come in. I had no idea where Ilya was. No one else was in the house.

"Stay there," I replied, "I will be right out."

I put on my coat and boots and went to the driveway gate but did not open it.

"You should not be here," I warned.

"I had to see you, Cassandra. Are you okay? I worry about you," Slava said.

Enormous snowflakes fell slowly through the still air, and the little bit of daylight was fading quickly, but I saw concern in his big green eyes.

"Why do you care about me? I mean nothing to you," I asked.

He seemed surprised.

147

"I think of you always. I worry for you, alone, here, with Karpov. He is violent. You deserve better," he said, struggling with English but expressing himself well.

"Sergei loves me. He would never hurt me," I rebutted.

"What about brand? What man brand wife?" He asked. "Tell me you wanted, I go, but I see truth in, your, uh, eyes," touching a finger near his right eye for clarity as he spoke.

I paused, not knowing what to say.

"Go," I said finally. "You are the one who is causing me trouble. I got the brand because of what you did to me in the laundry room. It was your fault. I want nothing to do with you. Leave us alone."

His face fell in disappointment, but he was not ready to give up.

"Come with me. Let me take care of you. You are not safe here," Slava pleaded. "If you do not want me, stay with Lena. You have friends, Cassandra. Let us help you."

He reached through the iron bars and lightly touched my face with his fingertips. My resolve wavered as I remembered the moment of searing shock as Sergei pressed hot metal into my skin and the terror of being tied up and beaten with a belt. Was I in mortal danger?

"Please, Cassandra. I not leave you here. My, uh, conscience not allow it," he said, glancing at English words written in Cyrillic letters on a piece of paper pulled from his pocket.

"Conscience? Where was your conscience the night we met? I am a married woman. You started this whole thing on purpose to provoke my husband!" I cried.

My loyalty to Sergei won.

"Cassandra, please. You are in danger. Come with me," he pleaded.

Floodlights snapped on, exposing the unplanned rendezvous. I took a step back from the gate and turned around, my eyes burning in the bright lights. Sergei and Ilya were striding toward us.

"Come with me!" Slava called desperately.

It was too late. Sergei was already upon us.

"Leave!" Sergei ordered as he grabbed my upper arm roughly, jerking me back from the gate.

My eyes connected with Slava's, and I mouthed the word,

148

"Go."

Sergei stood rigidly between me and the gate, his arms folded over his chest and his feet spread apart. He spoke commandingly,

"You have 10 seconds to get out of here. Ilya?"

Ilya drew a deadly-looking black handgun and pointed it at the big man.

"*Dyes-yat, dyev-yat, vo-syem, syem, shest,*" Sergei counted backward from ten.

Slava scrambled to get back in his car and quickly pulled out of the driveway. Snow spun in spirals behind the silver Mercedes as he drove away. I watched the red taillights of the sedan fade to pinpoints and disappear into the night.

I considered how easily I could have been in the car with him.

The snow continued to fall, as gently and peacefully as ever, bearing silent witness to the human drama playing out on this remote patch of earth. The world was hushed as I slowly turned to face my husband.

Sergei ordered Ilya,

"Change the security codes on the gates immediately and disconnect the remote controls. All of them. Then disconnect all of the phone lines except for the one in the library."

A chill coursed through me that had nothing to do with the weather. The prison doors in my mind banged shut. My whole body froze.

He turned to me stone-faced, with eyes so cold they looked like they belonged to a dead man.

I stepped backward in fear staring at him with wide-open eyes. Oh my God, you have lost your mind completely. And I am locked in here with you!

He clasped my arm and pulled me to face him directly. I could not look at him. I had to look away. I looked anywhere but at his soulless eyes.

"Look at me!" He ordered angrily.

I reluctantly lifted my eyes to his. What I saw filled me with terror.

"We need to discuss this in private. Come with me," Sergei ordered, pulling me roughly into the house and up the stairs to the master suite.

Once inside, he pushed me to my knees and stood above me with his arms crossed.

"Tell me what he said to you," he commanded.

I was in shock and could not speak.

149

Sergei grabbed a handful of my hair and twisted it painfully.

"He said I was in danger and wanted me to go with him. He said you are a violent man. I refused to go. Please, Sergei, don't hurt me," I nervously added.

I glanced up to see the dark version of my beautiful husband and quickly looked away.

"What am I going to do with you, Sanka? I told you to stay away from him. Then I find you alone together. He calls. Now he is coming to the farm. How many other times have you seen him that I do not know about?" He demanded in a voice full of threats.

My inner voice was screaming. Enough with the intimidation and pushing me around! I certainly was not going to grovel at his feet and let him beat me again. I'd done nothing wrong. I rose to my full height and looked him directly in the eye with strength and resolve that matched his own.

The games were over.

"Listen. I am your wife, and I demand your respect. If you hurt me again, I swear to God I will leave you the next chance I get. You think you can keep me locked up and cut off communication to the outside world, but guess what, you stupid asshole?" I laughed. Maybe I had gone crazy too.

"You will lose me anyway!" I screamed in his face.

He looked stunned as if my words punched him.

"Why is everyone so worried about me?" I demanded. "They seem to know something I don't know. What are you not telling me?"

Sergei's face fell, and he sat down heavily in his chair.

"No, Sandra. There are some things I cannot discuss with you," he spoke softly, his words stained with defeat.

His eyes were tearing. I watched him stand and slowly walk out of the room, shoulders slumped. I knew he would spend the night on the couch in the library. He was shutting me out, but that was fine. I needed space from him too.

Making love while angry would not fix this.

I paced the floor, my mind moving a million miles per minute, going over all that happened, from each person's perspective, their possible motivations, until I was exhausted. I kept coming back to the same conclusion. Slava might have ulterior motives, but no one drives eighty miles in a blinding snowstorm to check on someone unless they care. He needed to see me with his own eyes to know I was alright. Lena was also concerned about my safety. She did not like my husband, even though he had never done anything to her. Sergei seemed to be hiding something from me that everyone else knew. I needed more information.

I slid past the library without being seen. Sergei was facing the other way, the lighting dimmed, as he listened to Haydn's string quartets. I sought out Ilya. He'd been lifting weights in his room and was breathless and sweaty. I asked him for a cigarette and pushed a stack of US twenties into his hand to buy more. I had no idea how much cigarettes cost in Russia, but I figured that would cover it for a while. Then I stepped into the garage to commit my crime against Sergei's future children. I inhaled deeply and held the smoke, hoping it would calm me. My nerves were still on edge, and now I was dizzy and nauseous too.

A few minutes later, Ilya joined me, his large brown eyes brimming with concern. We spoke in halting Russian. I learned he had family near Moscow but no girlfriend. He came to work for Sergei after leaving the Army. He was a quiet person, answering my questions politely but not offering much conversation in return. That was okay. I didn't understand most of what he said anyway. Not knowing what else to say, I just smiled and accepted a second cigarette from him.

Sure, why not?

I slipped quietly back into the house to retrieve a bottle of wine and two glasses. I needed a friend, and I was far too tense to sleep tonight. After a while, the garage was full of smoke, the wine was gone, and I finally felt a little more relaxed. It was time to say good night. As I turned to leave, Ilya touched my arm. I turned to face him and found myself gazing into his deep brown eyes. He kissed me gently on the lips and placed his hand on my shoulder reassuringly. He pulled back to search my face, obviously worried he'd offended me. I smiled at the unexpected affection and nodded. I turned to leave.

"Cassie," Ilya spoke.

"*Da* Ilya?" I replied.

"Please. Call me Ilyusha," he requested.

A light brightened within me. I knew what that meant, but I would need to use the affectionate name only when we were alone together.

I was fond of him too.

"Ilyusha," I pronounced. His name felt like velvet on my lips.

He smiled, so I knew I got it right.

"*Spokoynoy nochi,*" he said.

"Good night," I replied.

I blew him a little kiss and skipped back into the house with a smile on my lips.

I would dream of a sweeter kind of love that night.

12

DARKEST DAYS

I lay low for a few days while Sergei sulked and slept on the couch in the library in self-imposed exile. I overheard him arguing loudly with someone on the phone and saw him pacing. He looked rattled. He was usually meticulously groomed but now sported unshaven scruff on his face and wore rumpled, slept-in clothing. My attempts at reconciliation met rejection. He waved me out of the library, saying,

"Go away. I need to work."

When I told him I was concerned and asked if he wanted to talk about what was going on, he said,

"Get out of my head, psychologist!"

All I could do was give him space and hope he would come around.

I went cross country skiing, visited the horses, and played with Velikan and Kukla. I even made a few snow angels. Sadly, the snow was too dry to make snowmen, or I would have made some friends. I missed having guests and going places.

We were right back to isolation mode.

One morning I got up early and mucked out the horse barn. My nerves were frazzled, and I needed to do physical work to burn off excess energy. Demeshko was shocked to see the lady of the house shoveling horse poop and tried to take the pitchfork from my hands. I laughed, smiled, and waved him away. I wasn't above getting dirty. This task was much more pleasant than dealing with the lord of the manor.

The weather was always overcast or snowing, and the days were cold and dark, with only a brief lightening of the sky at midday. We were quickly approaching the shortest day of the year. I hadn't been able to write in weeks, and I needed to produce something soon, or I would lose my job. I asked Sergei if it would be okay for me to go to the library at the university to do some research. I asked him to join me, but he did not want to spend a day in the city or with me.

He searched my face for signs of deceit for a long minute.

Finally, he said, "Fine, have Ilya drive you."

I kissed him on the forehead and left before he could change his mind.

I sat in the front seat of the Mercedes next to Ilya. When the gate closed behind us, my soul rejoiced! I was going somewhere! Ilya turned and smiled, the corners of his mouth curling up in the cutest way. He reached over to hold my hand. I was glad to have him as a friend. I had to admit, a part of me wished he could be more.

Do not go there. I cautioned myself. Sergei would ruin this young man's life without mercy if he ever had an inkling something was going on between us.

We drove through several snow squalls and took our time on the icy, snow-blown roads. The police pulled us over outside the city, but they seemed to be looking for someone else. No ticket was issued. The two-hour drive stretched to three, but we finally made it. I was getting used to the police, and the trips weren't scary anymore. I assured Ilya I would be fine in the library by myself and released him to do whatever he wanted to do. We planned to meet back in the lobby at 5:00 pm.

Once Ilya was gone, I found the nearest phone and called Lena. She was relieved to hear from me.

"Sandra, how are you? I've been trying to reach you for days!" She said.

I told her how Sergei freaked out when Slava came by the house and put us in lockdown.

"I don't know how you put up with him, *Cherie*, so far out in the country. He's a madman. Come stay with me," she offered.

It was tempting, but I was pretty sure Sergei would not be down with that.

154

"We will shop and go out dancing," she continued. "What's the point in having money if you can't enjoy it? There is so much to do in St. Petersburg. Have you been to the Hermitage?"

"*Non,*" I replied.

"That's a crime against culture, *Cherie.*" She declared dramatically. "Perhaps he can make you live out in the woods like a barefoot farm girl, but he can't deny you Russian culture."

I had to admit; she had a good point. Why bother living in Russia if I never got to see any of it? Surely Sergei would not deny me the chance to appreciate his culture.

"I will talk to him and let you know, but today I am here to get some work done," I said.

"Lunch, then. You must eat," she said. "I insist."

I glanced at my briefcase and thought of the boring cheese sandwich stashed inside and exhaled. Sergei would be pissed if he found out, but I deserved a friend and a nice meal out once in a while. I missed the freedom of being single in New York and doing whatever I wanted. I wished I had done a whole lot more when I had the chance.

"Okay, Lena, you win," I caved.

"Wonderful, I will pick you up in an hour," she said.

Stepping into Lena's limo was exhilarating. I felt like a spy on a mission. And this was a top-secret mission as far as Sergei was concerned. St. Petersburg reminded me of the James Bond movies. Intrigue seemed to be waiting around every corner. Why not have fun playing the part? Claiming some freedom from my overbearing spouse was thrilling. I lifted my dark sunglasses and took in the sight of my friend.

Lena was in full glamor mode. Her hair, makeup, and clothes added up to a vision of high society, Russian-style. She was even sipping a flute of champagne and offered me one of the same. I declined. I still planned to get some work done later.

We had lunch at a French restaurant in the heart of the city. Lena brought up the topic of Slava Valkov over cheese puff appetizers. I knew it was coming and was surprised she'd been able to hold off so long.

"He's a teddy bear, Sandra. He truly is," she said, "and he simply adores you."

"He adores me?" I asked incredulously. Recalling the laundry room debacle sent a shiver down my spine. I shifted uncomfortably in my seat.

"You have to understand a man like Slava is used to getting what he wants. He has gobs of money and very powerful friends," she explained.

It occurred to me 'powerful friends' was code for the Russian mafia.

"Sergei told me Slava is involved in organized crime," I whispered discreetly. "Sergei said he is a dangerous man."

Her surprised laugh caught mid-bite, and Lena coughed. An attentive waiter rushed to refill her water glass. She smiled her thanks and fluttered her eyelashes at him. I noticed he was attractive and lingered in her aura longer than necessary. Interesting.

Leaning in close, she said,

"My darling Sandra, can you be so naïve? Do you think anyone with money in Russia today is not involved in something illegal?"

"Sergei is a legitimate businessman," I said defensively.

She leaned back and stared at me, tapping a French manicured nail on the table.

I stared back, not knowing what to say.

"Is he?" She snorted.

I had to admit to myself I didn't know the full extent of Sergei's business dealings. Could he be a criminal? I'd never entertained the thought before. I must have looked shocked because Lena changed the subject.

"But, these matters are not for us to discuss, my dear. Our work is to enjoy life and these moments together," she said as she reached across to take my hands in hers.

"I am so glad we are friends," she winked.

"Me too, Lena, me too," I replied.

I would be totally lost without her.

She dropped me off at the library around 4:00 pm, which gave me enough time to establish visiting scholar credentials and open one book. Staring down at the Cyrillic letters, I wondered what I was thinking. It seemed like it would be years before I could read and write in Russian. This language wasn't coming as fast as French. I needed a three-step process for translation – converting the Cyrillic letters to their English counterparts, putting the words and phrases together, and translating from there. People like Sergei make it look easy, but the ability to learn foreign languages quickly was not one of my gifts.

I looked around the library nostalgically. It would have been a great place to work. I was out of the house and felt at home among the stacks of books and scholars. I missed academia, where life was quiet and predictable.

Ilya was visibly relieved to see me walk into the lobby at 5:00 pm, and we enjoyed an uneventful ride home. He didn't hold my hand this time, but he responded with a warm smile when I turned to look at him. The big loops of curly brown hair escaping from his fur hat softened the hard planes of his face in a flattering way.

I suddenly remembered he had a semiautomatic pistol beneath his coat, another gun strapped to his ankle, and a compact assault rifle under his seat. It occurred to me he could pull over anywhere along the way and force me at gunpoint to serve him sexually. What a delicious thought! My imagination played through several scenarios on the ride home. I became quite warm, naturally, but I kept my thoughts to myself. I looked to see if he knew what I was thinking, but he gave me the same sweet reassuring smile.

No. We can never be more than friends. I scolded myself. I am married to this man's boss. I wasn't about to ruin Ilya's life. We would never get away with fooling around under Sergei's nose, and it would end horribly. This romance was something that could not happen. No way. Never.

I went to see Sergei immediately and was pleased to see him shaved and in clean clothes. His mood improved as well. He welcomed me into the library and swept me down onto his lap, kissing me firmly on the lips.

"How was your day, my little bookworm?" He asked warmly.

"Wonderful," I replied, showing him my new library card.

"Good, very good," he responded with a proud look on his face.

His eyes were tired around the edges and the inner light dimmer than I liked, but he seemed to be coming around. I was glad.

"Will you sleep with me upstairs tonight, my love?" I asked.

"Yes, but I leave on business early," he responded.

My face must have fallen because he quickly added,

"Only for a few days, little bird. I have a problem in Turkey that cannot wait any longer."

That night we slept in the same bed, but we did not sleep together.

He was gone when I woke.

He didn't call.

I had no idea when he would return.

The positive was he restored the phones and internet before he left. My email inbox was full, but one message stood out.

> *"Dear Cassandra,*
>
> *Please accept my apology. I am very sorry for the way I behaved and for the trouble I caused you. Please consider me a friend. I would love to talk with you about America and hear what you think of my country.*
>
> *I will keep you in my prayers until I see you again.*
>
> *Merry Christmas,*
>
> *Slava"*

My heart melted because the tone seemed sincere, and he took the time to write it in English. He must have had help to get the grammar perfect. Plus, he said Merry Christmas. With everything that happened of late, I hadn't given the holiday much thought. December 25 was only a week away. There were no decorations in Sergei's atheist household, no presents, and no celebration planned. I was sad for him and his bleak outlook on life. I felt sorry for falling away from religion myself. Christmas was one of the things that made the shortest days of winter bearable. Life seemed empty without it, especially here in the cold and dark far north.

I reread the part where he said he was praying for me. That was completely unexpected, and it warmed my heart. People don't lie about prayers.

Either you pray, or you don't even think about it.

I replied, thanking him for his apology and wishing him a Merry Christmas as well. I obviously couldn't make any promises for friendship, or anything else, so I kept it brief and polite.

That evening, Lena called to invite us to a party at her house on New Year's Eve. I didn't know if Sergei would be home by then or if he would object, but I said yes anyway. I needed to mark the holidays somehow. I would find a way to make him understand.

When Sergei returned a few days later, he asked me to join him in the library. He didn't apologize for not calling. I let it go because I didn't want to start an argument.

To my surprise, he agreed to the party, but he called Piotr first to make sure Slava would not be on the guest list. Piotr promised to take care of it personally. Then he told me we would spend the night there and stay through dinner the next day. I was beyond excited.

With even more good news, Sergei said he was sending me to Lena's a day early to shop, dine, spa, and, incredibly, 'girl's night out' party with my friend. I was stunned Sergei would allow me to go clubbing, let alone spend a night at her home, knowing Slava Valkov could be lurking nearby. Then he told me Ilya would be with me as my bodyguard the entire time, and my heart sank.

He still didn't trust me.

He lifted my chin and looked deeply into my eyes, a hint of the man I loved. He said,

"I do trust you, Sandrochka. It is merely a precaution for your safety."

His fingers slid down, caressing my neck and then deftly unbuttoning my blouse. He lifted my breasts out of my silk bra and found my nipples, pinching and plumping them into firm pink hills. He raked his nails across them, sending pulses of hot electricity directly to my pussy, saturating my silk panties. A moan escaped my lips as he leaned over and took each nipple into his mouth, sucking one while he milked more height out of the other with his ruthless fingers. He took turns on each, taking his time, ramping up his offensive until he was biting and dragging his teeth over the soft, tender flesh. Looking down, I saw my poor nipples had doubled in size and were now beet red. They were sore, yes, but I wanted more.

"Please, Seryozha," I moaned wantonly. I wanted him inside me. I wanted him inside of me everywhere at once, filling me completely. He had the power to turn off my brain. I yearned for that black space beyond the stars where thinking is impossible. Only he could take me there. We hadn't made love in weeks.

I was leaning with my back against his desk, facing the glass window wall that was open to the rest of the house. I thought I saw Ilya pass by through my half-closed eyes, but I was so in need, I wouldn't have cared if the Pope was watching. I hopped onto the desk, and my skirt rode up as I opened myself to Sergei. He inhaled sharply and took a step back.

"Ah, I see my slutty wife hasn't lost her desire for me after all," he sighed with satisfaction.

"Please," I said, "I need you." I leaned back and spread wider.

Sergei responded with a few audible shutter snaps from his camera.

He was taking dirty pictures.

I didn't care.

"Please..."

Sergei slid two fingers past my ruined French panties into my starving vagina. He stroked in and out using his thumb to massage my clit with hard pressure at the same time. He masterfully sent me spiraling over the edge several times. Something burst inside of me, and a squirt of hot liquid shot into his hand.

"What's this?" He said, laughing, knowing. "You are full of surprises today, little bird."

I was too dazed to die of embarrassment, or I probably would have.

"Come," he said, leading me by hand to the sofa. He sat down and pulled his engorged manhood out of his dress slacks. I wasted no time kicking off my ravaged panties. I tossed my skirt aside and gladly accepted the invitation. I mounted him quickly and slid down the entire length of his shaft, finally feeling the primordial satisfaction I was craving. His penis reached deep inside my belly, feeding a hunger food could never satisfy. I was starving for him.

I rode him through a few more orgasms, each downward bounce meeting with a firm thrust from below. He pinched and twisted my devastated nipples savagely. Incredibly, the pain only seemed to heighten my pleasure. He gazed at me with half-closed eyes.

Sergei took my hips in his hands to slow me down. He moved to reposition me on my knees facing the back of the sofa. Then he fiercely pounded me from a standing position, using full strokes that threw me forward on impact. I braced my arms against the back of the couch to hold firm.

"Fuck me harder, Sergei," I cried out between moans.

A chorus of "Fuck me, fuck me" involuntarily escaped from my lips in between orgasmic crescendos. These vocalizations elicited a sharp smack on my ass and then another one. I felt the red hot handprint, but I didn't care. I wanted more. He did not disappoint – the spanks kept coming.

My pussy contracted violently on his ramrod cock, and my whole pelvic floor went into nonstop convulsions. I could no longer tell where one orgasm ended and the next began. Sex never felt quite like this before. I didn't know it was possible to be so out of control with sexual rapture.

Just when I couldn't possibly take anymore, Sergei spit on his thumbs and began rubbing my anus. In my current state, I didn't even care. A part of me hoped he'd shove his dick in there too, taking and filling me everywhere. He was unrelenting, rubbing in opposing circles and pushing in slightly, testing the give. This strange sensation sent off waves of a new kind of pleasure

"Mmmm…," I moaned.

Finally, he withdrew his cock and expelled his precious load across my back and into my hair.

"Sergei," I moaned. "What did you do to me?"

He collapsed onto me and held my still quaking form, his spent cock resting outside my pussy. The contractions from my pelvic floor came slower and slower for several minutes until finally, they ceased. We fell to the couch and held each other close, gazing into each other's eyes for a long time without speaking.

13

GIRLS NIGHT OUT

December 25 was just another day, marking the saddest Christmas of my life. Most Christians in Russia follow the Orthodox calendar, which celebrates Christmas on January 7. I called my parents to wish them a Merry Christmas and made sure they received the gifts I sent them. When I hung up the phone, I looked around and pledged to do Christmas right next year, whether Sergei liked it or not, with a Christmas tree, lights, cookies, holiday music, and a feast complete with egg nog. I would celebrate twice – both Christmases to make up for the dismal December this year.

On the 30th, I was so excited for my girl time with Lena I woke up early and roused Sergei with an under-the-covers oral wake-up call.

"Ah," he moaned, still half asleep. He grabbed handfuls of my hair and guided my head, so his full length went down my throat. I didn't do blow jobs that way, but I wanted to please him. Fighting a strong gag reflex, I tried to relax to give him the sensation he was craving. It wasn't working. My eyes watered with the effort. I wanted to finish what I started, but it hurt, plain and simple. I began to choke, and a whimper escaped me.

He let go of my hair, pulled the covers back, exposing my tear-stained face.

"Oh, Sandrochka, I am sorry," he said. "Why didn't you tell me?"

I looked down, embarrassed.
"Come here," he said softly.
I scooched closer.
He wiped the tears from my cheeks and kissed each of my eyelids.

162

"Look at me," he said.

I didn't want to look at him, so I didn't.

"Sandra," he repeated. "Look at me!"

I finally lifted my eyelids, heavy with the pain of disappointment, and met his gaze.

"What are you feeling that you can't share with me?" He asked.

I looked down again.

"I am sorry, Sergei. I was so happy this morning and wanted to surprise you with something nice, but now it is ruined."

He made a 'tsk' sound and stroked my hair softly.

Sergei rolled on top of me, parted my legs expertly with one knee, and slid his penis inside me in one practiced motion. He watched my face as he entered, looking for a reaction. A fresh well of tears sprang to the surface – definitely not the effect he expected. Sergei kept pumping, kissing me gently, but the tears did not stop. It did not take long for his patience to wear out.

"Turn over, Sandra," he directed.

I rolled over compliantly, lifted my hips, and let him screw me from the rear with my face buried deep in a pillow, so he didn't have to see me cry. I didn't climax. I felt dirty, used, and ashamed. When he finished, he went into his bath and closed the door. I flipped over the wet pillow, made the bed, and retreated to the seclusion of my own bath. "I'm fine," I said out loud to no one as I stepped under the dreary downpour of water from the overhead rain shower fixture.

My big bubble of excitement for the day had burst.

Ilya knew something was wrong when we set off for the city. He put his hand on my arm and had that all too familiar concerned look in his eyes. All I could do was show him a tired smile and tell him I was sad, and it would pass. The first hour of the trip was quiet. I watched the endless expanse of snow-covered countryside parade by the windows. Suddenly he laughed out of nowhere and started to tell me jokes. I only understood parts of them, but I got the gist, like the one about a drunk guy with a bear tied to his back who fell into the Volga River. I have no idea why it was funny, but it didn't matter. Ilya's laughter was contagious. Before I knew it, we were both laughing and listening to the radio. He found a station playing Christmas songs, and we sang along. The more distance from Sergei, the better I felt. My mood had taken a 180-degree turn by the time we reached the city, and I felt much lighter.

Lena welcomed us to her home with a characteristic flourish as if we were visiting royalty and showed us to our room. She chose a second-floor suite for us. There was a bedroom with a king-size bed for me and a sitting room with a pull-out sofa bed for Ilya. He would be firmly between me and any intruders which met Sergei's requirements. There was no balcony, and the windows were locked tightly against the winter chill. Ilya was pleased with the arrangement and called Sergei with an update.

My glamorous friend rolled her eyes dramatically at these precautions, but she approved of my bodyguard. She made a show of checking him out when his attention turned, made a 'big muscles' gesture with her arms, and secretly flashed me the American two thumbs up sign. The sound of a chuckle escaped my lips. Ilya turned to see what was going on, and I smiled at him. He smiled back in the cutest way.

This little getaway was going to be fun!

The day was a whirlwind of spa treatments, lunch, and shopping. She talked me into getting a full Brazilian wax, joking once I went smooth 'there' pointing downward with both manicured index fingers, I'd never go back. I wasn't so sure. I liked my little patch of lady fur.

I bit my lip as the esthetician ripped my most intimate hair out by the roots. It was shockingly painful, but lying still waiting for each next strip to be pulled was even worse. I figured the pain would be worth the look of surprise on Sergei's face when he discovered my super smooth coochie. Fortunately, the massage, facial, and mani-pedi balanced things out in the pleasure direction afterward.

Ilya and Lena's driver, David, joined us for a late lunch at an Italian restaurant, acting as our escorts. It could be worse, I thought, eyeing Ilya appreciatively. David was even younger and just as attractive. I wondered how Lena was able to keep her hands off of him. Reaching down to retrieve a dropped napkin, I saw her hand on his thigh. She was teasing the poor lad! I looked with amazement at my friend, who seemed perfectly innocent and proper above the table. She was a woman who did not deny herself many pleasures.

I wondered if Piotr knew.

Not my problem, I told myself. If Lena is banging her driver, that's between them, but she better stay away from my Ilya! I laughed at my possessiveness and wondered if there was more to it. I made a mental note to think about that later. Today was for fun, not self-reflection.

Neither David nor Ilya spoke French, so Lena and I conversed in relative privacy. I loved how she played the lady part to perfection and chose to reveal her salty side secretly to her close friends. She was full of life and making the most of her good fortune. I complimented her on her *joie de vivre*, and she laughed, saying,

"I try to live in the moment because we never know when life will turn to shit!"

I could learn a lot from Lena. I had a sense of humor, but I was much too serious. I felt bad about the past, worried about the future, and often forgot to be happy in the present.

We have to enjoy the good times while we have them.

And these were good times!

She came up with a code for Slava, calling him X, which sounds like 'ee-ex' in French. We would also cross our index fingers and flash the X to each other instead of saying it. The Cyrillic letter that looks like X sounds like an H, so maybe the boys wouldn't catch on. It was top secret, hush-hush, and therefore even more fun.

Lena gushed X just returned from a trip to Athens sporting a 'delicious' suntan. She said he always asks her how I am doing. Then she turned down the corners of her mouth like she was sad I wouldn't give him a chance.

I told her he sent an email apology and said he wanted to be friends. She leaned in, interested.

"And...?" She asked.

"And nothing," I said. "It is impossible with my...."

She nodded. I didn't want to say *'mari'* because David or Ilya might recognize the French word for husband. No names. If it wasn't clandestine with Lena, it wasn't fun.

"Do you want to be friends with him?" She asked with arched eyebrows.

"Maybe," I replied. "I might have been wrong about X. Maybe he's not so bad."

She leaned back with a contented smile and tented her fingers.

"Good. X is a very dear friend, you know. I just want everyone to get along so I can have one guest list again," she said. "Your husband is a pain in the ass."

I couldn't argue with that assessment.

I took a sip of full-bodied and delicious Italian amarone red wine. I noted the 'sin' of drinking it with my clothes on and laughed. What Sergei doesn't know won't hurt him. Somehow it made the wine taste even more delicious. I smiled, amused with myself for developing secret pleasures of my own.

"Now what about…?" Lena asked with her lips pursed, subtly motioning to Ilya.

"*Il est beau*," she added, dramatically fanning herself from the 'heat' he was giving off.

I laughed and leaned in close, looking around pretending I was about to divulge a big secret.

"He's mine!" I whispered, and we both gushed with laughter again.

My eyes darted to Ilya, who was eyeing me with interest. I smiled at him and felt telltale warmth spread over my cheeks. The wine was betraying me, but I didn't care. I giggled and happily turned back to my friend.

"He knows," she said with feigned portentousness as she winked.

We exploded into another round of raucous laughter.

We spent the rest of the afternoon shopping at ridiculously high-end stores I would never have dared step into in New York. With Lena's encouragement, I spent much more money than I care to admit. The charges to the black credit card were astronomical, but I figured Sergei owed me for ruining my morning.

Lena said we should plan a shopping trip to Milan, *sans* husbands. I told her I would have to make it to New Year's Day without getting into trouble first.

"Don't count on it!" She roared.

Dinner was a cozy affair back at their home. She hired chefs and party planners to do everything so she could relax and enjoy her guests. They had friends dropping by all the time, and she planned generously. There were ten guests for dinner this evening. Ilya was treated just as well as everyone else.

We sampled an assortment of Spanish tapas dishes that we passed around and shared. Piotr and his friends drank vodka shots in the customary way, as a group with lots of toasts. Ilya abstained since he was 'on the job,' and I decided to postpone my drinking until we hit the club. I explained I wasn't born with a Russian liver.

166

"We can get you one!" Piotr boomed, his deep laugh filling the room with warmth and a profound sense of welcome.

Lena rolled her eyes at his joke but laughed along anyway.

I understood why they had so many friends. There was so much joy in their home and not one note of depressing classical music.

A few of Lena's other girlfriends arrived after dinner, followed by a team of hairdressers who put our hair up in party styles for the nightclub. We took turns making up each other's faces until we looked like models in a pop music video. We had a six-girl party posse ready to hit the club!

Ilya rode in the front of the limo with David while the girls popped champagne bottles and pre-partied in the back. The bubbly flowed, and the effervescent energy continued to build. The girls talked about the hot guys at the club and how they would do some sexy bumping and grinding tonight.

Wild woman brigade! Woo!

We spilled out of the limo, champagne flutes in hand, and walked right into the club, bypassing the long line of people waiting in the freezing weather to get in.

VIP status! Woo!

Electronic dance music with lots of flashing lights greeted us inside the club. There were couches and tables around the periphery, but the center was all dance floor. Costumed scantily-clad women danced in big birdcages strung from the ceiling. The place was popping. I tried to act cool, but I was awestruck. I'd never been to a nightclub like this before. We made our way to the bar, and Lena ordered a round of their signature drink, vodka with God knows what else in a tall glass. I called it a Russian rocket because it immediately made my night take off.

There was a VIP area in an open mezzanine level upstairs where local celebrities hung out, but I didn't care about them. I just wanted to dance. Ilya was a conservative dancer, but he had no trouble keeping up with me. He was dressed stylishly in black slacks and a matching designer sweater that hugged the rugged terrain of his muscled upper body. To top it off, he wore a black fedora with a broad white band that made him look like a gangster. He was cool, funky, sexy, and far more fashionable than I ever expected. I wholeheartedly approved. There is no way Sergei would ever have been that much fun.

Hot date! Woo!

Ilya stayed close to me throughout the night. Giving the appearance we were a couple was one way to discourage unwanted attention, but I knew this must be a departure from the professional bodyguard handbook. The girls found no shortage of good-looking men for dancing. Ilya remained alert for signs of trouble, but that didn't mean we couldn't have fun. On breaks from dancing, we joined our party resting on the couches. Ilya leaned back and drew me close to rest on his arm. I was sure this affectionate display was unnecessary, but I could not object to the way his firm body felt against mine. I noticed how easy it was to let my guard down and relax with Ilya. I was always on edge with my husband, trying to avoid conflict.

An image of Sergei's scowling face flashed through my mind. He would not be pleased to see me so cozy with this young man. I had to remind myself once again this was just Ilya's job, not an actual date, biting my lower lip with regret.

The party didn't begin to wind down until after 4:00 am. We were taking one last turn on the dance floor with Lena and David when a large drunken man started dancing lewdly between them. He spewed a litany of indecent proposals on Lena. She dismissed him with an icy look, as only she could. Then he stumbled a jagged line toward me.

Ilya stepped in front of him and told him to back off. The drunk kept coming, trying to push the bodyguard aside. Ilya gripped his arm. By this time, the dancing stopped, and everyone backed away, the situation garnering the attention of two bouncers. The man lunged at Ilya, surprising him with a vicious head butt. A brief scramble ended with the vile man on his back with Ilya's boot on his neck. The bouncers picked up the drunk, who thrashed wildly, and dragged him to the rear of the club to throw out the back door like trash. Hot, sweaty, and stunned, I looked into the face of my savior and saw there was blood flowing down his cheek.

I ran to get towels from the bar, then carefully dabbed his face. There was a horizontal gash across his right cheekbone, a glancing swipe from the offender's signet ring, perhaps. I wanted to take him to a hospital for stitches, but he said no. Lena agreed that butterfly bandages would probably take care of it.

"What a night!" She declared, beaming. "Let's get this hero home."

Once locked safely in our suite, I tended to Ilya's wound with great care. He sat in a chair as I washed his face with a warm soapy washcloth and then cleaned the wound with hydrogen peroxide, cringing in empathy when it stung. I carefully closed the gap with two butterfly bandages, dabbing antibiotic ointment on top for insurance. There was not much to be done for the growing bruise on his forehead, but applying a cool compress made me feel better about it.

I couldn't help notice the bruise and bandages gave him a distinct after-the-game hockey player look. I always had a thing for hockey players but was too shy to date one.

Caution, Cassandra, I warned myself. After what happened with Slava Valkov, I most certainly knew better.

And yet, I found myself gazing into his smoldering brown eyes anyway. My breath caught. I glanced at his mouth and saw his firm, full lips slightly parted. Something about that made me salivate. I swallowed hard and risked another look at his beautiful eyes to see him watching me. I leaned in closer. With animal instinct overpowering intellect, I brushed my lips ever so slightly against his, shooting an arc of sparks across tinder skin.

I was being sucked into a black hole of desire and struggled to pull myself back from the brink.

"*Druz'ya,*" I whispered urgently, vainly. 'Friends'

"*Druz'ya. Da,*" he replied.

He lightly touched my lower lip with the tip of his finger, eliciting a slight involuntary gasp. My lips parted, and he advanced with a deep, soul-filled kiss full of sweet promises. My heart swelled with forbidden feelings, and my primed body responded like roses blooming for a honeybee. His tongue found mine, and we danced, slowly and deliberately, exploring, tasting, and feeling each other intimately, lighting a slow-burning fire that would be difficult to extinguish.

I dissolved into Ilya's kiss.

When he finally pulled away, I opened my eyes and gazed at him with wonder, appreciating his truly sensual nature for the first time.

"*Druz'ya?*" He asked huskily.

"*Da. Druz'ya,*" I repeated with a pout.

Ilya lifted me in his strong arms and carried me to the bedroom, where he placed me gently on the turned-down bed. He lay behind me and held me close in his protective arms.

My heart relaxed and opened, enveloped in the bubble of safety he provided.

"Ilyusha," I breathed.

He responded with a gentle squeeze.

I could fall in love with him so easily. Perhaps I already have, I wondered as we fell asleep nested like spoons.

14

S Novim Godom

Sergei arrived in the afternoon and released Ilya for two weeks, giving him a well-deserved vacation. He was traveling to Moscow to spend time with his family. I was sad to see him go and even sorrier his mother would see him with that ugly bruise and gash on his face.

I'd given him a pair of fine Italian deerskin gloves as a holiday gift earlier in the day. I admitted the Russian to English language learning program I gave him next was more of a gift for me. Finally, I'd handed him an envelope with ten $100 US bills inside. He said it was too much, but I insisted. A grand was nothing to me these days. The thought of contributing a little joy to his holidays with his family warmed my heart.

He wasn't alone. I'd given all of the staff generous bonuses on the sly.

"Don't tell the boss," I winked.

I knew he wouldn't.

Sergei seemed distant when he arrived. Something was weighing on his mind, but he didn't volunteer any information. He settled into our room and tiredly listened as I told him about the previous day's events. My husband seemed genuinely glad I had fun with Lena and was surprisingly unconcerned with Ilya's run-in with the drunk.

"That is what a bodyguard is for," he said calmly.

He was relieved there'd been no sign of Slava Valkov.

By 9:00 pm, the New Year's Eve party was in full swing, and the guests were enjoying Lena's lavishly decorated home with a 20 foot Christmas tree centered in their entrance hall between the two grand staircases that curved upward to the second floor. Meticulously prepared *zakuska* tables in three rooms offered delights from salads to meat-filled pastries, smoked fish, herring, meats and cheeses, *pirozhki,* caviar, and jellied fish. It was hors d'oeuvres on a grand scale. People were raving and insisting their companions try a taste of this one and that one.

Servers dressed like high fashion elves hustled to continually replenish the buffet and make sure no one's drink went dry. Beautiful young women dressed like sparkling snow fairies floated through the crowd offering flutes of champagne.

I felt ready to accept an Oscar descending the grand staircase in a plunging sleeveless crimson Versace gown with scandalously high side slits, my smooth bare legs and pedicured toes landing sweetly in a pair of Jimmy Choo party heels. I had help putting my hair up in a formal braided style that allowed a few meticulously ironed long corkscrew curls to escape down the center of my back. Diamonds flashed at my ears, neck, and ring finger. Sergei and I made the rounds to connect with influential people early in the evening while everyone was rational and we still looked good. Excitement was building among the revelers, and it promised to be a wild night.

I was becoming more comfortable playing model, holding onto my husband's arm and smiling demurely at the boring people he wanted to impress. These parties were a social game, and my husband expected me to play along. I felt confident, noting how far I'd come from when I met him. I gave myself credit for the change, but I had to admit diamonds and couture also make a strong bolster for poise.

Bored to death with a placid smile painted on my face, I allowed my thoughts to run freely. It occurred to me my role at these events was to simply provide a beautiful frame for a flattering portrait of my husband. I was an American trophy wife adoring her husband, eager to hear every brilliant word he spoke. A surge of anger rose from my gut. I wanted to shine and feel supported too! At least he seemed pleased. He gave me a little wink and a quick squeeze of the hand to let me know I was doing well. I tried to focus on the positives. Dressing up for an elegant party was far more fun than staying home.

After completing our circuit, Sergei settled into a political conversation with an older man with a shock of white hair and an off-putting arrogant attitude. Nothing interested me less than Russian politics. Even worse, this creep kept shooting furtive glances at me with his geriatric weasel eyes. I had to stand there and politely take it like a lady. Semyon Lukich was a shipping baron, a man my husband was eager to impress. I needed to extract myself discreetly but could not come up with a plan for a gracious exit. I'd been walking on eggshells trying to keep Sergei happy and didn't want to blow it on this important night.

Fortunately, the queen of the evening appeared to save me.

"Cassandra, darling," Lena declared with her characteristic flourish. "I've been searching for you all night. Please, there is something I absolutely must have your assistance with."

"Of course, anything," I replied enthusiastically.

"Forgive me for stealing your beautiful lady," she said to Sergei, "Don't worry. She will be in good hands."

She winked at me with an air of mystery, and with that, she whisked me away.

"What's happening?" I asked as she led me to the quiet south wing of the house.

"You started badly," she explained.

"What?" I asked.

"I want you to talk to him," she added.

"Who?" I asked.

"X, darling," she replied with a slight edge to her voice for having to state the obvious.

She paused.

"Please do not tell anyone he was here, or Piotr will never forgive me. Promise," she demanded, waiting for visual confirmation.

As if she didn't always get her way.

I nodded yes. I would never get my friend in trouble.

We arrived at a seldom-used sitting room, and there he was.

Suntanned and sexy Slava Valkov in a fur-trimmed black sheepskin coat that stated he wasn't planning to stay long. He was strikingly handsome for such a large man, with perfectly proportioned features, a strong nose, and full cherry lips. Here is the quintessential Russian man, I thought with admiration.

My pulse quickened.

He rose to his impressive height when we entered the room. He inhaled deeply and made a show of admiring us women in our finery.

I knew the view was good.

I'd never felt more beautiful than I did that night.

"*Zdravstvujtye*," I said, using the formal greeting.

"*Zdravstvujtye* Cassandra. You are radiant," he declared appreciatively with an expressive hand gesture. The way he said my name, 'Kah-SAN-drah,' jolted me with an unexpected buzz of electricity.

"*Spasibo*," I responded, politely accepting the compliment.

"May I?" He asked, taking my hands gently in his. He leaned down and gave me a light kiss on each cheek. I noticed his clean, manly scent.

He motioned for me to sit at a small table.

Lena glanced down the hallway, closed the door, and leaned her back against the inside to ensure privacy.

"You look, well," he said, searching for something more than health in my eyes.

His eyes were different tonight. Not hazel or green as they had appeared before, but as golden as a lion's eyes. Everything about him reminded me of the king of the beasts.

He was majestic, powerful, intelligent, alert, and very dangerous. Even his hands were impressive, with long, masculine fingers and well-groomed nails. The sight of his hands tugged a deep cord in my belly.

Slava Valkov was an incredibly sexy man.

I strained to hide my intense attraction.

A satisfied turn at the corner of his mouth told me I had not succeeded.

He was a man who did not miss much.

"I am sorry for September," he said sincerely, his voice deep and smoky. "I want you to know me as a gentleman."

He pulled a little box from his coat and pushed it across the table.

I flashed a question mark look to Lena. Her expression shouted, 'open it!'

Inside was a delicate gold bracelet with a single charm – a five-pointed crown with a small diamond at the tip of each point.

His strong hands moved swiftly to put it on before I could object.

"You are a princess, and I treated you poorly. I will not make that mistake again," he said with sincerity.

I was astounded. Then I remembered my manners and said,

"*Spasibo*, Slava. This is lovely."

He closed his eyes in a moment of silent gratitude. I don't know what pleased him more, accepting his gift or using his familiar name for the first time.

My perspective suddenly shifted. Maybe I was wrong. What happened wasn't entirely Slava's fault. The attraction was mutual, and we were both drunk. Perhaps I encouraged him to follow me into the laundry room, as Sergei insisted. The memory now seemed more like a misunderstanding.

Remembering the size of his erection and the press of it against me gave me a sudden 'woo' feeling in the naughty zone. Then a vision of the ungodly stain on his pants flashed through my mind. Oh, that is humiliating. How could I have had so little self-control?

The hot rise of shame burned my cheeks.

My attention turned back to the elegant man in front of me.

"You can tell your husband it was a gift from Lena," he suggested. "This is between you and me."

I nodded.

He stood, so I did too.

"Happy New Year, my American friend," he said, bending down to kiss both of my cheeks again.

"Happy New Year to you too," I replied.

He paused for a second and then spontaneously hugged me, making a deep 'Mmmm' sound as he did so. The vibration passed from his broad chest to my cheek, and I enjoyed the visceral feeling of creature contentment it gave me.

He nodded his thanks to Lena and stepped out through the patio door, leaving a swirl of frosty air in his wake.

"Wow," I said, looking at the bracelet and then up to my friend's happy face. "I never could have predicted this happening."

Lena beamed, "See? This is what I've been trying to tell you. Slava has a big heart. He has wanted to make things right with you for months."

"What should I tell Sergei about your emergency?" I asked.

"Tell him I had a wardrobe malfunction," she laughed as she slipped down the right strap on her gown to flash her breast at me. Sure enough, there was a perfectly pink, pretty little nipple perched atop a lovely globe of

175

lady flesh. The sight of her breast was so unexpected. I couldn't stop myself from staring.

She put a fingertip to her lips and painted an 'Oops, how did that happen?' expression on her face.

"*Mon Dieu* girl, you are too much!" I exclaimed as we both exploded into laughter.

Back at the party, Sergei was in the same place, still talking to the creepy old guy. I caught his eye, and he nodded slightly, acknowledging my return. The party was ratcheting up. I was in a great mood, and I had a little catching up to do. I accepted a flute of champagne from a passing server and headed to the party room, where a DJ led a lively dance party. I spotted some of Lena's friends from the night before and eagerly joined them on the dance floor.

After an hour or so, I noticed Sergei standing on the side watching us. I smiled and waved, encouraging him to join the fun.

I should have known better.

He stood with his feet firmly planted, his eyes calmly wandering over the crowd, taking in the scene.

So I went to him, flushed warm with happy energy.

"Let's go upstairs," he whispered in my ear.

He didn't have to tell me twice!

Sergei carefully laid his jacket on a chair, unzipped his pants, and reclined on the loveseat. He patted the seat for me to sit beside him and placed my hand over his partial erection, rubbing himself with my hand. Once he was ready, I started to take off my dress.

"*Nyet*," he said, harsher than needed to get my attention.

Looking to see what was wrong, I saw him pressing his cheek out from the inside with his tongue with a smirk on his face. This vulgar gesture for blow jobs is the same everywhere.

This kind of behavior was why I did not like most men.

It's all about what they want.

I did my best to hide my disappointment and dutifully went down on him. As if that wasn't bad enough, he wanted me to practice doing it the nasty way. With his hands on my head, he forced his dick down my throat

176

and kept it there firmly for a full minute before pulling out to let me breathe. Then he began using my throat like a pussy, stroking hard while holding my head in place. Gagging and upset, with tears running from my eyes, I couldn't believe he dragged me away from such a fun party for this. His ejaculate burned my throat and splattered onto my face as I pulled back in disgust. The taste was revolting. I ran to the bathroom and spat his venom into the sink, and splashed cold water on my face to rinse off the rest.

That's when I glanced in the mirror and saw he'd messed up my elegant hairdo.

I was pissed.

It had taken two people an hour to put up my hair and only a few minutes of his stupid selfishness to destroy their work. I took the pins out one by one and threw them in the trash. Then I unbraided the long accent pieces and started brushing it all out. I worked in a few drops of oil to smooth out the styling abuse and brushed my hair until it looked good enough to go back to the party.

Sergei followed me and leaned against the door jamb, silently watching as I did this.

I knew he was there, but I ignored him.

I figured it would only make things worse if he saw the flare of anger in my eyes. I carefully reapplied my makeup and turned to leave. I was going back downstairs to celebrate New Year's Eve, with or without him. He grabbed my arm as I tried to pass, twisting it backward until I had to face him.

"Where do you think you are going?" He asked derisively.

I glared at him and said nothing.

He twisted my arm even harder, cranking gears of pain through my shoulder until I felt things beginning to pop.

"Fuck you, Sergei. You don't fucking own me!" I shouted in his face.

And wouldn't you know? That bastard hit me!

He punched me right in the face. Luckily I reacted quickly, turning my head in time to take a glancing blow to the temple instead of a sock to the eye. His fist continued its trajectory past my face and hit hard into the wall, leaving a dent. Good, I hope that hurt!

I didn't wait for another punch to come. I stomped down on his foot as hard as I could, wrenched myself from his clutch, and shoved him backward with both hands knocking him off balance. I ran screaming away from him. My hand reached the doorknob as I was just about to escape to the safety of my friends when he grabbed a handful of my hair and hauled me back in a violent motion that pitched us both to the floor.

We wrestled for ten long minutes. I kicked, hit, bit, and scratched wherever I could, as hard as I could. I grappled, flipped, and rolled with him, my arms and strong legs scrambling wildly to purchase the upper hand.

I was sick of his shit.

I was full of pent-up energy, and it was on.

I gave it everything I had, holding nothing back.

Unfortunately, that only made the defeat more devastating when he ended up on top, triumphantly pinning me down. It was a hard-won victory. Sweat soaked his brow, plastered his fine hair to his head, and he was breathing hard from the exertion. I continued to struggle until I realized it was useless.

I wasn't going anywhere.

No one heard me scream with the party in full swing downstairs.

No one was coming to help.

He eyed me with a wicked smile.

"What a tiger you are, Sandra!" He said, sounding excited and genuinely impressed. "I had no idea you were such a fighter."

I spit in his face.

A little spit wasn't going to ruin his victory. He smiled and kissed my mouth open, forcing his tongue deep, showing me who was in charge. I chomped down on his tongue and used the surprise to my advantage, thrashing violently to the side, throwing him off. As I struggled to stand, he snatched the hem of my gown and pulled me back. A fierce tug of war ensued. The fine material gave, at last, the dress tore in half at the waist, pulling my delicate lace panties down with it. I tumbled forward clumsily, tripping over the falling skirt, tangled in my own underwear. He pounced and regained control quickly, pinning me on my back once again.

There would be no salvaging the $6,000 Versace evening gown from this utter destruction, but I wasn't concerned about that at the moment.

He'd just discovered my smooth Brazilian waxing.

"Hey, Tiger, where is your fur?" He asked lasciviously, running his fingertips over the smooth vulnerable skin.

It was supposed to have been a surprise. A sweet, sexy surprise I'd daydreamed about sharing with my beloved husband. It wasn't supposed to happen like this.

He ruined everything.

He always ruins everything!

My rage dissolved into despair as grief consumed me. Tears quickly escalated into heaving sobs. My eyes burned, tears mixing with mascara and staining my vision. I was crying so hard I could only breathe in wretched, ragged breaths.

Meanwhile, he probed me with his fingers, completely ignoring my emotional state. He savored his victory by licking my pussy. He seemed to find the taste favorable and began running his tongue over my labia, teasing me open and then swirling and flicking my clitoris until he got the response he wanted. As my sobs and tears subsided, he sunk his fingers in deep and finger-banged me until I came, shamefully, for him.

Sergei slithered on top of my body and kissed me with his pussy soaked face, forcing me to taste my own sweetness on his vile lips. He pushed his penis into me gently, using his privileged position to form the physical connection and sacred union of marriage. We were one, whether I wanted to be or not. His face was mere inches from mine. He locked eyes with me and stroked in and out slowly, maintaining the intense connection for as long as he could. I stared into his clear blue eyes, my mind roiling with thoughts, my heart burning with feeling.

I loved him. I hated him. I hated myself for loving him.

Despite my mental objections, I could not ignore the pleasurable sensation. An involuntary moan escaped me, encouraging him to pick up the pace. Before I knew it, I was coming in great crashing waves. I loathed myself for giving him the satisfaction so clearly evident in his impish grin.

Sergei Ivanovich Karpov won, again.

After he released his pleasure inside me, he rolled off and lay on his back next to me on the floor, breathing hard as he wound down from the prolonged exertion.

I stared at the ceiling and listened to the people counting down to midnight at the party below, everyone joyfully shouting, "*S Novim Godom!*"

Happy New Year!

Happy New Year indeed.

A single fat tear rolled from the corner of my eye.

On New Year's Day, I woke early to the sound of Sergei snoring like a broken snowblower. Looking back at him, I couldn't believe it was the same bed I felt so safe in the day before with Ilya. 'What a difference a *man* makes,' I joked to myself, playing on the words of the familiar phrase. It was a funny observation, but I was humorless.

I dressed quickly and slipped out the door without waking him. No one was up yet, so I helped myself in the kitchen. I found a French press and made a cup of black coffee. Coffee made me feel strong — American strong.

Safely wrapped in my fur coat, I ventured outside. From the frost quickly forming on my eyelashes and hair inside my nose, I figured it was about 20 degrees below zero. The air was still, the world quiet, and I enjoyed the solitude. The snow squeaked happily beneath my boots as I walked. The familiar sound pleased my ears and calmed my nerves.

I remembered Slava mentioning he lived nearby and wondered which house was his. Most of the homes were showy mansions like Lena's, set far too close to each other for their monstrous size. A columned home that reminded me of Caesar's Palace caught my eye. The one stood out from the others, set on a slight rise within a larger cushion of land.

I imagined Slava lived there. I pictured his suntanned body lying on a pile of fur blankets in front of a roaring fire. I smiled weakly at the thought and sent him good wishes. I prayed he was peacefully sleeping wherever he was.

I touched the gold charm, relieved the delicate bracelet survived the altercation. The diamonds twinkled innocently in the faint light of a streetlamp.

A sliver of hope soothed my tired heart.

Out of places to turn and risking possible frostbite, I decided to turn back.

There was still no one moving at Lena's, so I returned to my asshole husband upstairs. He was awake and lifted the covers, inviting me back to bed. I shed a trail of clothing as I approached and snuggled in next to him, skin to skin. Then I warmed my frozen hands on his stomach, jolting him with the icy surprise.

Ha! He deserved it.

Sergei kissed me gently and smoothed the hair back from my face. He kissed the bruise at my temple. He spoke loving words and made love to me sweetly, but I felt broken inside.

Punching me crossed a line.

A man should never hit his woman.

When love is no longer a sanctuary, what is left?

I took inventory of the damage I inflicted while we showered. Sergei had scrapes and bite marks all over his arms, a deep scratch down his cheek, a painful-looking bruise on the top of his right foot, and several purple bruises from kicks on his shins. He looked worse than I did. That gave me a sense of satisfaction.

Hopefully, I taught him a lesson.

I covered my bruise with concealer and hid the lump at my temple by styling my hair to that side. Then I touched up Sergei's facial scratch with a dab of makeup. His clothing would hide the rest of the damage except for his scraped knuckles. He was on his own with that.

We spent the rest of the day pretending to be a happily married couple. Lena's concerned looks told me she knew something was up. The story would have to wait because I wasn't about to ruin her holiday with my marital problems. I honestly didn't know if I could ever tell her what happened. I could barely explain it to myself.

Why would the love of my life ever hit me?

At last, our social obligations were over, and Sergei drove us home to our uncertain future.

15

MIDNIGHT CORNUCOPIA

Sergei's stress over the business deal in Turkey escalated in the New Year. He lashed out at me whenever I asked, so I stayed out of his business. His secrecy and black moods were driving the wedge in our relationship deeper.

I was back to rambling around an empty house devoid of guests while he traveled back and forth to Istanbul. He avoided me most of the time he was home. Sergei was angry because I refused to give him oral sex after the way he treated me on New Year's Eve. He thought an apology was enough, but I refused to concede. He then imposed sanctions of his own and stopped giving me oral too. We were at an impasse.

The cold war was back on.

Sex became mechanical and lacked the emotional connection we had before. There was no kissing or tenderness, just a minimal effort to get me wet and stick it in. Sergei mounted me from behind. After he came, he rolled away and pretended to sleep. I knew he was only doing it to keep up his end of the deal, but I felt worse than if we weren't having sex at all. The loneliness of the disconnect dug a hole deep in my heart. I'd felt closer to Sergei when he was on the other side of the planet than I did in our marital bed that January. Meanwhile, the pregnancy tests kept coming up negative, and I was beginning to give up hope we'd ever have children.

His dark mood was contagious, so I had to keep my mind busy, or I would fall into an emotional pit beside him. So I shoved my feelings aside and threw myself into my work. I was writing profusely, making up for lost time, and narrowly avoided a breach of contract for failing to deliver on deadline. I started writing in the family room on my laptop with the television on to immerse myself in the language. The sound of people talking gave the unruly part of my mind something to chew on while I focused on work. I hoped it would magically help with my Russian language comprehension.

I made a point to change channels whenever the news came on. They would show video of fire and accident victims, no matter how bloody or dismembered they might be. There were frequent terrorist attacks on government buildings and high-profile murders, including a rising number of car bombings. They even showed the corpse of a murdered government official with bullet holes in his forehead, covered in dirt from a shallow grave. Russia seemed much more violent and unsettled than New York. Explosions seemed as common as the potholes that cratered the roads.

What upset me most was the footage from trials. The defendants appeared for hearings within a prison-like cage inside the courtroom. The Stanford Prison Experiment, one of the most influential studies in psychology, clearly demonstrated the tendency for people to dehumanize those they perceive as 'prisoners.' They are presumed guilty regardless of the circumstances. How could anyone get a fair trial from inside a cage? I already had a fear of the police, but the idea of being subjected to the Russian legal system was a nightmare. I didn't need anything else to worry about, so I tried to push those thoughts from my mind too. I put on talk shows or sitcoms that were easier to ignore.

Ilya's injuries healed by the time he returned from his two weeks in Moscow, but it looked like he might end up with a small scar on his cheek. Of course, that only made him more attractive. He told me he gave his parents the money to make overdue home repairs. Then he showed me photos from the holiday at their ramshackle story and a half farmhouse in a village southeast of the city. I was curious and encouraged him to talk about his visit. His brother and sister were also home for the holidays, so the entire family was together for two weeks. They seemed to get along well and enjoyed their holiday traditions. Listening to him talk about his happy family relaxed me. His family seemed so normal compared to what my life had become. I sighed, genuinely glad he had a good vacation, but I missed him dearly and felt much better once he returned to the farm.

When he asked how things were going with Sergei, I held up my palm and said,

"Nekhorosho."

'Not good' was an understatement. Things were not good at all.

Concern flashed over his face. He nodded slightly and didn't ask for details. Feeling upset and on the verge of tears, I excused myself and went upstairs to be alone.

Ilya's English was slowly improving, and so was my Russian. It was fun to learn new words and help each other with pronunciation. I had difficulty saying words correctly, but I was beginning to understand conversations better. English was a struggle for him too. We developed a hybrid language that we continually added new phrases to, often laughing at the combinations we created. Ilya had patience for me that Sergei lacked, and spending time with him always put me at ease. I began to look forward to Sergei's trips so I could relax and feel normal.

We continued to keep our friendship a secret. Ilya called me 'Madam' and avoided eye contact whenever my husband or anyone else was around. He acted in the same bashful, socially awkward manner he did before, pulling it off perfectly. The subterfuge pleased me immensely and felt like 'wins' because I knew something Sergei didn't know.

My husband kept plenty of secrets from me. Whatever was happening in Turkey was burning a hole of stress right through him. Watching him carry that weight alone hurt even more because he didn't trust me enough to tell me what was going on. I felt excluded, unable to help. We were no longer partners. There was no 'us against the world' united front like he promised on our honeymoon. I'd become just another obligation to him, something to manage and control. After only seven months, our marriage was falling apart, and I wondered what chance we had of making it to our first anniversary. I pushed these depressing thoughts down too, but they were like acid percolating under the surface, slowly eating away at me.

I'd decided to reinstate a daily yoga practice for my New Year's resolution, following along to recorded yoga classes on the big TV in the family room for an hour every morning. After maintaining the schedule for a few weeks, I felt more grounded and could buffer Sergei's moods better. As I transitioned from Warrior One to Warrior Two pose on my mat one morning, I noticed Ilya had quietly joined in beside me. His face was turned away, holding his arms out in the pose correctly. The workout leggings and fitted tank top he was wearing left little to the imagination. I couldn't help but marvel at his sculpted muscular rear, solid arms, and strong legs. Even the muscles on his back and shoulders were well-defined. I sighed with appreciation and almost missed the cue to transition to the next pose.

He caught my eye and gave me a shy smile. I shot him a friendly, encouraging grin in return before I shifted into the one-legged balance stance of Warrior Three. He was a welcome distraction, especially when he went into Downward Dog, effortlessly forming a perfect upside-down V with his body, his magnificent behind pressed high in the air with his hands and heels flat on the floor.

Who doesn't appreciate a limber man?

Ilya remained through the end of the lesson, then pressed his hands into prayer position over his heart and said *"Namaste"* to me with a slight bow. What a surprise he was! He joined me whenever the others were not around, and yoga became one of our little secrets. He seemed to take the practice seriously, but I knew there had to be more to it. I loved sharing the practice with him, of course. Sometimes the memory of him saying *'Namaste'* to me that first time would pop into my mind on a bad day and make me smile out of the blue.

I'd asked Sergei to join me for yoga to help lower his stress, but he refused.

"I'll take more Vitamin D," he said in yet another marital eye-rolling moment.

Then there was the evening I was watching a St. Petersburg SKA hockey game on TV, and Ilya came into the family room, casually plopped down on the sofa beside me, and started talking hockey. He was a Moscow Dynamo fan and knew everything about the league, players, and coaches. He even knew personal details, like the star player who was going through a divorce, showed up to practice drunk and got benched, and about the hot-tempered coach known for throwing chairs when upset. So much drama! Insider information brought the personalities alive and made hockey even more fun.

Since I'd already pledged my loyalty to St. Petersburg, a friendly rivalry was born between us. He rooted for any team against mine, especially Dynamo or any of the other Moscow teams. Sometimes we drank beer and made wagers on games, guessing which players would score. He usually won because he knew the league better, but I didn't mind losing a few dollars here and there. The playful goading and trash-talking were what I loved most. Watching games was so much better with a fellow hockey fan, but of course, we could only share this special joy when my husband was out of town.

Sergei had no interest in sports. The only sport he ever played was polo. Rich boys in preppy clothes riding horses did not intrigue me like the grit and drama of hockey. Nothing compares to ice hockey, and hockey friends are precious even when they root for the wrong team.

I was surprised when Sergei encouraged me to ask Ilya to escort me outside the fence to make use of the trails blazed through the wilderness. The bodyguard loved a physical workout, and he was always up for a trek. The snow was too deep for the horses in the dead of winter, so we began to cross country skiing nearly every day, no matter how cold or dark it was. We had all the gear needed to be safe, warm, and comfortable. He always carried a gun and a GPS in case we got lost. There was nothing to fear with Ilya beside me, and I loved the way my body felt, powerfully gliding over the beautiful snow, becoming stronger every day. We didn't talk much, but there was something solid building in the silence between us. Spending those hours in the woods with Ilya, swooshing over the gorgeous plentiful snow, far from the emotional pain and restrictions at the farm, was healing for me. The distance helped me gain a perspective on my relationship with Sergei I may not have had otherwise.

This burgeoning friendship was hush-hush, of course. I was developing an ability to keep secrets and hide my feelings. The more I felt Sergei's control over me, the more freedom I required to compensate. My husband shut me out emotionally, so I opened up to someone else. Maybe it was a passive-aggressive way to get even. I'm not saying it was right, only that our marriage was complicated.

Humans are messy.

Sergei and I had a dynamic relationship.

Yin and Yang always find balance.

· I was becoming addicted to the thrill of getting away with something without getting caught. It didn't matter what it was. Smoking cigarettes in the garage, letting the dogs sleep on the bed, and taking Sergei's BMW out for a joy ride were risky. Early on, I thrilled in the rebellion of wearing shoes in the house and putting my feet up on the furniture because I knew he wouldn't like it. Of course, I thought those restrictions were silly, but they would never have given me any pleasure if Sergei hadn't forbidden them.

My actions were juvenile, I admit, but it was harmless enough in the beginning.

The problem with thrill-seeking is that we tend to need bigger and bigger thrills to stay satisfied. This was a dangerous game, like building a tolerance for alcohol.

How do we know when we have gone too far?

I decided to take Lena up on her offer to explore Russian culture. Sergei did not object. He was surprisingly eager to get me out of the house.

"Go, go," he said brusquely, waving me off, "but stay with Ilya at all times."

I nodded my acceptance of his oppressive terms with a somber expression on my face. Of course, I was secretly thrilled he didn't know the bodyguard had become my special friend. 'Discovering Russian culture' was a brilliant ruse. I owed Lena for that idea. I wished I had thought of it myself.

Lena and I planned to spend three days exploring the Hermitage while I stayed with her in town. The Hermitage is a vast museum, one of the largest in the world. I marveled at the elegance of the staterooms in the historic winter palace, and the enormous amount of art Catherine the Great collected during her travels across Europe.

Ilya followed along with us the first day, my ever-present protective shadow. By the afternoon, I began to feel guilty because he was bored. Not by the art, necessarily, but by being constantly excluded from our nonstop French chatter.

There was plenty of security at the museum. Whenever anyone tried to touch anything in the collection, someone was right there to intervene. I released Ilya from museum duty the following day. I had nothing to fear within the museum. Sergei did not need to know about this lapse, so we agreed not to tell him.

Ilya walked us to the museum door. I told him I would call his cell when we were ready to leave for the day. Lena rolled her eyes at all of this.

"Your husband treats you like a child," she observed.

I supposed she was right. I'd lived alone in New York City, and nothing happened to me there. I'd taken a self-defense course in college and knew how to take care of myself. My husband was the only person I ever had to use those moves on.

187

Off we went to continue our tour of the millions of pieces in the museum's collection. I wanted to see everything slowly enough to appreciate the essence of the people who created the art. Sometimes one of us would linger behind and catch up later, rubber banding our way through the halls together.

I lingered for a long time in the hall of Egyptian antiquities, looking over the objects, trying to feel the culture they embodied. I paused for a long time in front of a stele of Anubis, the jackal-headed god of death. He was seated, strong and regal, as a human stood before him with his hands held up in apparent worship. Something about Anubis was reassuring, like a promise.

I gazed deeply upon his image.

I indulged in a mental exploration of death, resurrection, and reincarnation. I wondered if any religion got the mystery right. I couldn't know with certainty, but I felt reincarnation was possible. I sensed I was born into this world many times before. Interesting, since that was a completely different view from what Catholicism taught me. And yet, reincarnation simply felt true compared to the one-and-done life of Christianity. I was standing before Anubis, completely lost in thought, struggling to access secret inner knowledge that seemed tantalizingly just out of reach, when I heard a familiar voice.

My attention returned from the mist of my reverie.

I turned and looked up into the familiar face of Slava Valkov. The big man's appearance in the hall of antiquities seemed perfectly natural. He appeared to be waiting for a response.

"*Privet* Slava," I greeted with the informal hello used between friends and asked him to please repeat what he'd said.

"I adore the Egyptian collection," he repeated with a warm smile. By his pronunciation and use of the word 'the,' I knew he'd been practicing English. I was honored. "This is Ipi, scribe of Pharaoh Tutankhamen," he added, pointing to the human supplicant.

My ears rode the tone and tempo of his voice, his words flowing into my mind like warm honey. I turned again to face him, and he took my hands in his, kissing me lightly on both cheeks in greeting.

I knew this was not an accidental encounter, suspecting his accomplice Lena must be right around the corner watching. She was fixated on me getting to know Slava better. I wondered about her motivations. Surely it couldn't just be for all of her friends to get along. She did not like Sergei and thought I could do better. My husband was the antithesis of fun from her perspective, but there seemed to be more to it.

After we exchanged pleasantries, Slava and I toured the rest of the hall. He translated the placards of the more unusual pieces for me, and we discussed the dynasties of Ancient Egypt. I enjoyed the intellectual banter and interest we shared in the topic. I found it easy to be with him, viewing the exhibits side by side.

We paused before a black basalt statue of Cleopatra VII, one of the prized pieces in the collection. She was a magnificent, stately nude with a corkscrew wig. She held a cornucopia in her left hand. The concept of cornucopias as mystical portals that bring things from another dimension into this world intrigued me.

I remarked the symbol is also found in Greek and Roman mythology. Zeus was nourished from the 'horn of plenty' as a child hiding in a cave from his destructive father, Kronos. I then noted in America, cornucopias are a part of harvest celebrations and symbols of abundance.

Slava nodded and pointed to Cleopatra's belly.

"Women, also," he noted.

I never thought of that. Yes! The vagina even looks like a cornucopia through which children come from the 'other side.'

Women are doorways into this world.

It was a compelling insight that struck a clear bell inside me.

I looked up at him with genuine appreciation.

This man had depth.

Slava's eyes appeared green with pretty golden flecks today. He gazed at me softly for a long moment, saying nothing. I unexpectedly felt a deep spiritual connection with him that went far beyond physical attraction. It wasn't love, exactly, more of a sudden recognition of the divine presence of God within him. I was 'seeing' him for the first time, and I liked what I saw.

The moment was profound. I was speechless.

He smiled a big, unreserved, American-style smile. I smiled back at him in wonder.

We soaked in the richness of this moment, feeding an invisible vine growing between us.

And then he laughed. The deep rolling sound of a cheerful bear flooded my soul with waves of comfort and light. The dark empty places that had taken root inside of me drank deeply from his well. I had no idea how much I needed joy until I felt it. And then I wondered how I lived so long without it.

He gave me something I was lacking.

It was a powerful gift.

Suddenly filled with happiness, I started laughing too.

Our behavior drew curious looks from other people in the hall, but I didn't care what anyone thought for once in my life. I felt free!

He took my hands and held them for a moment.

"Cassandra," he said.

"Slava," I replied.

It was as if we were meeting for the first time.

Wow, this man was full of surprises.

He touched my wrist where the crown charm sparkled and danced happily on its slender tether. I'd worn it every day since he'd given it to me. Oddly, Sergei never asked about the bracelet. He didn't even notice. Ugh. Thinking of my moody husband was like a dark cloud passing over the sun on a cold day. I didn't want to spoil the good feeling I had at this moment, so I shooed the thought of him away.

"I love it," I said. "Thank you."

He looked at me with a contented smile.

"Are you ready?" He asked.

"Yes," I replied with a grin.

He put his arm around me and gave me a sideways squeeze as we walked to the next hall, where Lena was waiting. Her eyes brightened to see us, her ruse an apparent success.

"I am starving," she announced. "What's for lunch?"

A twinge of guilt poked my belly as I stepped into Slava's silver Mercedes, but after glancing over my shoulder, I pushed the feeling aside. It was only lunch, I rationalized. Besides, Lena was starving!

We went to a Moroccan restaurant where we sat on cushions at a low table while servers brought various delectable entrees for us to share. The caravan music was lively, the food spicy, and the atmosphere fun. We shared a bottle of Spanish wine. When it was empty, Slava ordered another.

I felt another twist of guilt as I raised the glass of ruby wine to my lips, but when I said 'Shut up, Sergei' in my mind, I felt better.

The wine warmed my heart and eased any further guilty feelings. We took our time enjoying a prolonged mid-day feast. At the end of our meal, the waiter brought a decorative silver pot of sweet Moroccan mint tea. Then a beautiful woman dressed in sexy red Arabian garb stepped in front of our table. We clapped along to the lively drum beat as she danced, performing belly rolls, figure eights with her hips, and other feats of seductive feminine athleticism with the red silk of her costume flowing around her like the flames of a passionate fire. Her bell-covered hip skirt jingled brightly, and she chimed finger cymbals for dramatic counterpoints to the music. I sipped the sweet tea and delighted in the joyful feeling spreading throughout my body. I felt like I was glowing.

I stealthily glanced over the edge of my teacup at Slava's reclining form. He was magnificent! He was so tall, over six feet. His long arms and legs were thick with natural strength that stretched the fabric of his clothing as he moved, offering a teasing glimpse of what lay beneath. Everything about him seemed proportional, just larger than most men. I tried to imagine what he looked like undressed and wondered if he had a lot of chest hair. I hoped he did. When my eyes traveled back up his body to his face, I saw him looking back at me. I blushed, knowing I'd been caught in the act of checking him out, but I didn't care. Our eyes locked, we both smiled at the same time, and then he winked.

Heat flared in my belly as desire gave my vagina a firm anticipatory squeeze. My body was preparing for the inevitable. I knew it was only a matter of time before we finished what we started in the laundry room.

Some things were just meant to be.

Slava had business to return to, so he dropped us off at the museum after lunch. Lena exited the front seat of the car first. As I made my way to the door in the back, he whispered my name. I paused to look at him.

He discreetly passed me a folded up piece of paper and said,

"I hope to see you later."

I quickly tucked the note away before Lena could see it.

"It was nice to see you again, Slava," I said loud enough for Lena to hear. "Thank you again for lunch." I smiled at my subterfuge and stepped out, acting as if nothing unusual had happened.

My stealth ability was definitely improving.

Meanwhile, my pulse was racing with excitement. I couldn't wait to read the note, so I made a beeline for the restroom as soon as we were inside the museum. With a ridiculous amount of eager anticipation, locked in a toilet stall and feeling like a super spy, I carefully opened the note and read the handwritten English words inside.

"I want you. Come at midnight."

I could not believe this was happening! Could I have a clandestine tryst with Slava?

My mind and body both screamed 'Yes!'

I wanted to go, even though I kept seeing Sergei's scowl and hearing his specific order to stay away from Slava. What did he say? 'If you see him, run in the opposite direction?' Right. Why did he have to forbid me to do anything?

Didn't he know forbidden things are the most appealing?

This would be the Grand Prix of getting away with stuff!

I went through internal 'should I?' or 'shouldn't I?' debates for the rest of the day. 'Should' won every time.

Yes, I was married.

Yes, I loved Sergei.

Yes, I'd forsaken all others.

Would I regret it? Probably.

I wanted to do it anyway.

I casually asked Lena which house belonged to Slava, and she pointed it out for me. The Roman house. I guessed correctly on my frozen New Year's morning walk. I took that as a sign I was doing the right thing.

I feigned a headache after dinner and retired to my room early. Ilya was staying in an adjoining room this time, but I knew he would not disturb me unless I called for him. He didn't need to be there, and he knew it. There was no danger to me at Lena's.

I soaked in the tub for a long time to calm my nerves, shaved my legs twice, and blew my hair dry, long and straight. I messed up the bed to make it look slept in. Then I paced the floor until it was time to go. A few minutes before midnight, I went down the back stairway and slipped out of a patio door, leaving it unlocked to sneak back in later.

I walked briskly up the street and nervously tapped on the front door of the Roman house. Slava opened the door, and I stepped inside. We didn't make it past the vestibule. He had me up against the cold door, kissing me passionately as we tore off our clothes with lusty haste.

Slava lifted me by the hips and plunged his massive cock into me. I'd been anticipating him for hours, so I was wet and ready. I felt a satisfying tug of his firmness as I widened and lengthened within to accommodate. The exquisite stretch at the mouth of my vagina lit the flames of a thousand nerve endings. He filled me completely, pushing internal organs out of the way to claim even more space for himself. He lifted me up and down, using gravity to sink deeper with full, vigorous strokes. I never dreamed a man could be strong enough to do that while standing.

I didn't care how he did it. In less than a minute, I started to orgasm. He let out an 'Oof' sound as my strong pelvic muscles started contracting around him. Worried, I looked up at his face and saw his broad grin. Good, he can handle this. I suspected I was a bit of a freak. Some of my muscles get more exercise than others, I thought wickedly.

Slava carried me to a side table and set me down. I cried out, "No!" as he withdrew, but he kissed me quiet. Maybe he was too tall to do both at once, or perhaps he just wanted to slow down and not come too quickly himself. He took my breasts in his hands and massaged them, running his broad fingertips over my tender rock-hard nipples. Then he ran his hands down my sides to my hips. He hastily touched my vulva, orienting himself to my geography, and then took my clit into his mouth, sucking hard, eliciting another spontaneous orgasm.

I saw the surprise in his eyes as he came back up and kissed me again. He pulled me to the edge of the table, cupped his hands behind my rear, and went for re-entry. I cried out his name as he pushed deeper.

"Slava! Oh my God, Slava!"

He was inside my belly, satisfying the deep desire I had for him, the intense longing and the desperate need for whatever it was I couldn't get from Sergei, over and over. He filled my empty places entirely, forcing out the darkness and pain Sergei left behind. He stroked forcefully, banging the table loudly against the wall with every powerful thrust. My voice added to the din, crying out with pleasure.

"Yes! Yes! Yes!" I shouted. "Fuck me harder, Slava!"

My whole body tensed. I saw a shower of shooting stars in my eyes as I came fiercely, my body quivering and shaking, both feet cramping as my pelvic muscles compressed on his cock again and again in a series of multiple orgasms.

It was a do-over of the laundry room on a grand scale. I knew he wasn't disappointed. He gripped my hips and crushed himself into me even further, splaying my legs nearly 180 degrees apart. The tendons in my hips stretched uncomfortably, but I didn't care. I wanted all of him, and I wanted it now. He was a big broad man, and he needed room to maneuver. My job was to give it to him.

Slava jerked as he came inside of me. He shot me an 'Oh no' look, and I felt a stab to my heart. Oops. I hadn't thought about that. I hoped to God he didn't have an STD. Sergei would probably kill me if I gave him one. I had a mental flash of my husband coming at me holding an ax with a scowl on his face. I shuddered at the thought.

Holy shit! I thought soberly.

This was a risky game to play.

He closed his eyes and kissed me, but I didn't feel like kissing him anymore, so I pulled away. I quickly picked up my clothes from the floor and hastily put them on.

I was panicking and about to run out the front door.

"Don't you want to come in for a drink?" He asked.

I paused to look at him. He looked surprised and sounded hurt.

I couldn't believe I did this completely sober.

Maybe one drink wouldn't hurt. I was shaky. Besides, running would not change the facts. What is the etiquette for a midnight rendezvous anyway?

I didn't want to be rude.

He pulled on his slacks, leaving the rest of his clothing in the vestibule, and welcomed me into his home warmly. The imported Italian marble tile floors, sculptures, and fine art were exquisite and tasteful, but I was too dazed to appreciate anything in detail. I asked for vodka, and he poured me a double. I threw it back and asked for more. I tossed that one back too.

"Are you okay?" He asked.

Plump tears welled in my eyes.

"I'm sorry," I said. "I shouldn't be here."

He wrapped me with his strong arms, pulling me into his chest. I noticed it was covered with an impressive mat of black hair, just as I hoped it would be. The gold necklace I spotted in September held a three-barred Russian Orthodox cross pendant over his heart. He was warm and a little damp from the physical exertion, but he smelled clean like he just stepped out of the shower. I listened to his strong heartbeat as he kissed the top of my head reassuringly. He held me until I settled.

The vodka soon kicked in and began to take the edge off.

He brought me into the kitchen and offered me a seat at a wide white marble-topped island. He hummed a melody as he cut thick slices from a round loaf of black bread and dropped them into a toaster.

"No one should drink on an empty stomach," he explained. "You should take better care of yourself."

As peculiar as it was, we were eating crunchy buttered toast in the middle of the night like it was the most normal thing to do after committing adultery. The bread calmed me in a wholesome way, soothing deeper than alcohol could reach.

"What is wrong?" He finally asked.

I just broke my marriage vow to a man I loved so profoundly my soul hurt, a man who would be devastated if he ever found out. A fragile man I did not want to lose. The only promise I didn't break was remembering I was his wife. I was fully aware I was Sergei's wife while I had sex with this man. I didn't even know why I did it. Sergei wasn't perfect. He had mental health problems and was prone to possessiveness and cruelty, but he was a good lover. He went above and beyond his husbandly duty to satisfy me sexually. I didn't need to step out on him. There was no excuse.

"I just cheated on my husband," I confessed softly.

"He doesn't need to know," he said.

My eyes widened.

"He can never know," I urged. "Promise me."

He smiled and gently hugged me.

"Don't worry," he soothed.

He held me silently for a few minutes. Then he chuckled.

"You are amazing, Cassandra," he said.

He took my face in his hands and looked into my eyes.

195

His were golden. They looked soft and dreamy. Eyes I felt I could trust with anything, except perhaps to stay the same color.

"You are amazing too, Slava," I replied with a shy smile.

The truth was he was far more amazing than I ever expected.

He kissed me softly and deeply for several minutes, warming our passion again.

"Let's go upstairs and do this properly," he whispered.

I nodded. I already committed the big sin. Doing it twice would make little difference. If you are going to hell, you might as well have a good story to tell the devil when you get there.

He squeezed my hand and led me upstairs to his room.

Slava's bedroom was the polar opposite of Sergei's. It was light and cheerful with a warm cherry hardwood floor, thick white area rugs, a large bank of windows, and several skylights. A king-size bed piled high with pillows rested atop a built-in platform. The sage green and wheat textiles and cream-colored walls gave this open, inviting room a spa-like feeling.

A loveseat faced a fireplace with a cozy fire infusing the room with a warm glow and a smoky scent. A bottle of champagne in a bucket of ice and two glasses waited on a table beside the loveseat. The romantic scene touched my heart.

Slava opened the champagne with a loud pop sending the cork sailing across the room. He raised his eyebrow comically, which made me laugh, breaking the last bit of tension. I took a few sips of champagne and set my glass aside as we nested on the loveseat.

"Ah, Cassandra, so many nights I spent thinking of you," he said, taking my hands into his and gazing deeply into my eyes. "And here you are."

I smiled as I gazed back at him.

A solid border of dark green encircled the golden center of his iris, now flecked with green. I had no idea how an iris could change color. I made a mental note to research that later.

Slava was the most unusually handsome man.

His eyes were captivating.

He pulled me in to rest my head on his chest with his arm around me as we both faced the fire. He gently stroked my hair, rolling sections around his long fingers as he kissed the top of my head. The fire felt lovely, as did the warmth emanating from him. I was blissfully sandwiched between two divine sources of heat.

Something knotted began to relax at my core.

He sang what sounded like a lullaby, soft and low. The resonance of his voice vibrated through my body and tickled inside my ears with a most pleasant effect. The song was about a little bear in a forest who became angry when a pine cone fell on his head.

When he stopped, I turned to look up at him, and we kissed softly, easily, taking all the time in the world to savor the taste and precious feel of a new lover. He ran his tongue over my bottom lip and sucked it playfully, producing a deep pleasure sound from within me.

With half-closed eyes, he said,

"Let's go to bed."

We undressed and slipped under the covers, meeting in the middle to explore each other in the most sensual way. I ran my hands through the soft black hair on his chest while he kissed and nudged my neck with his nose while murmuring gentle words I scarcely comprehended. I massaged his muscular arms and shoulders, noting how mighty he was and yet, how tender. This big man did not need to dominate. He simply wanted to enjoy me.

Slava ran his hands along my back and pulled me closer for sweet kisses, lavishing them on me like a princess. He kissed me from my forehead to my belly button, and then he rolled me over so he could kiss the back of my neck, firing tiny sparks of feelings wherever he went. He reached around the front to cradle and gently massage my breasts. I felt cherished, and I gave myself over to the sensuality of it, feeling each previously unknown nerve ending pop with sweet, unhurried bliss.

I sighed deeply. A woman could get used to this royal treatment.

His fingers traced the outline of the brand on my lower back, and I stiffened. I'd forgotten the mark of my shame. He muttered "*zhivotnoye,*" the Russian word for 'animal' as he massaged the skin in gentle strokes, trying to heal the scarred flesh with the power of his fingertips. I looked over my shoulder worriedly, and he rolled me back over to face him.

"I am sorry, Sandrushka," he sighed, his eyes misty.

"It wasn't your fault," I said as I reached up to run my hands through his hair and appreciate the planes of his handsome face from the closer view.

"You were worth it," I added with a wink, suddenly feeling friskier.

197

"Was I?" He asked, scratching his chin and looking upward, pretending he'd forgotten the night we met and was trying to remember.

"Oh yes," he recalled with a wink, "You were the woman who ruined my favorite pants."

Yes. I was a bad wife indeed.

He was completely innocent.

I pummeled his chest playfully with my fists to jog his memory.

He rolled on top, squishing me gently, careful to hold up his weight with his forearms. I opened my legs in invitation, and he slipped inside me. He made love to me slowly, gently.

Then he moved his hands beneath my hips and rolled onto his back, taking me with him, still joined together. I planted my feet beside his hips and rode him gently, moaning,

"Mmmm, Slava, I love the way you feel inside of me."

He grinned with his eyes half-closed with pleasure.

I'm sure the view was good too, imagining what I looked like from his perspective with my breasts bouncing up and down with each stroke.

Every inch of him stroked inward, filling me with pleasure. I rode the narrow ridge of ecstasy for a while, building toward a powerful climax. I finally exploded into a billion stars, a new universe forming from a second big bang.

My mind flashed with insights about relationships as celestial bodies drifting away from each other, cooling off, until they come around again in their orbits to warm up and reconnect. I saw relationships and lifetimes, cycles that keep repeating. This wasn't the first time I was in Russia. We'd all been together before, all three of us, in another lifetime.

Sergei may have found me first, but I belonged to them both.

In that instant, I believed anything was possible, everything was okay, and all would be forgiven. I was exactly where I was supposed to be.

Of that, I was sure.

I opened my eyes with a new perspective on the world and gazed at the face of my new lover, reveling in the joy and wonder I found there. He reached up and pulled me close, down to his chest. He rolled back on top and kept stroking at a pace he found pleasing until he reached his own climax, coming inside of me a second time.

Afterward, we lay side by side holding hands, looking up at the darkened skylights in the ceiling, allowing our breathing to calm as our bodies cooled.

Life kept surprising me.
Either I was suddenly supremely spiritual or completely delusional.
I preferred the first explanation.

16

HOT SLAVA X2

A fierce gust of wind struck my face as I slipped out of Slava's front door. The excited air whipped my hair wildly around my head and blew bits of salty grit into my eyes. The wind smelled like the sea swirled with a trace of cigarette smoke. An electrical charge lifted the fine hairs on my arms. Flashes of blue light lit the sky to the west. I wrapped my fur coat tightly around me and hurried back to Lena's. The first bolt of lightning struck as I opened the patio door. Then a sudden deluge fell from the sky the moment I stepped inside. I stood at the door watching the storm for some time, marveling at the ferocity with which the rain slapped the earth. Great arcs of lightning speared from the sky.

Zeus is angry tonight, I thought, awed by the power and majesty of nature. When I made it back to my room and crawled into the cold bed, it was after 4:00 am.

When I woke hours later, nearly two feet of fresh snow covered the ground from the passage of a strong springtime cold front. I was pleased to see the thick blanket of white covering my crimes from the night before. The sun shone brightly, and the world looked clean and new.

Lena was at her laptop at the kitchen table when I went downstairs.

"Good morning!" She said warmly, "How are you feeling?"

"Wonderful," I answered enthusiastically.

She raised an eyebrow, knowing something was up. I was not known for morning cheerfulness.

"Did you, and...?" She asked, knowingly making the 'big muscles' gesture to represent Ilya. He was a convenient treat she probably would not have passed up.

"*Mon Dieu, non!*" I laughed.

"But I do have a secret...," I teased.

She looked at me expectantly.

"Coffee first," I said, helping myself to a cup of the black stuff and taking a sip before I spoke.

"And?" She asked.

"This is big. You have to swear to keep my secret." I demanded.

"*Oui, Oui*, absolutely, what is it?" She asked excitedly.

"Pinky swear," I said in English, holding out my hooked little finger. She joined her pinky to mine, and we shook on it. That made the oath binding.

Looking over my shoulder to make sure we were alone, I breathed, "X"

"*C'est quoi, ça?* Oh my God, darling, that is wonderful!" She exclaimed, beaming.

"When?" She asked.

"I went to him last night," I confessed.

"What about...*beurk?*" She frowned, not wanting to speak Sergei's name. He wasn't worth a secret letter to her.

My heart sank, the reality of the situation bursting the bubble of my happiness. I would have to end the affair with Slava.

Why couldn't I have them both?

Sergei was coming home from Turkey tomorrow night. I had one more night at Lena's before I would face my husband with a heart laden with secrets. How could I possibly hide something so big from him? He knew me so well.

I shivered in the warm sunlight.

Lena looked at me with sympathy shining in her eyes. No doubt she'd had similar dilemmas.

"We still have today, darling. What do you want to do?"

I glanced outside to see Ilya smoking a cigarette as he shoveled a path to the door. A great plume of smoke swirled around his head as he exhaled. I

201

noticed a truck had already been by to plow the street, and the driveway was clear. There was nothing to keep us in.

Lena and I spent the afternoon at the museum, and then we met Piotr for a lavish dinner out in the city. We walked the brightly lit Nevsky Prospekt avenue and along the bank of the Neva River, enjoying St. Petersburg's colorfully painted illuminated buildings and their charming reflections dancing cheerfully upon the water. The city had an elegance that transcended time. They call St. Petersburg the Venice of the North, and it was easy to see why. The river and canals crisscrossed throughout the city.

At last, we returned home and called it an early night. I gave Ilya the slip again and knocked quietly on Slava's door precisely at midnight. The door opened instantly, and I stepped from the cold right into his warm embrace. He hugged me hard, lifted me off the floor, and spun me around, his face beaming.

"Ah, Sandrushka," he exclaimed, kissing me wildly.

We ran upstairs and fell into each other on the bed, fumbling with clothing, kissing, and touching everywhere in our desire to melt into each other. If this would be the last time we could be together, I wanted to make it count. I cried out in pleasure as he pushed his penis into me, calling his name.

"Slava!" I cried again as he drove himself deeper.

I loved his name and the way he felt, the touch of his hands, the feel of his body on mine, his kisses on my lips, deep smoky voice, and sexy words in my ears. Everything about him was pure pleasure, comfort, and joy. I wanted to connect with this great man, to feel him fill me with his happiness, and never let it go. I rode a spiral of pleasure to a pinnacle peak. I clung to the edge for a moment, marveling at the height, then suddenly broke free and crashed like an avalanche in a wave of ecstasy, flowing down the steep slope, taking imaginary villages and trees with me as I went.

Slava was caught up in my cascade and lost control too. He came thundering down Pleasure Mountain alongside me. We lay exhausted and breathless, side by side, gazing into each other's eyes for a long time.

"Stay," he requested.

"You know I can't," I replied softly, looking away.

He took me into his arms and kissed me, holding onto me tight.

"I can't bear the thought of you with him," he finally spoke. "I will worry every minute you are there."

I was worried too. Sergei's moods were unpredictable, and he was potentially violent, but he was still my husband. I had to go home. I hoped I could mask my guilt. Assuming I could get away with it, what would happen next?

"Why does he hate you so much?" I asked finally.

Slava chuckled softly.

"Your husband does not like to lose. I beat him on a big deal a few years ago, and he never got over it," he explained.

That sounded like Sergei.

"Do you know his secret?" He asked somberly.

I shook my head, no.

"He has a thing for beating up prostitutes," he said softly, watching for a reaction, ready to catch me emotionally if needed.

"He told me about a girl in Holland," I said. "Have there been others?"

Slava nodded, looking ill. He knew more than he was saying but did not want to be the one to tell me.

"Everyone was surprised when he brought a pretty wife home from America," he said. "No one thought Sergei was the marrying kind. He did not date. He never had a girlfriend."

That explained why everyone seemed so worried about me.

I supposed I could hire a private detective to get the story from an unbiased source. Ilya would probably know someone.

I wondered if it was still going on.

Slava seemed to know what I was thinking. He asked,

"With so many opportunities to build a new Russia, why would he need to travel so far, so often?"

I felt as if someone punched me in the stomach. The implication in his words rang true. I always thought it was odd Sergei never invited me to join him on his trips. Before we married, I assumed we would be traveling around the world together. No one can do business 24 hours a day. What did he do with all of his free time? I felt sick.

And yet, incredibly, a part of me could not accept this. I was defensive. Sergei wasn't perfect, but he had many fine qualities. I loved him. As a psychologist, could I have misjudged him so completely? Surely he wasn't the monster he was being made out to be. That was impossible. I would have known!

Perhaps Slava was trying to make Sergei look bad, so he could take me as a prize, rubbing it in his rival's face he could take his deals and his woman. It would be the ultimate victory for a vindictive man.

I was being expertly played.

Alarm bells started to ring in my head. I bolted upright, suddenly aware of my nakedness. I was Sergei's wife, and he was coming home tomorrow. I was in bed with his enemy, whose sperm was swimming around inside of me. The invisible hands of anxiety circled my neck, choking my breath. With my heart pounding, I looked around in a panic.

I had to get out of here!

Where were my clothes?!

Slava gripped my shoulders with his gigantic hands and pulled me into him. I fought to pull away, but he held me firmly, gently pressing his mouth to my ear, saying,

"Tssss Sandrushka. It's okay. Tssss."

A lump the size of a fist formed in my throat. I fought to hold back the well of tears that were building inside of me.

I wanted to be strong. I needed to be strong for Sergei.

I kept trying to shove the lump back down to my stomach, but it wouldn't budge until it suddenly broke loose. Great sobs racked my body as a flood of tears spilled onto Slava's furry chest. He held me firmly, patiently, never letting go until the last tear fell. A great river of feelings rushed through me. Disappointment in my great beautiful love, memories of the mistreatment I suffered at my husband's hands, and shameful feelings of my betrayal mixed with grief and raw fear of what would happen when Sergei found out. Eventually, the torrent slowed to a stream and then to a trickle. Finally, I turned to face Slava and felt a warm glow of gratitude when I saw his reassuring smile and kind eyes.

"It's not your fault you fell for a Russian," he said proudly. "But you shouldn't have married the first one you met."

I couldn't believe he was teasing me in this vulnerable moment, but the humor caught me by surprise. It was true, of course. I'd fallen for Sergei hook, line, and sinker like a silly schoolgirl. I started laughing at my foolishness, and he joined me, his great belly laugh vibrating the broken pieces of my heart back into place.

We locked eyes, staring silently at each other for a moment before we began kissing passionately again. We made love at a leisurely pace, feeding our emotional connection, seeking pleasure of a different kind. I held off my orgasm until I felt him start to jerk, signaling his imminent release. Then I liberated the full fury of my climax on him in his critical moment, my vagina gripping and squeezing him while he came. A look of intense pleasure passed over his face. Perhaps he'd never seen that trick before, I thought with naughty satisfaction. I may have been the most naïve woman in human history, but there were a few things I learned to do well.

"I have a surprise for you," he said. "Stay here," he wrapped himself in a robe and stepped out of the room.

I propped myself up into a comfortable seated position and wondered what it could be. Suddenly a tiny white dog bounded into the room and jumped from a low bench onto the bed, a male Maltese with a short cut. The appearance of the little pooch was totally unexpected. I was delighted! He yipped and came onto my lap for petting. I was beside myself with joy to see the sweet little creature. Slava was leaning against the doorframe watching with a smile.

"His name is *Snezhok*," he said. "Snowball."

I laughed and said,

"Hello, *Snezhok*! What a handsome boy you are!"

Slava came back to bed, and *Snezhok* snuggled between us.

My heart melted to see the enormous man fuss over the delicate five-pound creature.

Once the little dog settled, Slava looked at me with a worried expression and asked,

"What is the plan?"

I thought for a minute and said,

"I have to go home. I can't leave my marriage without giving it serious thought."

"I'm sorry if you are disappointed," I added.

The pain on his face told me that he was.

He nodded, stoically accepting my decision.

What else could I do?

It was hard to imagine a path to a future together that didn't include Sergei detonating like a nuclear bomb and killing us all.

"I promise to call or email to let you know I am okay, but I don't know when I will be able to see you again," I said with regret.

I bit my lower lip. Slava deserved so much more than a married woman to hook up with from time to time. I was terrified to face Sergei with what I had already done. I couldn't imagine being able to keep the secret of an ongoing affair from him.

He hugged me and pressed his warm forehead to mine, lending me some of his strength.

"If you don't call me tomorrow night to let me know you are safe, I will come with an army to get you," he vowed.

I smiled a sad smile.

"I wish I could make you a promise," I said softly.

He saw me to the door.

"Be safe, Sandrushka. I will pray for you," he said sincerely.

"*Spasibo*, Slava," I said, standing on my tiptoes to kiss him goodbye.

"*Spokoynoy nochi*," I added.

Silent tears streamed down my face as I walked away from comfort and joy back to my life of shame and humiliation.

I loved them both so much.

17

TAKING THE BMW TO TOWN

Ilya was surprised by my request, but he knew someone who could do detective work in St. Petersburg. We stopped to meet his contact on our way back to the farm.

The grimy bar he pulled up to was near the port. Massive cargo ships were docked just a few blocks away amid a mountain of shipping containers. The air smelled of rotting fish. Rough-looking men sat at the bar, staring blankly at the TV hung on in the corner. There wasn't much conversation. This was the kind of place people come to drink their troubles away when fun is no longer an option. Business was good.

Anton Ruslanovich was a blond man in his 40s with a blotchy pockmarked face, pale blue eyes, and thinning hair. He wore a black Adidas tracksuit complete with a thick gold chain around his neck and eight massive gold rings on his fingers, four on each hand. I chuckled to myself at his stereotypical look, but there he was, a real live *Gopnik* in the flesh.

Ilya made the introduction and stepped away to give me privacy. Anton knew just enough English to make our conversation easier. I gave him Sergei's name and photograph. I asked him to find out if he was frequenting brothels in the city, if he hurt any of the girls and when he had last been there. He said, *"Da,* no problem." His rate was $500 American. I paid him $200 in advance. He said he would have a report for me in a few days.

That was easier than I expected, I thought as I walked out with Ilya. I felt more like a secret agent than ever.

At last, I was home with a few hours to kill before Sergei arrived. I wanted to call Slava and tell him I loved him but thought better of it. You don't tell someone 'I love you' over the phone the first time. I am just nervous, and everything will work out fine. I lied to myself.

I brought carrots out to the horses and petted them as I told them my troubles. Horses are good therapists. I liked the smell of the barn. The earthy smell of hay and manure soothed my soul and grounded me. Then I played with Velikan and Kukla, throwing snowballs for them to catch mid-air. The spring snow was clumpy, so I made a snow woman outside the library, complete with boobs, straw hair, and red pepper lips. I faced it toward the window so that Sergei would see it. Hopefully, it would make him smile. With less than an hour to go before he arrived, I went back indoors.

I planned to be in the bath. That way, I'd be relaxed, and any residual evidence from my affair would soak away. Being naked was a bonus. Who doesn't love a nude woman? The sight of breasts alone is enough to stop most people in their tracks. It was the perfect plan. With a bit of luck, he would be so distracted by my squeaky clean exterior he would completely overlook the enormous stain on my heart.

I was soaking in my beautiful bathtub overlooking the forest, surrounded by bubbles, candles, and the soft notes of Tibetan flute music, when I heard Sergei call my name.

"I'm in the bath," I sang out. "Please, come in."

He leaned over the tub to give me a little kiss on the lips. He was handsome in his unbuttoned white dress shirt and gray dress slacks, but he looked exhausted. The dark circles under his eyes were all I needed to see to know the Istanbul project was still not going well. I knew not to ask. It was like asking someone how their dissertation was coming.

Don't ask.

He made it abundantly clear that if he wanted to talk about something, he would bring it up. Sergei did not like to be questioned.

He moved the stool from the vanity beside the tub and sat down.

"Would you like to join me?" I offered sweetly, bringing my knees up to my chest to make room for two.

He shook his head no.

After a few minutes of silence, I opened the drain, feeling the heaviness of my body return as the water receded. I rinsed in the glass-walled shower and wrapped myself in a towel. Sergei watched me with distant eyes, his mind elsewhere. I wondered if his soul was still traveling and hadn't yet caught up to his body.

I removed his shirt and massaged his neck and shoulders with eucalyptus scented oil. His muscles were very tense. I couldn't recall ever seeing him this drained before, and I was genuinely concerned for his health. I gave him a good long massage until, at last, he seemed to loosen up a little.

"Are you hungry?" I asked.

"*Nyet*," he replied.

"You look tired, Seryozha. Would you like to lie down?" I asked. It was only 4:00 pm, but he'd obviously had a difficult day.

He nodded.

I helped him out of his clothes and into bed. I'd never seen him so out of it. He was like a zombie. I slid into bed and cuddled with him until he fell asleep. Then I watched his face as he breathed softly, his eyelids fluttering with dreams. He seemed so innocent, almost childlike.

I remembered what I had done with Slava Valkov and scolded myself for letting passion get the best of me. I felt pangs of guilt for betraying my marriage. If I had been able to restrain myself, I would not be in my current predicament. I felt weak, childish, and deeply ashamed.

And yet, as I lay next to my sleeping husband, I found myself thinking of Slava's great laugh and the way I felt when I was with him, warm, safe, and happy. I closed my eyes and saw his broad handsome face. I remembered the way his skin smelled and how good it felt to kiss him. A flush of warmth filled me.

Even if things didn't work out with Slava, I wanted to love a man like him – someone who could laugh and cry and share the ups and downs of life in a healthy way. As much as I loved Sergei, I was exhausted by him. I was always tense and walking on eggshells trying to avoid the next blowout. Our relationship wasn't sustainable on its present course. We were bound to crash and burn.

Some relationships come with expiration dates, I thought bitterly.

At that moment, I chose. I decided I wanted a chance at a real relationship with Slava, but only if I could let Sergei down easy. That seemed impossible. I racked my brain for a solution and came up with nothing.

So I decided to pray for help. I cringed at the irony of an unfaithful wife asking for favors, but maybe God would take pity on my situation. If not, perhaps I would give God a good laugh and get back into grace that way. Either way, I figured it couldn't hurt to ask.

Old fashioned kneeling-by-the-bed praying never seemed to do anything for me, so I went outside to stand before God in the cathedral of the Great Russian sky. The weather was clear for a change, and the sky lit with innumerable stars. I took that as a good sign. I kissed the prayer into my hands and lifted my arms to release it.

That's when I noticed the ethereal blue and green curtains of the aurora borealis appear to the north. I stood motionless for a long time, bearing silent witness to the miraculous display. How lucky was I to be alive in this time and place to see this? I asked philosophically.

'Because you were meant to,' came a reply from somewhere deep inside me.

What was that? I wondered. Nothing like that had ever happened to me before. Was it God talking back to me or some kind of inner guidance? I knew it wasn't an auditory hallucination because I didn't actually hear a voice, more like words forming inside my mind. As odd as it was, the message made me feel sure I was on the right path. Calm and steadfast, I made my way back inside.

I called Slava from the phone in the kitchen to let him know I was safe. I told him my decision and explained my desire to make my departure easy on Sergei. I didn't know how to do that yet. He was worried, but I promised him everything would work out if for no other reason than it had to.

A few hours later, I called Jack Hawthorne to check in. When I asked how he was doing, he burst into tears. Between sobs, he told me Jean found out about his affair and kicked him out. He went to see his Japanese girlfriend and told her he wanted to move in. She broke up with him, saying she didn't want a full-time boyfriend. His wonderful, albeit deceitful life dissolved within a matter of hours, losing both of his loves at once. My heart broke for him. While he spoke, I silently crossed my chest and asked God to protect me from a similar fate. I didn't bother telling him about my affair. It didn't seem as exciting now. I hung up the phone feeling more than a little freaked out by the timing of Jack's bad news and started having second thoughts about my plan.

Sergei was up early the following day making calls in the library. He barely glanced at me when I brought in the tea and bowl of hot kasha he requested. I didn't understand Turkish, but I knew things were going horribly wrong by his tone. He was visibly shaken. When he ended the call, I asked what was happening.

"It's complicated. I can't talk to you about it," Sergei replied.

"Why not? Maybe I can help," I offered.

I hated seeing him so upset.

He shot me a warning look. I knew better, but I persisted.

"Whatever it is can't be worth all of this," I said. "Why don't you just cut your losses and get out of Istanbul?"

"I can't do that," he said simply, slamming a folder down on the desk for emphasis.

His cold stare told me this discussion was over.

Frustrated, I threw my hands up in the air and walked out.

All I knew was he bought a shipping company, fired the management team, and put new people in to run the place. What could be going on to cause this kind of trouble? I had no idea.

Clearly, this was not the best time to tell him I was leaving our marriage for his arch-enemy. I wanted to get it over with as soon as possible, but I had to find the least hurtful way to do it. I still could not conceive of a scenario that did not end horribly.

Ilya was bored, as always, so he eagerly agreed when I asked him to go skiing. I tossed a thermos of hot tea into a backpack along with some snacks. The surprise late spring snow was quick and fun to glide over. We went two hours out, farther than we'd gone before, and stopped for a break. I wondered if Uvar might have said something to him about what was happening in Istanbul, so I asked, but Ilya didn't know anything.

I was at home in the wilderness, sitting on a fallen tree, drinking tea with my special friend. There was so much about being here that I would miss. I was already planning the summer vegetable garden and drawing up plans for landscaping the house. I choked up, thinking about how much I would miss Ilya. Would I ever see him again? Then there were the horses and dogs. I would have to let them go too. Everything belonged to Sergei. It would be hard to go back to living in an apartment after getting used to the expanse out here. Then, of course, there was Sergei. I would miss him the most. A dagger point jabbed my heart. I cleared my throat and shifted my thoughts before I started to cry.

I needed a distraction, so I asked Ilya if I could shoot his gun. He gave me a funny look and then nodded. Why not? We were so far out in the woods, and no one would hear the shots back at the house anyway. I'd plinked cans with a rifle back in the States, but I never held a handgun before.

The weight of the black weapon was impressive in my hand. It felt dangerous, cold, and deadly.

"Sig Sauer P226," he stated.

Ilya took the gun back and pointed to the various parts as he named them.

"Muzzle, barrel, slide, hammer, trigger guard, trigger, front sight, rear sight, grip, magazine release."

He pressed the release, and a cartridge loaded with bullets popped out. He eyed me for a second and then pushed it back into place with a click.

"Nine millimeter," he noted.

Then he demonstrated the stance, legs shoulder-width apart, right foot back a little opening the hips to the right, right hand on the grip first, pointer finger on the trigger guard, left fingers locked over the first set on the grip to support the weight of the gun. He held his arms out with his elbows slightly bent and held the gun level as he looked down the front and rear sights with his right eye.

We were both right-handed, so we matched. I supposed everything would be reversed for lefties.

He looked at me for confirmation, and I nodded, got it.

Then he set a thick dead branch vertically against the fallen log we'd just been sitting on, and we backed up about 20 feet.

"Show me," he said, handing me the gun.

I mimicked his stance and wrapped both hands around the gun as he had.

"Good," he said, moving my left thumb down a little to rest in the niche below the slide.

"Hold the grip firmly and keep tension between your hands, pulling slightly away from each other to reduce the kick," he counseled.

He stepped behind me and wrapped his thick arms around to support my forearms from below. The firmness of his warm chest pressed into my back covered me in a feeling of safety. The moisture from his breath teased my left ear as he spoke.

"A soldier keeps both eyes open to see a threat coming. Look down the sights with just your right eye until the target is just above the front sight," he instructed. "Understand?"

I nodded.

He pulled back the slide to pop one round from the magazine up into the chamber.

"Do not pull the trigger. Ease it back gently until it fires," Ilya instructed.

"Okay," I replied.

"One more thing. Pay attention to your breathing. Breathe normally and fire after the exhale pause. Try to relax."

As if I could relax with death in the form of metal in my hands!

"Ready?" he asked.

I couldn't believe how exciting this was!

"Yes," I replied soberly. Good soldiers do not gush with excitement.

"Line it up and take your shot," he said into my ear.

He remained wrapped around me, his supportive arms in place.

I firmed up my stance, gripped the gun tighter, added tension between my hands as he suggested, feeling the muscles in my forearms activate. Then I took my time lining up the shot, waited for my next exhalation, and gingerly eased the trigger towards me. The trigger went back farther than I expected, then the gun suddenly fired. The branch exploded with a loud 'Boom' that reverberated through the silent snow-laden forest.

A surge of adrenaline coursed through me.

"*Molodets!*" Ilya praised, smiling.

I laughed. I did it!

"Show me what you can do," I encouraged as I handed him the gun, careful to keep the barrel pointed well away from him.

He set up a row of tiny pinecones upright along the fallen tree and backed up to 30 feet. He stretched out on his belly in the snow like a sniper. I watched him take aim and fire the deadly weapon with expert precision. He picked them off one by one. Pleased with his work, he looked up and smiled proudly.

I beamed back, clapping my hands.

"Well done!" I exclaimed. "You are amazing!"

Damn, he's hot, I thought, as a volcanic surge of heat erupted in my lady parts. How easy would it be to make love with him right here, outdoors, with no one around for miles? All I would have to do is hold his gaze for 20 seconds, make out with him again, and our clothes would probably burn off from the steam. I immediately scolded myself. I was in enough trouble with one lover. I could never handle two, especially this precious one living under Sergei's roof. Was I going to cheat on Slava while I cheated on Sergei? What a mess I am! Maybe Sergei was right about me after all. So I stuffed those lusty feelings into a vault and told myself *'Druz'ya'* to lock the door.

This one had to stay 'Friends.'

On the way back to the farm, I noticed the buds on branches were thickening and shrubs developing a reddish color. There was still plenty of snow on the ground, but it was early April, and the signs were there. Spring gave my heart hope. After living like a mole these past few months, I looked forward to those super long summer days again.

Sergei was packing his suitcase when I returned to the house.

"You have to go back already?" I asked incredulously.

He did not seem happy about it either.

"I'm sorry, Sandra," he said, remorse weighing heavily in his voice.

He paused for a moment, actually stopping to look at me.

"You must have missed me," he said softly.

"I always miss you when you are away," I replied truthfully.

"I don't have much time, but...," he said with a familiar spark in his tired eyes.

He pulled me close and kissed me. I was sweaty from the extended trek, but he didn't seem to mind. His hands were all over me, and before I knew it, we were in bed making love with a heart-to-heart connection we had not shared in a long time. When we finally came to stillness, he stayed inside me for a minute and said,

"I love you, Sandrochka. I hope you never forget."

Tears welled in my eyes.

"I love you too, Seryozha!" I replied sincerely.

Twin trails of tears ran down from the outside corners of my eyes.

"Don't worry," he said, "I will always come home to you," actually showing sensitivity to my feelings.

A dagger stabbed my heart. He wasn't hopeless after all.

Sergei kissed me one last time, and then he was gone.

My heart exploded with pain.

I still loved him!

I waited until the following day to call Slava. I wasn't as settled in my decision and wanted to talk it over. I packed an overnight bag and went downstairs. When I told Ilya I was going to St. Petersburg for the weekend, he strongly objected,

"No, Cassie, please don't leave!"

I shook my head. Who was he to tell me what to do?

"Take me with you," he pleaded.

I was shocked and replied,

"Americans drive cars and go places on their own, Ilya. I am from New York!"

He glared, his face red, clearly fuming.

"Sergei can speak to me directly if he has a problem with my decision," I added as I turned and walked away.

No doubt he would, I thought, but I no longer cared. I had a cell phone now, and they both knew the number.

I was well within my rights, but the argument unsettled me and made me question what I was doing. I didn't expect Ilya to be upset. Why was he so upset? Was I really in so much danger I needed a man to escort me everywhere I went? Screw that, I concluded as I started the BMW. I am an independent woman, and I will do as I please!

After turning onto the highway with an open road ahead of me, I pressed the pedal to the floor, feeling a surge of energy flow through me. The brawny engine practically hummed with vigor. The car was responsive, and so was I. My heart raced as adrenaline flowed through me, lifting the fine hairs on my body with excitement. I was in the driver's seat for a change, and the power felt incredible!

The tough-looking guard at the gate phoned Slava to clear me to enter the highly secure enclave. I smiled at myself in the review mirror, watching the gate close behind me, knowing my husband would not be able to follow me here. Slava's garage door opened as I pulled in the driveway, and I parked inside for discretion. Not even Lena knew I was here. She probably wouldn't

215

have recognized the red beamer because we'd always taken the Mercedes SUV to the city. I don't understand why Sergei was so paranoid. If anyone wanted to kill us, they would find a way around an armored vehicle.

As I rushed to my lover's embrace, all thoughts of Sergei and his control issues vanished. I lost myself inside the light of Slava's golden eyes as he gave me a bear hug. We kissed happily, right there in the garage.

Oh, how I had missed him!

Yes! This is definitely what my heart wants!

Snowball greeted me inside the house with happy yips and ran circles around my legs. He was wearing a light blue sweater with white snowflakes stitched onto it. I was beside myself with joy to see the endearing tiny creature. Slava picked him up with one hand and held him close to his chest, scratching the pup's little head gently. Snowball's tongue hung from his mouth sideways, and he was panting, clearly deserving the title of happiest dog on earth. I'd never seen anything so adorable as the enormous man with his little buddy. Everything was right in my world, at least for the moment.

Slava led me to a cozy sitting room with two overstuffed chairs, a fireplace, and floor-to-ceiling bookcases lining three walls. A stack of old newspapers rested next to one of the chairs, telling me at a glance which one was his. The wear on the preferred chair further indicated this was a favorite room, and the complete lack of wear on the other told me visitors were rare.

Sunlight streamed through wooden blinds throwing horizontal bars of warm light across the room. A steaming pot of tea and a plate of cookies offered more inviting warmth as I settled into the comfy chair facing the worn one. I poured from a porcelain teapot elegantly painted in cobalt blue on white. The design resembled a fishing net with golden accents wherever the blue strands crossed. Slava took lemon and sugar with his tea. I prepared mine to match his.

Snowball quickly settled and fell asleep on the giant's thigh as we spoke. Such a good dog, he didn't even beg for a treat.

"What happened?" Slava asked after taking his first sip, looking at me over the brim of the cup.

There wasn't much to tell.

"Sergei came home from Turkey completely exhausted and left again in the morning," I replied. "He is dealing with a disaster in Istanbul, but I don't know what is going on."

I shook my head sadly and looked down.

"Sandrushka," he gently intoned, calling my attention back.

I looked up to see the concern in his eyes.

"I wanted to tell him about us, Slava, but I didn't know how to. He is my husband. Of course, I still care for him. I can't kick him when he is down. I owe him that much."

Tears started forming in my eyes, so I glanced away again, this time to the bookcase. The title Анна Каренина jumped out, recognizable even in the Cyrillic letters. I read Tolstoy's Anna Karenina in my youth and knew the story. Just because Anna's extramarital affair ended poorly didn't mean mine would. I was nothing like Anna. I had options. I could always go home to the United States and call my time in Russia cultural 'field experience' to boost my career in Psychology.

The surprise lift in confidence pleased me immensely. Knowing we'd read some of the same novels made me feel more connected with Slava. When I turned my attention back, he was waiting patiently for me to continue.

"I don't feel safe telling him at the farm," I added. The threat of being trapped within those brick walls with a madman was an unstated concern we shared.

Slava sipped from his teacup again and set it down.

"Packing my things and leaving when he isn't there seems too cold," I explained, exhaling sadly.

I glanced down at my bright pink socks, then back up to Slava. I'd left my leather boots by the garage when I entered the house.

"I prayed and asked for God's help," I finished.

He didn't say anything, but his slight nod encouraged me to continue.

I finished my tea and poured us some more.

I leaned back into the chair with my cup and spoke freely.

"I can tell him I need space and separate from him, rent an apartment in St. Petersburg, give him time to adjust and let him down gently. I have another year left on my book deal and some savings, so I can support myself. I may not be able to stay in Russia once I am divorced. But at least we will have time to get to know each other and see where our relationship is going, right?"

This sounded like a reasonable plan to me, but when he lifted his eyes, sadness had darkened them.

217

"What's wrong?" I asked.

He just shook his head and looked down.

"Slava?" I asked, moving to kneel by his chair so I could look up into his face. I put my hand on his knee.

"I want you, Sandrushka. I want you here with me," he said finally. "Why do you want to live in an apartment?"

Good question.

"I don't," I replied truthfully.

"Don't you think it's wrong for a woman to leave her husband and move in with another man?" I asked. "What will people think?"

"I don't care," he replied.

I studied his face for a moment and realized he was a lonely man.

"Why aren't you married?" I asked softly.

"I was," he replied. "We divorced a year ago."

"What happened?" I asked.

He shook his head.

"She was never happy. We fought constantly," Slava explained sadly.

"I am so sorry," I said, giving his leg a gentle hug, careful not to disturb sleeping Snowball.

I had difficulty imagining anyone not being happy with this charming man. His personality was so much easier than Sergei's.

"Do you have children?" I asked.

"Not living," he replied, his voice touched with regret. "My son died when he was two years old."

My heart broke in empathy as tears sprung to his eyes.

"Oh no," I said. "What happened?"

"He was born with a heart defect. They tried to fix it, but he died during surgery."

He drew a deep breath and shook his head sadly.

"Alexei was sickly from birth," he continued. "My son was always tired, and he didn't grow like other children. Alexei even looked a little blue. After he died, my wife was done. She did not want to have any more children."

I understood why she would feel that way.

"I couldn't do anything to help him. I was completely powerless," he added softly.

218

Tears were streaming down his cheeks. I retrieved a box of tissues from the bookshelf and handed him one. Slava dabbed his eyes and blew his nose, then smiled at me sadly.

"Oh, Slava," I said gently, taking his right hand in both of mine, "that sounds unbearably painful."

Losing a child is one of the worst things that can happen. I couldn't imagine how much pain he'd experienced. I hugged him and pressed my cheek against his. When I pulled back to look at his face, he nodded and looked at me stoically. He was fine. This was an old wound, but one that would never fully heal. How unfortunate it was for him to lose his child and then his wife. What a strain the death of their son must have been on their marriage.

We sat in silence for several minutes.

"Do you mind me asking? How old are you?" I asked finally, making this the last question. I didn't want him to feel interrogated.

"43," he replied. "You?"

"29," I answered.

Fourteen years was a pretty big difference, but it wasn't a deal-breaker as far as I was concerned. Slava was an intelligent, educated man with broad interests and a big heart. Those qualities outranked the difference in age for me.

I returned to my chair, sipped my tea, and thought. I decided I didn't care what people thought either. My mother would give me an earful for leaving my husband no matter what Slava and I decided to do.

"Are you sure you want me to move in with you?" I asked finally.

His eyes lit up.

"Yes," he replied enthusiastically.

"Okay, then that's the plan," I said, smiling. Lena is going to pee her pants over this. We will be neighbors!

A few minutes later, my cell phone rang. I excused myself and looked at the number. St. Petersburg. Relieved it wasn't Sergei calling to scold me for taking off with his car, I answered. The caller was Anton Ruslanovich, who said he had a report for me. We agreed to meet in an hour.

I asked Slava if he would take me to meet the detective, and he did not hesitate. Soon we were on our way to the Port of St. Petersburg in his silver Mercedes sedan. The big man needed no bodyguard and drove his own car. I could not have asked for a better escort.

Slava stood at the bar while I spoke with Anton at a nearby table.

"I have bad news for you," he said. "This guy, no good."

I swallowed hard and nodded for him to continue.

"He beat up at least 15 girls in St. Petersburg. Three went to hospital. He was told, no return."

I felt sick.

And then he pulled out a photograph of one of the girls, and I actually started to gag on the contents of my stomach. I jumped up and ran outside, taking deep gulps of cold air trying to stuff the puke back down to my gut. I closed my eyes but could not shut the image out. The young woman's face was beaten severely, with laccrations, black eyes, and puffy dark bruising everywhere. Even the whites of her eyes were filled with blood.

That kind of assault can cause brain damage!

What kind of animal would do that to another human being?

My husband did that!

I lost the esophageal battle and vomited explosively on the sidewalk.

How vulnerable I'd been with him! I was lucky to be alive!

Any part of me that still wanted to stay with Sergei was off the fence and firmly on board with Plan X.

Slava came outside and put a comforting hand on my shoulder.

"Are you okay?" He asked gently.

I looked at him wide-eyed, nodding.

There was still something else I needed to know. I took a deep breath, popped a breath mint into my mouth, and went back inside.

"Anton," I said calmly, "Did you find out when this happened?"

"*Da*," he replied. "Two years ago. There might have been others," he added with a shrug. He couldn't know everything.

It wasn't much consolation to know this happened before I met Sergei. The violence probably only stopped because he lost access to victims. Slava was right. A serial offender with money would have just taken his show on the road. Sergei spent his life traveling.

My husband was a psychopath.

I was an expert writing books about personality disorders.

How could I have been so blind?

I thanked Anton and paid him the rest of the money. I apologized to the bartender for the mess I made out front and handed him a $20 bill as a tip. From the looks of the place, I wasn't the first to puke here and surely would not be the last.

I was physically shaking by the time I got in Slava's car. I jumped when he closed the door. He put his face next to mine.

"What do you need?" He spoke into my ear.

"Hold me," I requested.

He wrapped his strong arms around me, pulling my cheek firmly against his chest, and hummed a tune I had never heard before. His voice had a powerful effect. Within minutes I felt stronger.

I was resolute.

I was done with Sergei forever.

Slava gave me a plateful of toasted chewy black rye bread spread with fresh cream butter to soothe my stomach while he warmed a beef and root vegetable stew on the stove. It was just the kind of comfort food I needed. Then we went upstairs, where we snuggled in front of the fire for a long time without speaking. I felt safe with him. I loved how big he was physically and his calm inner strength. Lena was right when she called him a teddy bear. That was the perfect description.

I turned to look at his contented expression. He looked into my eyes and gently smiled. Love was written on his face, but it was too soon to tell him how I felt. I didn't want the memory of our first expressions of love to be tainted by what I learned about Sergei today.

That revelation would take a long time to process. There were so many details in my mind to be analyzed. I had to figure out where I went wrong in my assessment of Sergei's character, but it was a project I wasn't willing to start tonight. I chose to be present in this moment with Slava instead.

So I set those thoughts aside and gazed into Slava's eyes and touched his face lightly. He was so handsome. I couldn't believe how lucky I was to be here with him. How did we get from the laundry room to this tender place? I laughed to myself at the memory, feeling more acceptance and a little less shame. Our story was crazy. We will have to make up another tale to tell our grandchildren about how we met! I laughed out loud at the thought.

He wanted to know what I found funny, but I deflected.

"Will you kiss me?" I requested.

His lips met mine, and I melted into a pool of warm, gooey love. He was incredibly sensual, running his hands over my hair, touching my fingertips, kissing my neck, and loving every inch of me with his gentle touch. We took our time, and our clothing fell away slowly. With each kiss and caress, the bond between us grew more solid.

Slava carried me to the bed and gently set me down, kissing and holding me, warming me with his body. I relished the comfort and care he lavished on me. When we made love, an unexpected peacefulness filled me. What we were doing felt pure, almost holy.

I was his, he was mine, and we twirled together among the stars, weaving our love for each other. I was far too relaxed to have a mind-blowing orgasm, but my gentle climax was pleasurable, and he came soon after. We lay on our sides, gazing into each other's eyes. I thanked God for bringing us together.

My heart swelled with feelings I could no longer contain.

"I love you, Slava," I said softly.

His face shone with happiness.

"I love you too, Sandrushka," he replied, his eyes wet with tears.

He hugged me tightly.

I'd fallen for the big man with the tiny dog, and he'd fallen for me.

I fell asleep wrapped safely in his arms with little Snowball tucked in under the covers.

Slava's bed was a little piece of heaven on earth.

And I could stay all night this time.

We lingered over tea and toast in the morning inside a bubble of peaceful ease. My phone rang, and I braced for an angry exchange with my husband, but it was Ilya. He was all business and spoke rapidly, telling me the news in a factual manner. After agreeing to meet him at the airport, I ended the call.

"What is it?" Slava asked with concern in his voice.

"Sergei is missing," I replied. "I have to go to Istanbul and talk to the police."

"I will go with you," he offered.

"Thanks, but no," I replied. I couldn't bring my lover on this trip. What would the police think? That I was responsible? Plus, I could only imagine what would happen if Sergei turned up and saw me with Slava.

I was in shock. Missing? What did that mean? How does a grown man disappear? Was Sergei dead? Wouldn't I have felt something when he died? I felt sure that I would have. No, he was definitely alive. I knew it. Where was he?

I called Lena, confessed where I was, and told her what had happened. She immediately volunteered to go on the trip with me. Lena was a bored housewife, always up for an adventure. I was grateful and thanked God for giving me this wonderful friend.

Slava unloaded our suitcases from his silver Mercedes at the curb and gave me a warm kiss and long hug before letting me go.

"Call me when you get there," he requested.

I promised I would, and we said our goodbyes.

This affectionate display moved Lena. As Slava drove away, she touched my forearm and said.

"I knew you would be perfect for each other!"

I glanced at Ilya, whose pained face met my gaze briefly before he turned his attention to the bags. I knew he was upset about my affair with Slava and was probably shocked to see us kiss. Ilya and I were *Druz'ya*, more than friends. He was exceedingly special to me. My heart churned, a cement mixer of emotions. I never meant to hurt Ilya. Of course, I loved him too, but there was no way we could be together. Not only did he work for my vindictive husband, who would destroy Ilya and his family if he ever found out, but he was a good man who deserved so much more than scraps of love from another man's table. I didn't want to ruin his life or keep him from finding true happiness. Slava was my husband's equal. He had the money and connections to defend himself, and me, from Sergei's wrath.

With nothing to be done now, I vowed to find a way to make it up to him later. As I turned my attention to following Ilya into the terminal, my mind flashed to Sergei.

Where could he be?

SEARCHING FOR GHOSTS

Uvar picked us up at the airport and drove us to the hotel where he and Sergei stayed. Uvar said Sergei went to his room the night before and was gone in the morning. There were no signs of forced entry or a struggle. Everything was tidy. His clothing was folded neatly and laid out on the back of a chair. His watch, cell phone, and wallet were resting on the bedside table. Sergei's laptop lay beside his briefcase, and the bed looked like someone slept in it.

The scene looked like he vanished into a dream.

When I gave Ilya the slip for my midnight trysts with Slava, this was precisely how my room looked. I would know he left of his own free will if he took the plastic hotel key card with him. Somehow, I already knew he had.

Where did you go, Sergei?

We were careful not to touch anything. I'd watched enough TV crime dramas to know we needed to dust for fingerprints and look for fibers or other clues. If there was any evidence, we had to find it.

Sergei's life might depend on it.

I stopped by the front desk, found a clerk who spoke English, and explained our situation. I gave her a photograph of Sergei and asked her to tell the staff to keep an eye out for him. I gave her my cell phone number to call if anyone saw him. I offered a $500 cash reward for any information and gave her $50 to get the word out to the rest of the staff right away.

Our next stop was the *Polis* station. None of us spoke Turkish. After a very frustrating and loud exchange, they finally found someone who spoke English to deal with the pain in the ass American woman.

The officer's name was Bartu Yilmaz. Dark haired and tan, Officer Yilmaz looked to be about thirty. The blue uniform made him look intimidating, but he was surprisingly friendly. He listened to me explain the problem.

"People go missing every day. He's probably drunk and sleeping it off," he suggested.

I recoiled at the stereotype of the drunken Russian.

"No," I insisted. "Wealthy businessmen do not go missing every day. My husband is not a drunk. His money and clothing are still at the hotel. I strongly suspect foul play."

"There's nothing we can do until he's been gone for a few days. A man can walk away from his life if he wants to. As far as we know, there has been no crime," he said, shaking his head. "If he was kidnapped, you may hear from the kidnappers with a ransom demand."

"But we will lose evidence, and the trail will go cold!" I cried.

He just shook his head and said,

"Sorry."

I was dejected.

Lena elbowed me. Oh yes.

I took out the five $100 US bills folded up in my pocket, pushed it toward him, and asked for special consideration.

"Please. Help me," I pleaded with eyes brimming with tears.

He pushed the money back, not even tempted.

"I can file a report. That's all I can do."

And so we went through the grim task of completing the report. The most disturbing part was describing the body so the police could identify remains. Sergei had no markings other than the few God gave him. I pulled out the photograph Anton Ruslanovich used in St. Petersburg to discover Sergei's history of assaults on prostitutes. I noted the grim irony of handing it to a police officer for assistance on Sergei's behalf.

He gave me a copy of the report along with his card.

"Call if you hear anything," he said, turning to leave.

"Wait," I said, "do you know a private investigator I can hire?"

"No," he responded flatly.

I wanted to scream at his face in frustration, but I stayed calm.

"Thank you," I said. "I will be in touch."

Our next stop was the Russian Consulate. The staff was sympathetic to our situation, especially after being charmed by Lena, but there wasn't much they could do to help. They referred us to a local private detective agency with a reputation for getting results.

By then, it was too late to call the agency, so we went for dinner. The Turkish food was fresh and tasty, but I had no appetite for the grilled chicken *tavuk sis kebab* they set in front of me. I was more interested in the local sauvignon blanc wine the waiter paired with it. Thankfully one glass was enough to take the edge from my nerves. Afterward, we went to the hotel bar and talked to people, showing Sergei's photo. No one had seen him. We fanned out to local bars, still nothing. Eventually, we called it a night because we could not think of anything else to do.

We went to the private investigation firm early the following day. I ordered the works – a full workup of the hotel room, interviews with guests and staff, questioning employees at the shipping company, and finally, a survey of the local brothels to see if anyone had seen him. I cringed, but it was necessary to cover all of the bases. The investigation would cost a fortune, but I didn't care. I was spending Sergei's money, and I figured he would want the best investigation money could buy. If not, he should have left a note.

I went with the team to process the hotel room. They collected fingerprints, but the room was clean. Then I collected Sergei's possessions, took one last look around, and released the room to housekeeping. I went through everything he left behind. Sure enough, the plastic room key card was missing.

He went on his own free will and took that key with him in case he forgot something and needed to come back.

I didn't know what he'd packed, so I couldn't tell what was missing. Most of his clothes were business, but he also wore jeans and casual clothing. I figured he was wearing dress slacks and a button-down shirt when he disappeared.

I couldn't guess the password, so I had the detective agency hack into his computer. Once in, I carefully went through his documents and email. There was nothing of interest, just spreadsheets and business correspondence. I cringed as I hit the button to check his internet browser history. He'd visited numerous pornography sites but no escort services. I saw searches for local restaurants and stores, but there was nothing to suggest what his destination might have been the night he disappeared.

We went to the shipping company next. The sheet metal-clad building appeared run down, and the ships that were there looked rusty and outdated. This dump was not the kind of place I could see Sergei wasting his time. And yet, there must have been money to be made, or he wouldn't have invested. I wished Slava was here so I could ask him what the attraction could have been. I was not impressed.

I told a worker outside I wanted to see the boss. He didn't understand any of the languages I offered, but he recognized we were visitors and pointed to an office on the second floor of the nearly empty warehouse. All four of us went up. The man sitting at the old metal desk covered in empty take-out food containers seemed nervous. He didn't speak English, Russian, French, or even Spanish, so we hit a language wall. I held up my finger and called Slava.

"Hi Slava, do you speak Turkish?" I asked.

"Yes, a little. I am better with Greek," he replied.

"Good. This guy can probably speak Greek. I am with the boss of the shipping company. Will you please talk to him and tell me what he says?" I asked.

"I will try," he said.

"Thank you," I replied, sending a wave of gratitude through space.

What a blessing it is to have friends with skills.

"Please tell him I am Sergei's wife, and Sergei is missing, and I am mad as hell. That means I own this company, and he works for me. Ask him if he's seen Sergei since Saturday and try to get him to tell you what the problems were at the company. You can threaten to come down and ask him in person if you have to, or we can have Uvar and Ilya soften him up right now." I said, laughing to myself at the last part, remembering Ilya's boot on the drunk's neck at the nightclub. Violence isn't funny, but we needed to find out what happened to Sergei.

Our future depended on it.

I handed the phone to the man, who was now sweating. Who wouldn't be with two beefy Russian men, a pissed-off American woman, and a Russian diva would-be-baroness crowding the space in his small office?

I was sick of Turkey and had been since Sergei bought this crappy company. There was nothing but trouble since the start.

Looking around, I wondered what the real deal was. This place wasn't worth the gasoline needed to burn it down. I suspected it wasn't the ships or the company but the cargo that was important. Sergei kept me out of that end of his business, assuming he was doing anything illegal at all. I never had a reason to doubt Sergei until Lena planted the seed in my mind. But once there, it took root. There were no alternative explanations for his secrecy. Sergei was doing something shady here. What else could it be?

As the dark-eyed man spoke to Slava, his eyes kept darting nervously to me. I stood like a mountain with my legs slightly apart and arms crossed. You don't screw with Americans, I thought confidently. Which reminded me I should probably check in with my own consulate, just in case there was any blowback from this. I might be kicking over a hornet's nest, and God only knew what would fly out. I was new at playing the heavy hand, but I needed to do it the best I could.

If this guy had answers, I intended to get them.

Eventually, he passed the phone back to me, nodding, bowing, and flinching like I was about to hit him. Excellent.

"Thanks, Slava, so what did he tell you?" I asked.

"He hasn't seen Sergei since Saturday afternoon. The problem is missing cargo. It sounds like they were transporting something for someone else, and a third party stole it. This guy is an idiot. He doesn't know what is going on," he summarized.

"It does sound like you are doing an excellent job of intimidating him," he added with a touch of pride in his voice.

"Thank you," I replied.

Turning away from the group, I asked, "What should I do?"

"Take the computers and paper files before they can destroy evidence. Then hire someone else to decipher them for you," Slava suggested.

"What about the ships at sea?" I asked.

"Have them finish their runs and return to port. Cancel future shipments. You can sell the ships and whatever real estate there is later. Gut the company and take the loss," Slava advised. "If Sergei couldn't run it, neither can you."

"Thank you, Slava. I would be lost without you," I said sincerely.

"Can you tell him what we are doing? I will continue payroll until we sell it off. I will give him half of his annual salary in bonus for managing the close." I said.

"Yes, put him on," he replied.

I silently thanked God once again for putting Slava in my life.

Then I put the business face I learned from Sergei on and handed the phone back to the dark-eyed weasel.

I told Uvar and Ilya we were taking all of the computers and paper files with us.

Once the call was over, I stuck out my hand, gave him my best bitch-in-charge American power smile, and said, "Cassandra Davidovna Karpova." There was real power in my name, I realized for the first time. It felt good to say it out loud. I was proud to have Sergei's surname.

The feeble man took my offered hand, shook it limply, and identified himself as "Aköz Zeybec." He made a weak attempt to smile back. This guy had the backbone of a jellyfish. Why did Sergei hire someone like him? Nothing about this made sense.

I snapped my fingers and pointed to the computers. Ilya and Uvar immediately started dismantling the computers and packing up the hard drives for decryption at the detective agency. They ended up taking an entire cabinet of paper files, metal cabinet and all, rolling it away on a dolly for transport to the accounting firm to audit and summarize.

I imagined Sergei would be proud I learned so much under his tutelage.

Where the hell was he?

We regrouped over lunch at the hotel. Everyone seemed pleased with how things went at the shipping company. I thanked them profusely for playing their roles and promised Ilya and Uvar a big bonus for this. We were like a team of action heroes, but we were no closer to finding Sergei than before.

I suggested posting a substantial reward for information about his whereabouts. We could hire people to put flyers under windshield wipers, hand them out at street corners, and put ads in newspapers and on television. I didn't care how much it cost.

I decided on $50,000 US for the reward. That was a lot of money in this part of the world, and the news would travel fast. If he had amnesia, someone would turn him in for the money. If he was dead, we might get a lead on a body. Blond men with blue eyes and pale skin tend to stick out in the south, where people have darker complexions.

He would not escape detection for long.

I didn't want to deal with the particulars, so I hired a public relations firm to handle it. I was planning to stay long enough to make sure they got the job done. I wanted a big media blitz and needed to see the results for myself.

The detective company processed the fingerprints and concluded there was no sign of foul play in the hotel room. The evidence strongly suggested he was alone and simply left in the middle of the night. I wondered why he felt he needed to hide his plans from Uvar. They'd been together for years, and the man was so devoted, he would take Sergei's secrets to his grave. Uvar was just as upset as I was.

The agency was still talking to brothels, but there had been no hits on Sergei's photo so far. I was relieved by that initial news, knowing how many lonely nights he spent in Istanbul in the last few months. He looked so different from most people here. I was sure they would have remembered him.

The next day there was nothing to do. We'd been hanging around the hotel waiting for a sign or word from Sergei with no success. The *Polis* still didn't care, especially when I told them there was no sign of foul play at the hotel. No one had heard from him back home. And there hadn't been any activity on his bank and credit cards.

It occurred to me people don't vanish unless they are kidnapped, murdered, or don't want to be found.

There was no ransom demand from a kidnapper. We had the entire population of Istanbul looking for a corpse, which left the third explanation. I believed he was still alive, but I couldn't fathom why he would run. He was Sergei Ivanovich Karpov, the biggest badass I had ever known.

He would not run from anyone.

Lena and I decided to take a break from the search to do some sightseeing in the city. I wanted to see Hagia Sofia, the ancient domed Orthodox Church converted to a mosque and now a museum. So we went there and walked around, with the two bodyguards shadowing our every step. Any other time, I would have thrilled at the majesty of this special place, but I had a heavy heart.

Then we went to the Grand Bazaar and walked for hours. Lena loved the shopping, purchasing rugs and artwork, making arrangements to have everything shipped home. I wasn't in the mood. I didn't know where I would be living when I returned to Russia, and I felt very unsettled.

Damn you, Sergei. I was planning to leave, and you pulled this stunt. Now I don't know what to do. I was still very much his wife, which meant I would have to keep up his house and business while he was gone. Of course, I would probably sleep with my eyes open, waiting for his return.

If he turned up dead, I would grieve for him. He was the great love of my life, even if he turned out to be a monster. Some people are too tough to die, however, so I believed he was still alive. He had to be. Various soap opera storylines played out in my mind, but no explanation I came up with felt right.

What could possibly make Sergei abandon his life?

Would he run from his partners because shipping cargo went missing? I could not imagine him running from anyone. Sergei was not a coward. He would turn to face his problems and do whatever he could to make things right.

The accounting company would oversee the payroll and sell-off of assets at the shipping company. I made sure Aköz Zeybec would get the bonus I promised for his assistance in that effort. Whatever secret cargo there might have been was lost to us. If anyone was angry about losses, no one contacted me about it. An organized crime boss would surely hit me up for any money my husband owed, but there was only silence.

The detective agency finished their canvas of brothels the next day, and there were no hits on his photograph. No one had seen him.

I launched upright in bed one night with the sudden realization that the real reason Sergei waited so long to be intimate with me was that he needed the time to gain control over his rage. If he'd given in to sex with me on our first date, he might have turned my face into a pizza as he had done to those other girls. I was very disturbed by what I'd learned in St. Petersburg. Seeing the photograph hammered home how violent his rages were and how truly dangerous he was. No doubt, that image would haunt me for the rest of my life. My love for him completely blinded me to the truth.

There was no way for me to know if he'd stopped hiring prostitutes after we met because he traveled to so many cities. I could not possibly check them all. I took a small amount of comfort in the fact he seemed to have resisted the temptation all of those weeks he'd spent in Turkey this past year. If he still indulged in professional sex, he certainly would have done it here with all of the stress he was under here. That was a positive indication he'd developed some self-restraint.

Plus, I noted grimly, he didn't beat me on the night I fooled around with Slava in the laundry room. Sergei was trying to change, but I didn't know if it was out of love for me or to keep me around long enough to give him the family he wanted.

We went to see the Basilica Cistern on our last full day. The ancient underground palace beneath a central square was built to supply the city with water by Emperor Justinian in the 6th century. A forest of beautiful columns and sculptures holds up the ceiling, creating a sanctuary unlike any other. The cavernous space suited my mood to wander underground, far from the harsh sunlight and bustle above. I imagined Sergei hiding down there in the dark and half expected him to pop out from behind a column and say, 'Did you miss me, Sandrochka?'

A week passed, and we still had no leads. I had enough. We could continue the search remotely, so I decided it was time to go home. No one objected. We were all exhausted from the ordeal.

Getting back on the plane with no resolution felt like a significant loss.

19

LOST AND FOUND

I spent one night wrapped in Slava's arms in St. Petersburg before driving Sergei's BMW home to the farm. Once there, I went through Sergei's desk and found a sealed envelope with 'In case anything happens to me' written on it in his handwriting. I opened it and found a will leaving everything he owned to me, a list of his assets and accounts, to which he had already named me joint-owner. I didn't need to do the math to know he was a wealthy man. There was more than 25 million US in diversified assets scattered across the globe. That didn't include his businesses, real estate, and other complex holdings. I could easily live the rest of my life on the interest from his investments alone, but that knowledge was little comfort.

I sat on the floor behind his desk and cried for hours. I didn't care about the money. I wept for our lost love, that he thought so highly of me, and that I cheated on him and never had the chance to confess. I lamented that he let a stupid Turkish shipping company drag him down when he already had so much. I wept because he'd been so driven to accumulate wealth when he could have experienced the joy of sharing what he had, done something noble to improve the lives of others, or just stayed home and enjoyed everyday life. I cried for his horrible childhood, his fear, and his pain. I grieved for all of those beautiful young women he beat so mercilessly. I wept because maybe our relationship helped heal some of his trauma. But most of all, I cried because I let him down. He was lost out there somewhere in the world, and I couldn't find him.

Where are you, Sergei? I wondered hopelessly.

I went upstairs and stood in his closet, hugging his clothes around me. The smell of him in the closet made me feel better, but it was empty. I crawled into the big bed and slept for 16 hours straight. I thought I heard him enter the room in the middle of the night, and my heart jumped, but it was only my imagination. I cried myself back to sleep with racking sobs.

Ilya was worried, but his concern made me feel worse, so I told him to leave me alone as I went into an emotional tailspin. He called Lena and asked her for help.

Slava and Lena came over together and found me a naked unwashed emotional mess in bed. I hadn't eaten for a few days because my stomach had been bothering me. Every time I stood up, I became dizzy and found myself retching. I figured it was either guilt or my bad nerves failing me at last. I talked about wanting to die so I could see Sergei on the other side. The look they exchanged made me wince. I knew it sounded insane. I felt bad enough without being judged for expressing myself honestly.

Slava was extremely upset seeing me in this state, but he did his best to hide his feelings. He sat next to me on the bed and held my hand. I felt horrible and didn't want him to see me at my worst, but I did feel stronger with him there.

Lena brought me a tray with tea and salty crackers. Once that stayed down, she led me into my bath so we could talk privately. She handed me a pregnancy test stick and said,

"Pee on it."

I looked at her like she was crazy. I wasn't fertile. We'd tried for nearly a year and got nothing but failures every month.

I wasn't strong enough to handle another disappointment.

I didn't want to do it.

"Pee on it," she insisted.

Miraculously, a plus sign appeared. It took a minute to register because I'd never seen one before. A positive! I did three more tests and couldn't believe the result was positive each time. I put my hands on my belly and felt joy. Lena's face lit with excitement.

"You have to tell Slava," she said elatedly.

"Why?" I asked.

"It's his baby, right?" She asked, a question mark crossing her face.

"Um," I said as my sluggish brain struggled to do the calculation.

"Actually, it could be either Sergei's or Slava's," I confessed, looking down. There had been some overlap, I remembered, wincing.

"Still," she said. "This is your baby. That's all that matters, right?"
She had a point.
I smiled. Yes, this is my baby! Oh my God, I am going to have a child!
Tears of joy streamed down my face.

I took a shower while she went downstairs to warm up solid food for me.
When I padded downstairs in fresh clothes and slippers, I knew Lena had already spilled the beans to Slava. His face was lit with enthusiasm like a kid at Christmas. He went to hug me but didn't want to squish the precious gift of life growing inside, so he carefully put his arms around my shoulders instead. He kissed my cheek, and with his golden honey voice thick in my ear, he said,
"Congratulations! You will be a good mother!"
Slava pulled back and kissed me on the lips.
"I love you, Sandrushka," he added softly.
The golden light of his love filled my heart.

"Enough, enough, let the poor girl eat," Lena insisted.
That's when the pampering and telling me what to do every step of the way started. There is no shortage of women who will give unsolicited maternal advice in Russia, even strangers, but I didn't mind. They seem intrusive, but they watch out for each other. This is one of the ways the community protects children.

Months passed, and there was still no sign of Sergei. We'd get a hit once in a while on our reward campaign, and I'd get excited, but then nothing came of it. The shipping company sold. We never figured out why Sergei had been so upset. I wondered if his disappearance had anything to do with the shipping company or something else entirely. I spent many sleepless nights trying to figure it out and continually came up empty.
Jack Hawthorne was very sympathetic to the changes in my life. A sympathy card for my missing husband and a congratulations card for my pregnancy came in the mail on the same day. I was glad I never told him about my affair with Slava. I would prefer my boss to think of me as a

bereaved good wife than a woman getting some on the side when her husband went missing under mysterious circumstances.

Jack called one evening with good news. His wife Jean took him back, and they were in marriage counseling, working on reconciliation. I congratulated him and wished him luck. I knew how difficult it is for couples to recover from infidelity, but it wasn't impossible. He felt like a schmuck for having done it. Jean was a loving woman. The prognosis for their relationship was good.

I was very relieved to hear this and wished him luck.

I spent weekends with Slava and the rest of the time in the country, knocking around the farm with Ilya. I didn't want to waste the summer sitting in Slava's house after earning those gloriously long days through the darkest winter of my life. They call the weeks around the summer solstice 'white nights' because it stays light most of the night.

People seemed manic in summer compared to the depression of winter. Was the entire country bipolar? My mood was markedly better with the extended daylight. Having a baby to look forward to was another boon to my spirit.

I lovingly tended the vegetable garden and planted trees and bushes around Sergei's house to soften the brick home. We built another hay barn, expanded the hayfields, and added sheep, goats, and chickens to the growing little farm.

My parents came to visit for two weeks over the summer and actually enjoyed Russia. The countryside wasn't much different than upstate New York, and of course, Russians are just like Americans in many ways. They liked Slava, even though my mother chastised me for not holding out longer for my husband's return before dating someone else. I was pregnant, so this was especially unseemly. Of course, my parents assumed the baby was Sergei's.

I wasn't so sure. Sergei tried to get me pregnant for nearly a year with no luck. But the minute I slept with someone else, it miraculously happened. If the baby was Sergei's, perhaps his sperm needed a little competition to swim faster.

Those two were rivals to the end.

I didn't care who the father was. Half of me wished the baby was Slava's, and the other half hoped for Sergei. I loved them both. I was happy I resisted the temptation to sleep with Ilya. The situation was embarrassing enough with two potential fathers. I winced every time I remembered Ilya shooting pinecones in the forest and how badly I wanted to romp with him that day.

What a disaster that would have been!

Slava and I did not bother to hide our relationship. He spared no effort introducing me to St. Petersburg's high culture. We visited every museum and church in the city, attended gallery openings, and went to society parties together. We frequented the Mariinsky Theater, where we saw ballet and opera performances and became regular patrons of the St. Petersburg Philharmonia.

When an internationally renowned Austrian pianist visited to perform a collection of piano concertos with the symphony, I was unexpectedly struck with intense emotion hearing the haunting opening notes of Liszt's Consolation Number Three. I burst into tears, overcome by grief. It was Sergei's song, the one I had come to associate with his gloomy moods. I fled to the exit of the Grand Hall, running in heels and a sapphire blue evening gown, desperate to get outdoors. Slava followed, patient and kind, understanding the depth of my anguish and perhaps, helping me to see the beauty in it. We walked the paths of Mikhaylovskiy Park until the intensity of my feelings subsided. Then he took me home and made love to me sweetly, making everything right within me again.

Losing Sergei wasn't just a loss. It was a gut-wrenching mystery. I didn't know if he was alive or dead. Perhaps he'd been murdered or taken his own life. If he was alive, I could not imagine where he could be or why he didn't call. Without a death, you can't have a funeral, grieve and get on with your life. Not knowing what happened to him was torture. Hearing the melancholic song he once loved, played so beautifully in the concert hall, unexpectedly drove a dagger deep into my chest and twisted it.

Slava was a man well acquainted with sorrow, yet he still had the remarkable ability to laugh and feel joy. I realized I'd used avoidance most of my life to cope with a fear of negative emotions. That strategy blunted all of my feelings, including the positive. Slava showed me I could trust the full range of my emotional experience.

"Sad feelings change into happy ones, just as spring storms give way to warm summer days. Like the weather, no emotional state lasts forever. Experiencing emotions is the richest part of our human experience," he explained in a combination of Russian and English words. I finally understood the poetry of this simple truth, spoken from the depths of the big man's heart.

I began to trust that I could feel intense sadness or anger and not be swept away, growing more confident those feelings would pass and not harm me. I could simply allow the emotions and then let them go.

As a trained therapist, I knew this intellectually, but I was unaware of how limited my feelings had been for most of my life. I never experienced ease of emotional fluidity until this healing time with Slava. I achieved considerable personal growth in those months following Sergei's disappearance with his loving support and mature guidance.

My anxiety was resolving. I was no longer afraid to live my life.

I became a mature, confident woman.

Slava gave me an encouraging smile as we entered Kazan Cathedral to attend the Russian Orthodox Sunday service. He was incredibly handsome, dressed in a dark suit with special shiny black shoes he only wore on Sundays. I was nervous the first time we went to mass but quickly grew to enjoy it. We'd come here several times, and the Cathedral was beginning to feel like home.

He squeezed my hand as the service began.

The church was modeled after St. Peter's Basilica in Rome, complete with a horseshoe-shaped, column-lined courtyard. He promised to take me on a trip to Rome to see the original once the baby was old enough to travel. He was fluent in Italian and wanted to impress me with his language skills and familiarity with the city.

I was initially shocked to see there are no pews in Russian Orthodox churches. Slava explained Russians consider it disrespectful to sit while in God's presence. They stand for the entire two-hour service unless they are elderly or infirm, in which case they can sit on a bench set off to the side. I noticed no one took a seat, no matter how elderly or infirm they seemed to be. Russians are tough people, I thought with admiration. I quickly learned to wear comfortable shoes.

The Kazan Cathedral is as peaceful as a place can be, rich with the scent of incense, candles, and flowers. I lit two candles each week. One candle for Sergei to find his way home, and the other was for the baby's safe passage from the other side of the cornucopia.

During the service, the priest intones the liturgy, and the choir responds. They go back and forth in a musical way while the people in attendance mill about freely. I noticed only a handful of people received Communion on any given Sunday. Slava explained that preparing to receive communion takes about a month, so most people only do it once or twice a year. That was interesting, and it made a lot of sense to me. If you are going to take a piece of God into your body, you should take it seriously. I wasn't ready for that and glad I was not the only one passing on communion. I always felt like a pariah when I went to church with my parents and stayed behind because I wasn't caught up on my confessions and other Catholic obligations.

The ladies wore modest long dresses and silk scarves on their heads. Pants are not allowed for women, and they must cover their hair. This is not optional. The rule seemed sexist, but I didn't care. If you go to the world's oldest Christian church, you should expect things to be old-fashioned. I loved wearing dresses anyway, and it gave me an excuse to buy a few longer ones and some of those babushka scarves I told Sergei I would never wear. I imagined he would be amused to see me dressed like a proper church lady. He'd probably take me home and spank me for being there with Slava, I thought naughtily, laughing to myself. But church was not the place for such irreverent thoughts, so I shooed them away. The truth was I missed him, and he was never far from my mind.

Kazan Cathedral is home to many beautiful icons. The soulful images are so moving I could understand why Sergei's mother Sofia clung to hers for inspiration during her darkest days. I'd assumed the icons were initially intended to tell bible stories in pictures to those who could not read, but I realized they are far richer than mere words when I meditated on them during the Sunday service. Icons communicate feelings in a way words cannot. Images of the holy family and saints are sacred and revered in this tradition, and I developed an authentic appreciation for this serene form of spiritual expression.

I planned to get an icon for the baby's room to watch over and inspire the little one. Reproductions of the beautiful icons were easy to find, and many people had them in their homes. I wished I knew which one Sofia held onto because that was the one I wanted. I wondered if it was the Kazan Icon, a somber image of Mary and Jesus set into a golden background. I will ask Sergei when he comes back.

My heart sank. I did it again. 'If' he comes back, I corrected myself. This happened all of the time, and it never stopped being depressing. Unfortunately, it seemed less likely he would ever return with each passing day.

I didn't convert. I was just a visitor feeling the divine presence of God in a rich new way. My mother pressured me to get the baby baptized as soon as possible after the birth, and I didn't know what to do. I was pretty sure neither the Roman Catholic nor Russian Orthodox Church would baptize the child of an adulteress who wasn't enrolled in their congregation. As if having two potential fathers wasn't bad enough, one of them was a hardcore atheist. I planned to have a paternity test done when the child was born and decide what to do then. If the baby was Slava's, maybe he could work a deal on the baptism based on his own good standing in this church.

The kindly, bearded Russian priests seemed more approachable than the Catholic ones of my youth. Perhaps because they had wives, they would understand women better and be less judgmental about the complexities of romantic relationships. Still, I was not in a hurry to explain my situation to them or anyone else.

Since my husband was gone, but not necessarily dead, I committed adultery every time I was with Slava. What is the point of confession while you are still actively sinning? I had no intention of stopping. I promised to get right with God later and prayed I wouldn't die in the meantime – or I'd be on an express elevator to somewhere hot. I laughed to myself at the irony of having these thoughts during mass.

It was a miracle I didn't burst into flames walking in the door.

Slava squeezed my hand to pull my attention back to the present moment and the beautiful service in progress. He could always tell when my mind was wandering. I smiled at him gratefully and inhaled deeply, finding the sensual warmth of the candles and powerful incense profoundly calming. I listened to the choir singing 'Lord have Mercy' in rounds of three and appreciated all the beauty surrounding me here. This sacred place made me want to believe in forgiveness, resurrection, and a glorious afterlife.

If Slava believed it, why couldn't I?

If Slava could sin and receive forgiveness, why couldn't I?

Maybe there was hope for me after all.

Perhaps the Orthodox concept of God was more loving and less judgmental than the Roman Catholic. Slava didn't seem to be racked with guilt like I was. And he didn't question every article of faith as I did. He simply breathed in the peace the service offered and let it purify him.

He said when it comes to spirituality, I think too much and feel too little.

This powerful truth struck me deeply.

Strangers assumed Slava and I were married and expecting our first child. We received congratulations regularly. Of course, I was still wearing Sergei's wedding ring because I never took it off. Slava never asked me to. I looked down at the wide golden band on my right hand and thought of the words engraved inside, 'Sergei & Cassandra Forever.' Tears formed in my eyes.

I didn't bother to correct them.

I simply said *spasibo* because I didn't want to be rude.

At last, the service was over, and we walked out into the bright sunshine feeling renewed. When you leave a Russian Orthodox Church, the scent of the incense and feeling of peace stay with you the rest of the day. Sometimes they give you blessed fruit or bread to take home to boost your spirit later. I can't say I understood everything that happened during those services, but I felt something at work easing my troubled heart.

I believed God knew where my husband was and would bring him home at the right time or release my heart if he was truly lost. I spent a lot of time reflecting on faith, patience, and trust. A tremendous burden lifts when we leave what we can't control up to Spirit. I began to feel lighter as I focused on letting go of the need to know everything and simply accepted the uncertainty of my situation.

Throwing myself into my work helped me cope, and I managed to keep up with my publisher's deadlines throughout all of this. I was on the last book, the one about my people, the Anxious Personality types. I was even a little ahead of schedule and determined to see the project through to the end.

When I finished the series, I planned to turn my attention to a hands-on project. I considered making Sergei's farm into a sanctuary for Russian teens in crisis. Those eight idle guest bedrooms could be making a difference. Perhaps this could be my way of undoing some of the ugliness in the world.

If I couldn't help Sergei, I could help others in his memory. I owed him that much.

Sometimes I would think of Sergei and cry.
Sometimes I would watch my belly grow and laugh with joy.

Slava and I had a normal, healthy relationship. He was not as exciting as Sergei, no one could be, but he was rock solid and would be a good father whether the child was his or not. We were in love and talked about getting married, but that meant waiting years until Sergei could be declared legally dead, or I would have to divorce him in absentia on the grounds of abandonment. The thought of doing that made me sick. So we tabled the discussion indefinitely and simply enjoyed our time together.

I tried to focus on the positives. I was looking forward to seeing Slava hold the baby and hearing him sing lullabies. Our child would feel safe and never have to fear his father or anyone else. I couldn't wait to meet him, or her. I didn't want to know the sex until the baby was born. I'd become a bit superstitious and didn't want to jinx anything by expecting too much happiness. Something niggled at the edge of my awareness, warning me to proceed with caution or something terrible would happen. I couldn't tell if it was intuition or just my old friend, anxiety.

I had an irrational fear something would come and clutch the baby away at the last minute. Perhaps this is a common phobia for first-time mothers, but I wasn't taking any chances. I didn't want a baby shower or set up the nursery until after the baby arrived. I didn't drink or smoke and took daily prenatal vitamins, ate healthy food, and exercised. I wanted to give my child every chance for a good start in life.

I was lucky to have so much support. My friend Lena was itching for a reason to power shop. My mother planned to come to help for a few months when the baby was due in December. I could trust her with her grandchild if I had to go out and get things done. Slava would be as gentle with a baby as he was with his little dog Snowball, so I would never worry. Ilya was always eager to help, and I could count on him completely. Everything would work out one way or another.

The pregnancy was going well, and we didn't need to curtail our lovemaking, though admittedly, we slowed down a lot. I think that would have happened even if I wasn't growing to the size of a small whale. To

Slava, love was about so much more than sex. I chalked that up to his greater maturity, but it is more accurate to say he was emotionally intelligent.

He was a good man.

We never argued. Not even once.

We were enjoying our typical lazy Saturday morning time together at his house, bathed in the great beams of golden light from a late autumn sunrise. I was plump with a big belly at seven months, playfully kissing and cuddling with golden-eyed Slava in his heavenly bed while the baby danced inside of me and Snowball happily played with a squeak toy.

For once in my life, I was living within a blissful, perfect moment, thinking of nothing else. My mood was as bright as the golden light in Slava's eyes.

My cell phone rang, and I lumbered out of bed to answer it. I recognized the number immediately and responded cheerfully.

"*Allo* Ilyusha, what's happening?" I asked.

There was static on the line and then a muffled sound. Then Ilya's familiar voice whispered in an urgent hushed tone,

"Sergei is home. He is asking for you."

"What should I tell him?"

ABOUT THE AUTHOR

An American with maternal Slavic ancestry, named by her mother in remembrance of Catherine the Great, Catherine Ivers Norton developed an early interest in St. Petersburg and the Russian people. A precocious child, she read every work by Russian writers at her local public library, including Tolstoy and Dostoyevsky, while still in primary school. She spent her childhood writing short stories and composing poetry, planning to become a writer someday, with the dream of traveling to Russia close in her heart. Finding English studies painfully dull, she changed her academic course once in college.

The author earned a bachelor's degree in Psychology with the highest honors from Alfred University in New York State. She went on to pursue a Ph.D. in Clinical Psychology at Syracuse University. The degree eluded her as she needed more practical work during a time of upheaval involving a difficult divorce. This story was born with urgency during that tumultuous period. Writing became a recreational outlet, an escape from emotionally intense work in the field of adolescent psychology.

A woman of insatiable curiosity, Catherine lives in Ithaca, in the heart of New York State's beautiful Finger Lakes region. She is looking forward to the moment she arrives in St. Petersburg, takes her first breath of Russian air, and wanders the city that has always felt like home in her heart. Здравствуйте друзья, скоро увидимся.

Made in the USA
Las Vegas, NV
28 October 2021

33254346R00144